鳥 山 明

I don't think there's anything good about being near-sighted. When you go to the pool or the beach, you can't see any of the girls in their bikinis! Darn it! Quickly, I'll put on my glasses, but it'll turn out that the girl is actually an old lady! Then I'll take my glass-es off as quickly as I can. This happens to me quite often. Once, I went to a mixed-bathing hot spring but I couldn't see anything because I wasn't wearing my glasses! It made me want to cry. Darn this near-sight-edness! Everyone please take care of your eyes.

—*Akira Toriyama, 1987*

Artist/writer Akira Toriyama burst onto the manga scene in 1980 with the wildly popular **Dr. Slump**, a science fiction comedy about the adventures of a mad scientist and his android "daughter." In 1984 he created his hit series **Dragon Ball**, which ran until 1995 in Shueisha's bestselling magazine **Weekly Shonen Jump**, and was translated into foreign languages around the world. Since **Dragon Ball**, he has worked on a variety of short series, including **Cowa!**, **Kajika**, **Sand Land**, and **Neko Majin**, as well as a children's book, **Toccio the Angel**. He is also known for his design work on video games, particularly the **Dragon Warrior** RPG series. He lives with his family in Japan.

DRAGON BALL VOL. 10
SHONEN JUMP Manga Edition

STORY AND ART BY
AKIRA TORIYAMA

English Adaptation/Gerard Jones
Translation/Mari Morimoto
Touch-Up Art & Lettering/Wayne Truman
Cover Design/Sean Lee & Dan Ziegler
Graphics & Design/Sean Lee
Senior Editor/Jason Thompson

In the original Japanese edition, DRAGON BALL and DRAGON BALL Z
are known collectively as the 42-volume series DRAGON BALL. The
English DRAGON BALL Z was originally volumes 17–42 of the Japanese
DRAGON BALL.

Printed in the U.S.A.

Published by VIZ Media, LLC
P.O. Box 77010
San Francisco, CA 94107

10 9
First printing, May 2003
Ninth printing, January 2019

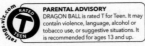

SHONEN JUMP MANGA

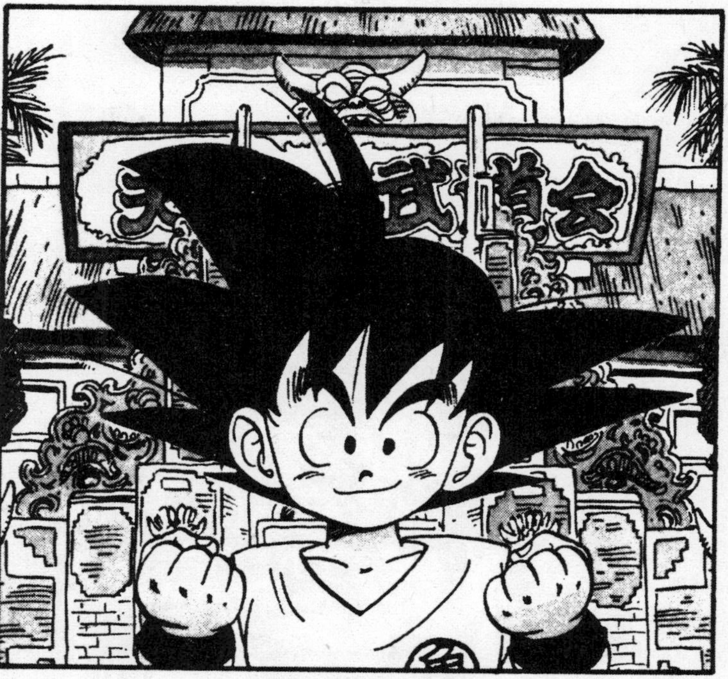

DRAGON BALL

Vol. 10

DB: 10 of 42

STORY AND ART BY
AKIRA TORIYAMA

THE MAIN CHARACTERS

Son Goku

Monkey-tailed young Goku has always been stronger than normal. His grandfather Gohan gave him the *nyoibô*, a magic staff, and Kame-Sen'nin gave him the *kinto'un*, a magic flying cloud.

Bulma

A genius inventor, Bulma met Goku on her quest for the seven magical Dragon Balls.

Yamcha

Yamcha used to be a desert bandit, but he went to the city to be Bulma's on-and-off boyfriend. He uses "Fist of the Wolf-Fang" kung-fu.

Lunch

A strange woman whose personality changes whenever she sneezes.

Kuririn

Goku's former martial arts schoolmate under Kame-Sen'nin.

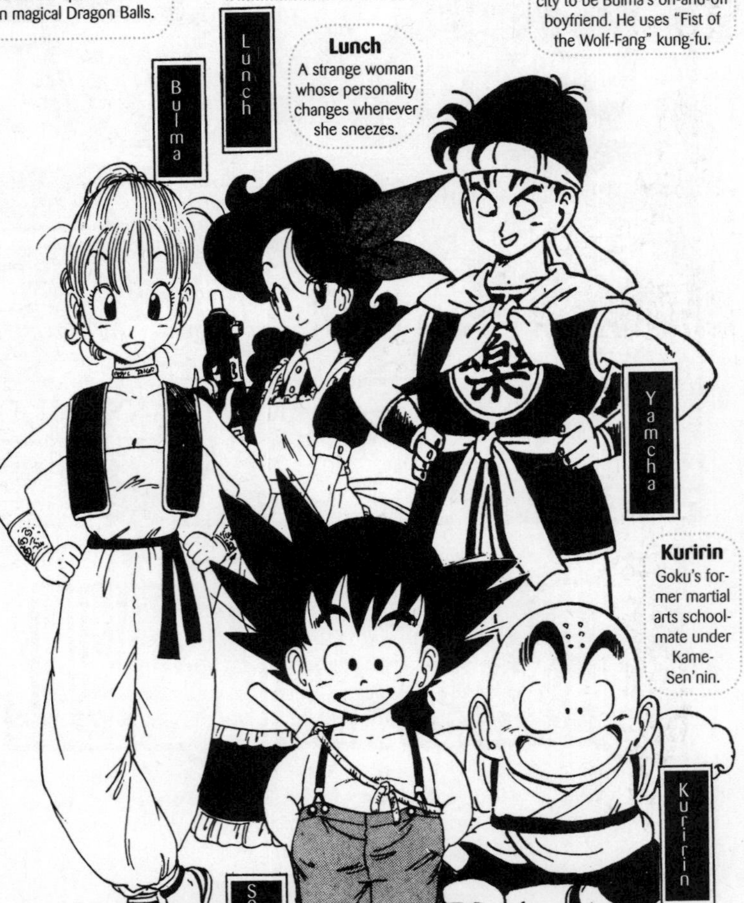
Lunch
Bulma
Yamcha
Kuririn
Son Goku

Chaozu | Tsuru-Sen'nin (The "Crane Hermit") | Tenshinhan

Upa and Bora
A father and son who lived in the area around the Karin Tower. When Bora was killed by Taopaipai, an assassin working for the Red Ribbon Army, Goku vowed to gather the Dragon Balls and wish him back to life.

Upa and Bora

Tsuru-Sen'nin (The "Crane Hermit") Tenshinhan • Chaozu
The rival of Kame-Sen'nin, Tsuru-Sen'nin is a mighty martial artist himself. Chaozu and Tenshinhan are his pupils.

Kame-Sen'nin (The "Turtle Hermit")
A lecherous but powerful martial artist (also known as the *muten-rôshi*, or "Invincible Old Master"). He taught Goku the *kamehameha* attack. In disguise as "Jackie Chun," he narrowly defeated Goku at the "Strongest-Under-the-Heavens" martial arts tournament.

Pilaf and Co.

Pilaf and Co.
A little emperor who wants to get the Dragon Balls so he can wish to rule the entire world.

Kame Sen'nin

Legend says that whoever gathers the seven magical "Dragon Balls" will be granted any one wish. Son Goku, a young boy from the mountains, first heard the legend from a city girl named Bulma. After many adventures with Bulma, Goku decided he wanted to be stronger, and so he trained under Kame-Sen'nin, the great martial artist. With his new strength he defeated the evil Red Ribbon Army, who had killed many people, including Upa's father Bora. Goku swore to Upa that he would gather the Dragon Balls to wish his father back to life. With the help of the All-Seeing Crone, Goku found the last missing Dragon Ball...in the hands of his old enemy Pilaf!

DRAGON BALL 10

CONTENTS

Tale 109 • A Second Helping of Pilaf

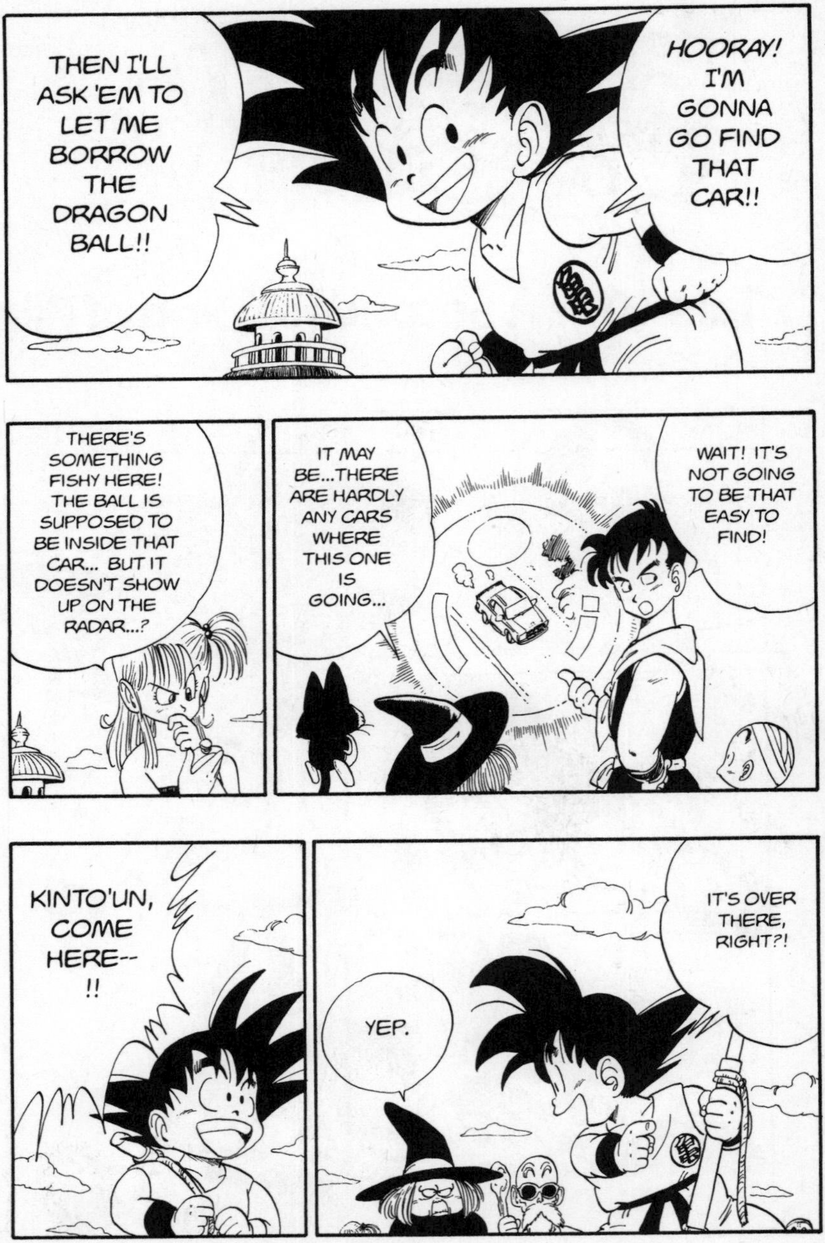
HOORAY! I'M GONNA GO FIND THAT CAR!!
THEN I'LL ASK 'EM TO LET ME BORROW THE DRAGON BALL!!
WAIT! IT'S NOT GOING TO BE THAT EASY TO FIND!
IT MAY BE...THERE ARE HARDLY ANY CARS WHERE THIS ONE IS GOING...
THERE'S SOMETHING FISHY HERE! THE BALL IS SUPPOSED TO BE INSIDE THAT CAR... BUT IT DOESN'T SHOW UP ON THE RADAR...?
IT'S OVER THERE, RIGHT?!
YEP.
KINTO'UN, COME HERE-- !!

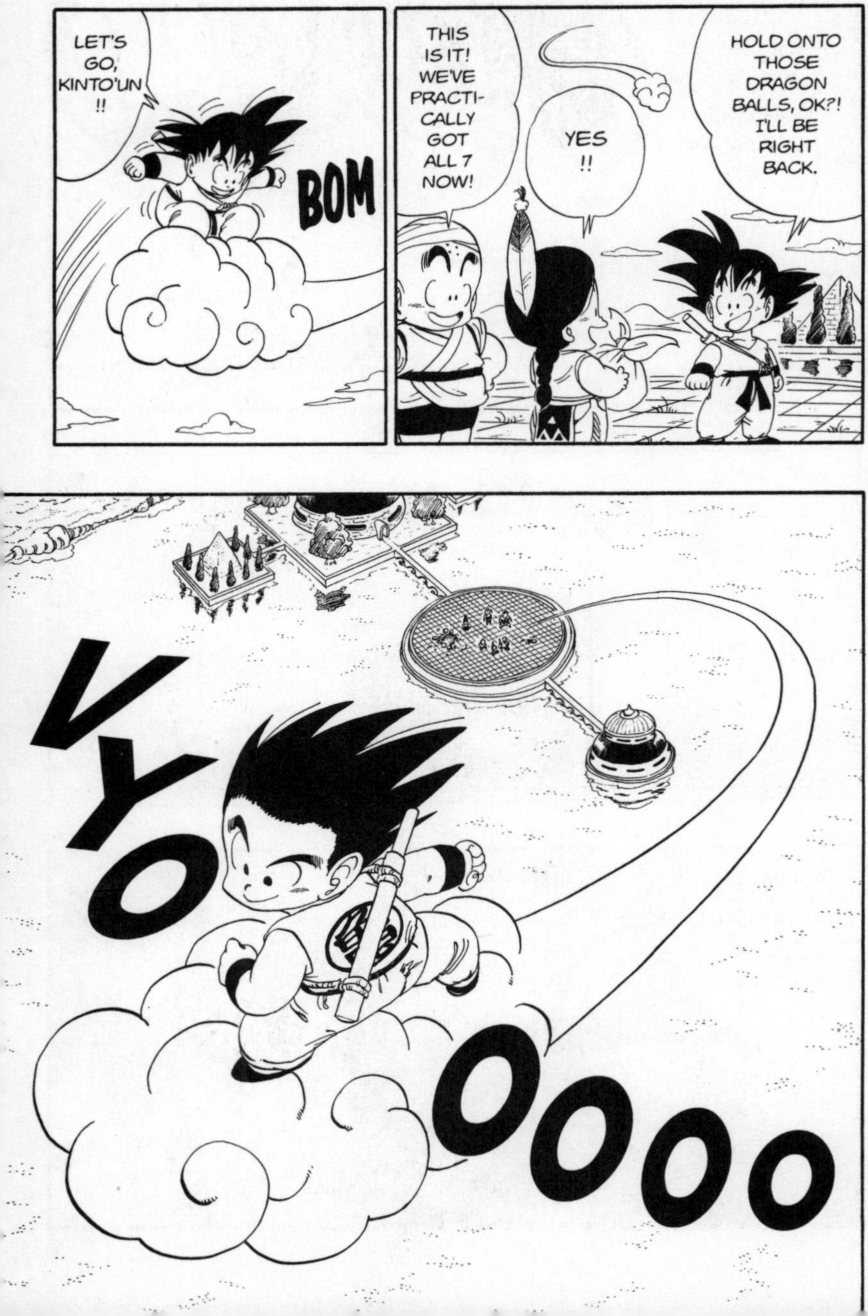
HOLD ONTO THOSE DRAGON BALLS, OK?! I'LL BE RIGHT BACK.
YES !!
THIS IS IT! WE'VE PRACTI-CALLY GOT ALL 7 NOW!
LET'S GO, KINTO'UN !!
BOM
VYOOOOOO

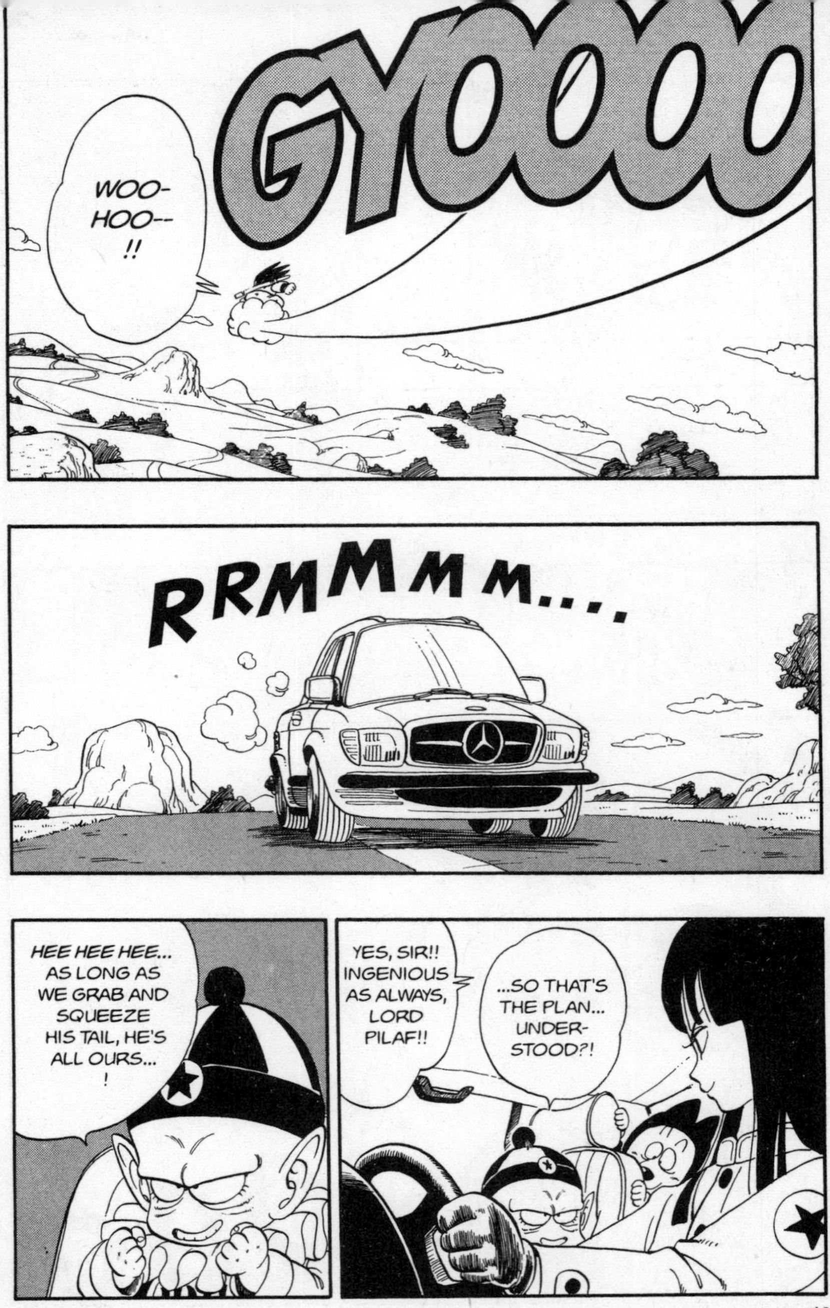
GYOOOO
WOO-HOO--!!
RRMMMM....
...SO THAT'S THE PLAN... UNDERSTOOD?!
YES, SIR!! INGENIOUS AS ALWAYS, LORD PILAF!!
HEE HEE HEE... AS LONG AS WE GRAB AND SQUEEZE HIS TAIL, HE'S ALL OURS...!

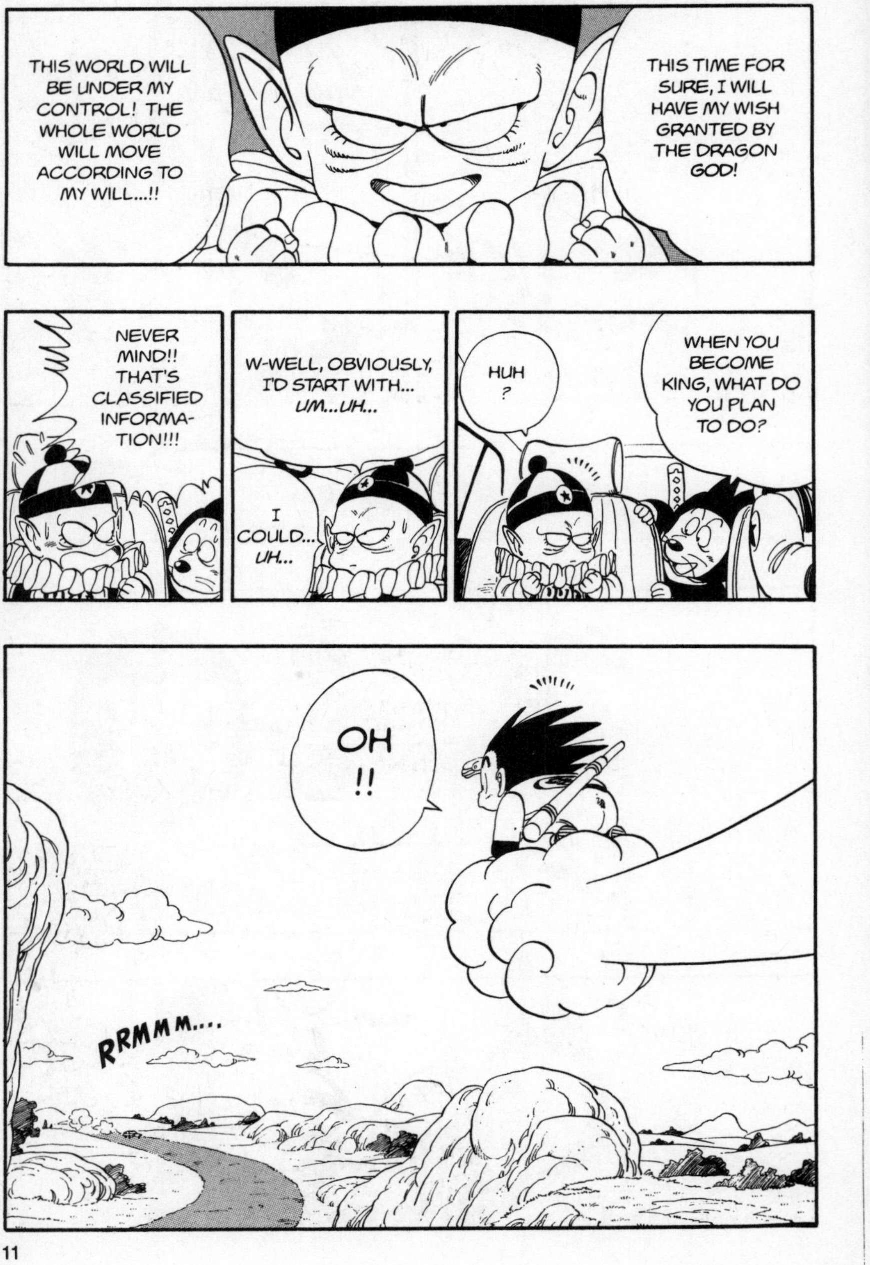
THIS TIME FOR SURE, I WILL HAVE MY WISH GRANTED BY THE DRAGON GOD!
THIS WORLD WILL BE UNDER MY CONTROL! THE WHOLE WORLD WILL MOVE ACCORDING TO MY WILL...!!
WHEN YOU BECOME KING, WHAT DO YOU PLAN TO DO?
HUH ?
W-WELL, OBVIOUSLY, I'D START WITH... UM...UH...
I COULD... UH...
NEVER MIND!! THAT'S CLASSIFIED INFORMATION!!!
OH !!
RRMMM....

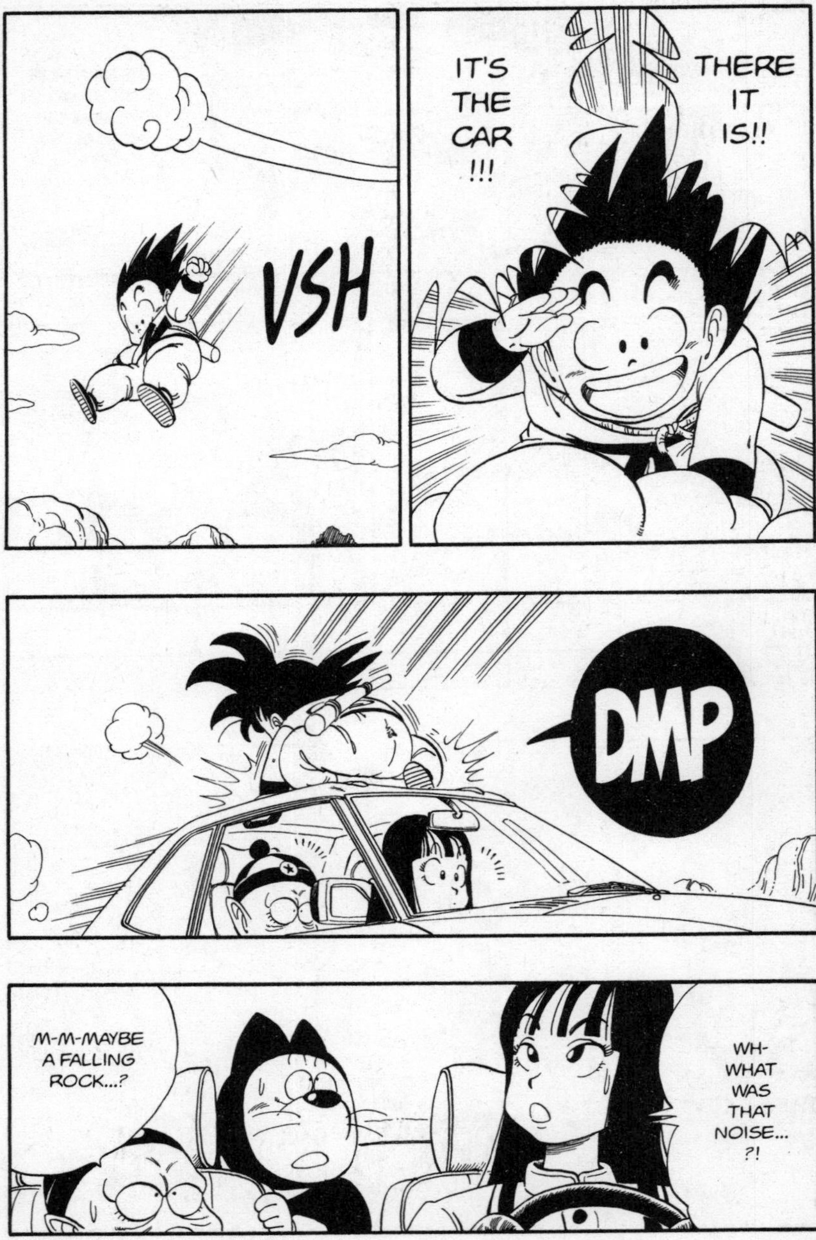
THERE IT IS!!
IT'S THE CAR !!!
VSH
DMP
WH- WHAT WAS THAT NOISE... ?!
M-M-MAYBE A FALLING ROCK...?

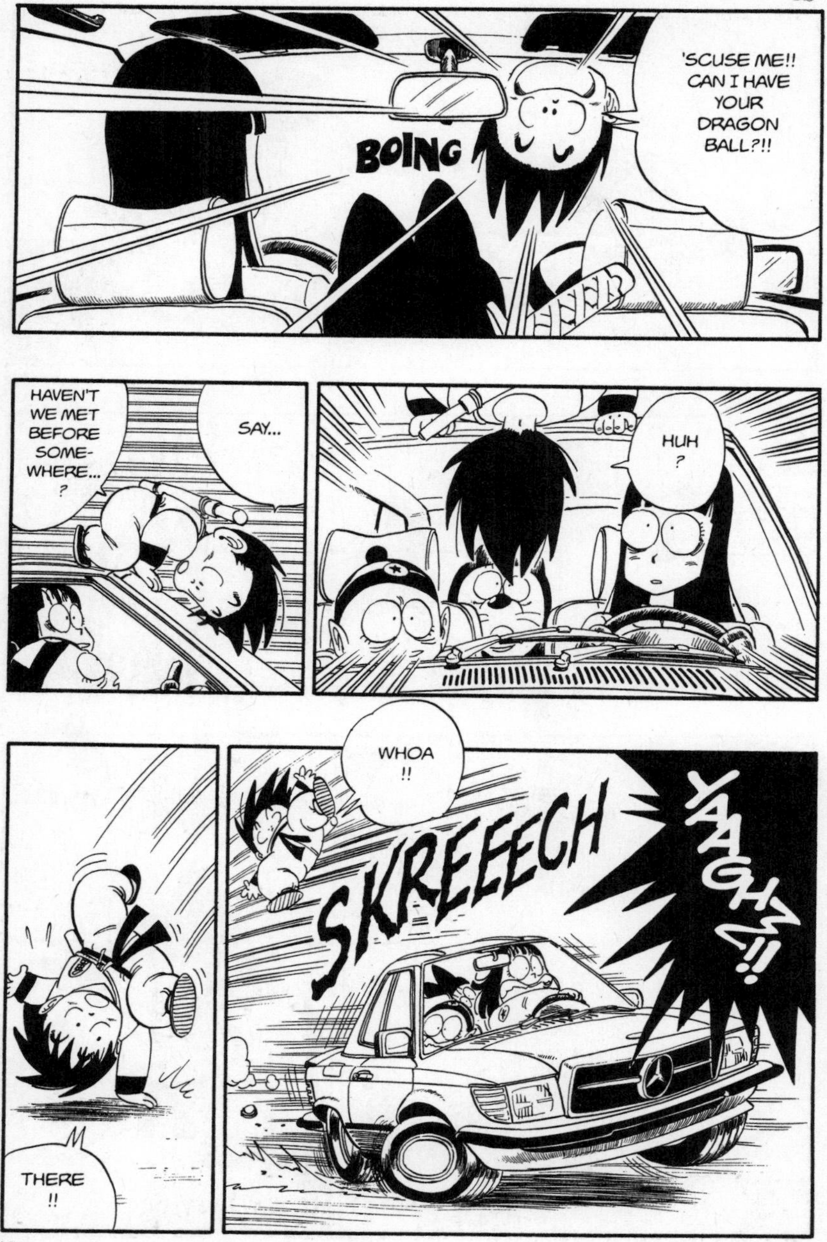
BOING
'SCUSE ME!! CAN I HAVE YOUR DRAGON BALL?!!
HUH ?
SAY...
HAVEN'T WE MET BEFORE SOME-WHERE... ?
WHOA !!
SKREEECH
YAAGHZZ!!
THERE !!

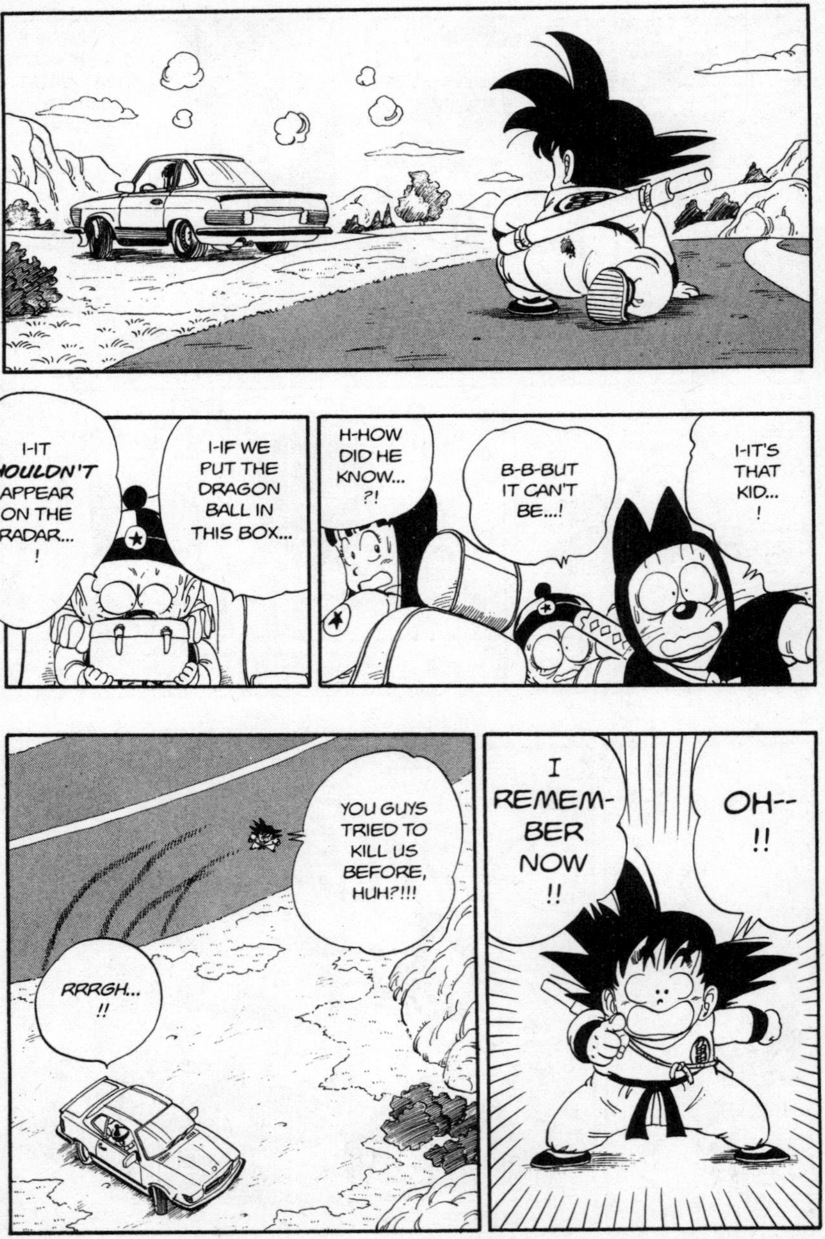
I-IT'S THAT KID...!
B-B-BUT IT CAN'T BE...!
H-HOW DID HE KNOW...?!
I-IF WE PUT THE DRAGON BALL IN THIS BOX...
I-IT *SHOULDN'T* APPEAR ON THE RADAR...!
OH--!!
I REMEMBER NOW!!
YOU GUYS TRIED TO KILL US BEFORE, HUH?!!!
RRRGH...!!

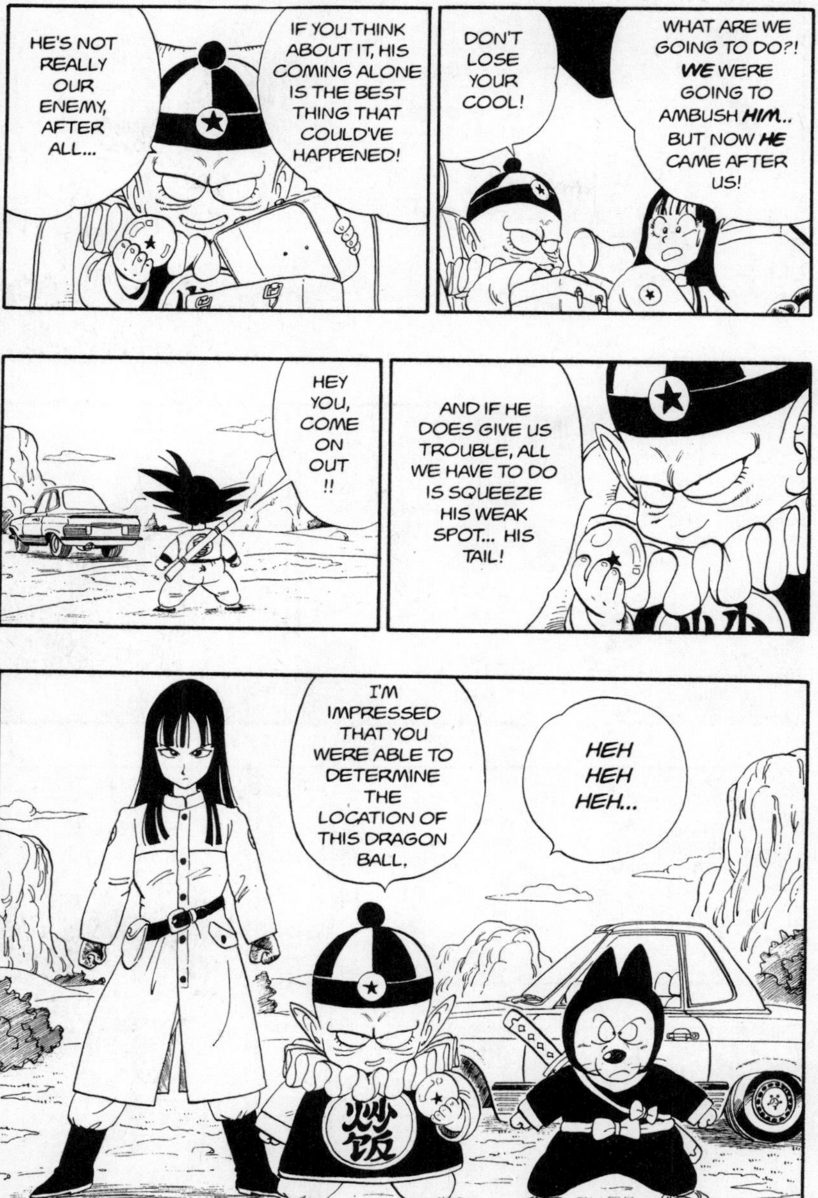
WHAT ARE WE GOING TO DO?! **WE** WERE GOING TO AMBUSH **HIM**.. BUT NOW **HE** CAME AFTER US!
DON'T LOSE YOUR COOL!
IF YOU THINK ABOUT IT, HIS COMING ALONE IS THE BEST THING THAT COULD'VE HAPPENED!
HE'S NOT REALLY OUR ENEMY, AFTER ALL...
AND IF HE DOES GIVE US TROUBLE, ALL WE HAVE TO DO IS SQUEEZE HIS WEAK SPOT... HIS TAIL!
HEY YOU, COME ON OUT !!
HEH HEH HEH...
I'M IMPRESSED THAT YOU WERE ABLE TO DETERMINE THE LOCATION OF THIS DRAGON BALL.

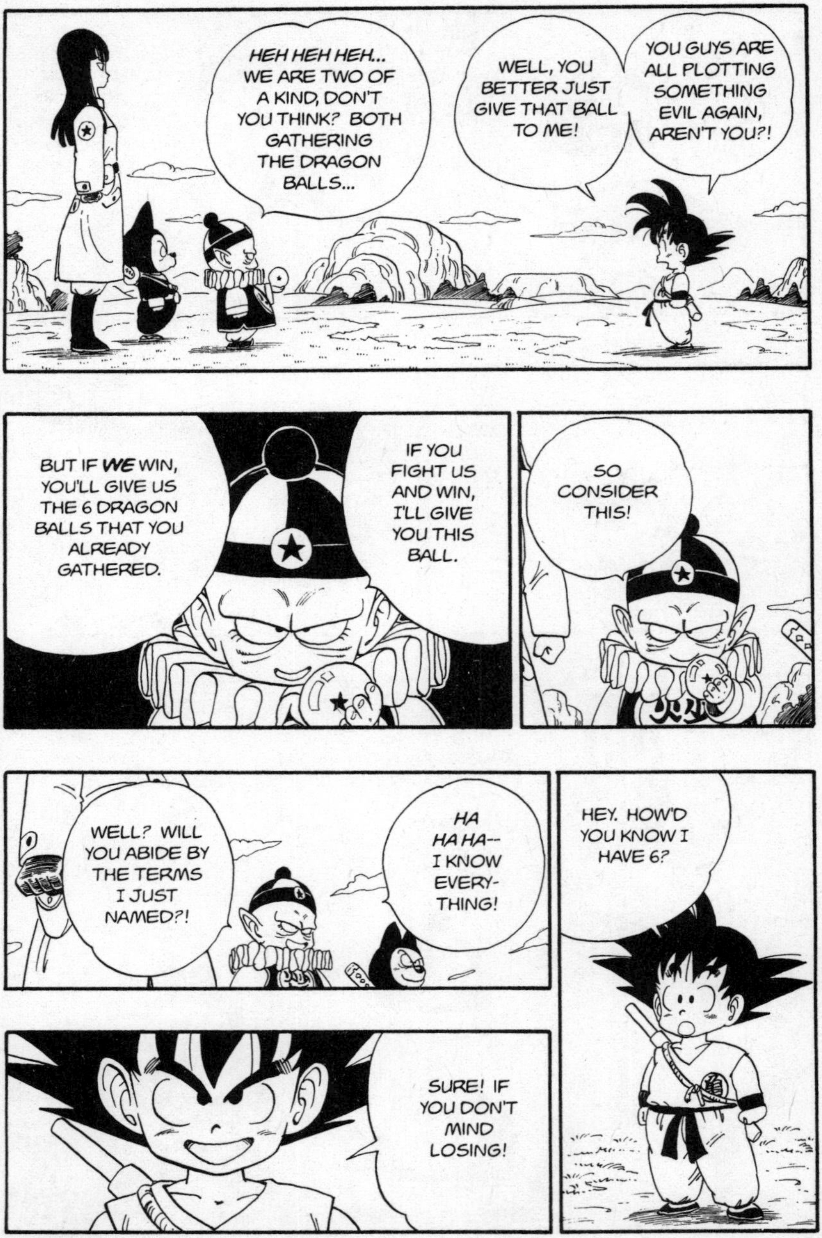
YOU GUYS ARE ALL PLOTTING SOMETHING EVIL AGAIN, AREN'T YOU?!
WELL, YOU BETTER JUST GIVE THAT BALL TO ME!
HEH HEH HEH... WE ARE TWO OF A KIND, DON'T YOU THINK? BOTH GATHERING THE DRAGON BALLS...
SO CONSIDER THIS!
IF YOU FIGHT US AND WIN, I'LL GIVE YOU THIS BALL.
BUT IF ***WE*** WIN, YOU'LL GIVE US THE 6 DRAGON BALLS THAT YOU ALREADY GATHERED.
HEY. HOW'D YOU KNOW I HAVE 6?
HA HA HA-- I KNOW EVERYTHING!
WELL? WILL YOU ABIDE BY THE TERMS I JUST NAMED?!
SURE! IF YOU DON'T MIND LOSING!

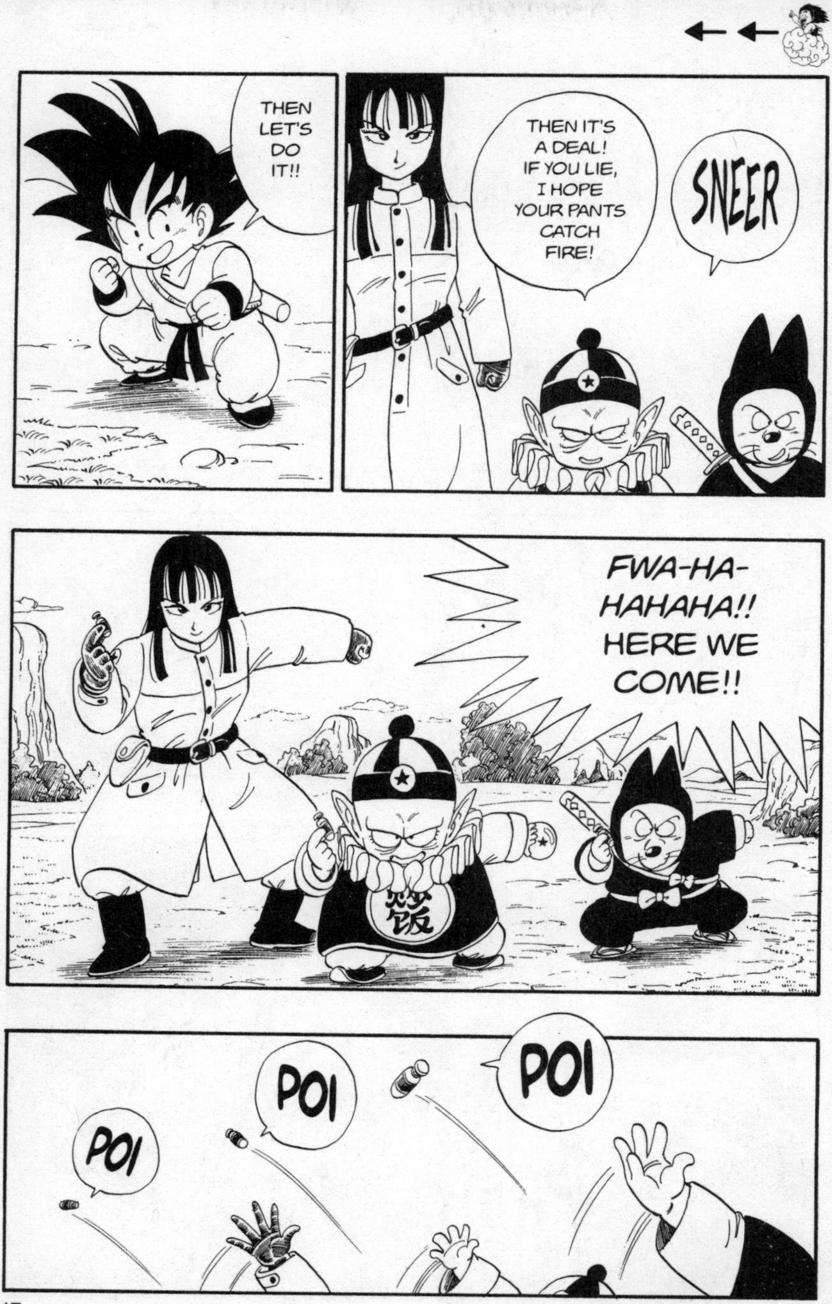
THEN IT'S A DEAL! IF YOU LIE, I HOPE YOUR PANTS CATCH FIRE!
SNEER
THEN LET'S DO IT!!
FWA-HA-HAHAHA!! HERE WE COME!!
POI
POI
POI

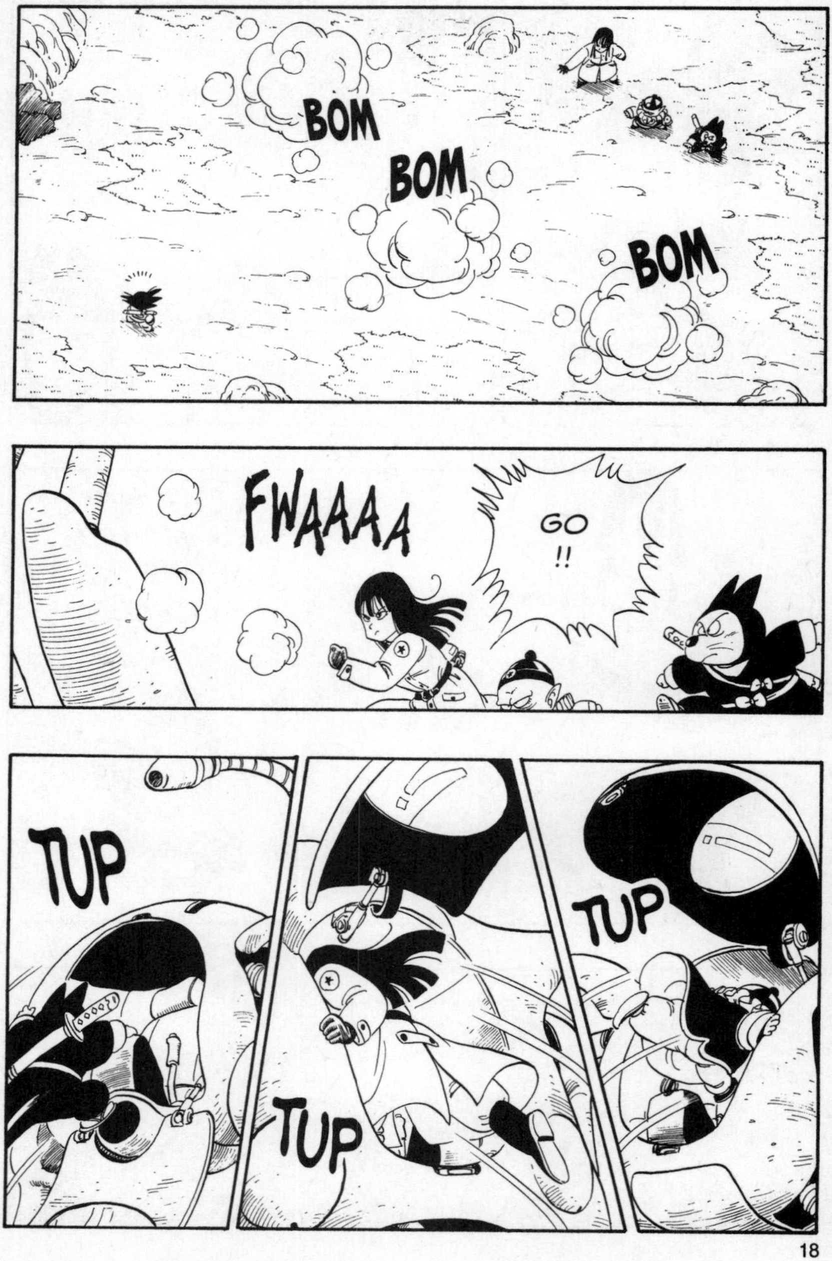
BOM
BOM
BOM
GO !!
FWAAAA
TUP
TUP
TUP

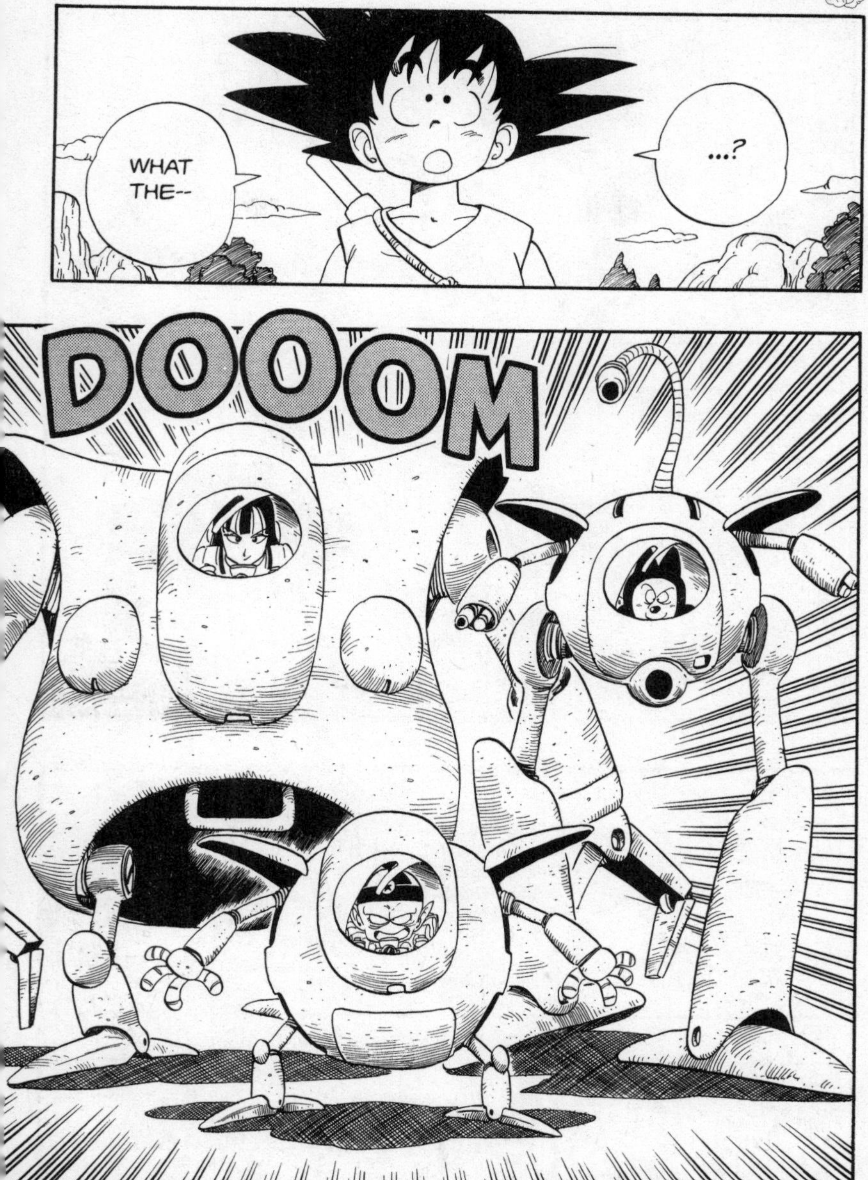
...?
WHAT THE--
DOOOM

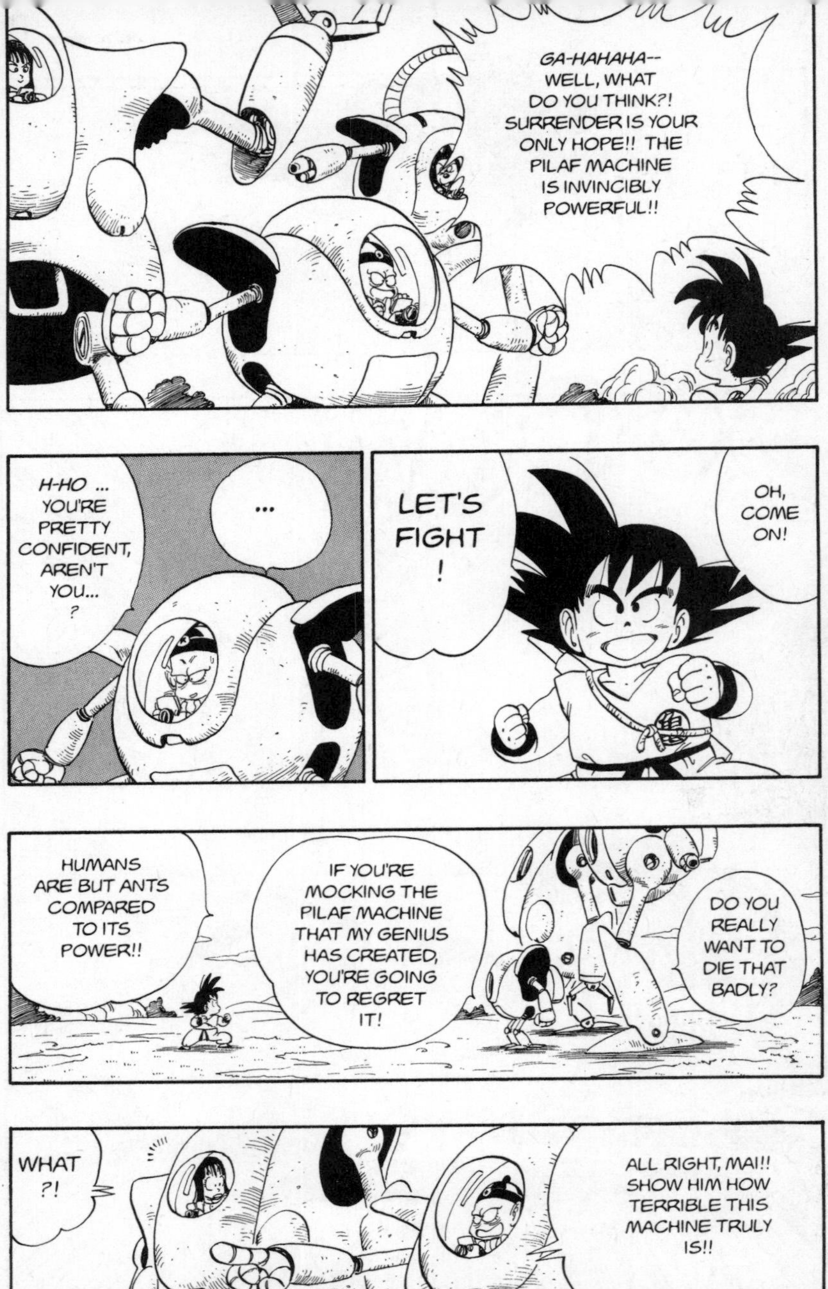
GA-HAHAHA-- WELL, WHAT DO YOU THINK?! SURRENDER IS YOUR ONLY HOPE!! THE PILAF MACHINE IS INVINCIBLY POWERFUL!!
OH, COME ON!
LET'S FIGHT !
...
H-HO ... YOU'RE PRETTY CONFIDENT, AREN'T YOU... ?
DO YOU REALLY WANT TO DIE THAT BADLY?
IF YOU'RE MOCKING THE PILAF MACHINE THAT MY GENIUS HAS CREATED, YOU'RE GOING TO REGRET IT!
HUMANS ARE BUT ANTS COMPARED TO ITS POWER!!
ALL RIGHT, MAI!! SHOW HIM HOW TERRIBLE THIS MACHINE TRULY IS!!
WHAT ?!

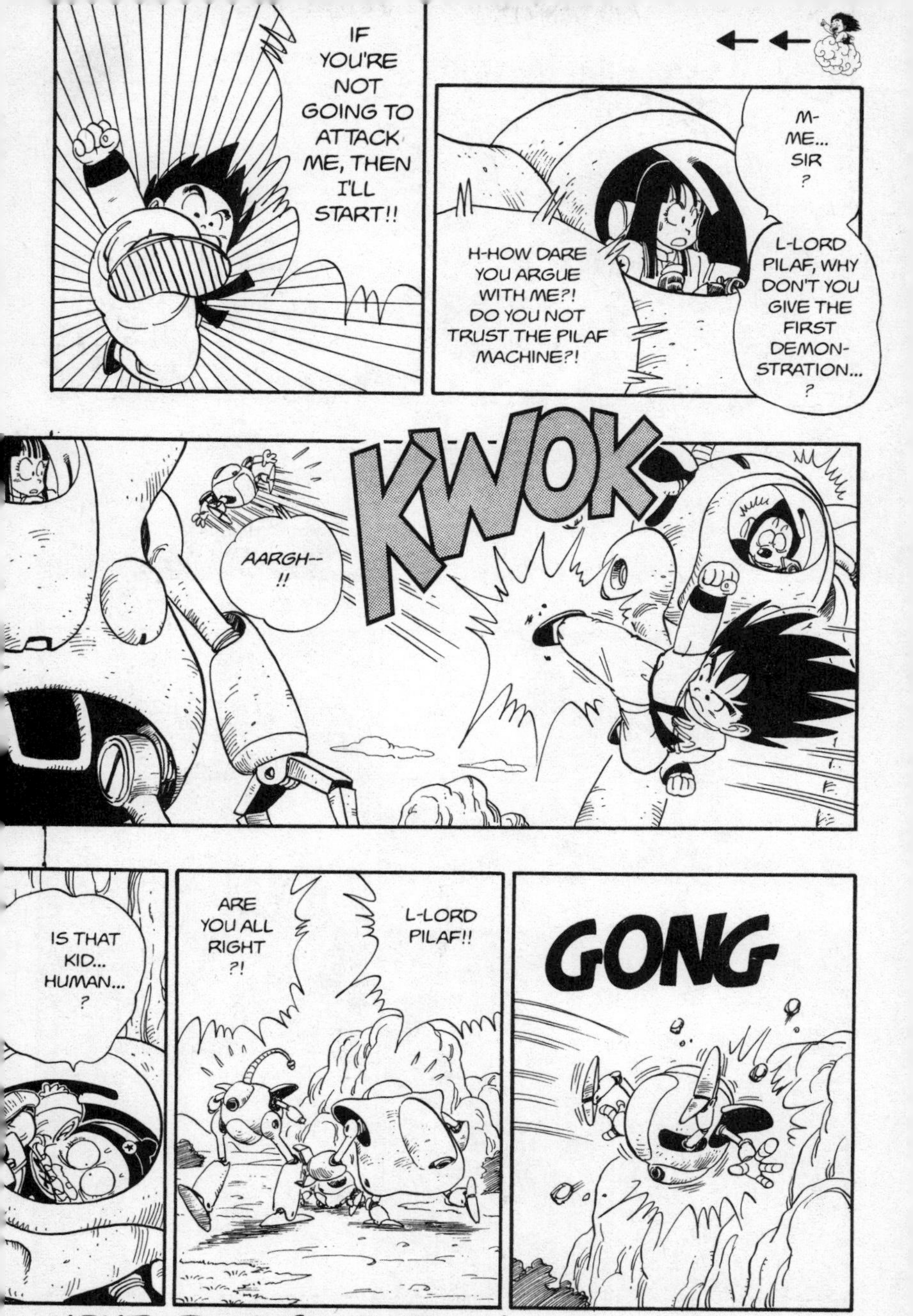
M-ME... SIR?
L-LORD PILAF, WHY DON'T YOU GIVE THE FIRST DEMONSTRATION...?
H-HOW DARE YOU ARGUE WITH ME?! DO YOU NOT TRUST THE PILAF MACHINE?!
IF YOU'RE NOT GOING TO ATTACK ME, THEN I'LL START!!
KWOK
AARGH--!!
GONG
L-LORD PILAF!!
ARE YOU ALL RIGHT?!
IS THAT KID... HUMAN...?

NEXT: Battle for the Pants!

Tale 110 • The Pilaf Machine

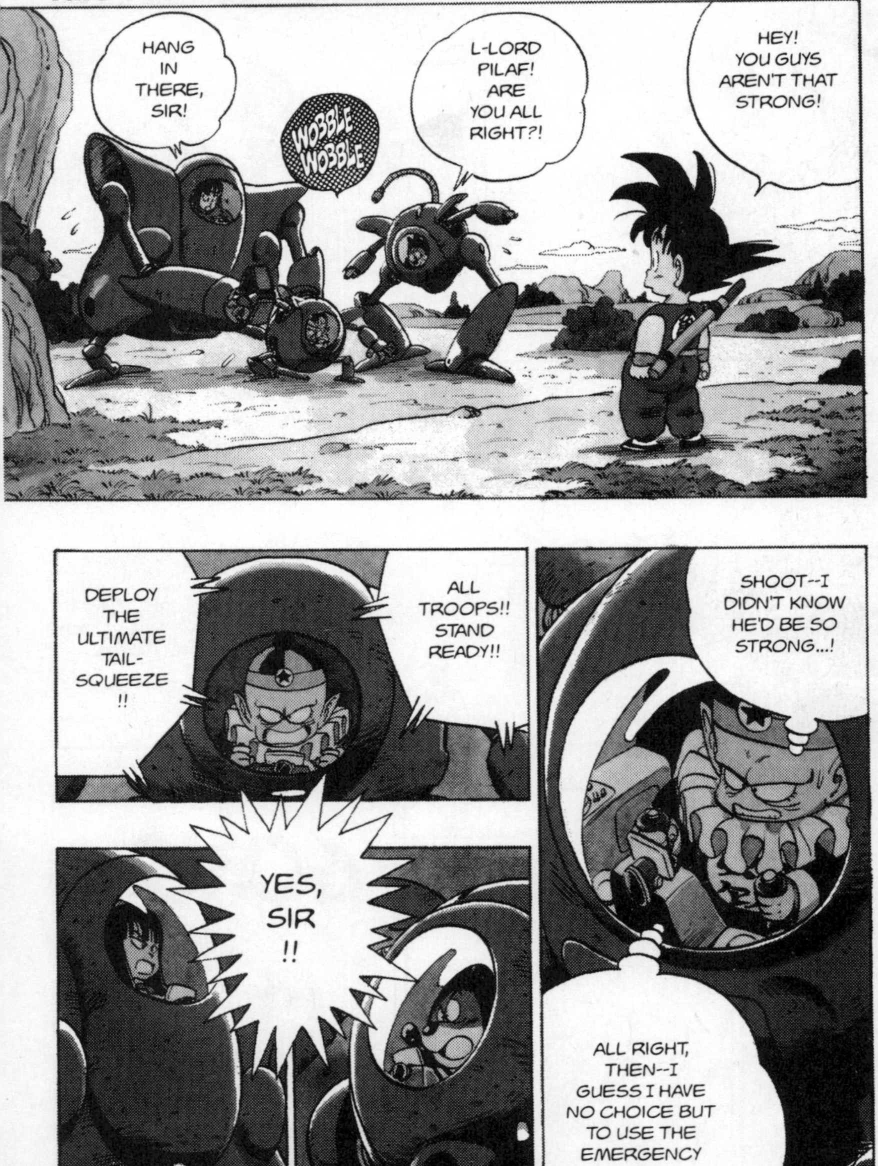

HEY! YOU GUYS AREN'T THAT STRONG!
L-LORD PILAF! ARE YOU ALL RIGHT?!
WOBBLE WOBBLE
HANG IN THERE, SIR!
SHOOT--I DIDN'T KNOW HE'D BE SO STRONG...!
ALL RIGHT, THEN--I GUESS I HAVE NO CHOICE BUT TO USE THE EMERGENCY PLAN...!
ALL TROOPS!! STAND READY!!
DEPLOY THE ULTIMATE TAIL-SQUEEZE !!
YES, SIR !!

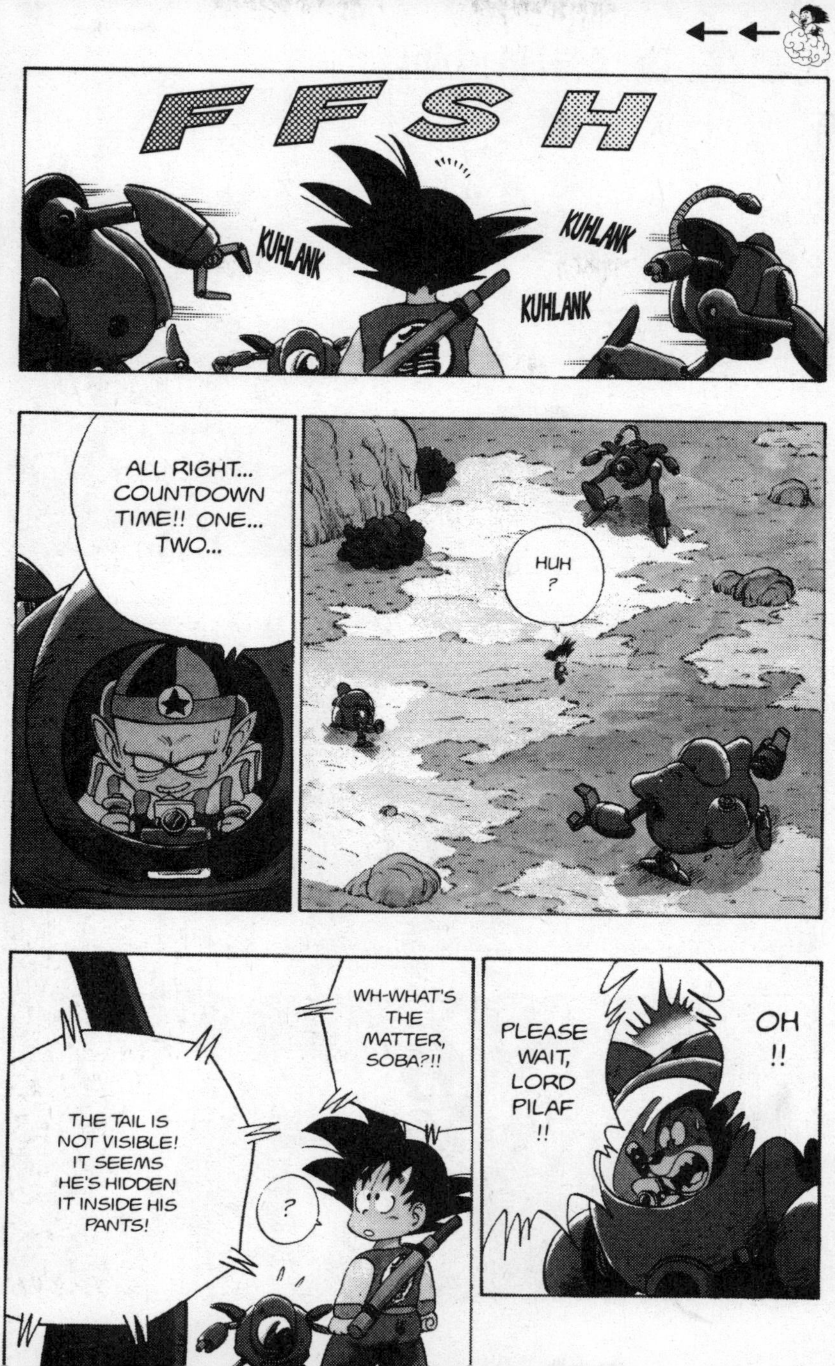
FFSH
KUHLANK
KUHLANK
KUHLANK
HUH ?
ALL RIGHT... COUNTDOWN TIME!! ONE... TWO...
OH !!
PLEASE WAIT, LORD PILAF !!
WH-WHAT'S THE MATTER, SOBA?!!
THE TAIL IS NOT VISIBLE! IT SEEMS HE'S HIDDEN IT INSIDE HIS PANTS!
?

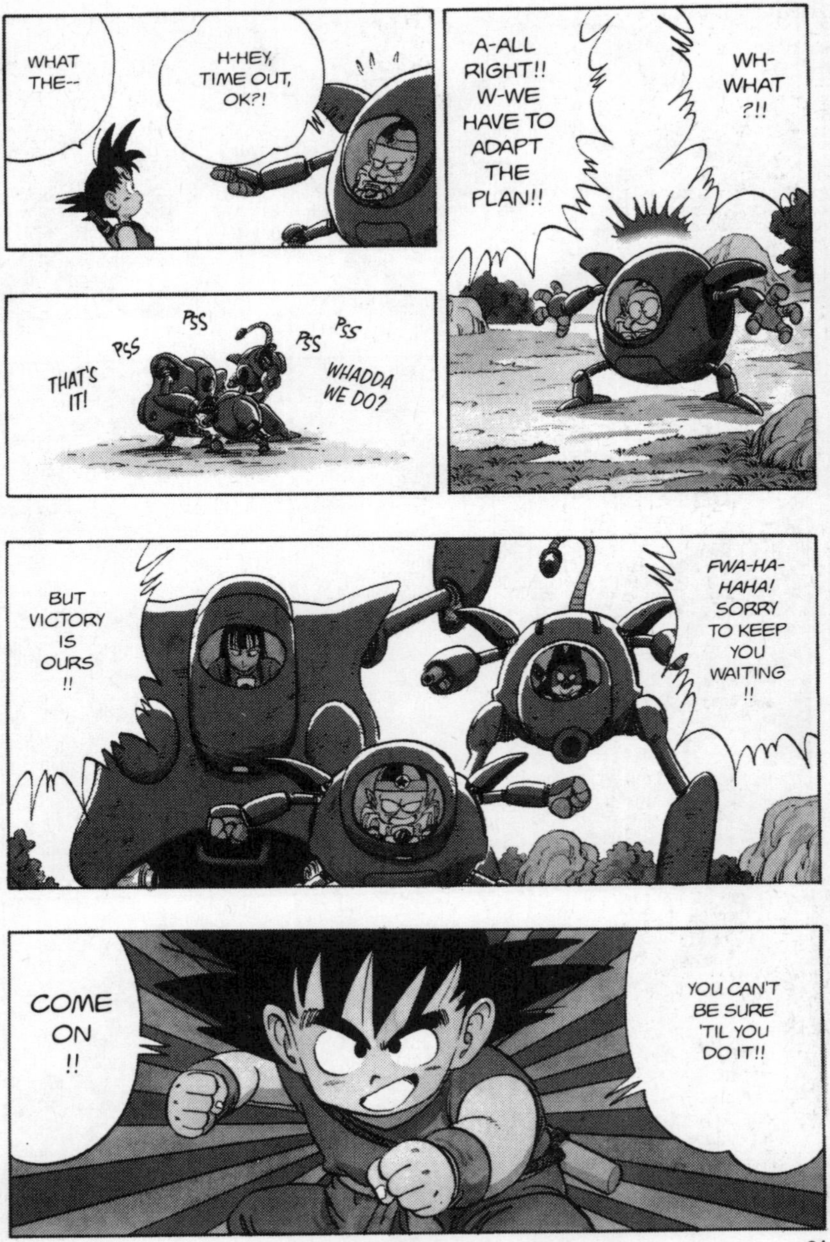
WH-WHAT ?!!
A-ALL RIGHT!! W-WE HAVE TO ADAPT THE PLAN!!
H-HEY, TIME OUT, OK?!
WHAT THE--
PSS
WHADDA WE DO?
PSS
PSS
PSS
THAT'S IT!
FWA-HA-HAHA! SORRY TO KEEP YOU WAITING !!
BUT VICTORY IS OURS !!
YOU CAN'T BE SURE 'TIL YOU DO IT!!
COME ON !!

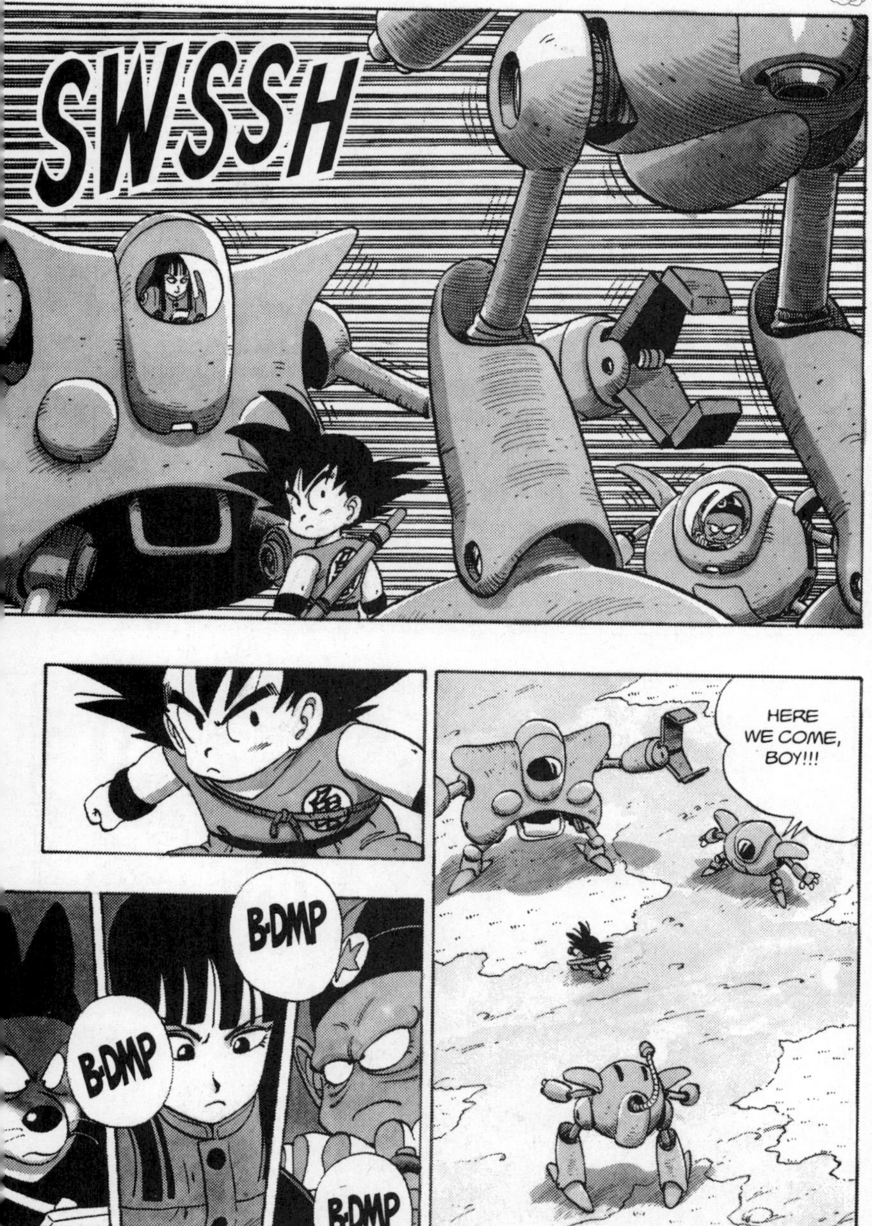
SWSSH
HERE WE COME, BOY!!!
B-DMP
B-DMP
B-DMP

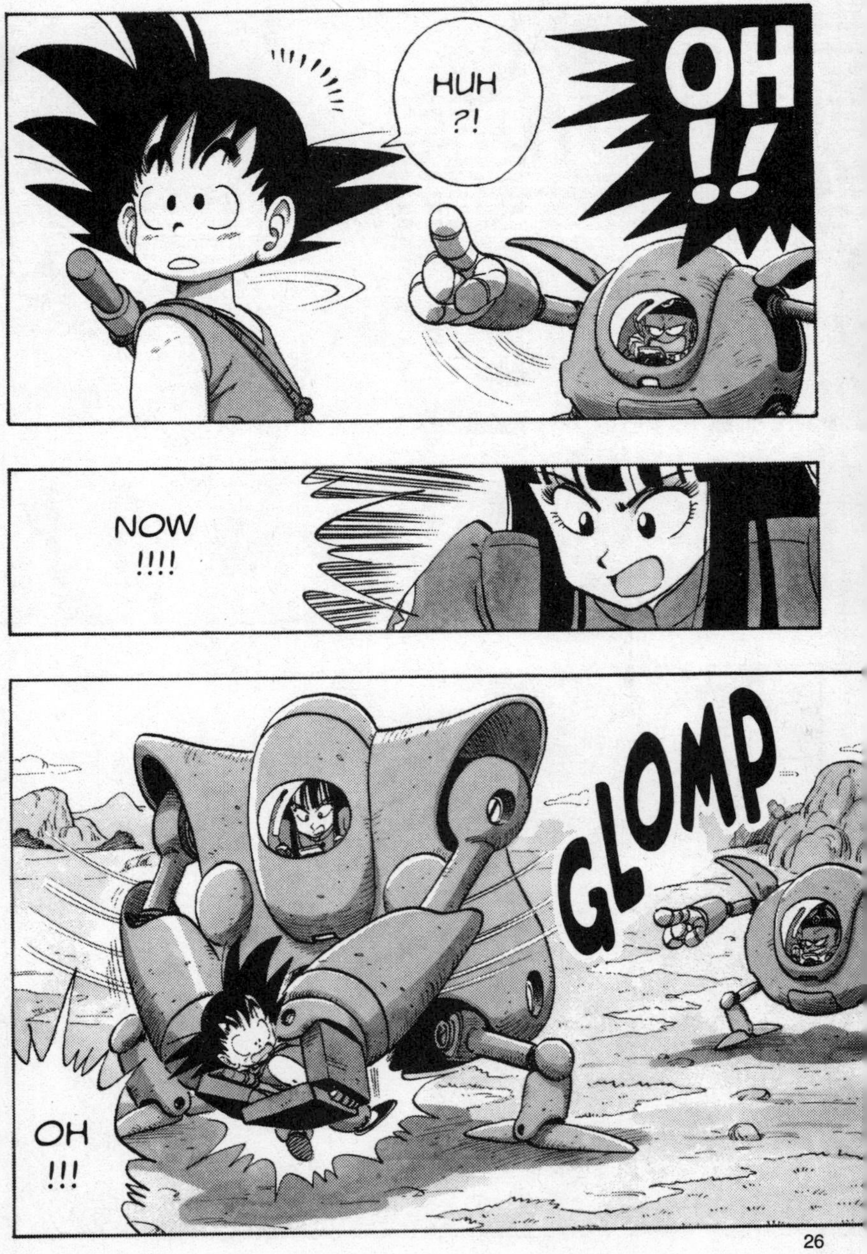
OH!!
HUH?!
NOW!!!!
GLOMP
OH!!!

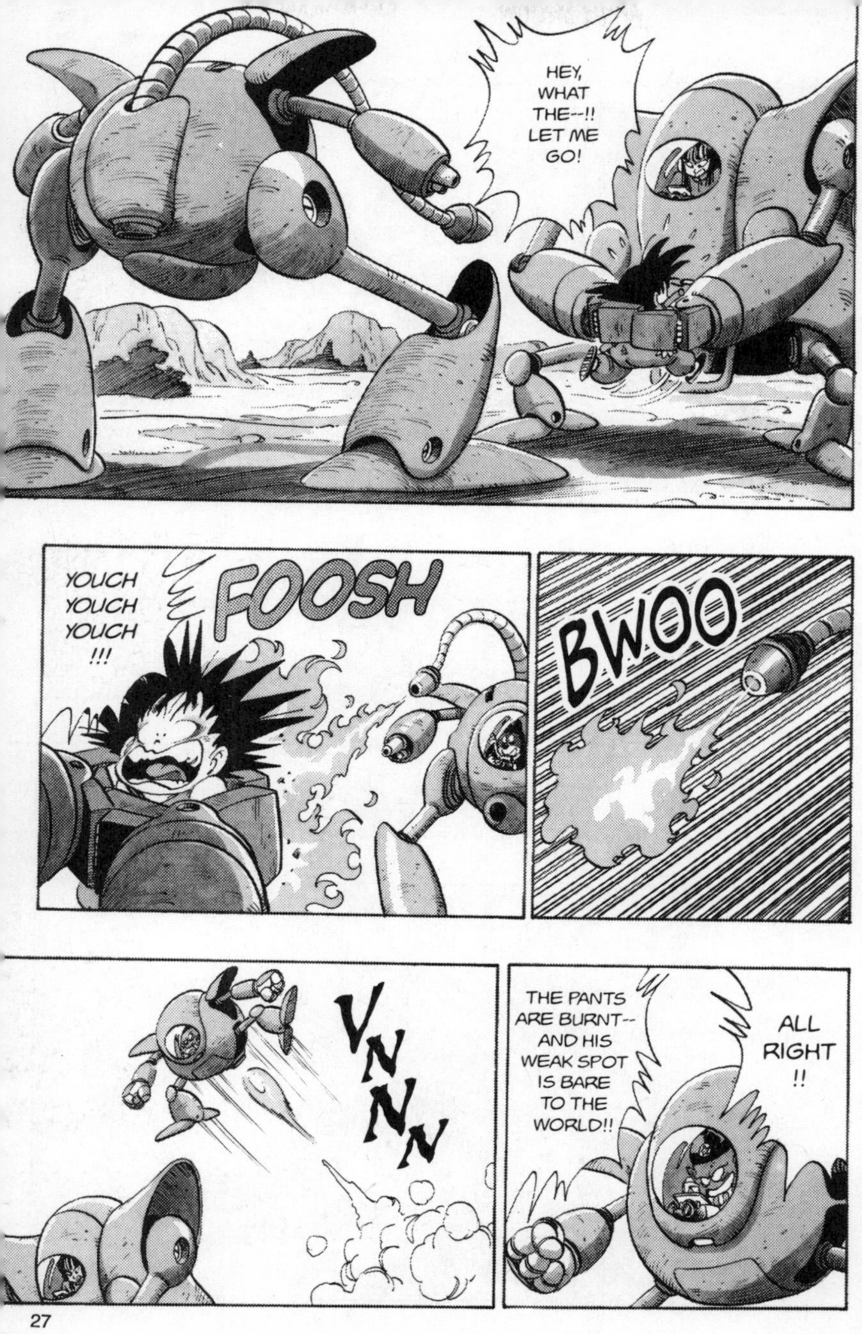
HEY, WHAT THE--!! LET ME GO!
BWOO
YOUCH YOUCH YOUCH !!!
FOOSH
ALL RIGHT !!
THE PANTS ARE BURNT-- AND HIS WEAK SPOT IS BARE TO THE WORLD!!
VNNN

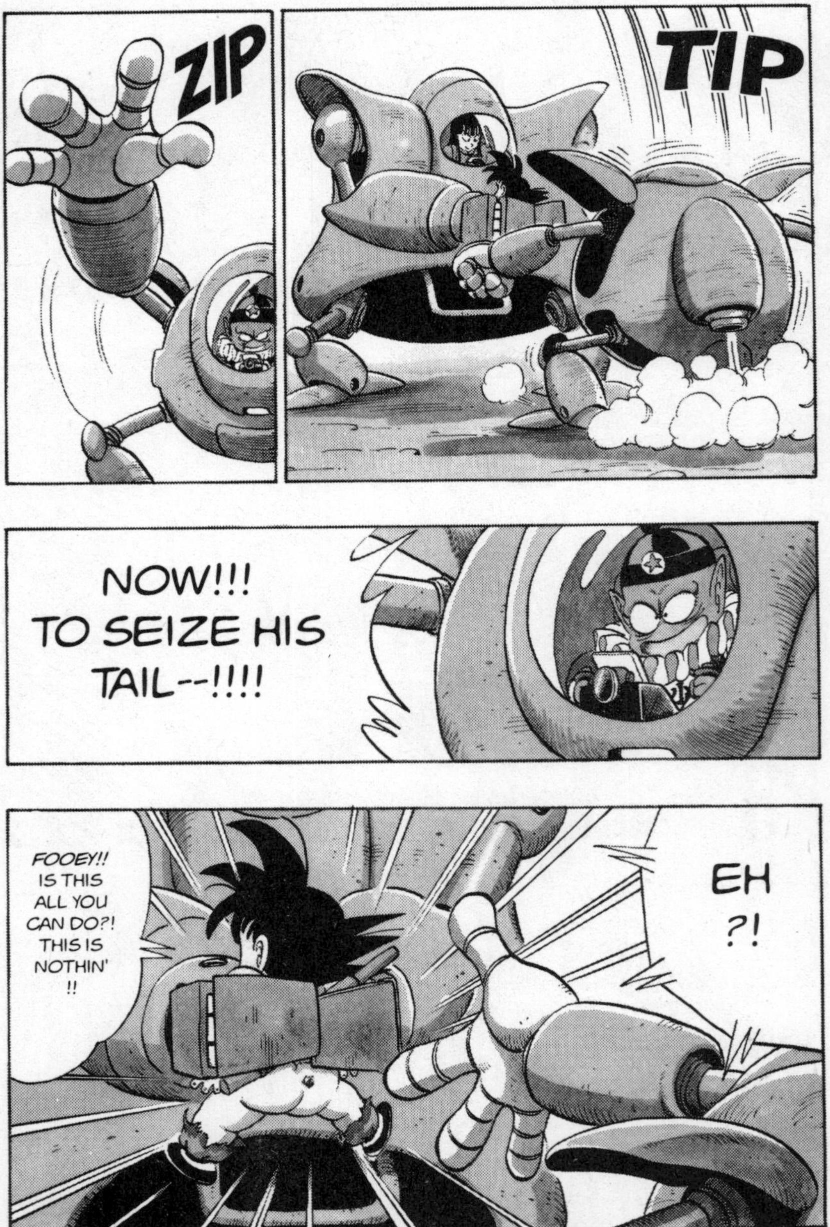
TIP
ZIP
NOW!!! TO SEIZE HIS TAIL--!!!!
EH ?!
FOOEY!! IS THIS ALL YOU CAN DO?! THIS IS NOTHIN' !!

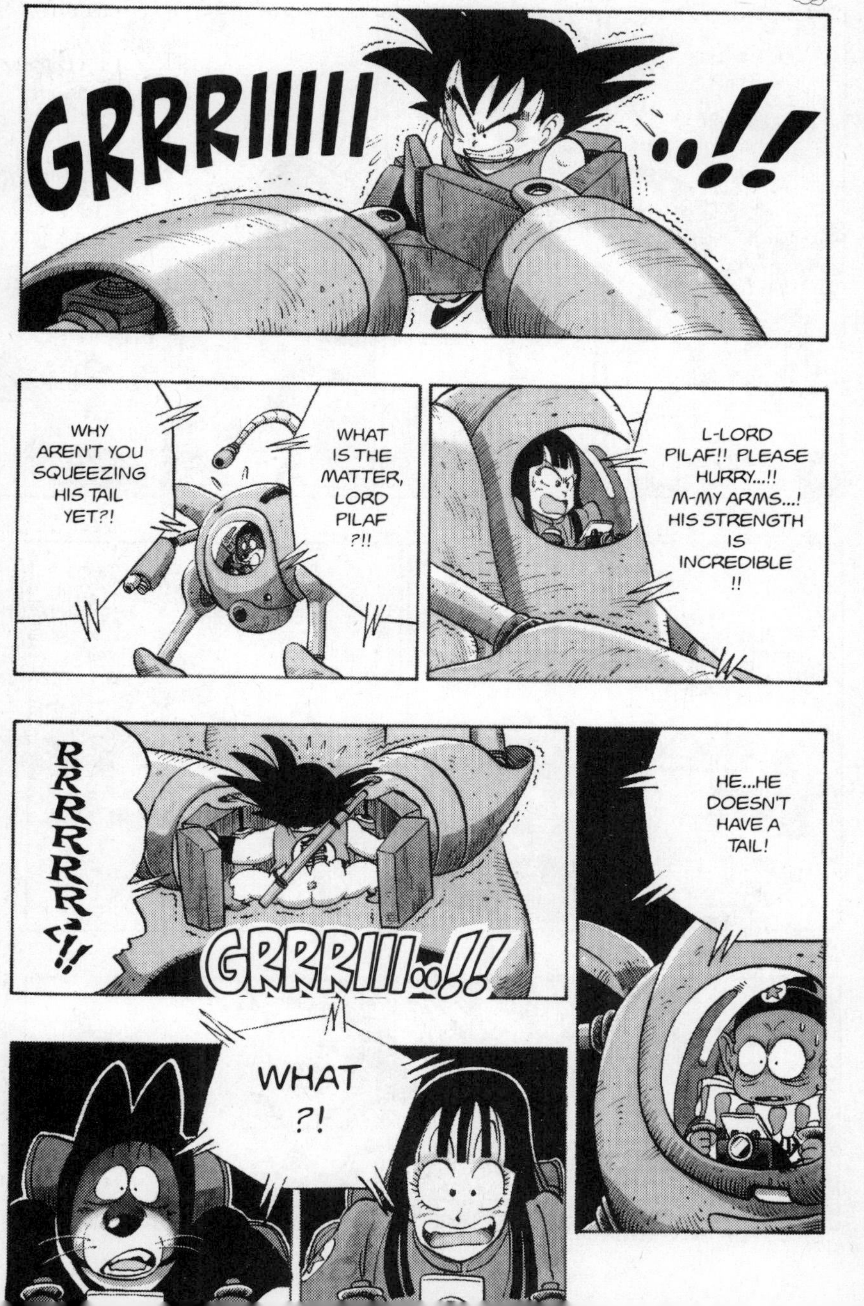
GRRRIIIIII
..!!
L-LORD PILAF!! PLEASE HURRY...!! M-MY ARMS...! HIS STRENGTH IS INCREDIBLE !!
WHAT IS THE MATTER, LORD PILAF ?!!
WHY AREN'T YOU SQUEEZING HIS TAIL YET?!
HE...HE DOESN'T HAVE A TAIL!
RRRRRR~!!
GRRRIII..!!
WHAT ?!

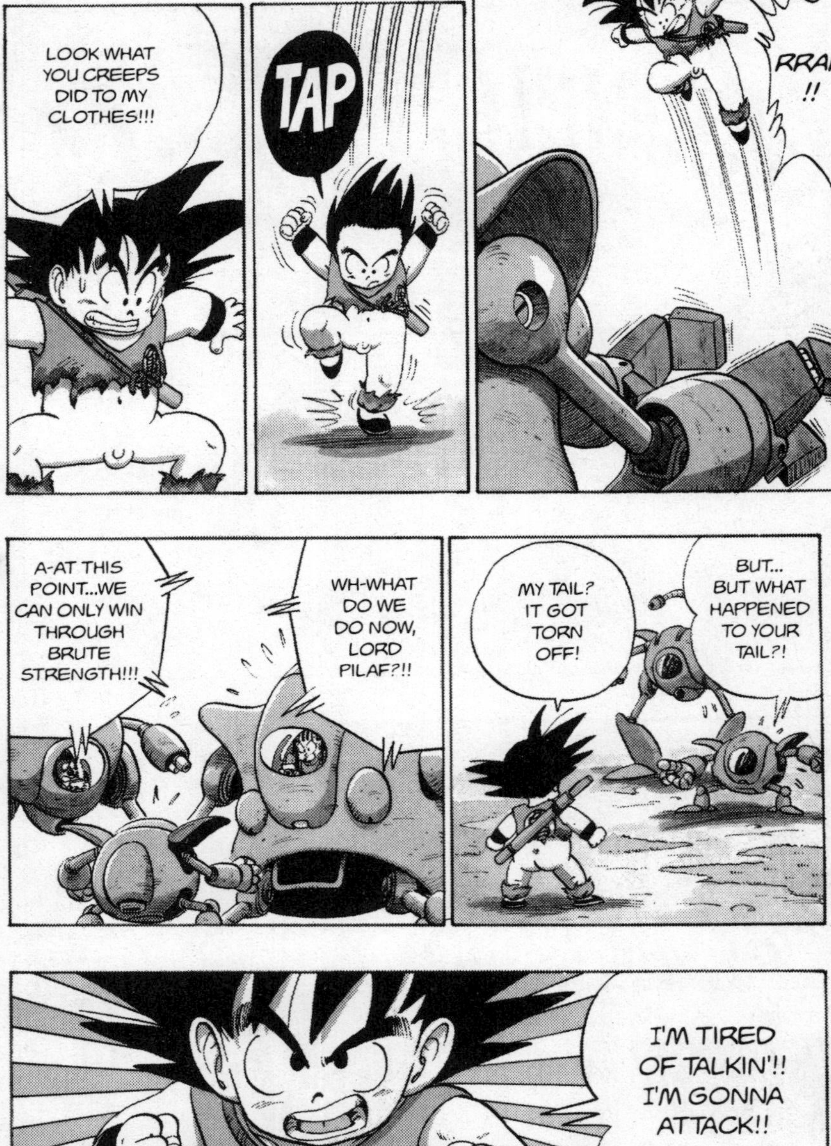
RRAH !!
TAP
LOOK WHAT YOU CREEPS DID TO MY CLOTHES!!!
BUT... BUT WHAT HAPPENED TO YOUR TAIL?!
MY TAIL? IT GOT TORN OFF!
WH-WHAT DO WE DO NOW, LORD PILAF?!!
A-AT THIS POINT...WE CAN ONLY WIN THROUGH BRUTE STRENGTH!!!
I'M TIRED OF TALKIN'!! I'M GONNA ATTACK!!

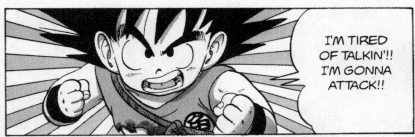

MERGE
!!!!

ALL
RIGHT
!!!

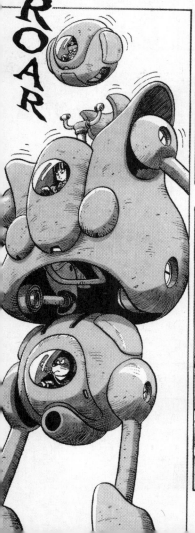

ROAR

WIIIN
WIIIN

BOMM

KYUUUN

WIIIN

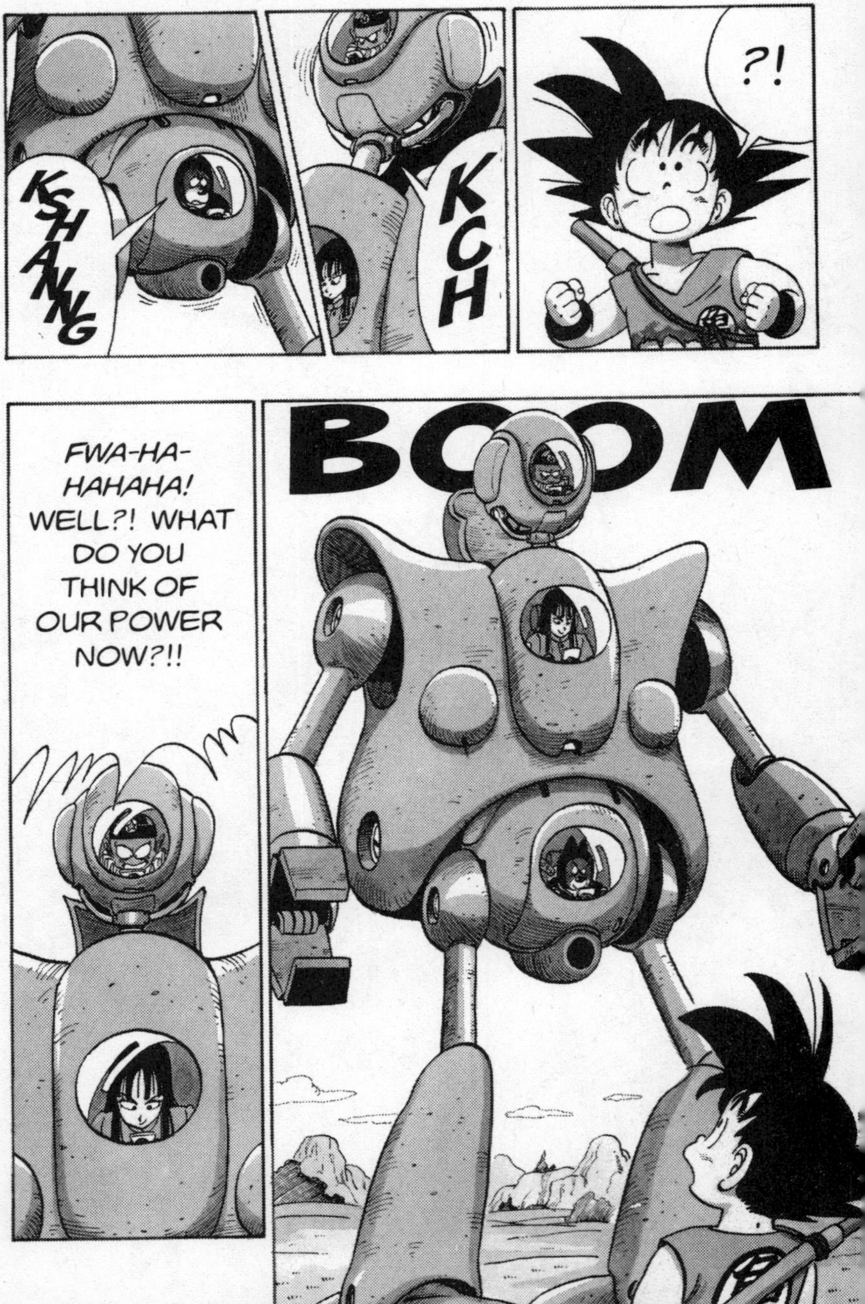
?!
KCH
KSHANNG
BOOM
FWA-HA-HAHAHA! WELL?! WHAT DO YOU THINK OF OUR POWER NOW?!!

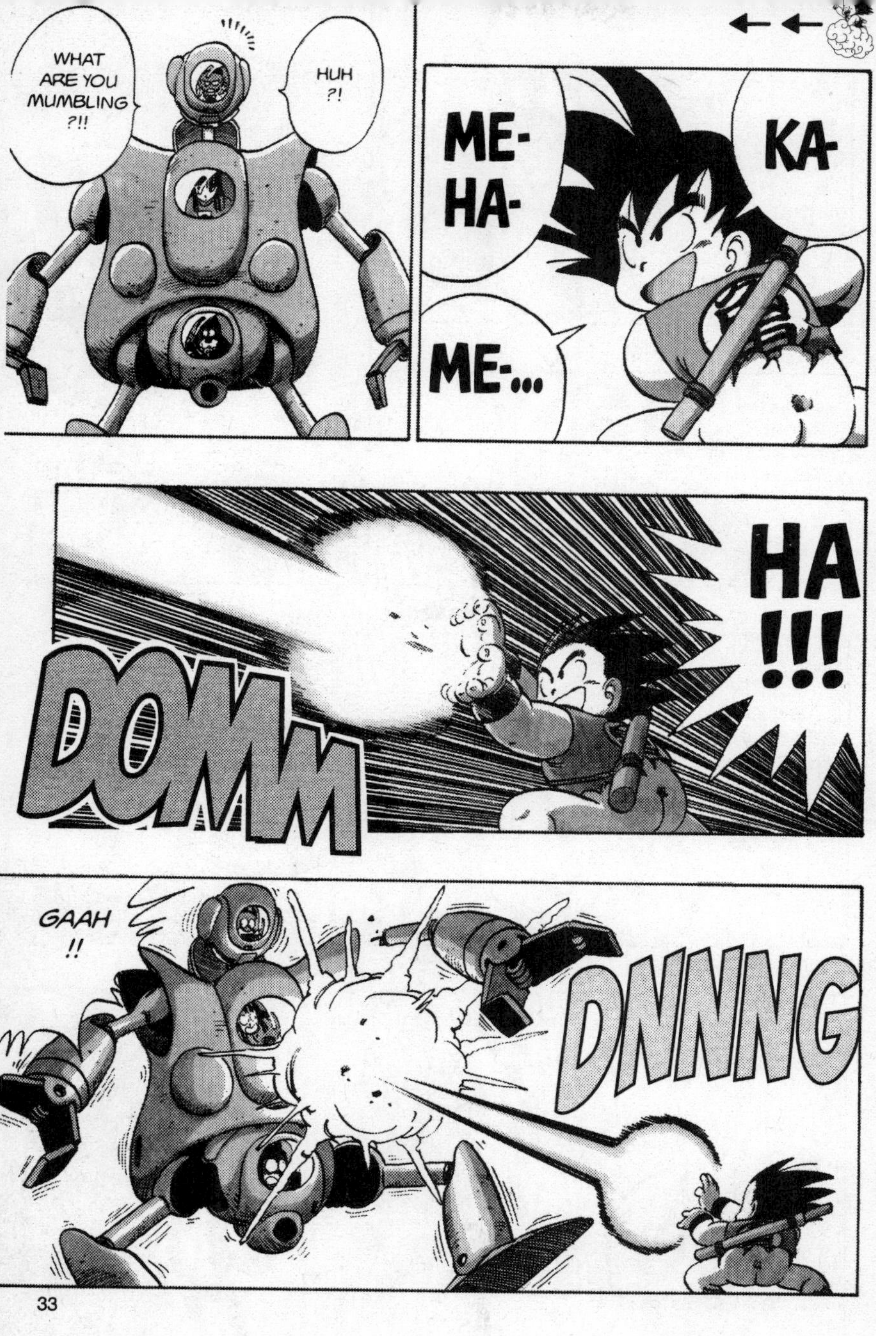

KA-
ME-HA-
ME-...
HUH ?!
WHAT ARE YOU MUMBLING ?!!
HA !!!
DOMM
DNNNG
GAAH !!

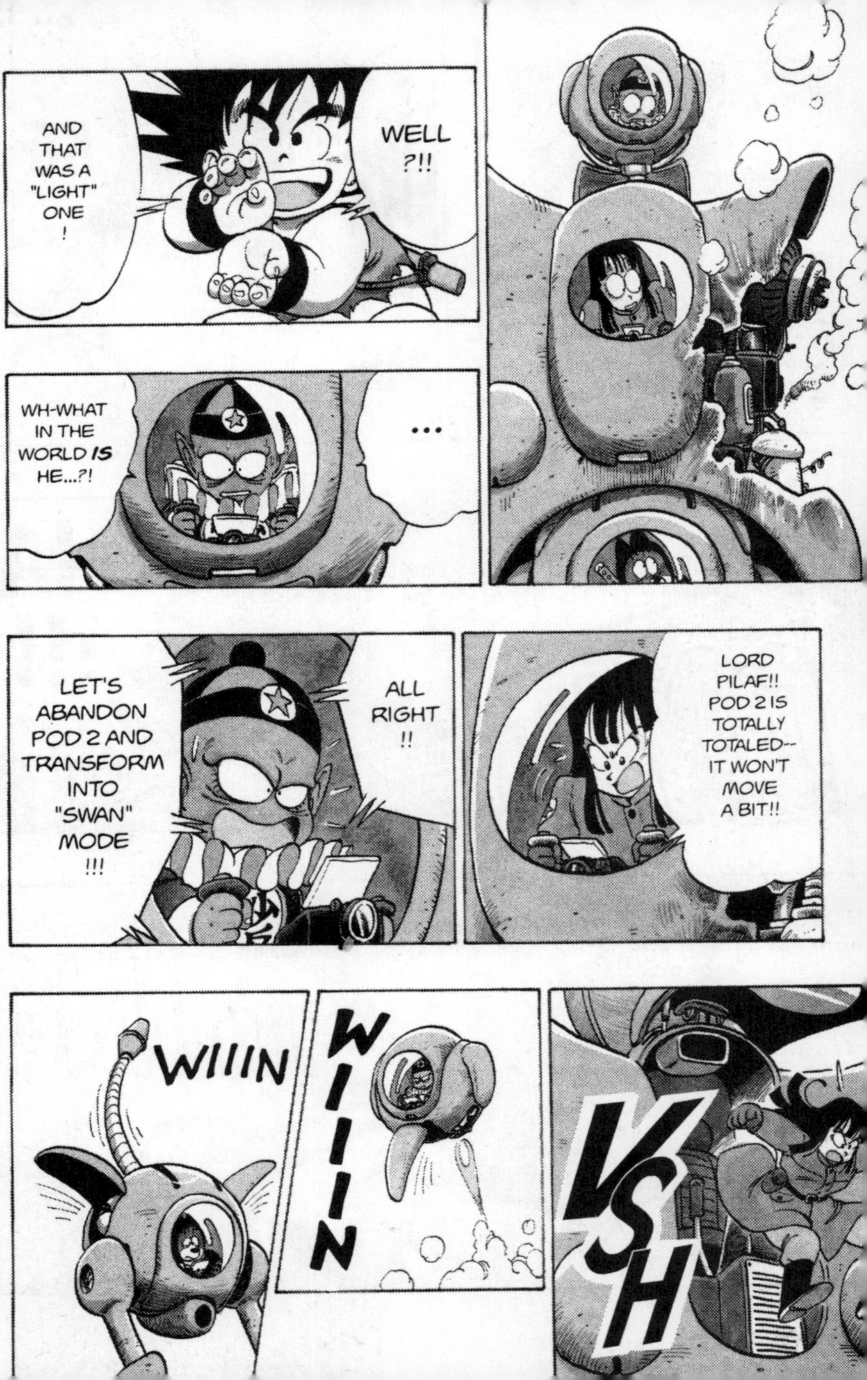

WELL ?!!
AND THAT WAS A "LIGHT" ONE !
...
WH-WHAT IN THE WORLD *IS* HE...?!
LORD PILAF!! POD 2 IS TOTALLY TOTALED-- IT WON'T MOVE A BIT!!
ALL RIGHT !!
LET'S ABANDON POD 2 AND TRANSFORM INTO "SWAN" MODE !!!
VSH
WIIIN
WIIIN

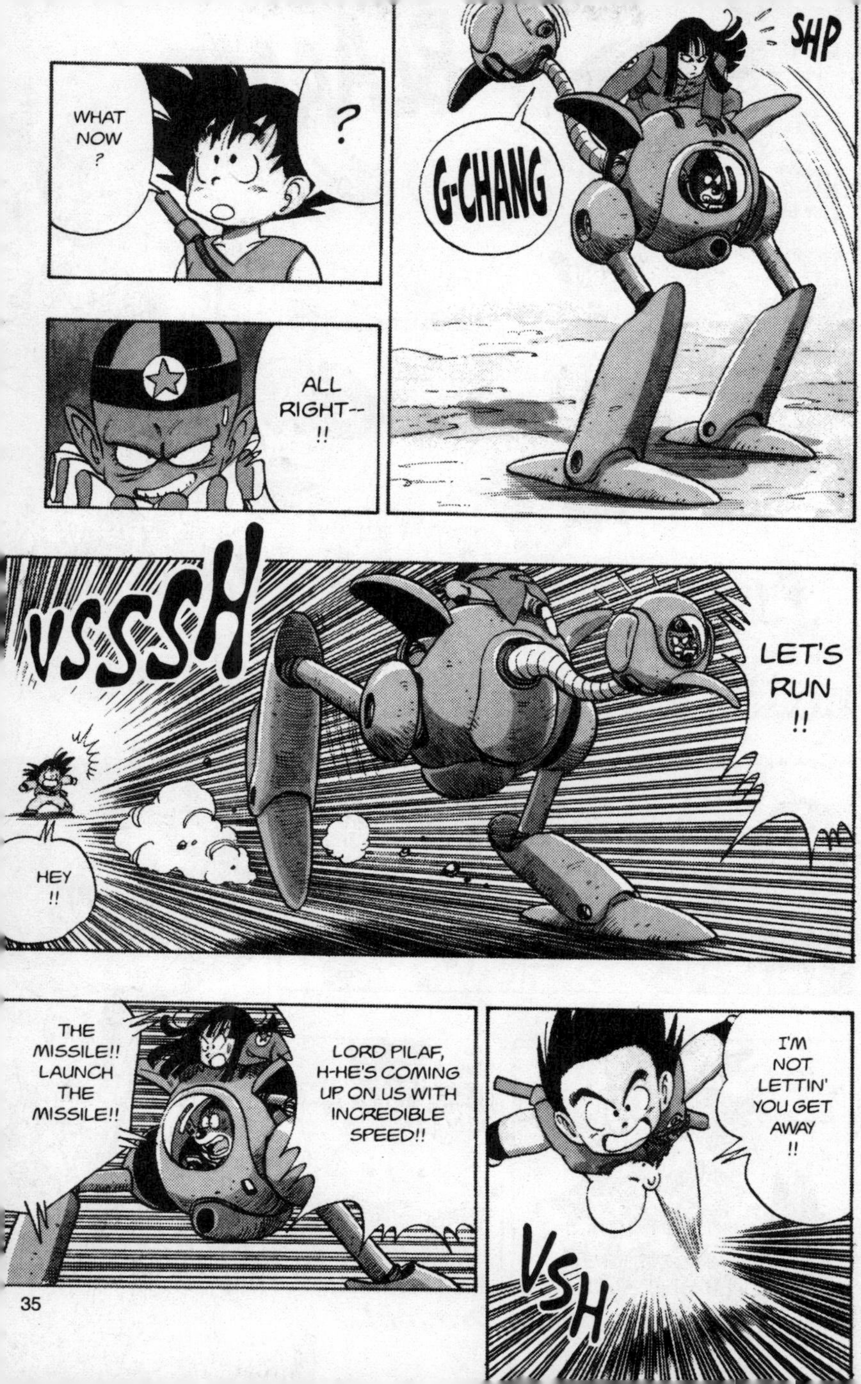
SHP
G-CHANG
WHAT NOW ?
?
ALL RIGHT-- !!
LET'S RUN !!
VSSSH
HEY !!
I'M NOT LETTIN' YOU GET AWAY !!
VSH
LORD PILAF, H-HE'S COMING UP ON US WITH INCREDIBLE SPEED!!
THE MISSILE!! LAUNCH THE MISSILE!!

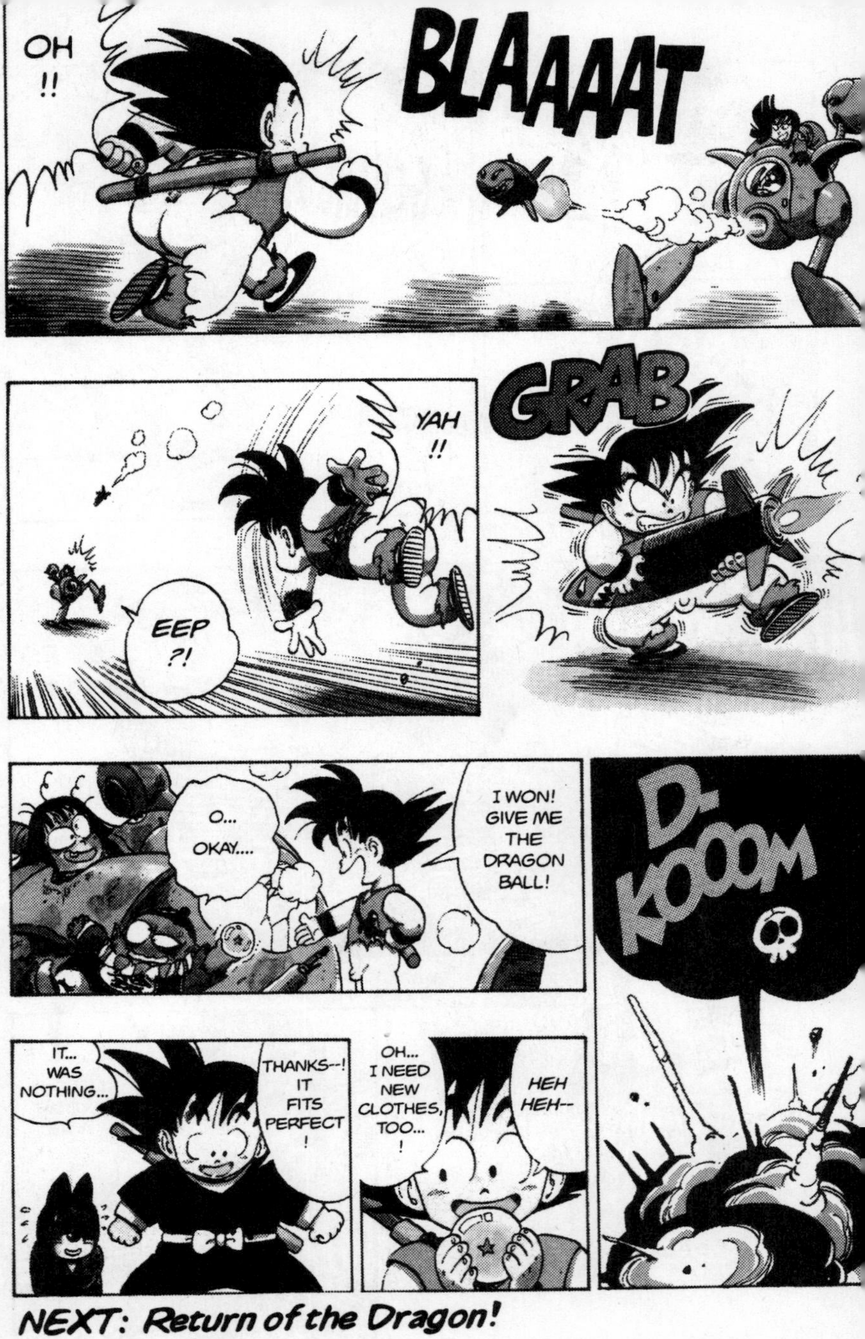

BLAAAAT
OH !!
GRAB
YAH !!
EEP ?!
D-KOOOM
I WON! GIVE ME THE DRAGON BALL!
O... OKAY....
HEH HEH--
OH... I NEED NEW CLOTHES, TOO... !
THANKS--! IT FITS PERFECT !
IT... WAS NOTHING...

NEXT: Return of the Dragon!

Tale 111 • Reenter the Dragon!

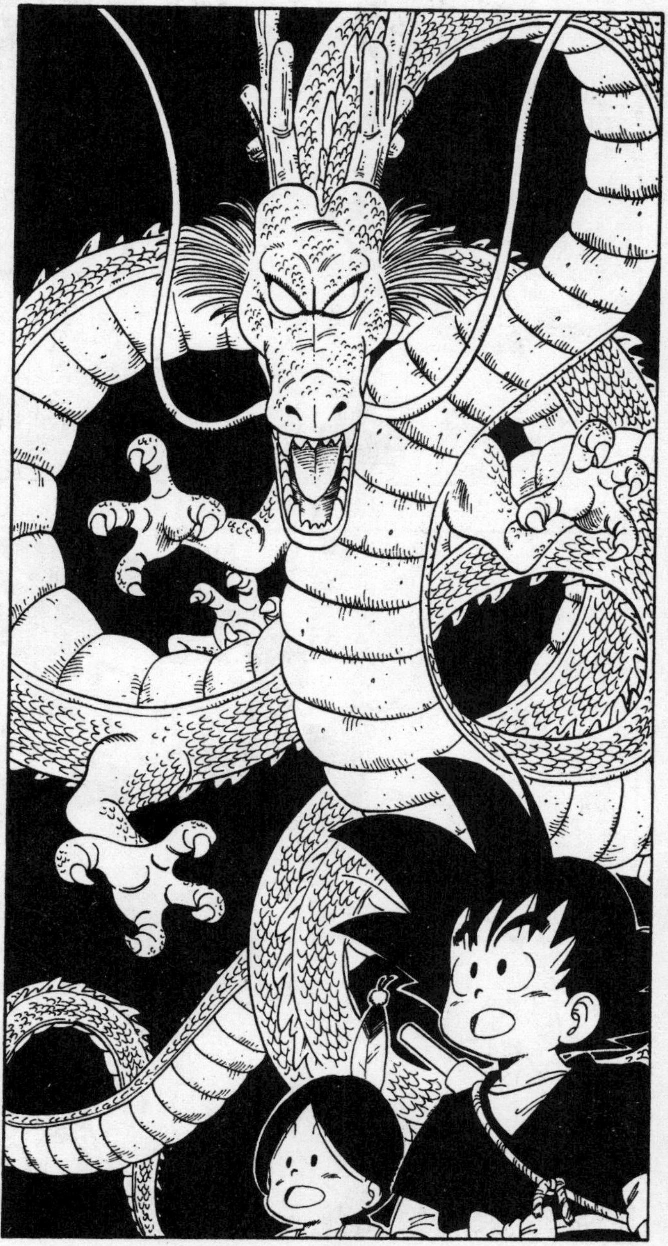

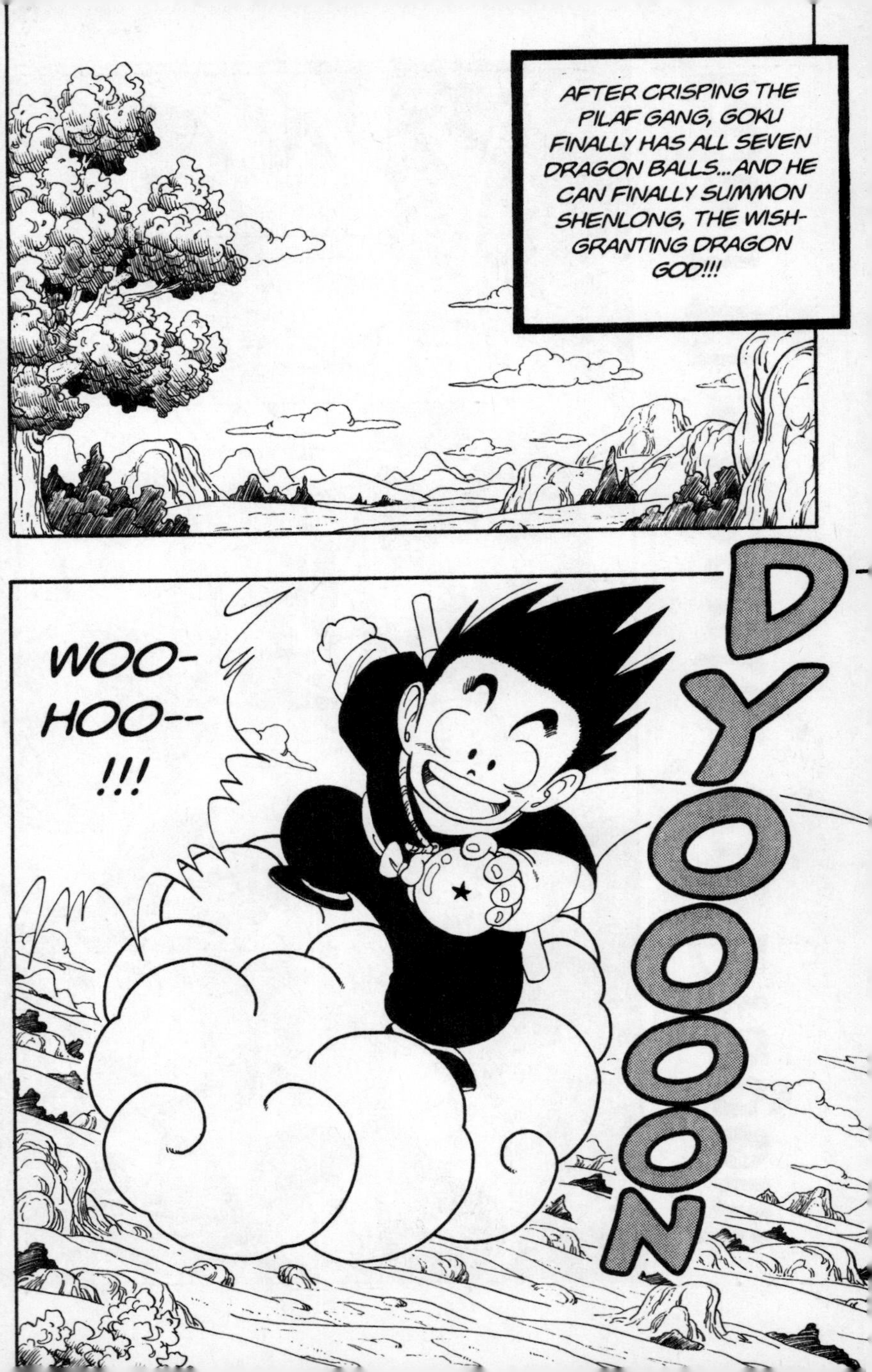
AFTER CRISPING THE PILAF GANG, GOKU FINALLY HAS ALL SEVEN DRAGON BALLS...AND HE CAN FINALLY SUMMON SHENLONG, THE WISH-GRANTING DRAGON GOD!!!
DYOOOOON
WOO-HOO--!!!

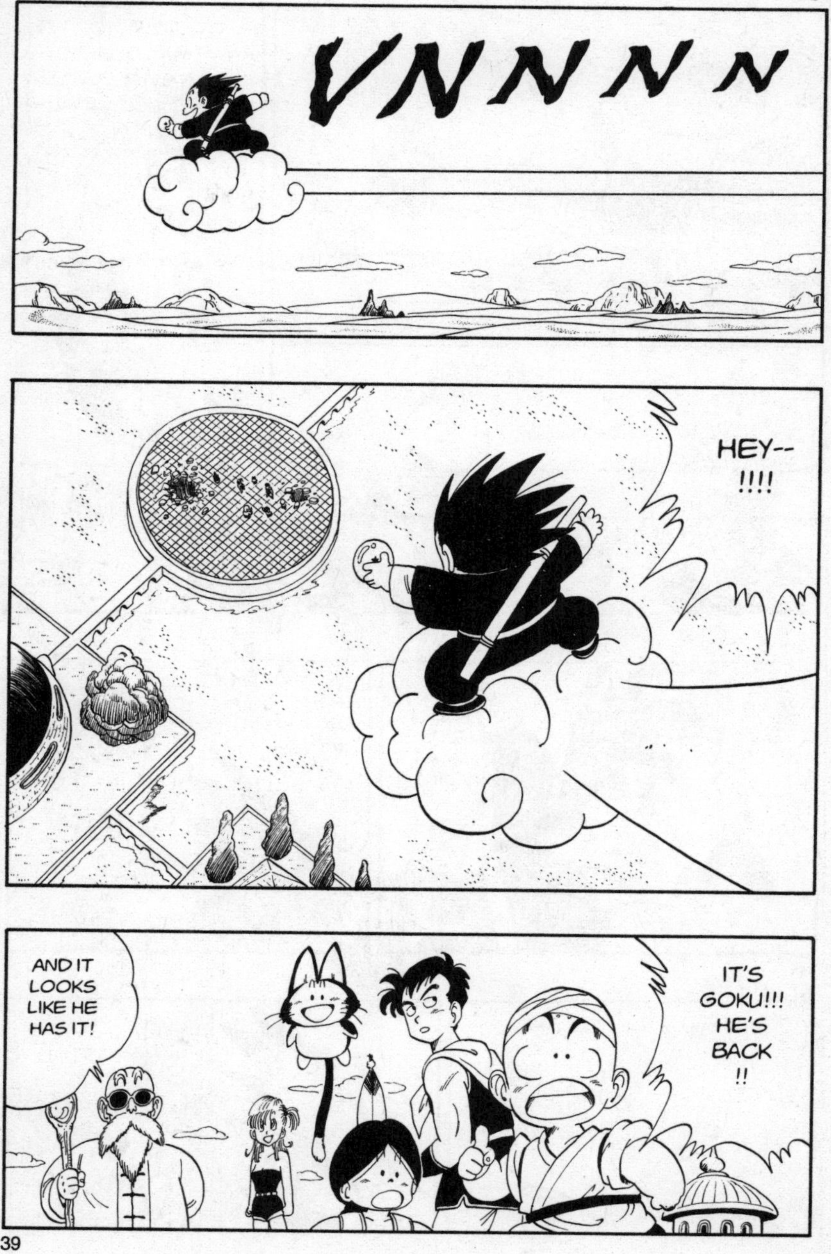
VNNNN
HEY-- !!!!
IT'S GOKU!!! HE'S BACK !!
AND IT LOOKS LIKE HE HAS IT!

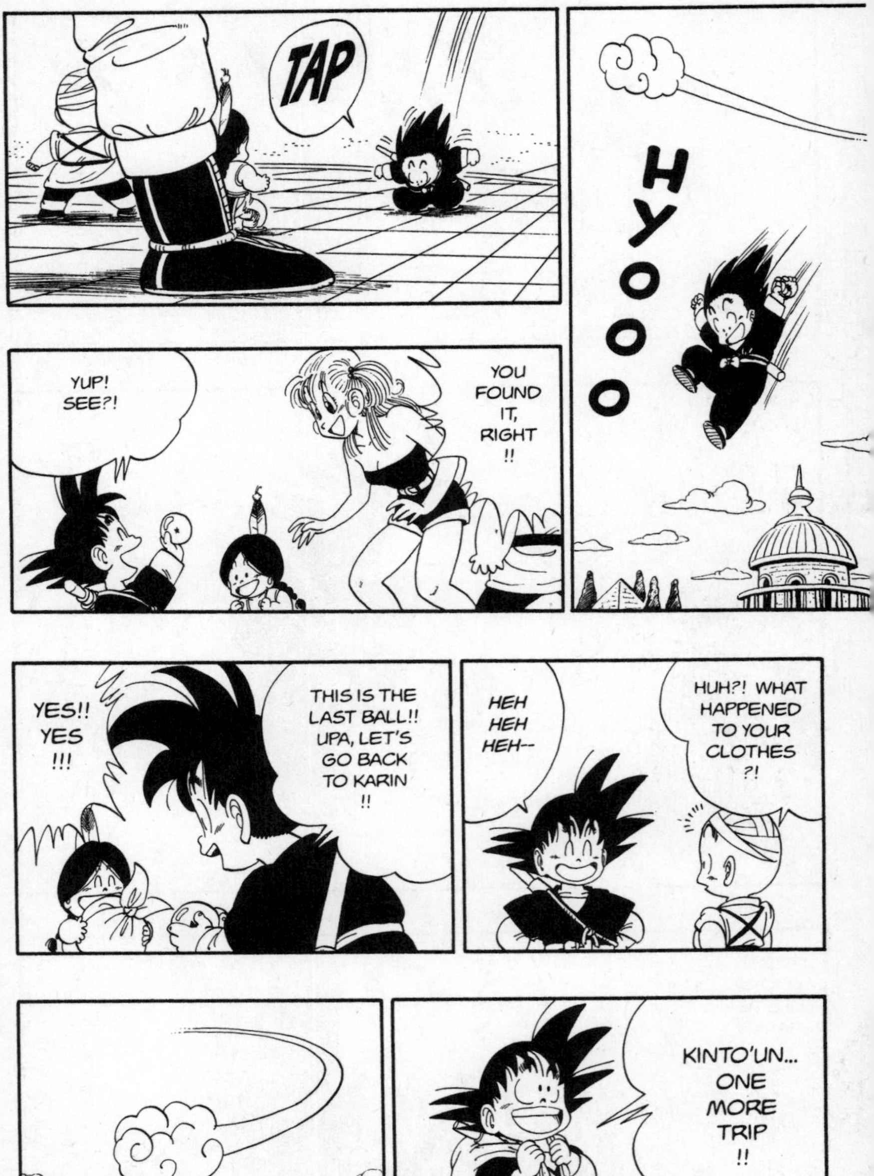
HYOOOO
TAP
YOU FOUND IT, RIGHT !!
YUP! SEE?!
HUH?! WHAT HAPPENED TO YOUR CLOTHES ?!
HEH HEH HEH--
THIS IS THE LAST BALL!! UPA, LET'S GO BACK TO KARIN !!
YES!! YES !!!
KINTO'UN... ONE MORE TRIP !!

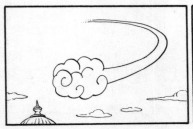

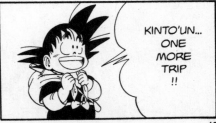

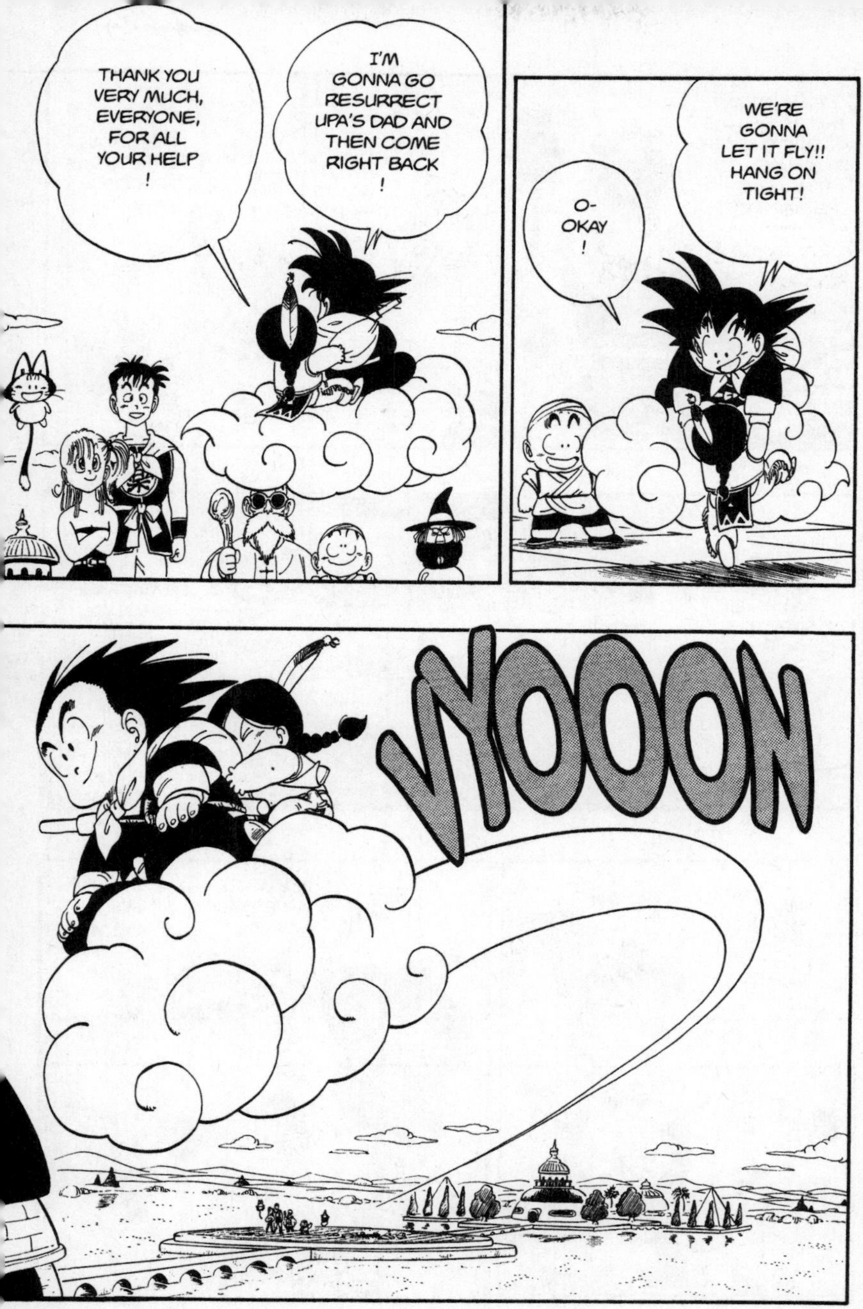
WE'RE GONNA LET IT FLY!! HANG ON TIGHT!
O-OKAY!
I'M GONNA GO RESURRECT UPA'S DAD AND THEN COME RIGHT BACK!
THANK YOU VERY MUCH, EVERYONE, FOR ALL YOUR HELP!
VYOOON

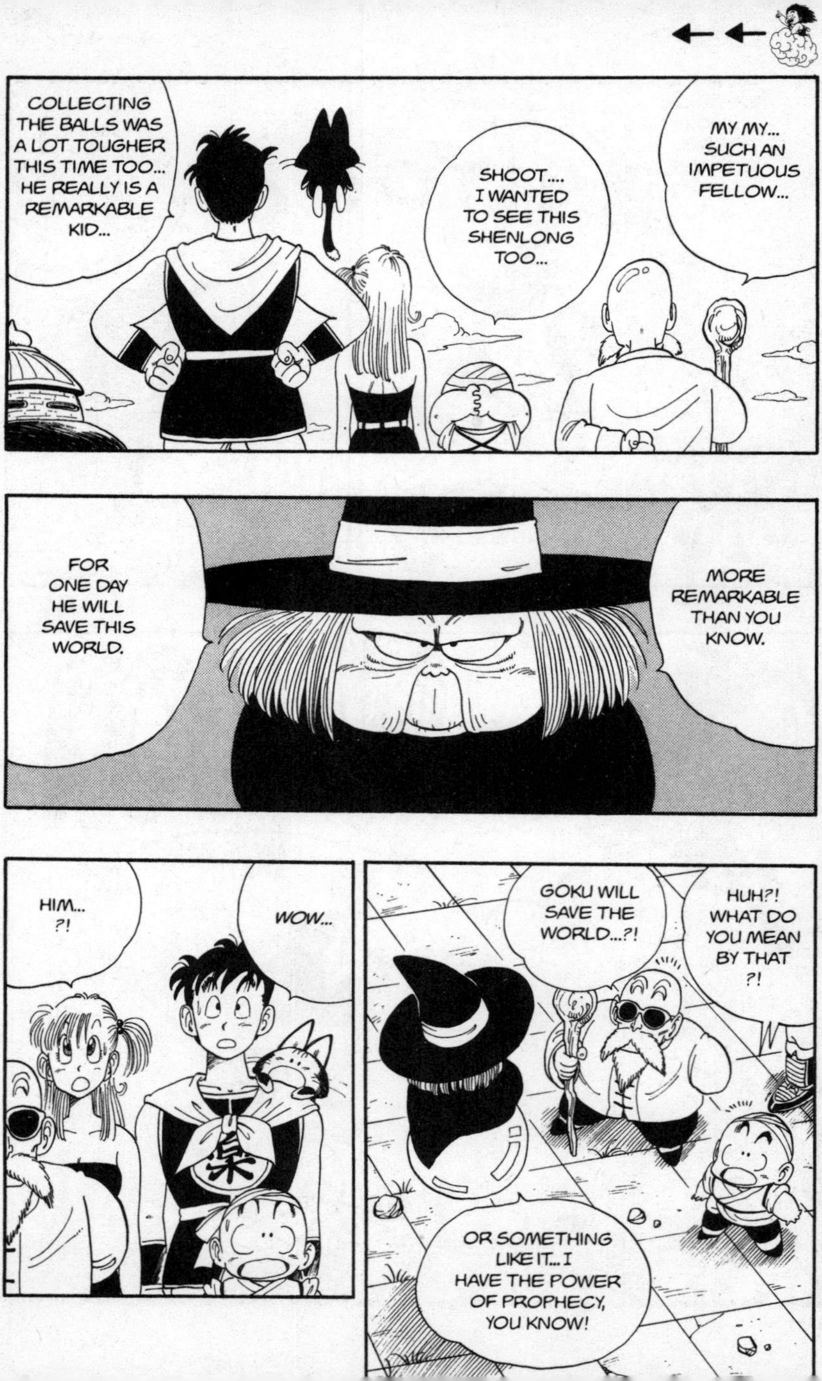
MY MY... SUCH AN IMPETUOUS FELLOW...
SHOOT.... I WANTED TO SEE THIS SHENLONG TOO...
COLLECTING THE BALLS WAS A LOT TOUGHER THIS TIME TOO... HE REALLY IS A REMARKABLE KID...
MORE REMARKABLE THAN YOU KNOW.
FOR ONE DAY HE WILL SAVE THIS WORLD.
HUH?! WHAT DO YOU MEAN BY THAT ?!
GOKU WILL SAVE THE WORLD...?!
OR SOMETHING LIKE IT... I HAVE THE POWER OF PROPHECY, YOU KNOW!
WOW...
HIM... ?!

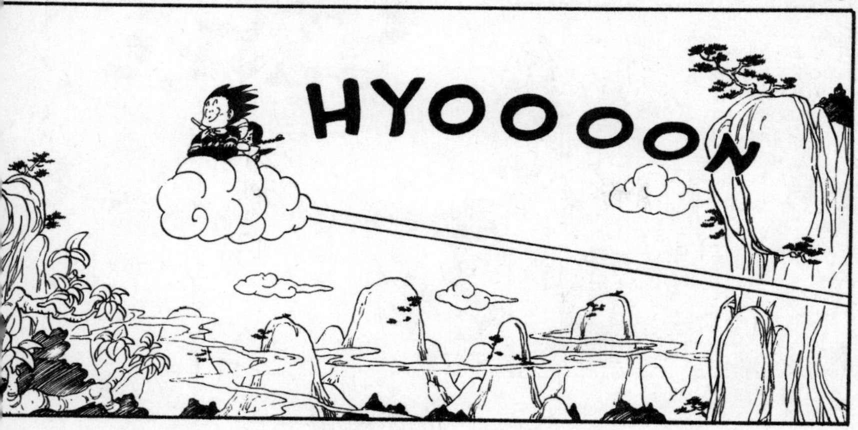
HYOOOOON

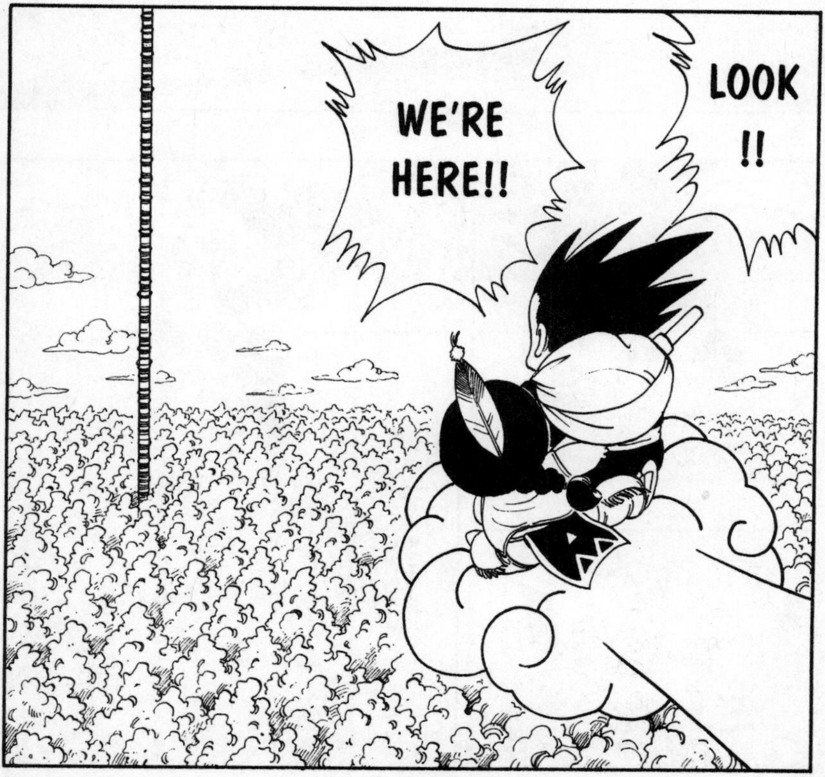
LOOK !!
WE'RE HERE!!

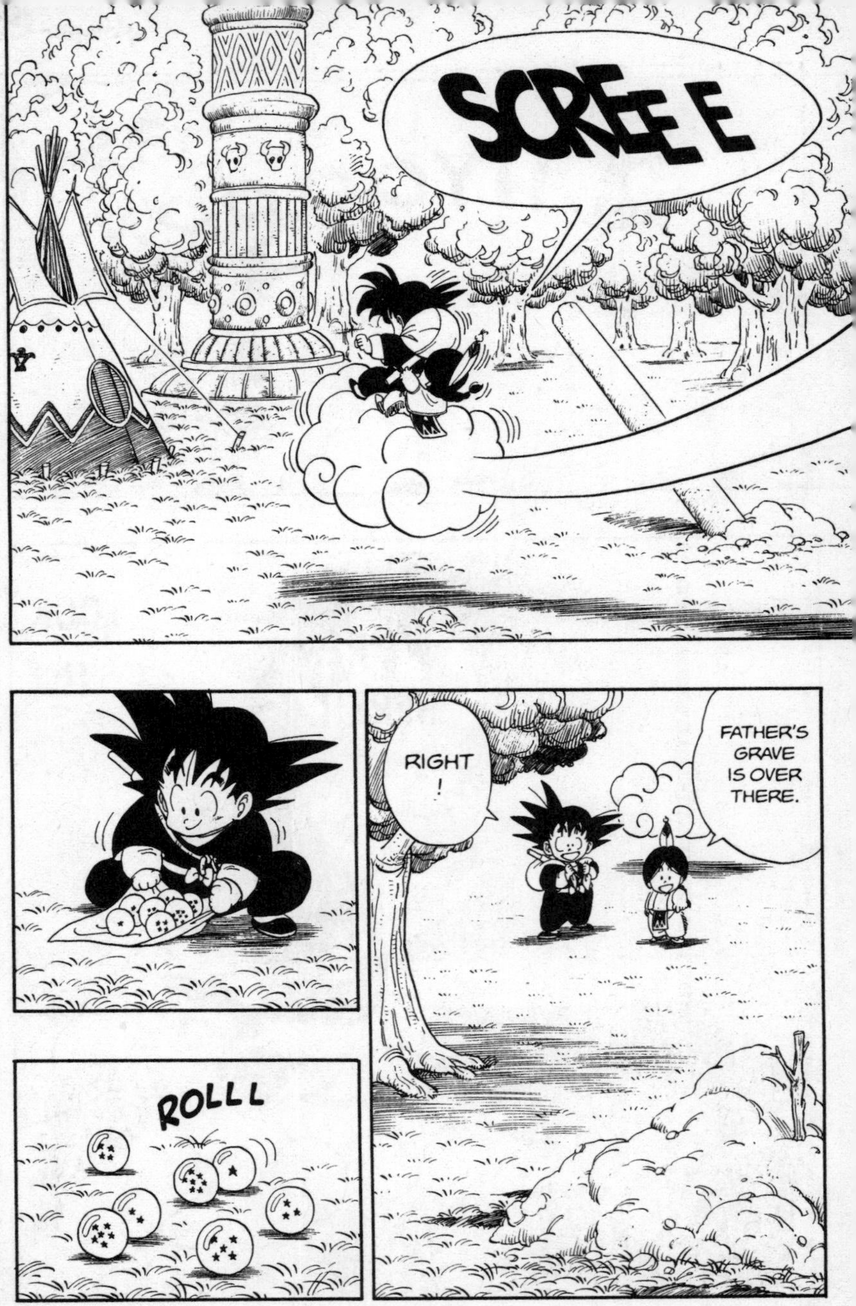
SCREEE E
FATHER'S GRAVE IS OVER THERE.
RIGHT !
ROLLL

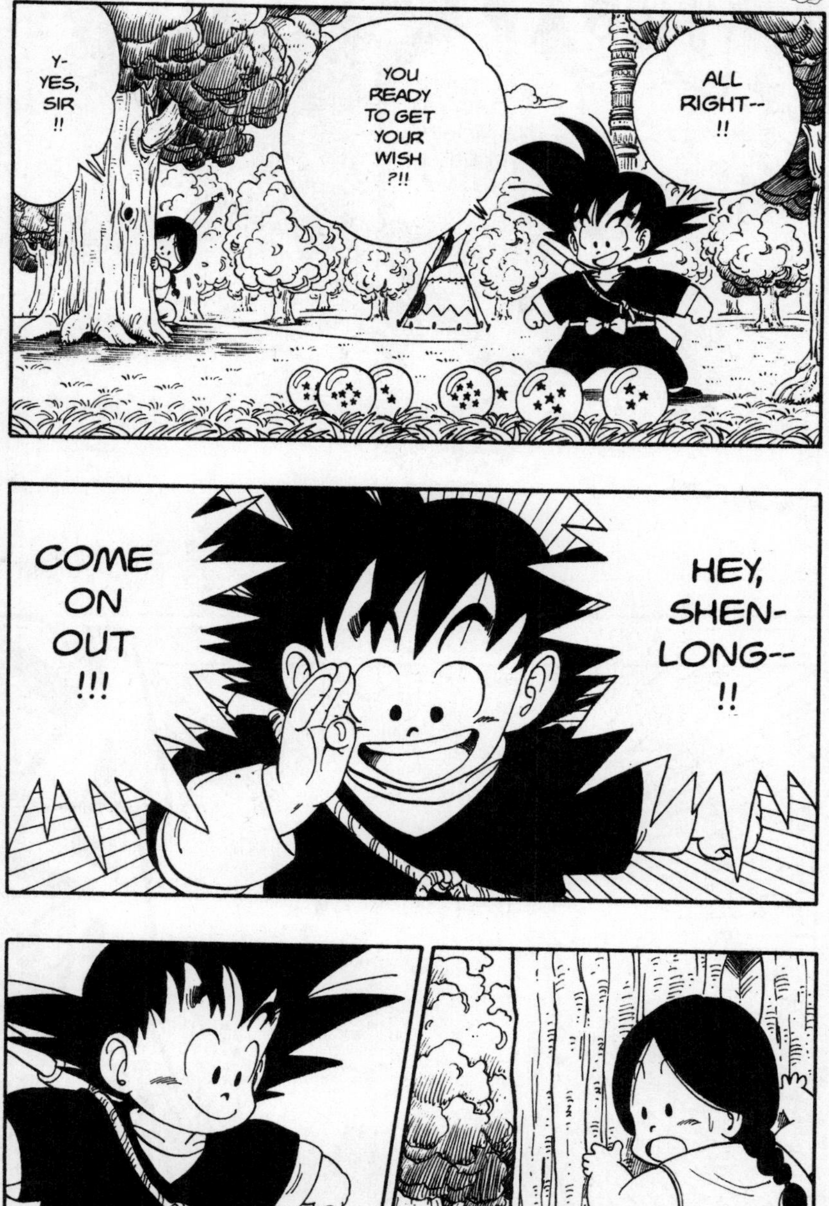
ALL RIGHT--!!
YOU READY TO GET YOUR WISH?!!
Y-YES, SIR!!
HEY, SHEN-LONG--!!
COME ON OUT!!!

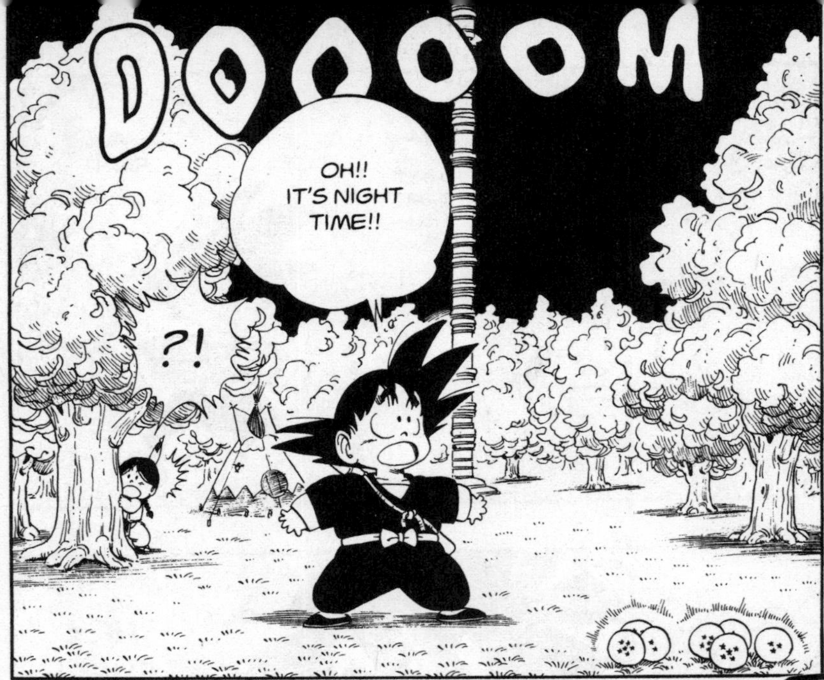
DOOOOM
OH!! IT'S NIGHT TIME!!
?!
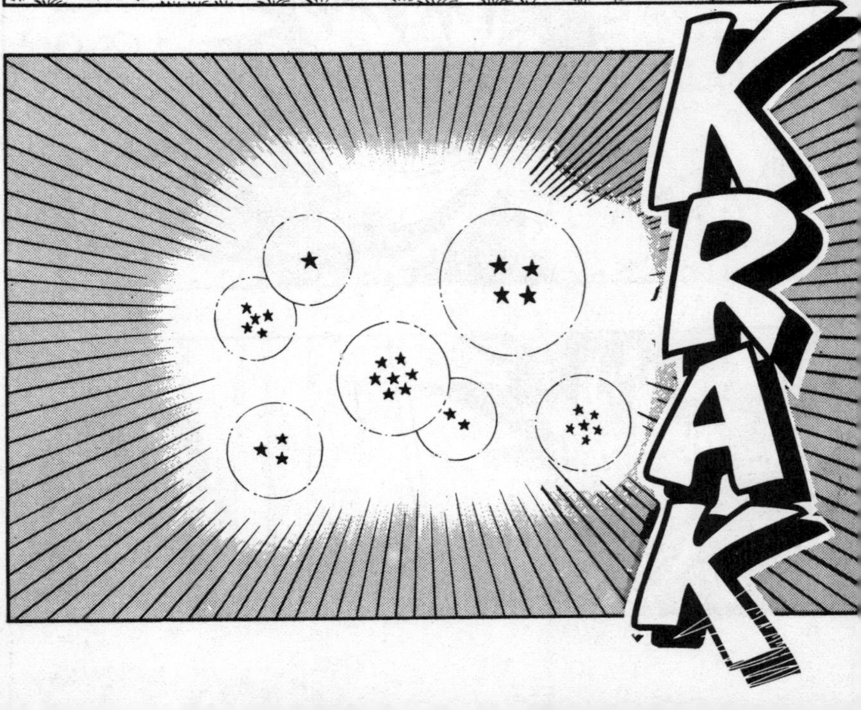
KRAK

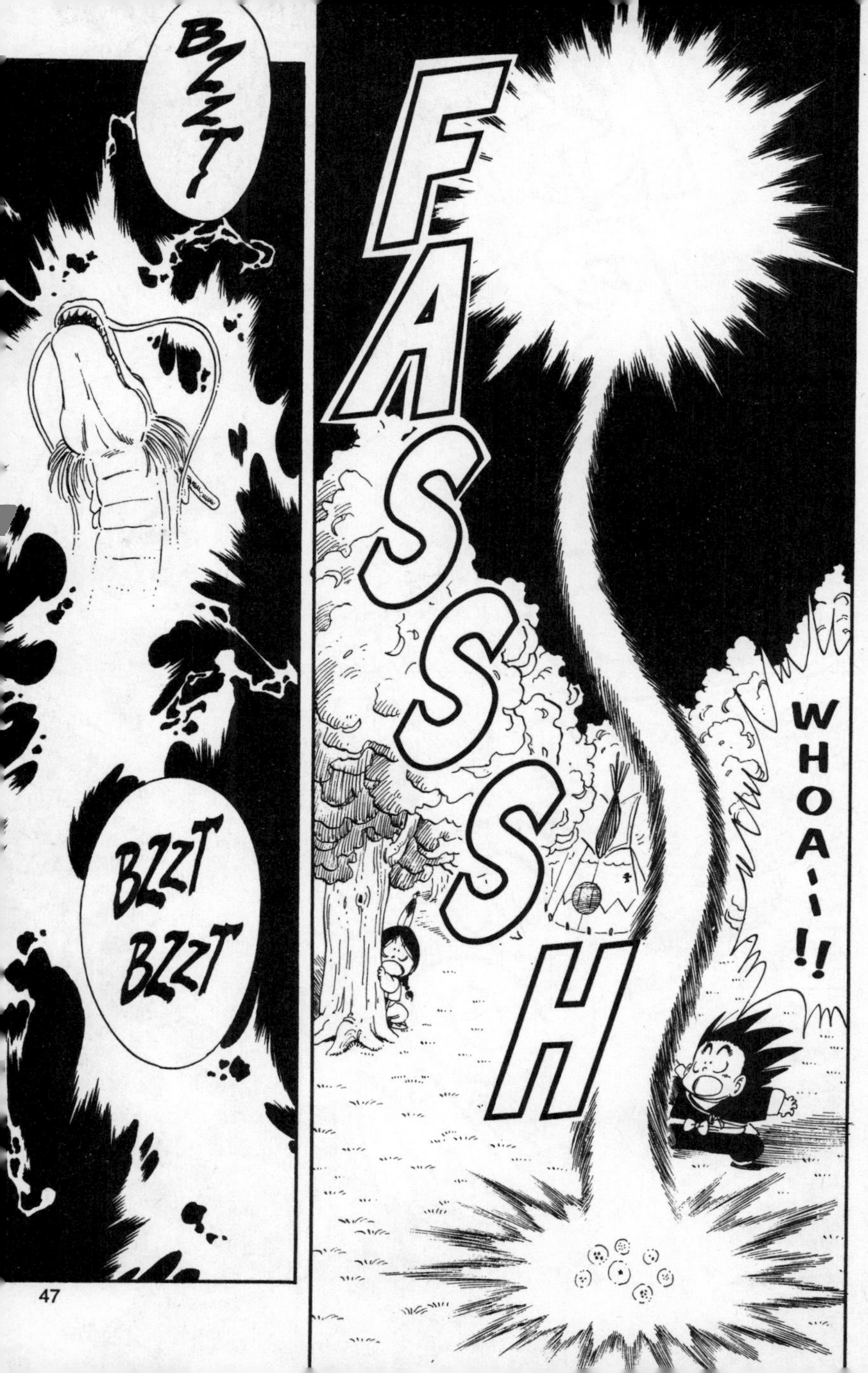
FASSSH
WHOA!!
BZZT
BZZT BZZT

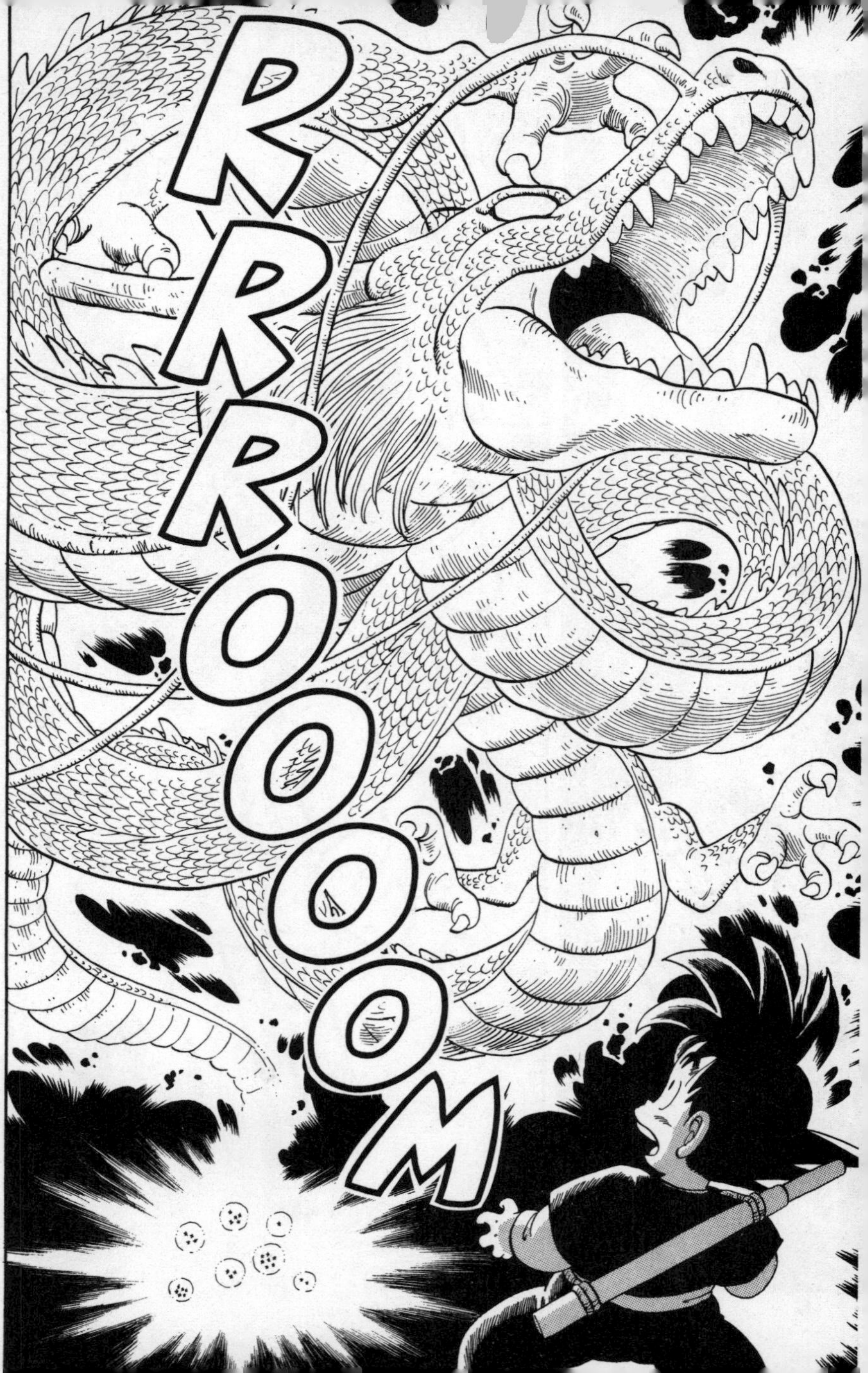
RRROOOOM

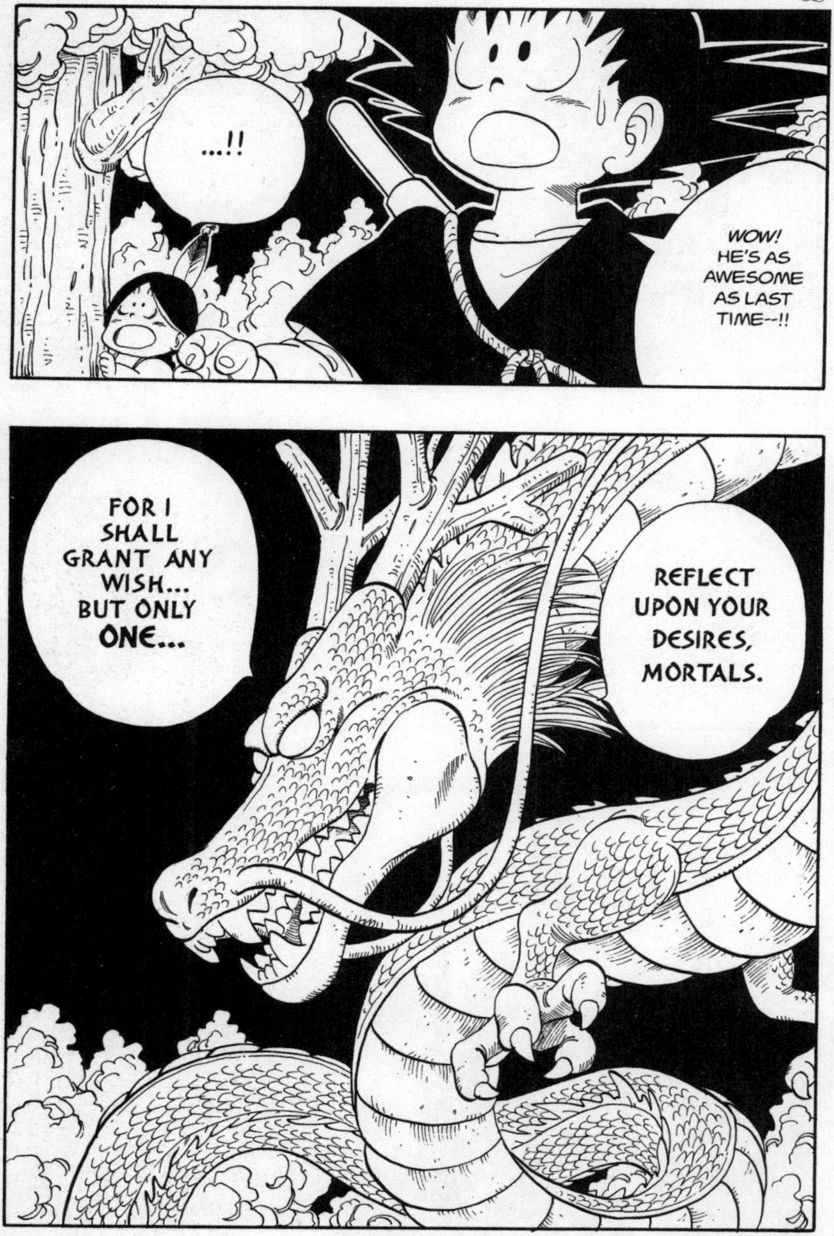
WOW! HE'S AS AWESOME AS LAST TIME--!!
...!!
REFLECT UPON YOUR DESIRES, MORTALS.
FOR I SHALL GRANT ANY WISH... BUT ONLY ONE...

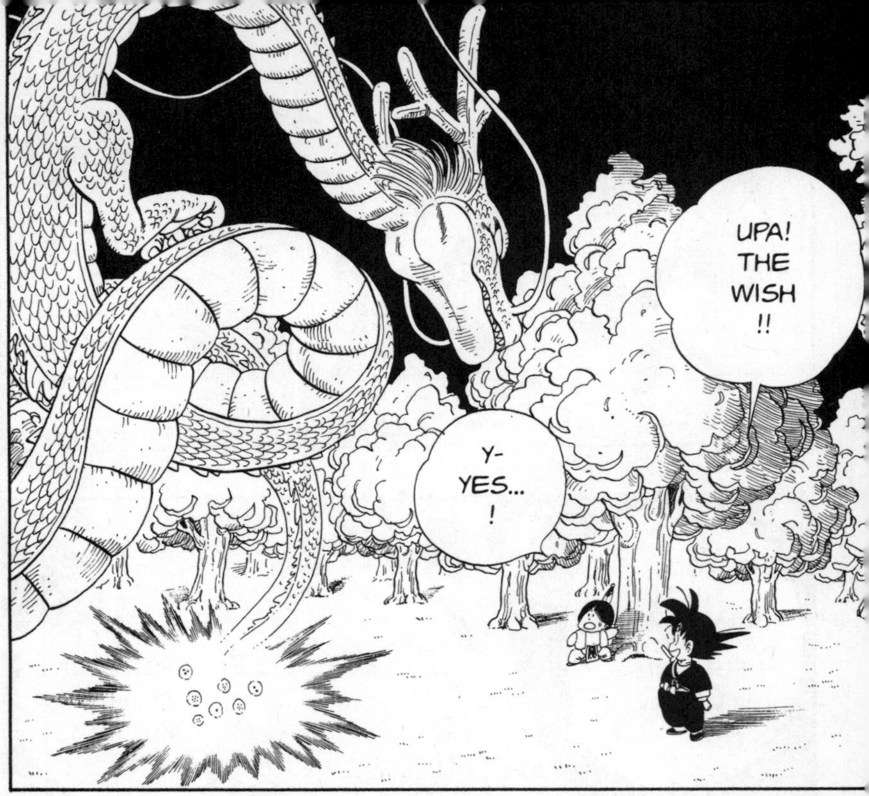
UPA! THE WISH !!
Y- YES... !

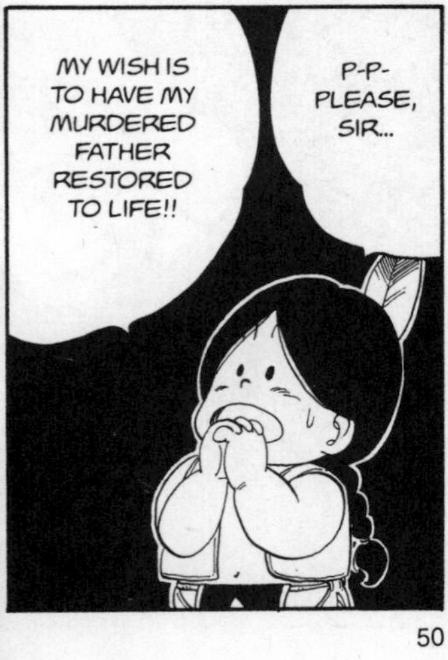
P-P- PLEASE, SIR...
MY WISH IS TO HAVE MY MURDERED FATHER RESTORED TO LIFE!!

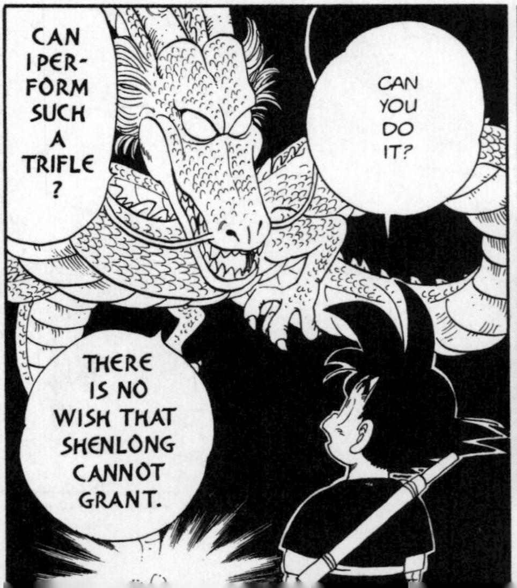
CAN YOU DO IT?
CAN I PER-FORM SUCH A TRIFLE ?
THERE IS NO WISH THAT SHENLONG CANNOT GRANT.

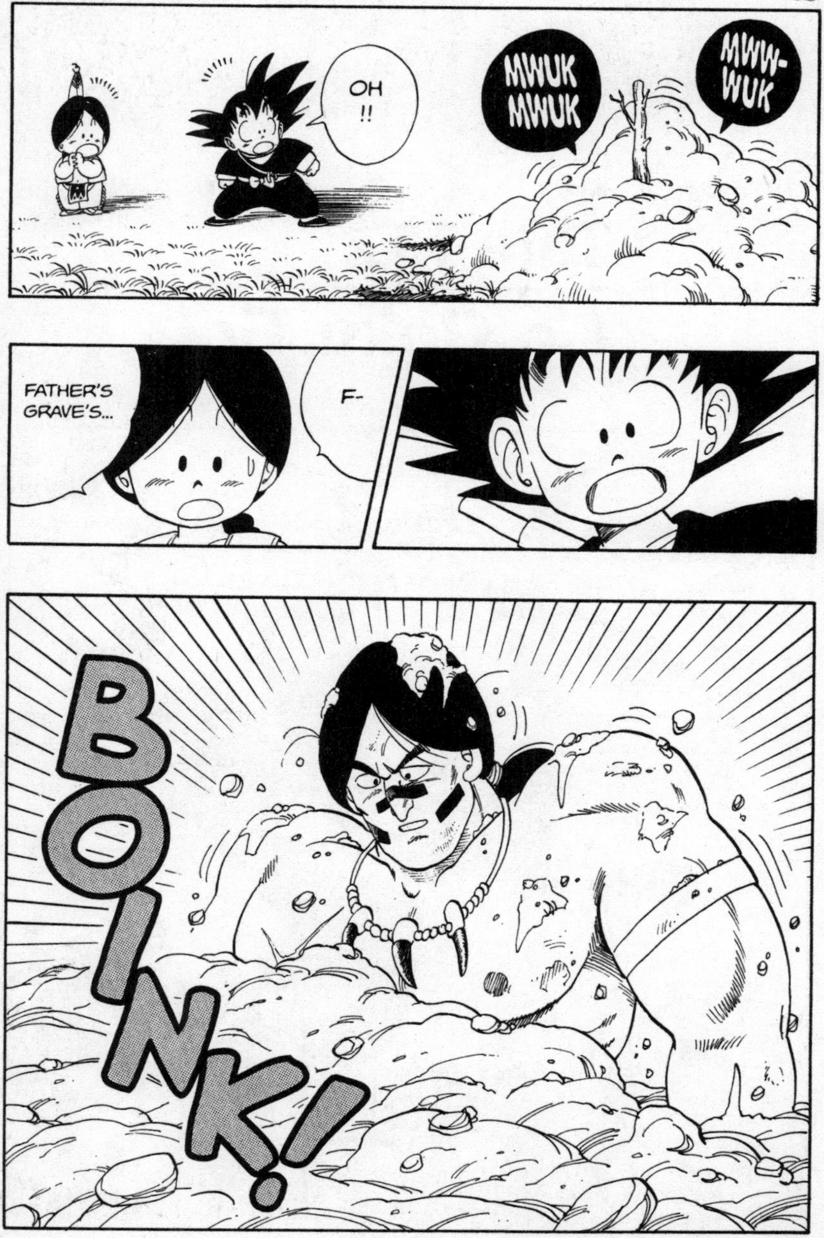
MWW-WUK
MWUK MWUK
OH !!
F-
FATHER'S GRAVE'S...
BOINK!

Tale 112

Go, Goku, Go!

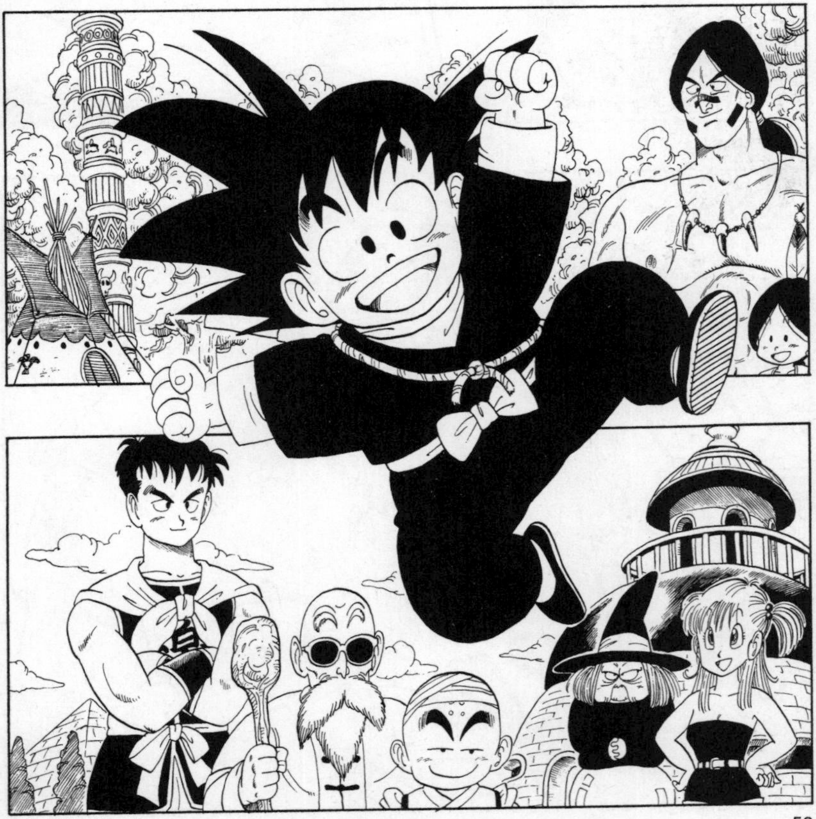

FA...

F...

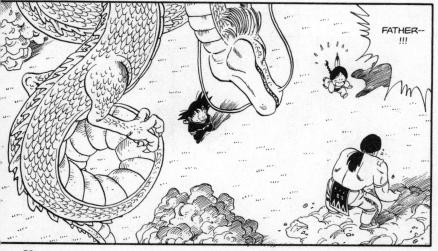

FATHER--!!!

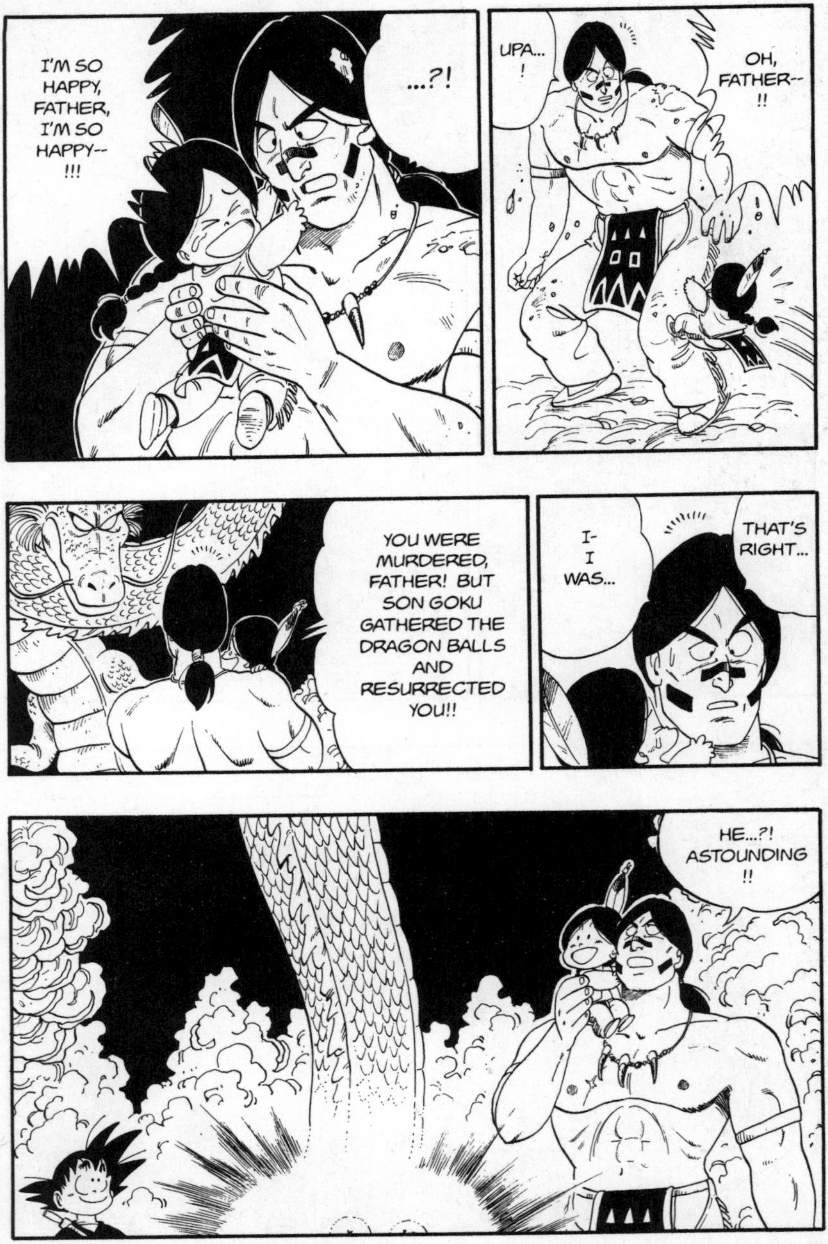

OH, FATHER-- !!
UPA... !
...?!
I'M SO HAPPY, FATHER, I'M SO HAPPY-- !!!
THAT'S RIGHT...
I- I WAS...
YOU WERE MURDERED, FATHER! BUT SON GOKU GATHERED THE DRAGON BALLS AND RESURRECTED YOU!!
HE...?! ASTOUNDING !!

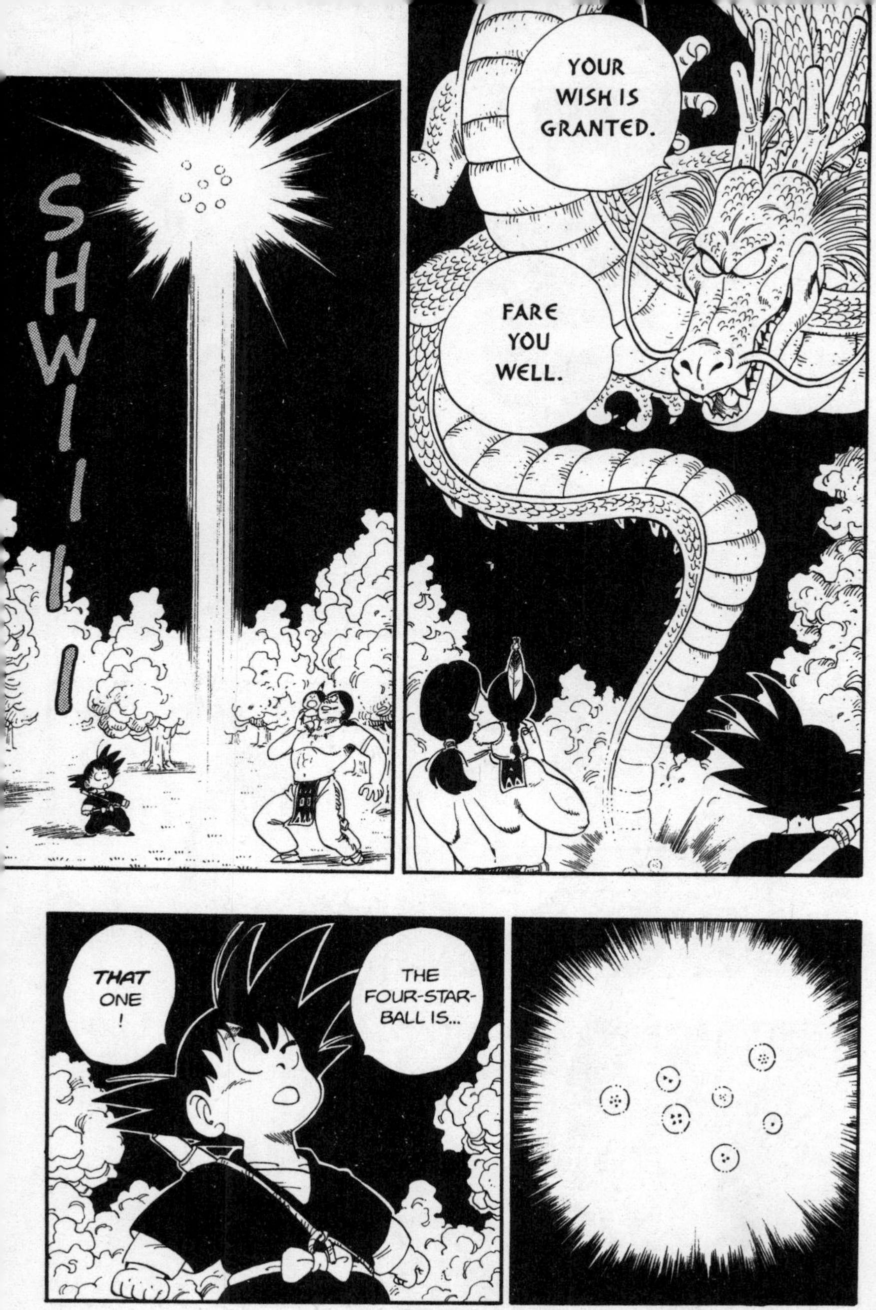
YOUR WISH IS GRANTED.
FARE YOU WELL.
SHWIIII
THE FOUR-STAR-BALL IS...
THAT ONE!

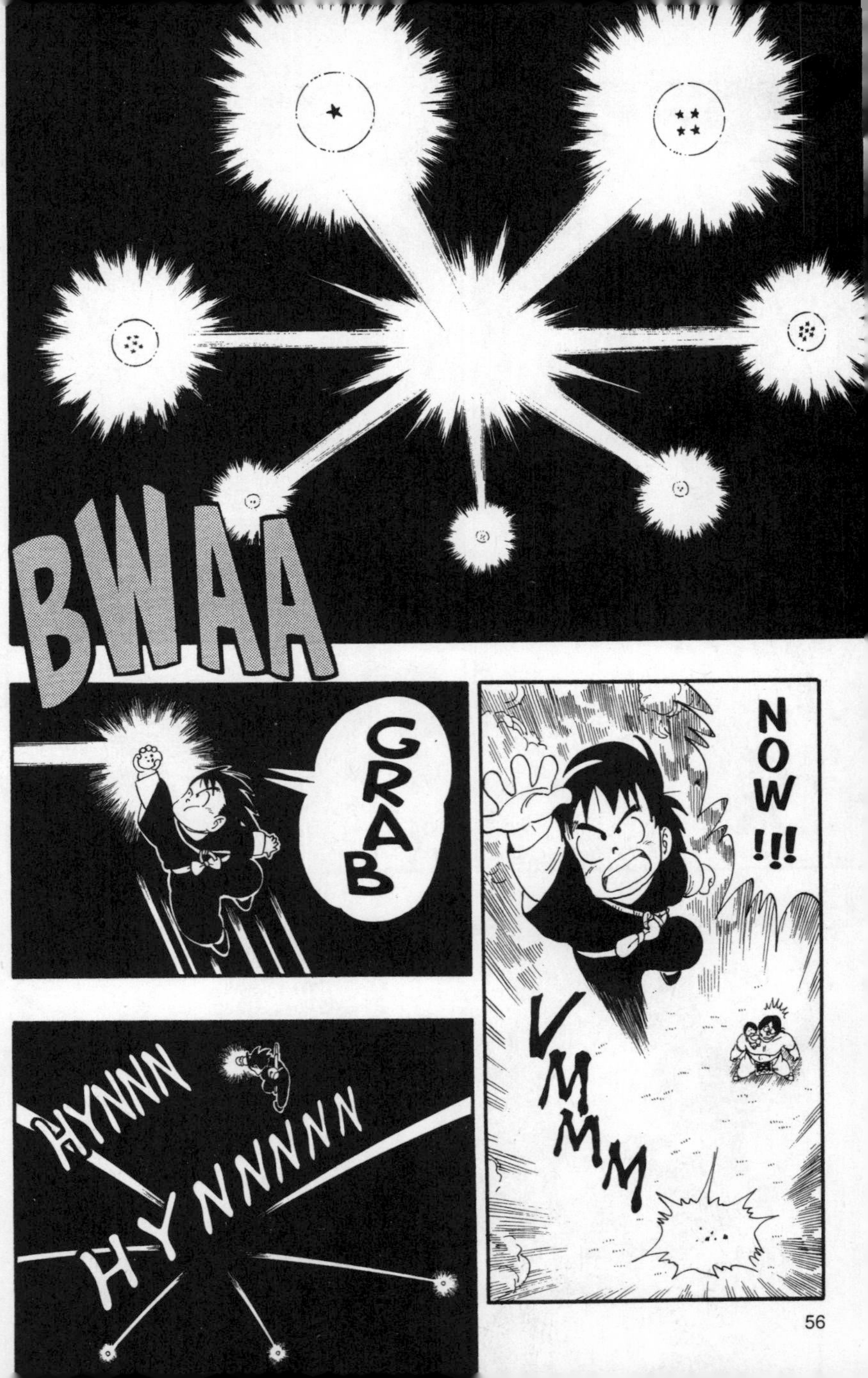

BWAA
NOW!!!
VMMM
GRAB
HYNNN
HYNNNNNN

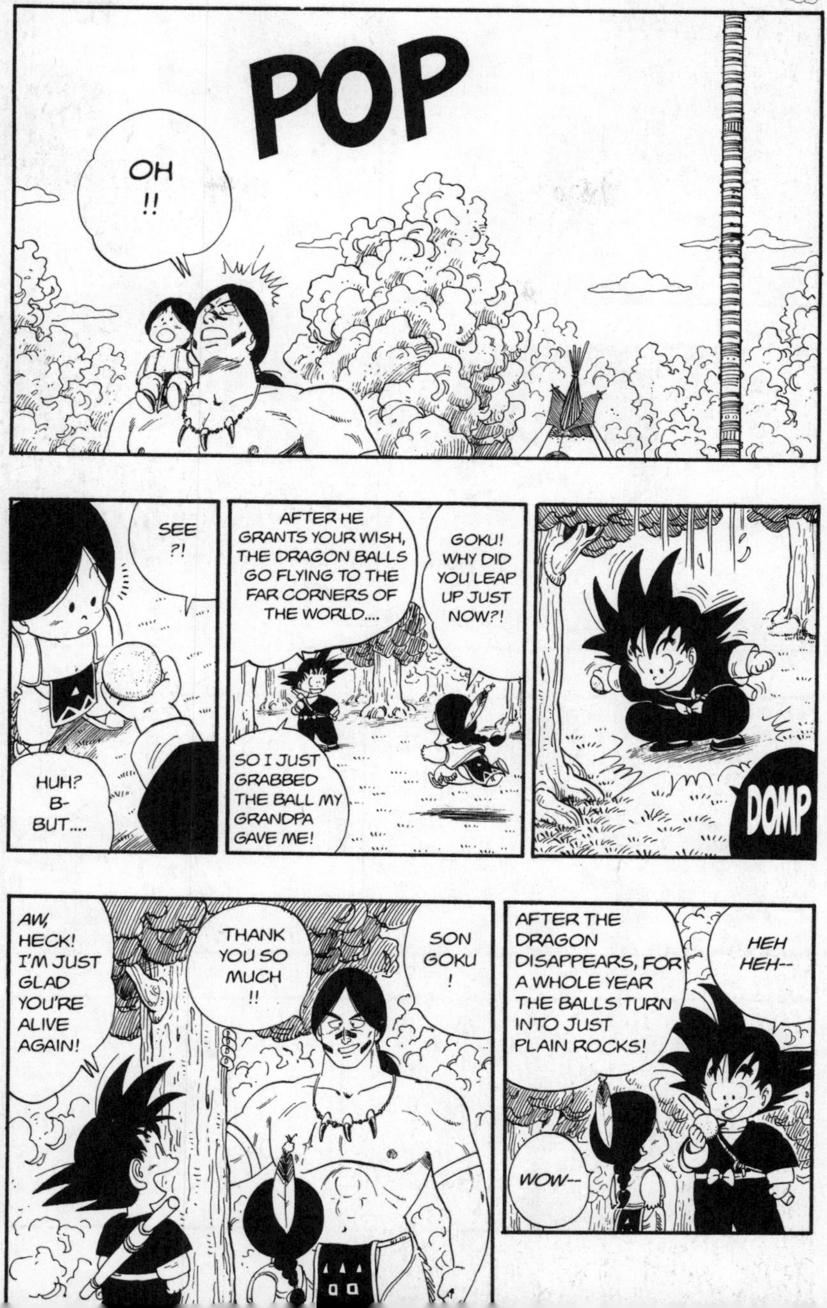
POP
OH !!
DOMP
GOKU! WHY DID YOU LEAP UP JUST NOW?!
AFTER HE GRANTS YOUR WISH, THE DRAGON BALLS GO FLYING TO THE FAR CORNERS OF THE WORLD....
SO I JUST GRABBED THE BALL MY GRANDPA GAVE ME!
SEE ?!
HUH? B-BUT....
HEH HEH--
AFTER THE DRAGON DISAPPEARS, FOR A WHOLE YEAR THE BALLS TURN INTO JUST PLAIN ROCKS!
WOW--
SON GOKU !
THANK YOU SO MUCH !!
AW, HECK! I'M JUST GLAD YOU'RE ALIVE AGAIN!

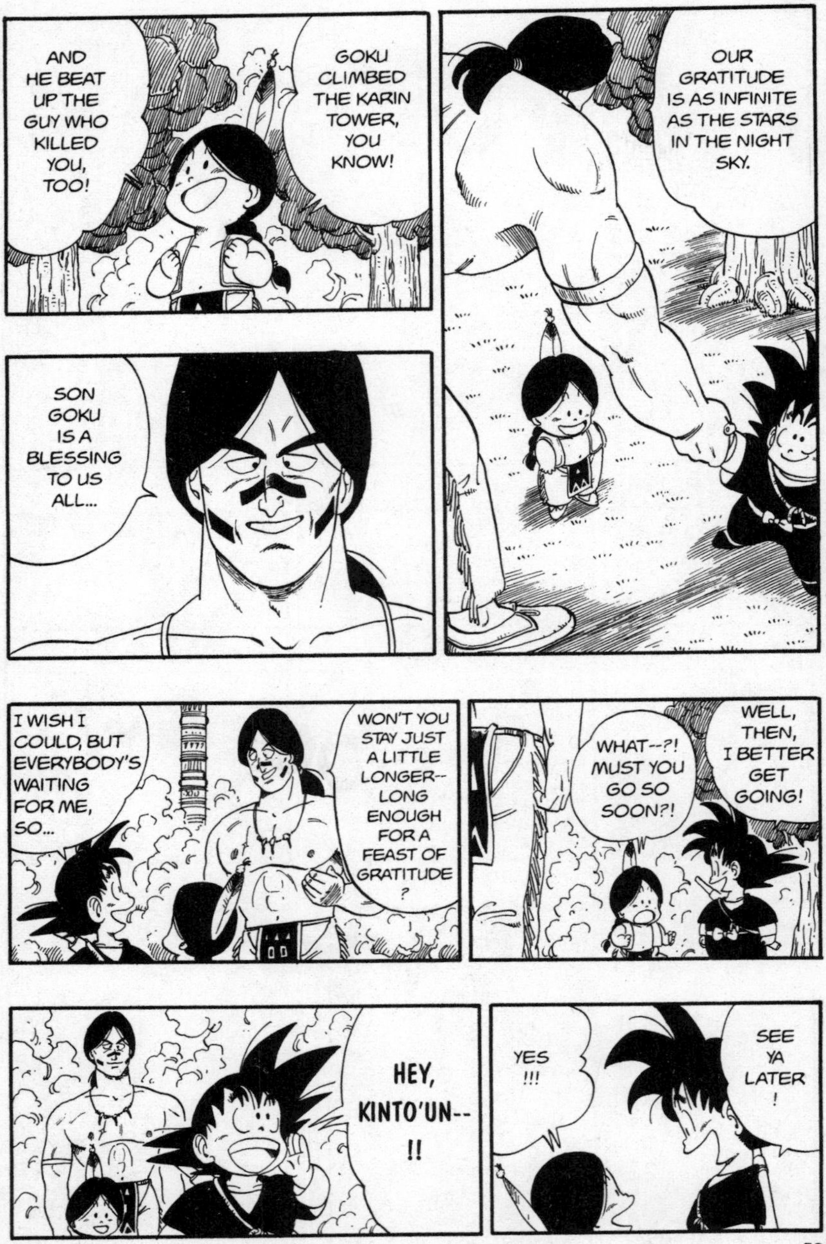
OUR GRATITUDE IS AS INFINITE AS THE STARS IN THE NIGHT SKY.
GOKU CLIMBED THE KARIN TOWER, YOU KNOW!
AND HE BEAT UP THE GUY WHO KILLED YOU, TOO!
SON GOKU IS A BLESSING TO US ALL...
WELL, THEN, I BETTER GET GOING!
WHAT--?! MUST YOU GO SO SOON?!
WON'T YOU STAY JUST A LITTLE LONGER-- LONG ENOUGH FOR A FEAST OF GRATITUDE?
I WISH I COULD, BUT EVERYBODY'S WAITING FOR ME, SO...
SEE YA LATER!
YES!!!
HEY, KINTO'UN--!!

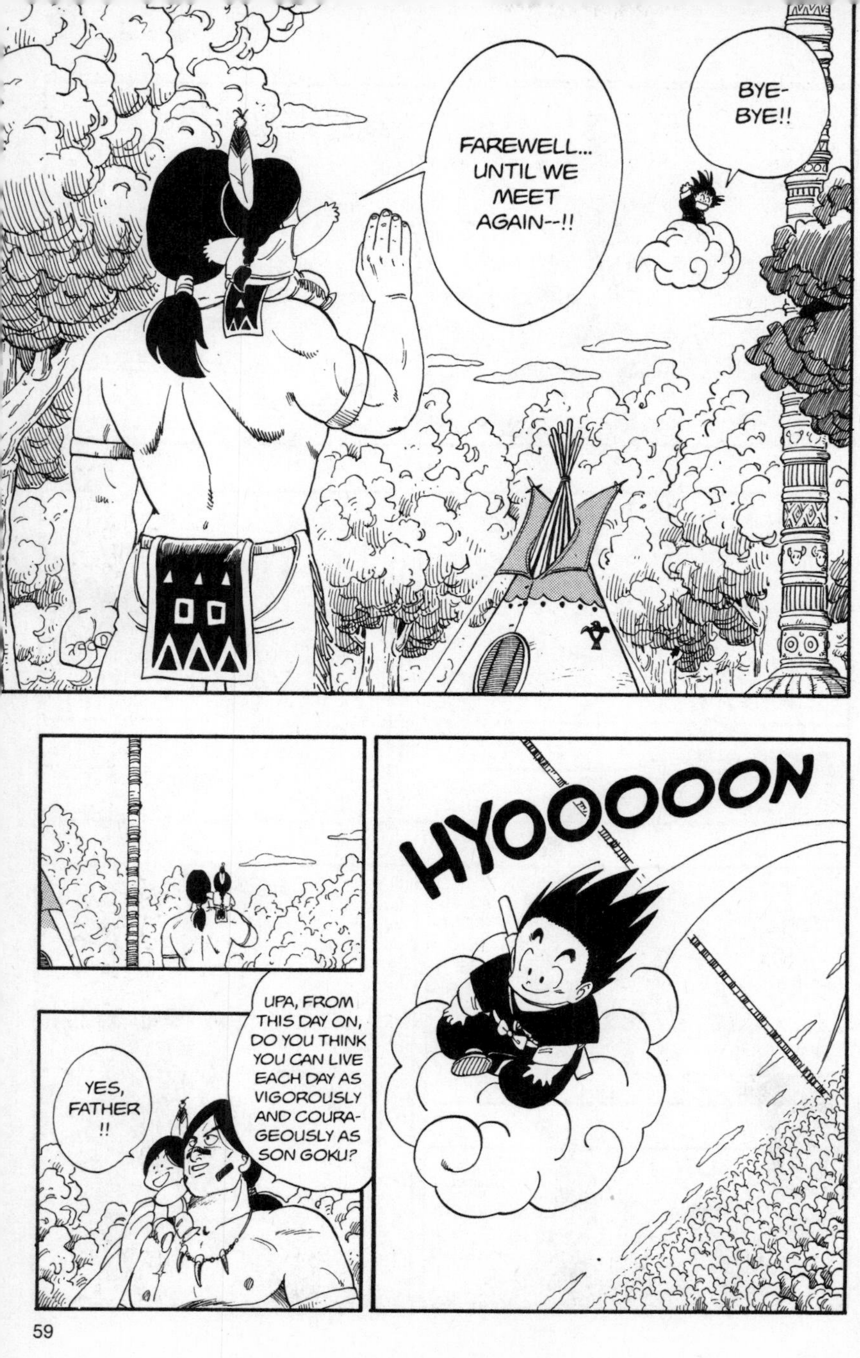
BYE-BYE!!
FAREWELL... UNTIL WE MEET AGAIN--!!
HYOOOOON
UPA, FROM THIS DAY ON, DO YOU THINK YOU CAN LIVE EACH DAY AS VIGOROUSLY AND COURAGEOUSLY AS SON GOKU?
YES, FATHER!!

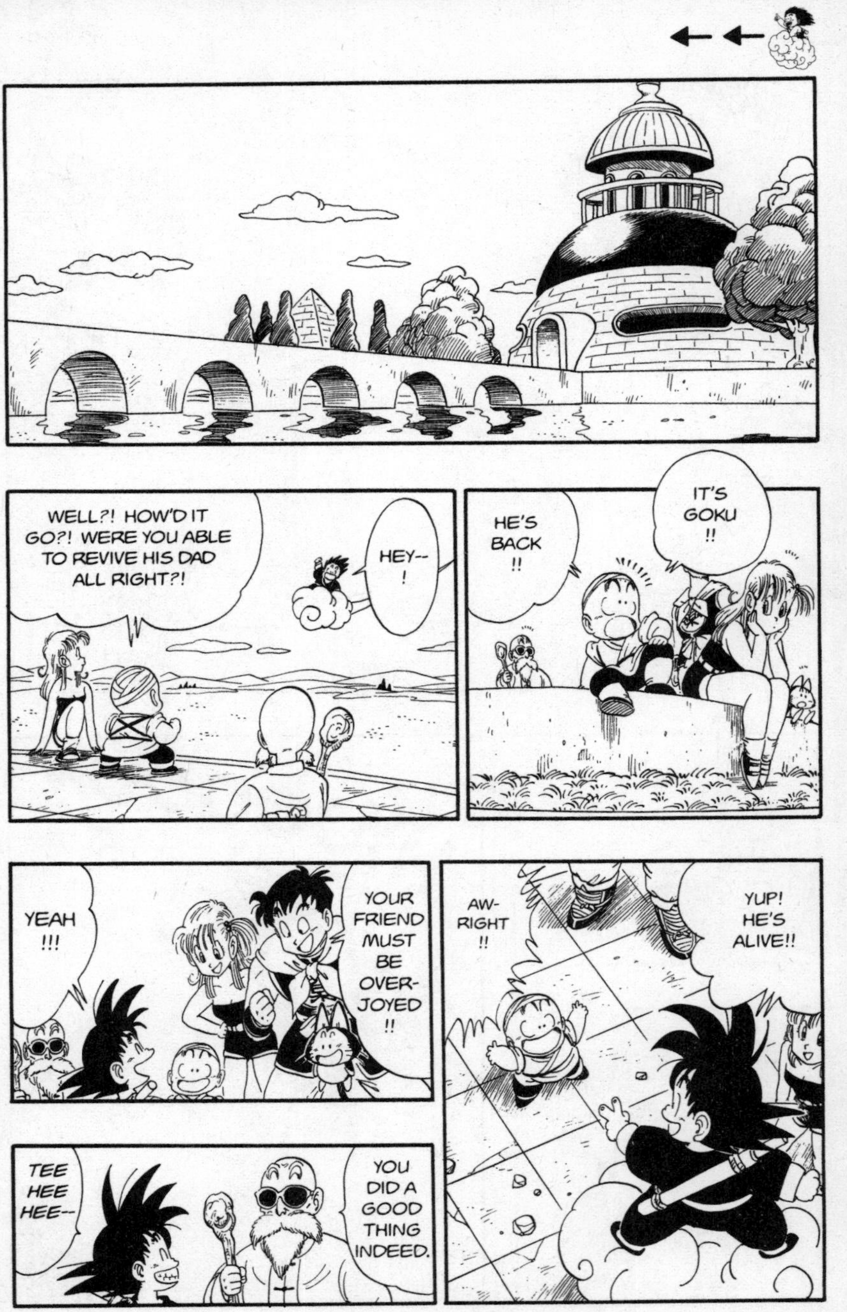
IT'S GOKU !!
HE'S BACK !!
HEY--!
WELL?! HOW'D IT GO?! WERE YOU ABLE TO REVIVE HIS DAD ALL RIGHT?!
YUP! HE'S ALIVE!!
AW-RIGHT !!
YOUR FRIEND MUST BE OVER-JOYED !!
YEAH !!!
YOU DID A GOOD THING INDEED.
TEE HEE HEE--

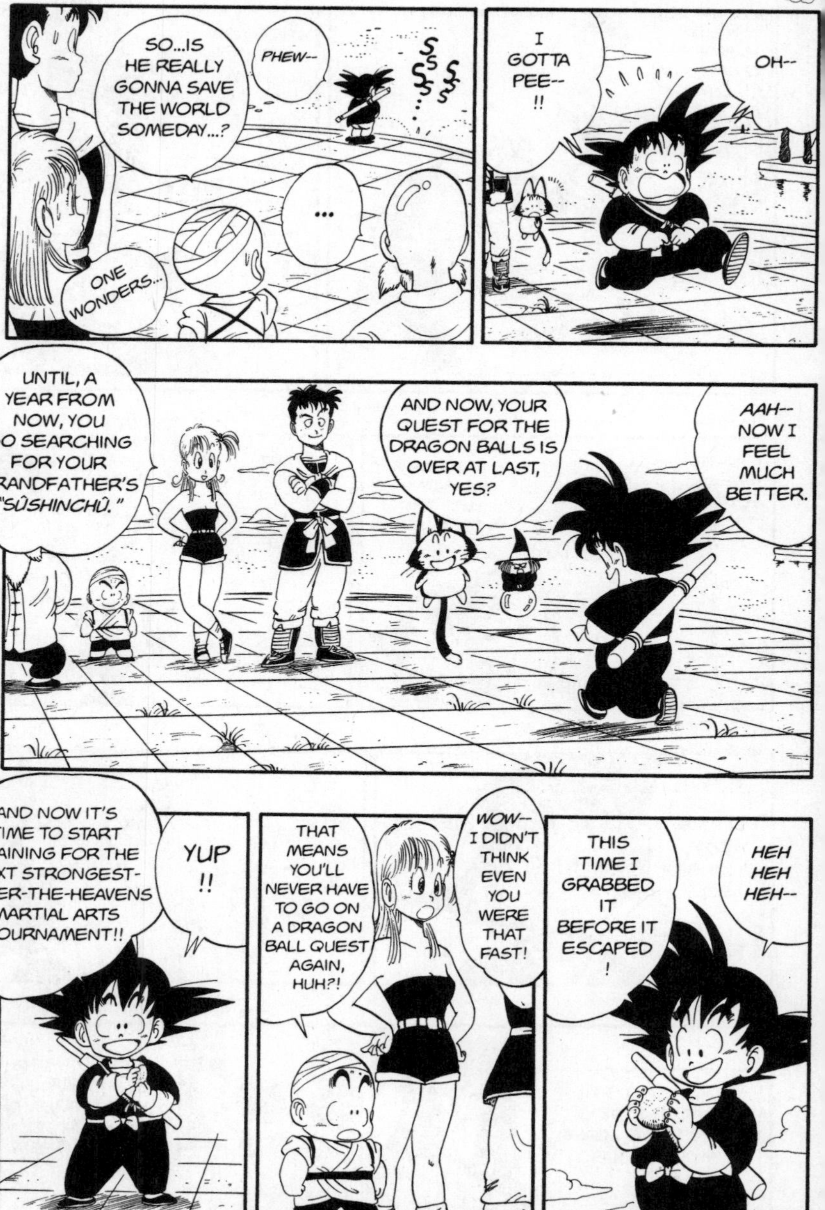
OH--
I GOTTA PEE-- !!
PHEW--
SO...IS HE REALLY GONNA SAVE THE WORLD SOMEDAY...?
...
ONE WONDERS...
AAH-- NOW I FEEL MUCH BETTER.
AND NOW, YOUR QUEST FOR THE DRAGON BALLS IS OVER AT LAST, YES?
UNTIL, A YEAR FROM NOW, YOU GO SEARCHING FOR YOUR GRANDFATHER'S "SÛSHINCHÛ."
HEH HEH HEH--
THIS TIME I GRABBED IT BEFORE IT ESCAPED!
WOW-- I DIDN'T THINK EVEN YOU WERE THAT FAST!
THAT MEANS YOU'LL NEVER HAVE TO GO ON A DRAGON BALL QUEST AGAIN, HUH?!
YUP !!
AND NOW IT'S TIME TO START TRAINING FOR THE NEXT STRONGEST-UNDER-THE-HEAVENS MARTIAL ARTS TOURNAMENT!!

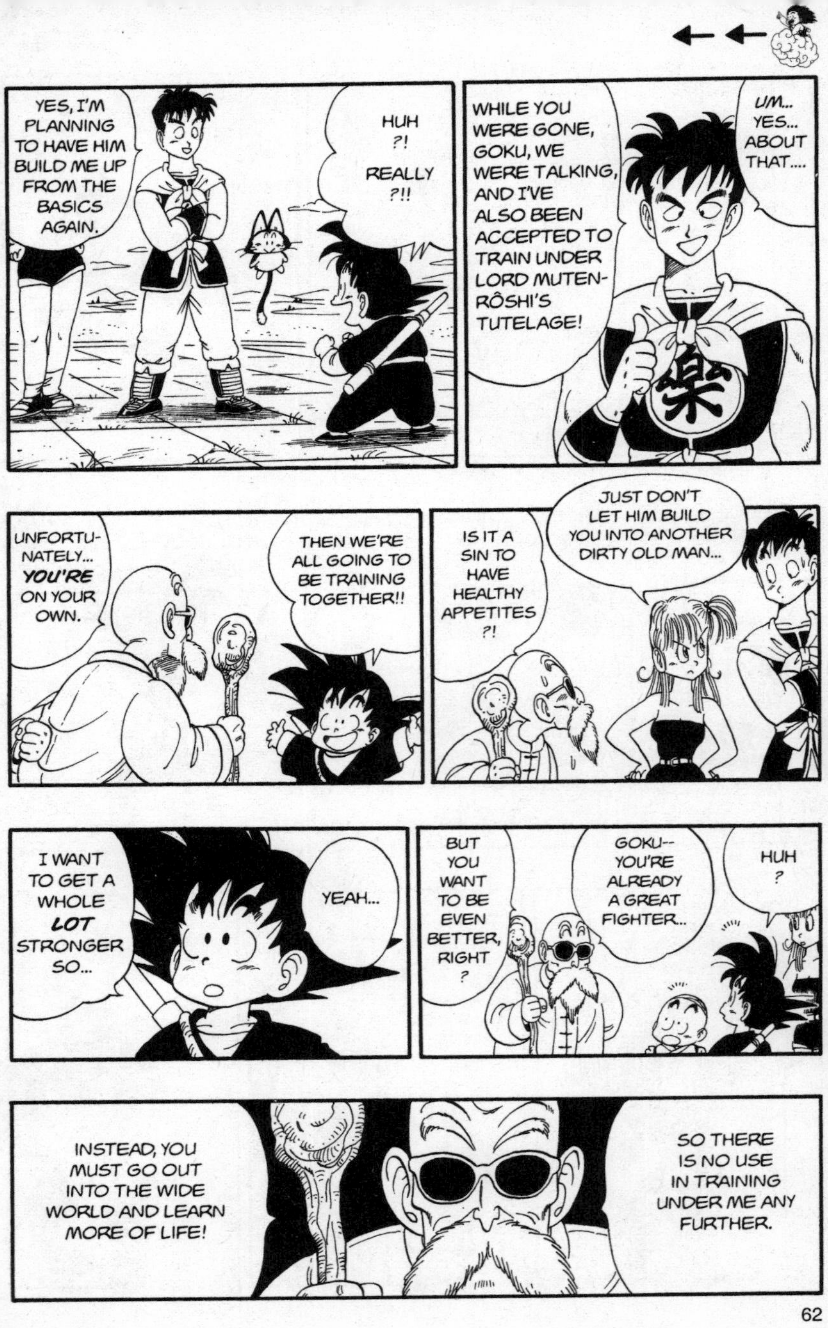
UM... YES... ABOUT THAT....
WHILE YOU WERE GONE, GOKU, WE WERE TALKING, AND I'VE ALSO BEEN ACCEPTED TO TRAIN UNDER LORD MUTEN-RÔSHI'S TUTELAGE!
HUH ?! REALLY ?!!
YES, I'M PLANNING TO HAVE HIM BUILD ME UP FROM THE BASICS AGAIN.
JUST DON'T LET HIM BUILD YOU INTO ANOTHER DIRTY OLD MAN...
IS IT A SIN TO HAVE HEALTHY APPETITES ?!
THEN WE'RE ALL GOING TO BE TRAINING TOGETHER!!
UNFORTU-NATELY... *YOU'RE* ON YOUR OWN.
HUH ?
GOKU-- YOU'RE ALREADY A GREAT FIGHTER...
BUT YOU WANT TO BE EVEN BETTER, RIGHT ?
YEAH...
I WANT TO GET A WHOLE *LOT* STRONGER SO...
SO THERE IS NO USE IN TRAINING UNDER ME ANY FURTHER.
INSTEAD, YOU MUST GO OUT INTO THE WIDE WORLD AND LEARN MORE OF LIFE!

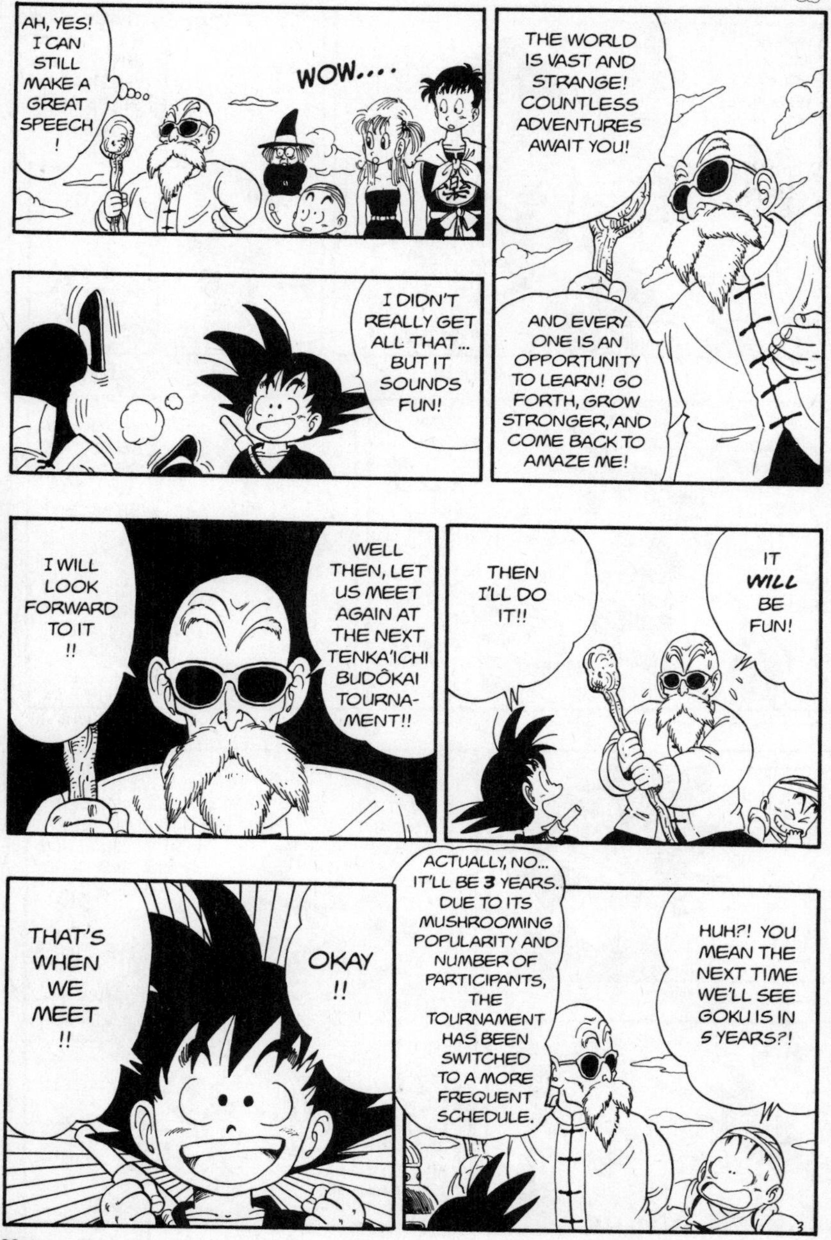

THE WORLD IS VAST AND STRANGE! COUNTLESS ADVENTURES AWAIT YOU!
AND EVERY ONE IS AN OPPORTUNITY TO LEARN! GO FORTH, GROW STRONGER, AND COME BACK TO AMAZE ME!
WOW....
AH, YES! I CAN STILL MAKE A GREAT SPEECH !
I DIDN'T REALLY GET ALL THAT... BUT IT SOUNDS FUN!
IT **WILL** BE FUN!
THEN I'LL DO IT!!
WELL THEN, LET US MEET AGAIN AT THE NEXT TENKA'ICHI BUDÔKAI TOURNA-MENT!!
I WILL LOOK FORWARD TO IT !!
HUH?! YOU MEAN THE NEXT TIME WE'LL SEE GOKU IS IN 5 YEARS?!
ACTUALLY, NO... IT'LL BE **3** YEARS. DUE TO ITS MUSHROOMING POPULARITY AND NUMBER OF PARTICIPANTS, THE TOURNAMENT HAS BEEN SWITCHED TO A MORE FREQUENT SCHEDULE.
OKAY !!
THAT'S WHEN WE MEET !!

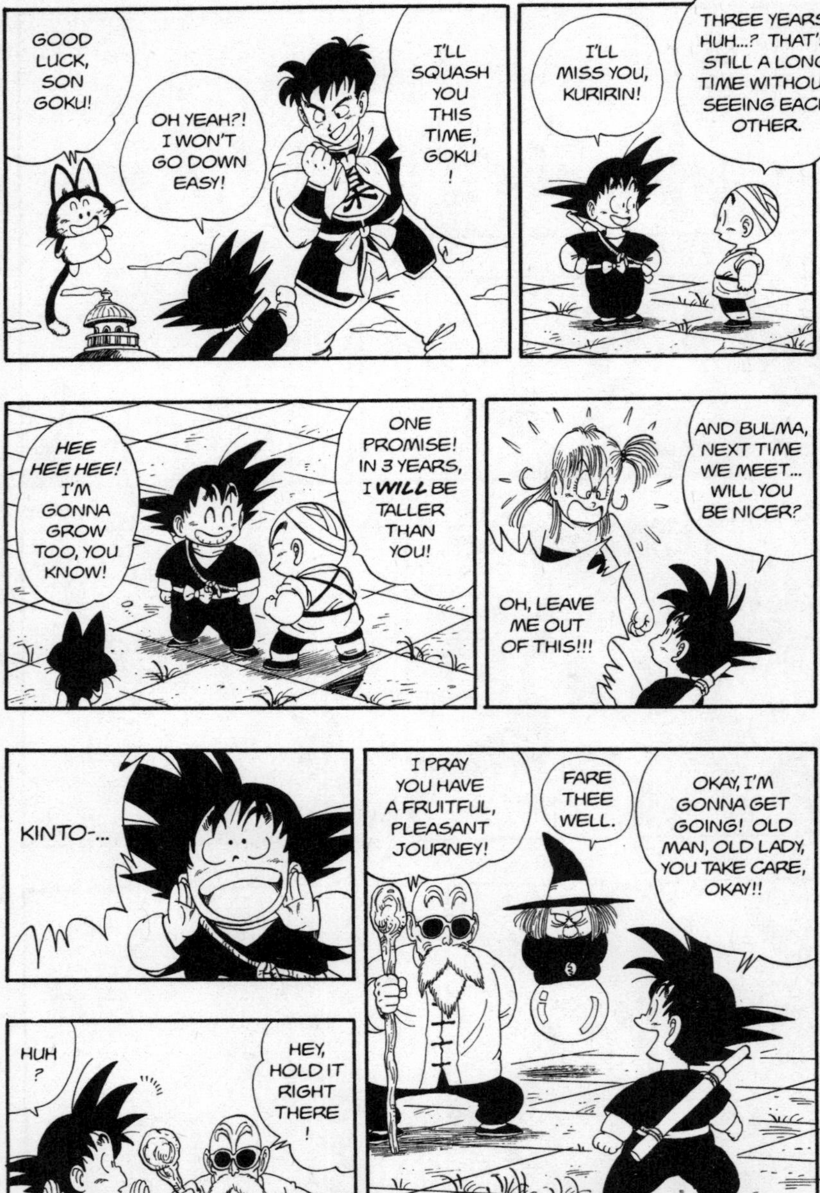
THREE YEARS, HUH...? THAT'S STILL A LONG TIME WITHOUT SEEING EACH OTHER.
I'LL MISS YOU, KURIRIN!
I'LL SQUASH YOU THIS TIME, GOKU!
OH YEAH?! I WON'T GO DOWN EASY!
GOOD LUCK, SON GOKU!
AND BULMA, NEXT TIME WE MEET... WILL YOU BE NICER?
OH, LEAVE ME OUT OF THIS!!!
ONE PROMISE! IN 3 YEARS, I WILL BE TALLER THAN YOU!
HEE HEE HEE! I'M GONNA GROW TOO, YOU KNOW!
OKAY, I'M GONNA GET GOING! OLD MAN, OLD LADY, YOU TAKE CARE, OKAY!!
FARE THEE WELL.
I PRAY YOU HAVE A FRUITFUL, PLEASANT JOURNEY!
KINTO-...
HEY, HOLD IT RIGHT THERE!
HUH?

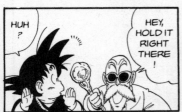

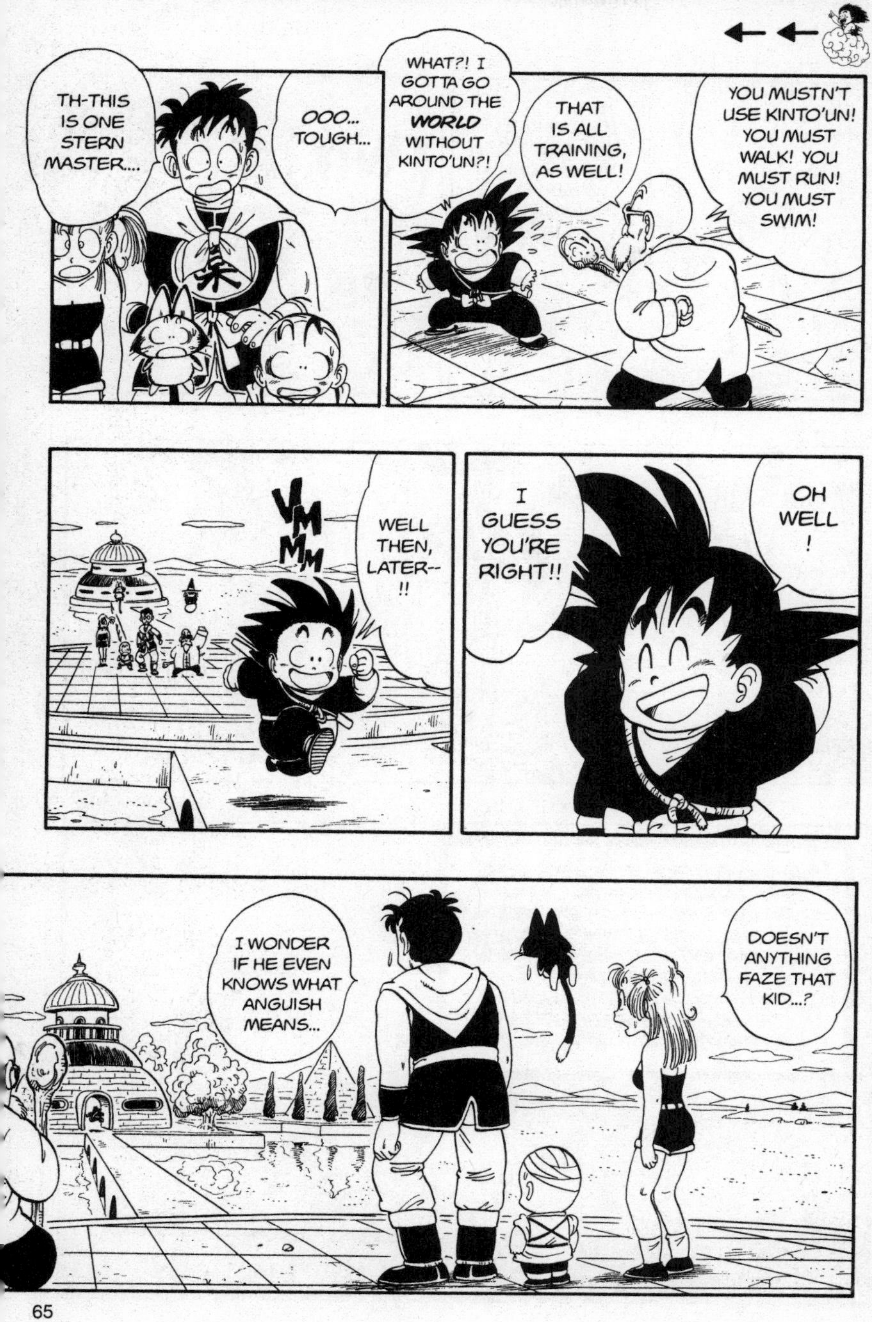
YOU MUSTN'T USE KINTO'UN! YOU MUST WALK! YOU MUST RUN! YOU MUST SWIM!
THAT IS ALL TRAINING, AS WELL!
WHAT?! I GOTTA GO AROUND THE WORLD WITHOUT KINTO'UN?!
OOO... TOUGH...
TH-THIS IS ONE STERN MASTER....
OH WELL !
I GUESS YOU'RE RIGHT!!
WELL THEN, LATER-- !!
VMMM
DOESN'T ANYTHING FAZE THAT KID...?
I WONDER IF HE EVEN KNOWS WHAT ANGUISH MEANS...

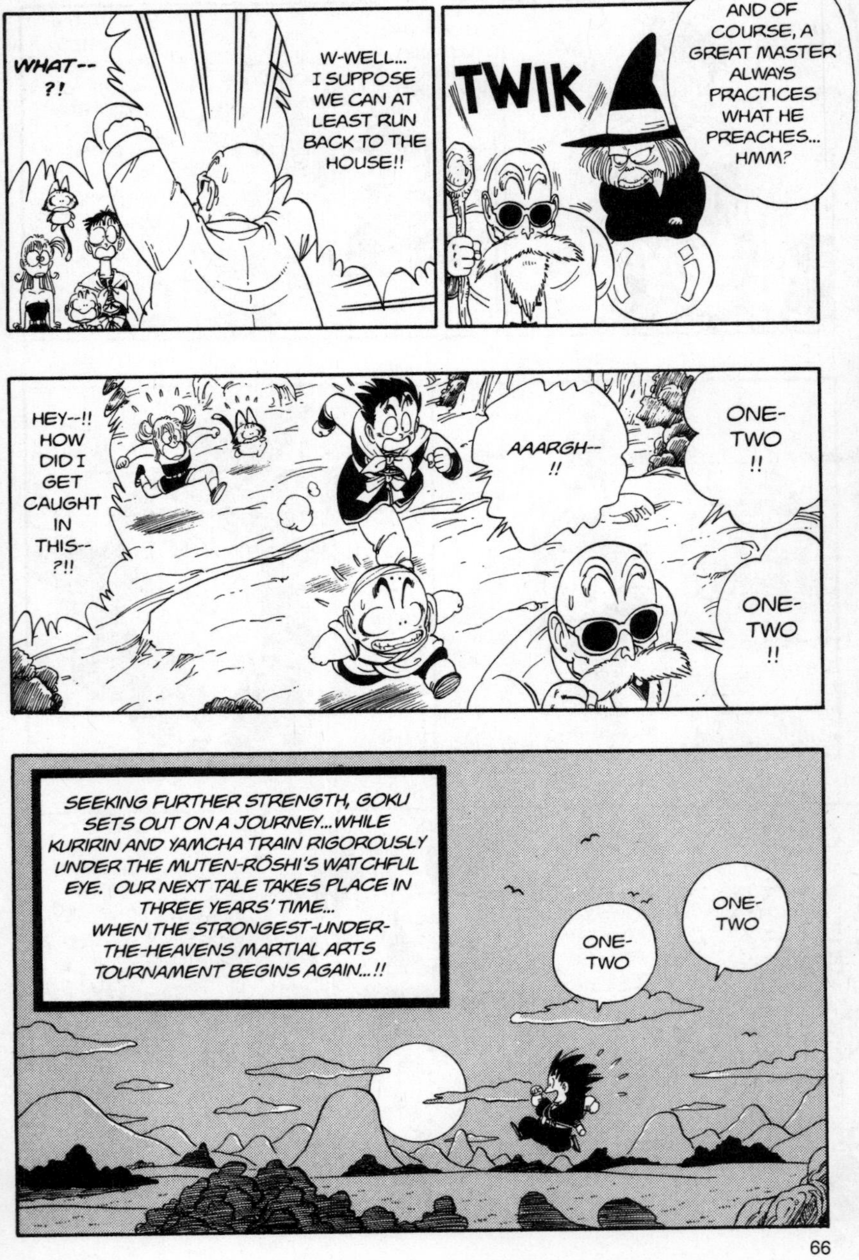
AND OF COURSE, A GREAT MASTER ALWAYS PRACTICES WHAT HE PREACHES... HMM?
TWIK
W-WELL... I SUPPOSE WE CAN AT LEAST RUN BACK TO THE HOUSE!!
WHAT-- ?!
ONE-TWO !!
AAARGH-- !!
HEY--!! HOW DID I GET CAUGHT IN THIS-- ?!!
ONE-TWO !!
SEEKING FURTHER STRENGTH, GOKU SETS OUT ON A JOURNEY...WHILE KURIRIN AND YAMCHA TRAIN RIGOROUSLY UNDER THE MUTEN-RÔSHI'S WATCHFUL EYE. OUR NEXT TALE TAKES PLACE IN THREE YEARS' TIME... WHEN THE STRONGEST-UNDER-THE-HEAVENS MARTIAL ARTS TOURNAMENT BEGINS AGAIN...!!
ONE-TWO
ONE-TWO

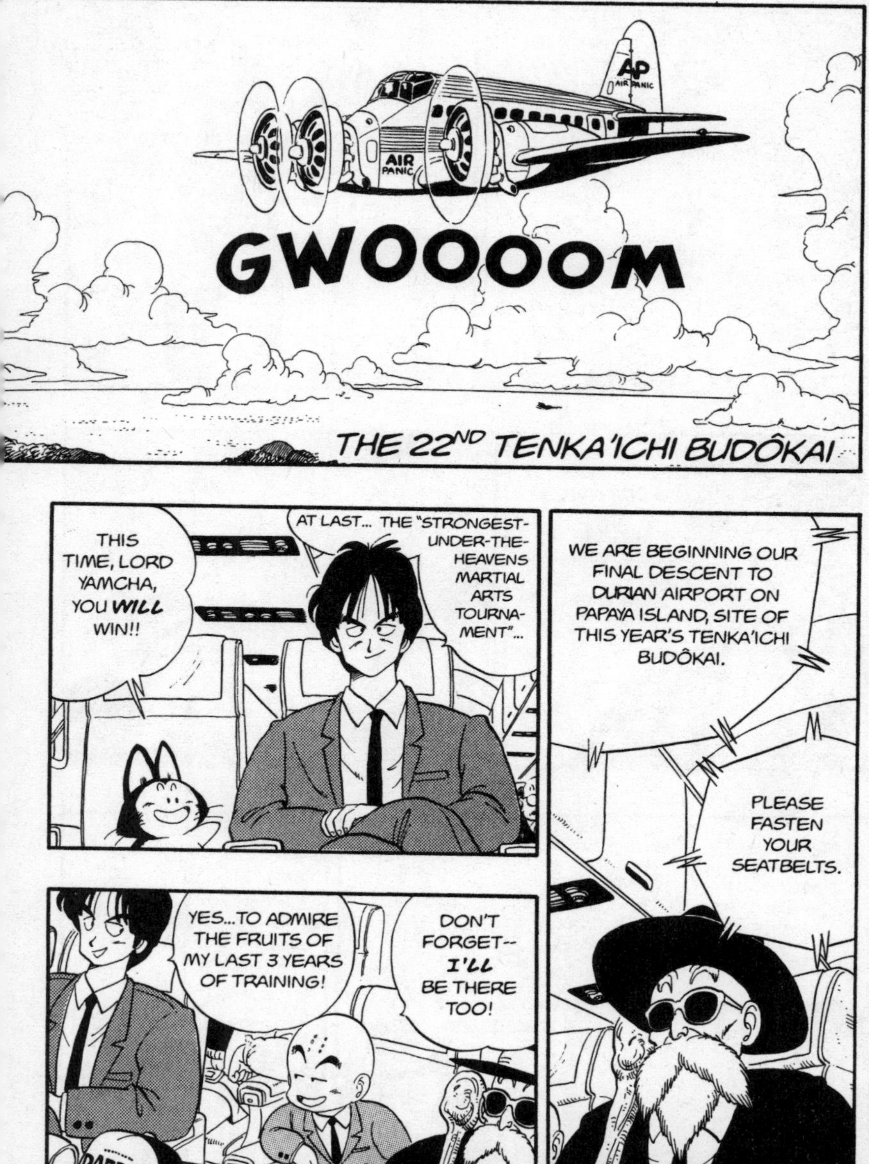

AP
AIR PANIC
AIR PANIC
GWOOOOM
THE 22ND TENKA'ICHI BUDÔKAI
WE ARE BEGINNING OUR FINAL DESCENT TO DURIAN AIRPORT ON PAPAYA ISLAND, SITE OF THIS YEAR'S TENKA'ICHI BUDÔKAI.
PLEASE FASTEN YOUR SEATBELTS.
AT LAST... THE "STRONGEST-UNDER-THE-HEAVENS MARTIAL ARTS TOURNAMENT"...
THIS TIME, LORD YAMCHA, YOU WILL WIN!!
DON'T FORGET-- I'LL BE THERE TOO!
YES...TO ADMIRE THE FRUITS OF MY LAST 3 YEARS OF TRAINING!
PAFPAF

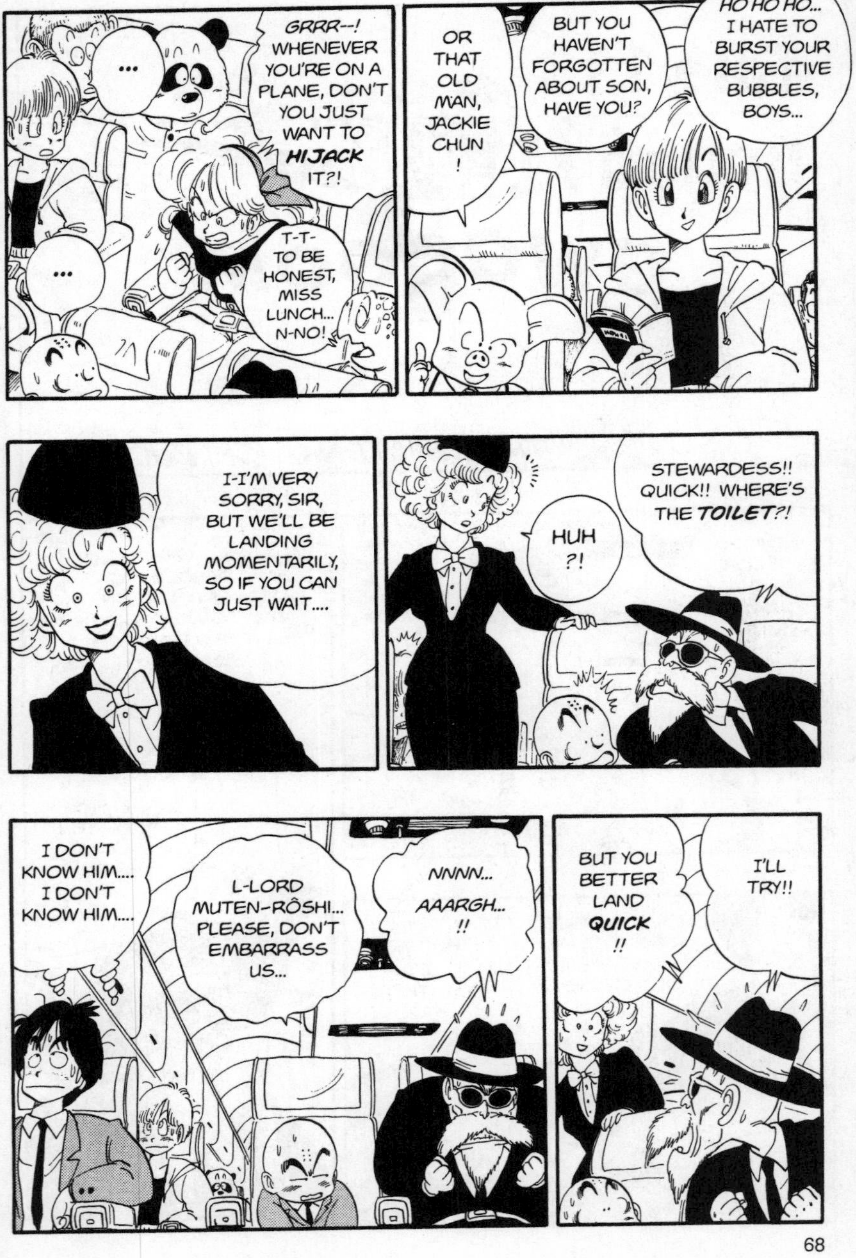
HO HO HO... I HATE TO BURST YOUR RESPECTIVE BUBBLES, BOYS...
BUT YOU HAVEN'T FORGOTTEN ABOUT SON, HAVE YOU?
OR THAT OLD MAN, JACKIE CHUN!
GRRR--! WHENEVER YOU'RE ON A PLANE, DON'T YOU JUST WANT TO HIJACK IT?!
...
...
T-T-TO BE HONEST, MISS LUNCH... N-NO!
STEWARDESS!! QUICK!! WHERE'S THE TOILET?!
HUH?!
I-I'M VERY SORRY, SIR, BUT WE'LL BE LANDING MOMENTARILY, SO IF YOU CAN JUST WAIT....
I'LL TRY!!
BUT YOU BETTER LAND QUICK!!
NNNN... AAARGH...!!
L-LORD MUTEN-RÔSHI... PLEASE, DON'T EMBARRASS US...
I DON'T KNOW HIM.... I DON'T KNOW HIM....

Tale 113

Return to the Tournament

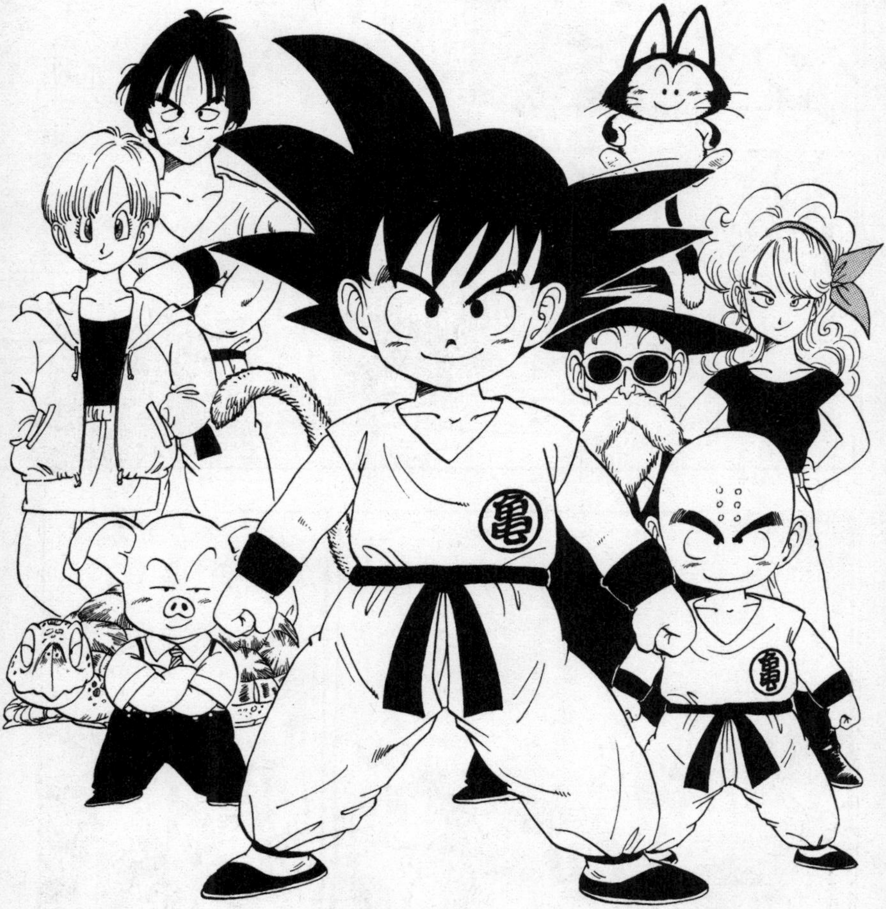

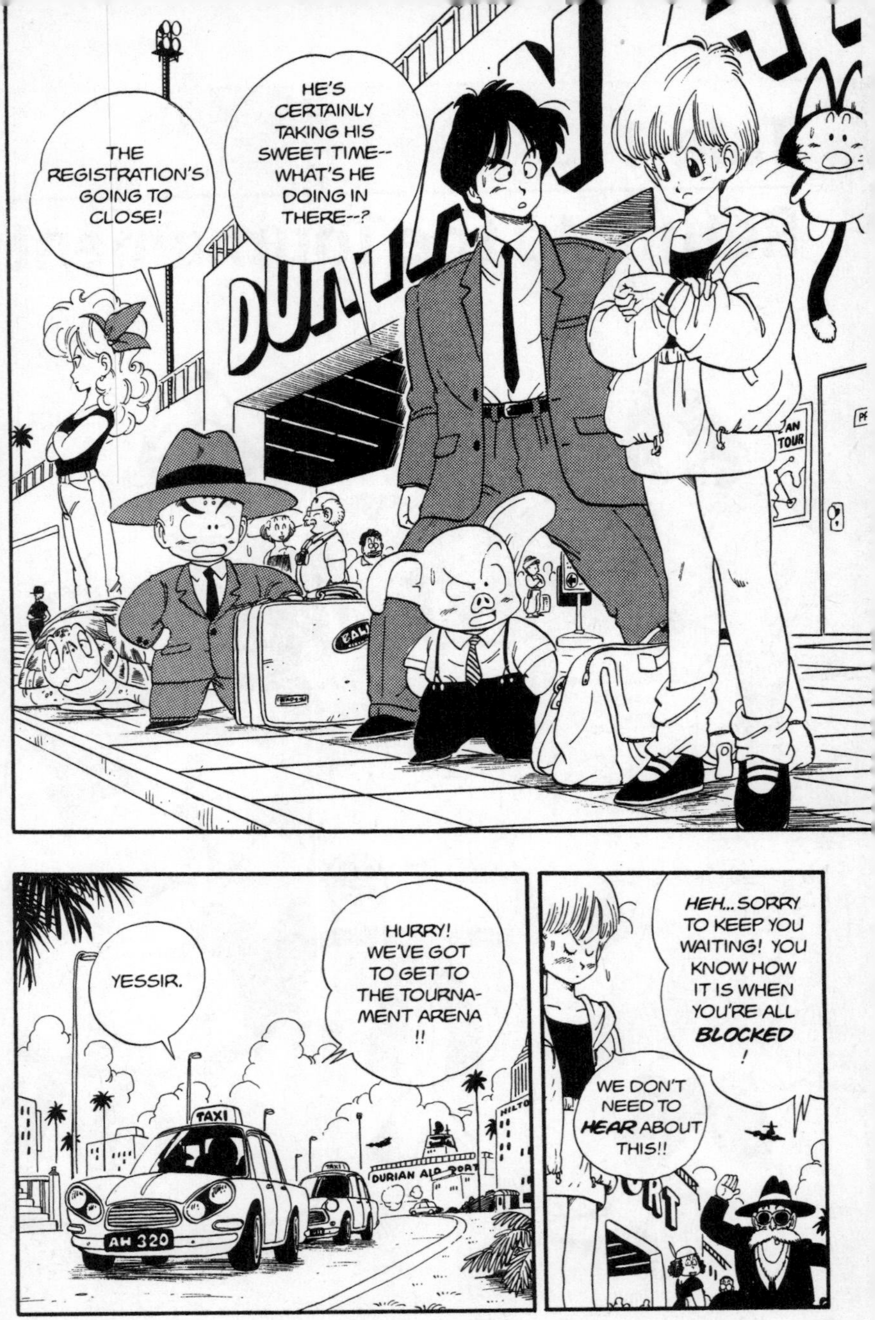
HE'S CERTAINLY TAKING HIS SWEET TIME-- WHAT'S HE DOING IN THERE--?
THE REGISTRATION'S GOING TO CLOSE!
HEH...SORRY TO KEEP YOU WAITING! YOU KNOW HOW IT IS WHEN YOU'RE ALL BLOCKED!
WE DON'T NEED TO HEAR ABOUT THIS!!
HURRY! WE'VE GOT TO GET TO THE TOURNAMENT ARENA!!
YESSIR.
TAXI
AH 320

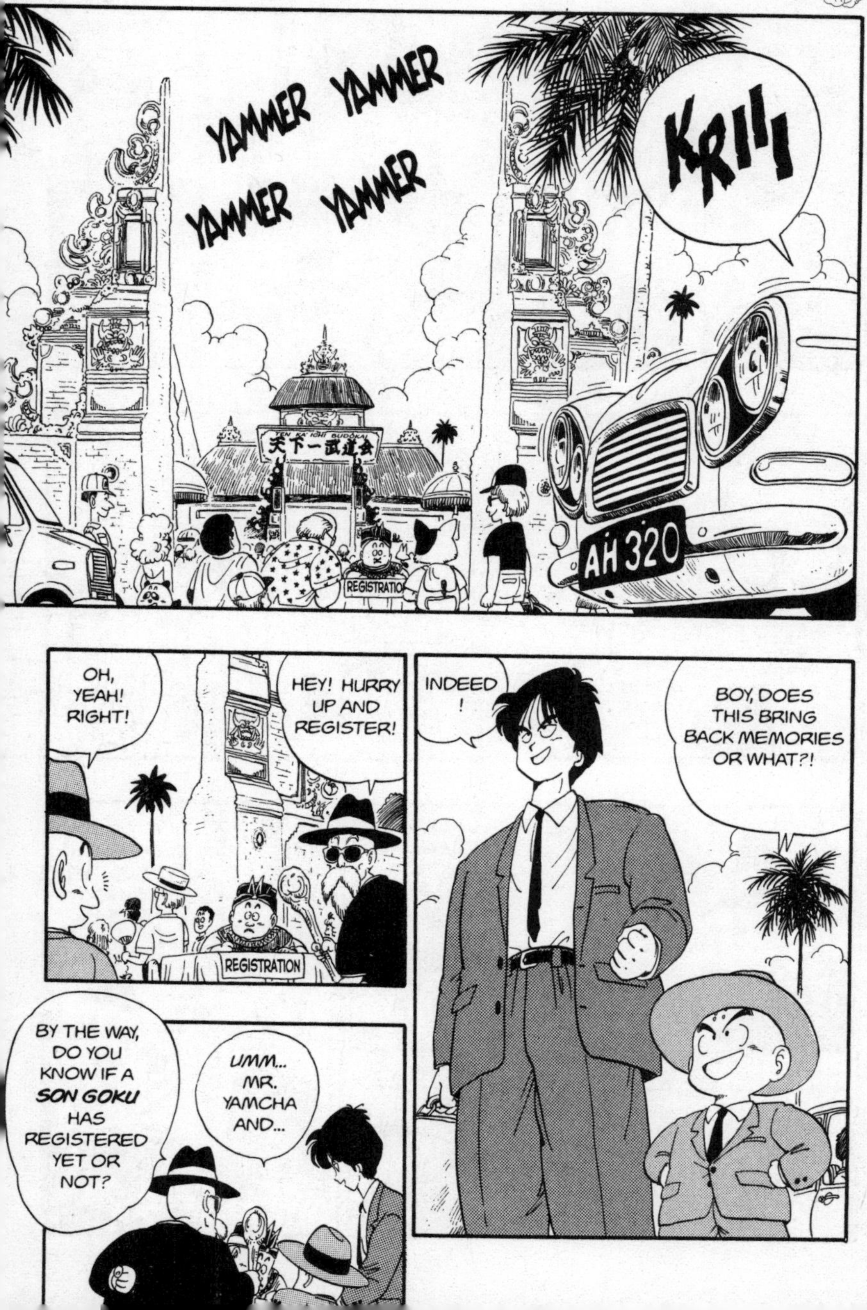
KRIII
YAMMER YAMMER
YAMMER YAMMER
TEN KA'ICHI BUDOKAI
天下一武道会
AH 320
REGISTRATION
BOY, DOES THIS BRING BACK MEMORIES OR WHAT?!
INDEED!
HEY! HURRY UP AND REGISTER!
OH, YEAH! RIGHT!
REGISTRATION
BY THE WAY, DO YOU KNOW IF A *SON GOKU* HAS REGISTERED YET OR NOT?
UMM... MR. YAMCHA AND...

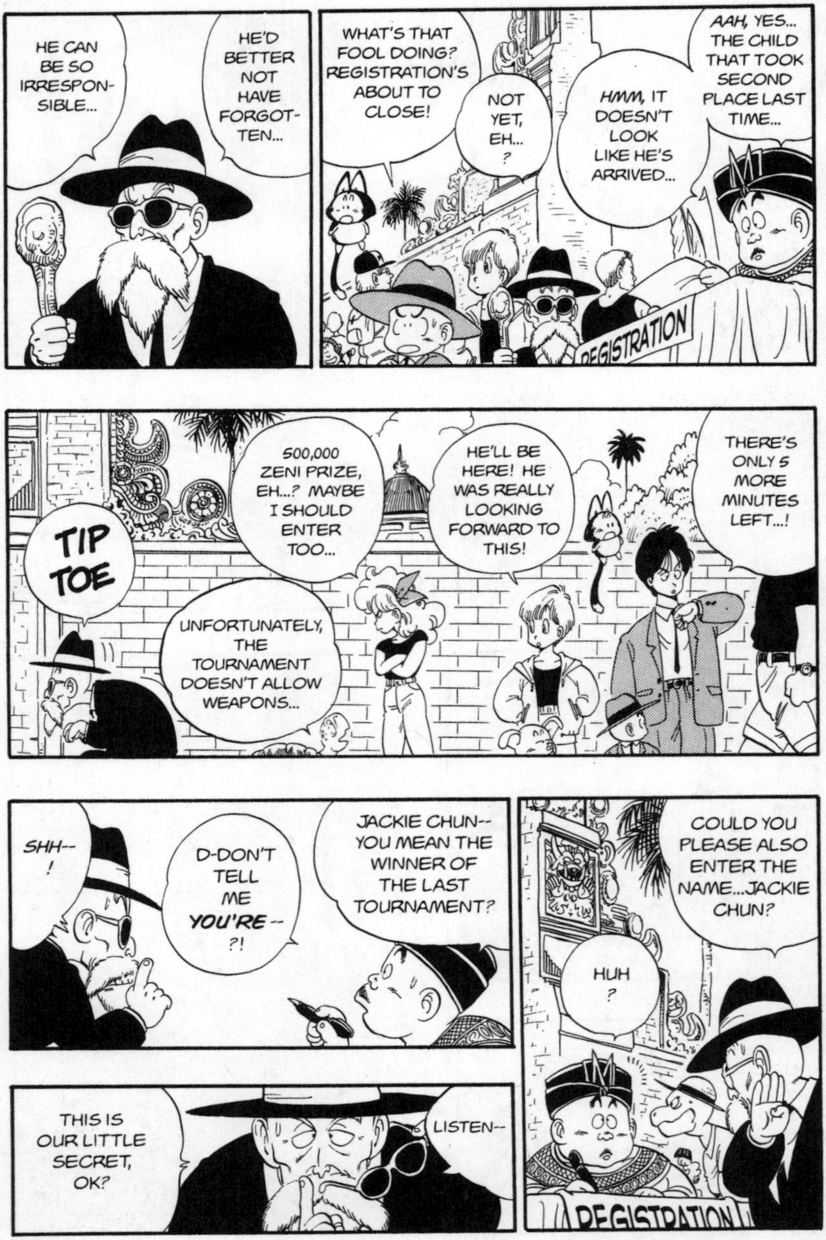
AAH, YES... THE CHILD THAT TOOK SECOND PLACE LAST TIME...
HMM, IT DOESN'T LOOK LIKE HE'S ARRIVED...
NOT YET, EH...?
WHAT'S THAT FOOL DOING? REGISTRATION'S ABOUT TO CLOSE!
REGISTRATION
HE'D BETTER NOT HAVE FORGOTTEN...
HE CAN BE SO IRRESPONSIBLE...
THERE'S ONLY 5 MORE MINUTES LEFT...!
HE'LL BE HERE! HE WAS REALLY LOOKING FORWARD TO THIS!
500,000 ZENI PRIZE, EH...? MAYBE I SHOULD ENTER TOO...
UNFORTUNATELY, THE TOURNAMENT DOESN'T ALLOW WEAPONS...
TIP TOE
COULD YOU PLEASE ALSO ENTER THE NAME...JACKIE CHUN?
HUH?
REGISTRATION
JACKIE CHUN-- YOU MEAN THE WINNER OF THE LAST TOURNAMENT?
D-DON'T TELL ME YOU'RE--?!
SHH--!
LISTEN--
THIS IS OUR LITTLE SECRET, OK?

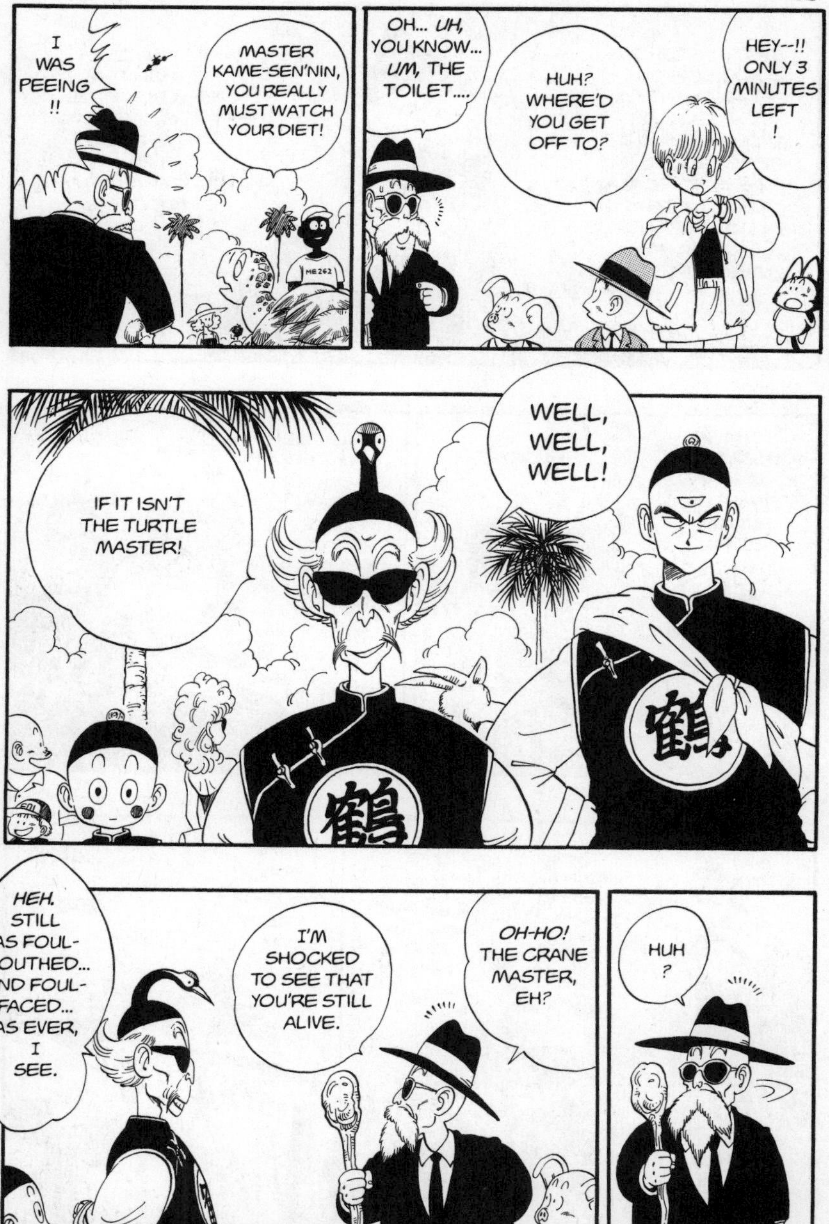
HEY--!! ONLY 3 MINUTES LEFT!
HUH? WHERE'D YOU GET OFF TO?
OH... UH, YOU KNOW... UM, THE TOILET....
MASTER KAME-SEN'NIN, YOU REALLY MUST WATCH YOUR DIET!
I WAS PEEING!!
ME262
WELL, WELL, WELL!
IF IT ISN'T THE TURTLE MASTER!
HUH?
OH-HO! THE CRANE MASTER, EH?
I'M SHOCKED TO SEE THAT YOU'RE STILL ALIVE.
HEH. STILL AS FOUL-MOUTHED... AND FOUL-FACED... AS EVER, I SEE.

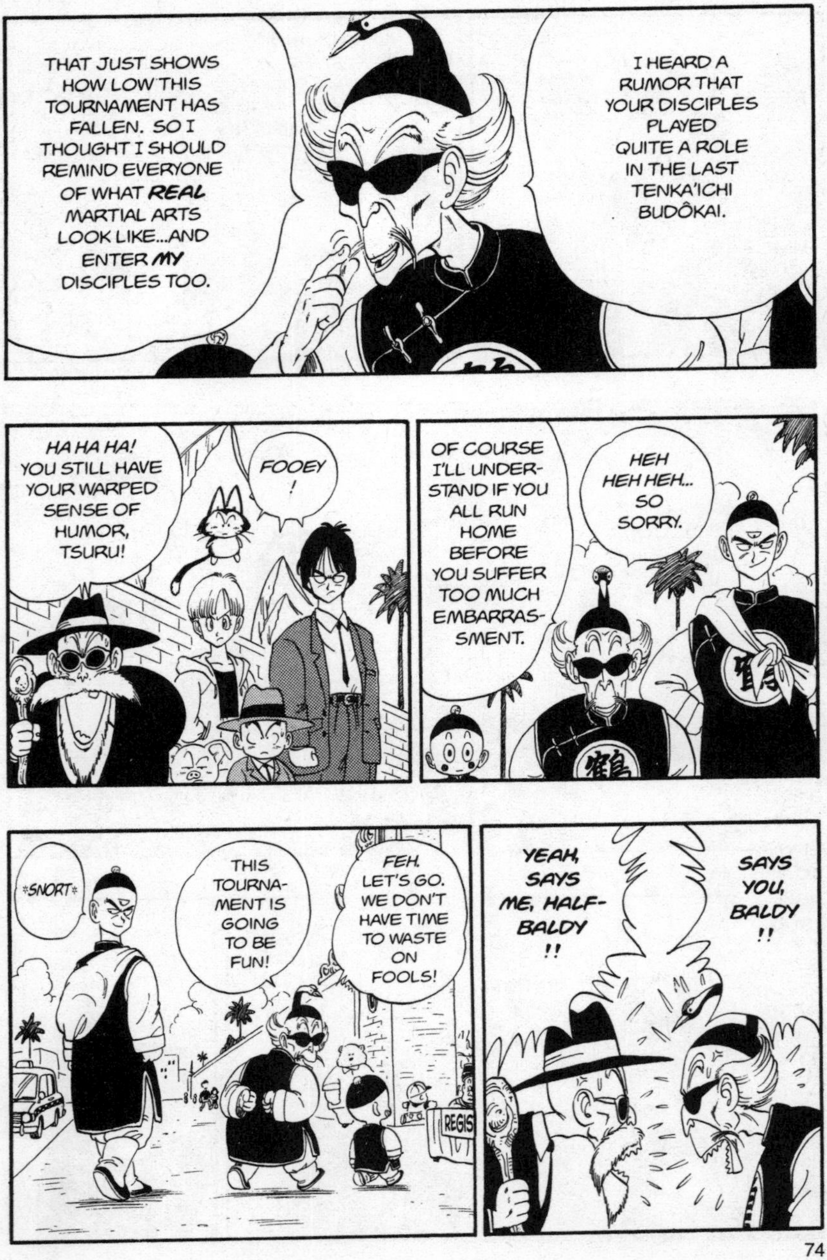
I HEARD A RUMOR THAT YOUR DISCIPLES PLAYED QUITE A ROLE IN THE LAST TENKA'ICHI BUDÔKAI.
THAT JUST SHOWS HOW LOW THIS TOURNAMENT HAS FALLEN. SO I THOUGHT I SHOULD REMIND EVERYONE OF WHAT *REAL* MARTIAL ARTS LOOK LIKE...AND ENTER *MY* DISCIPLES TOO.
HEH HEH HEH... SO SORRY.
OF COURSE I'LL UNDERSTAND IF YOU ALL RUN HOME BEFORE YOU SUFFER TOO MUCH EMBARRASSMENT.
FOOEY!
HA HA HA! YOU STILL HAVE YOUR WARPED SENSE OF HUMOR, TSURU!
SAYS YOU, BALDY!!
YEAH, SAYS ME, HALF-BALDY!!
FEH. LET'S GO. WE DON'T HAVE TIME TO WASTE ON FOOLS!
THIS TOURNAMENT IS GOING TO BE FUN!
SNORT
REGIS

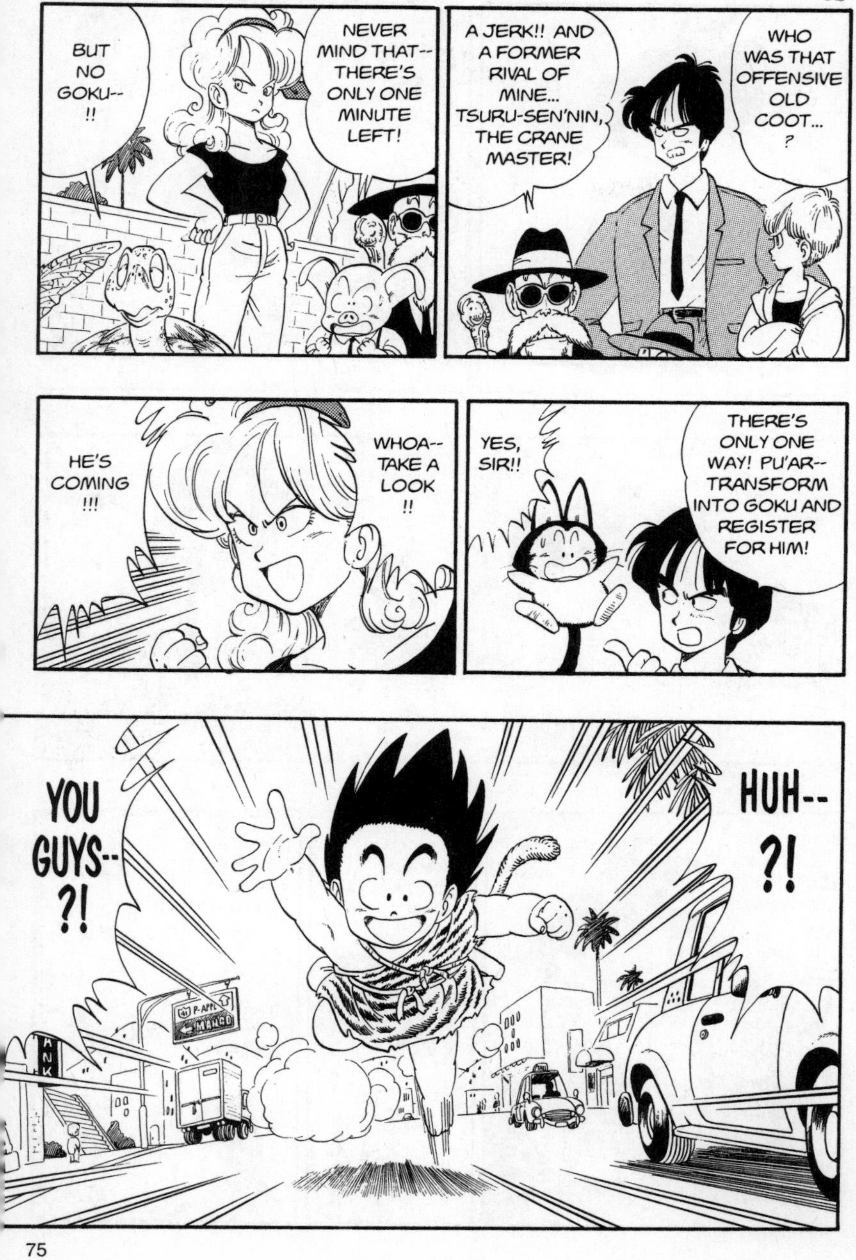
WHO WAS THAT OFFENSIVE OLD COOT...?
A JERK!! AND A FORMER RIVAL OF MINE... TSURU-SEN'NIN, THE CRANE MASTER!
NEVER MIND THAT-- THERE'S ONLY ONE MINUTE LEFT!
BUT NO GOKU--!!
THERE'S ONLY ONE WAY! PU'AR-- TRANSFORM INTO GOKU AND REGISTER FOR HIM!
YES, SIR!!
WHOA-- TAKE A LOOK!!
HE'S COMING!!!
HUH--?!
YOU GUYS--?!
P-APPL
MANGO

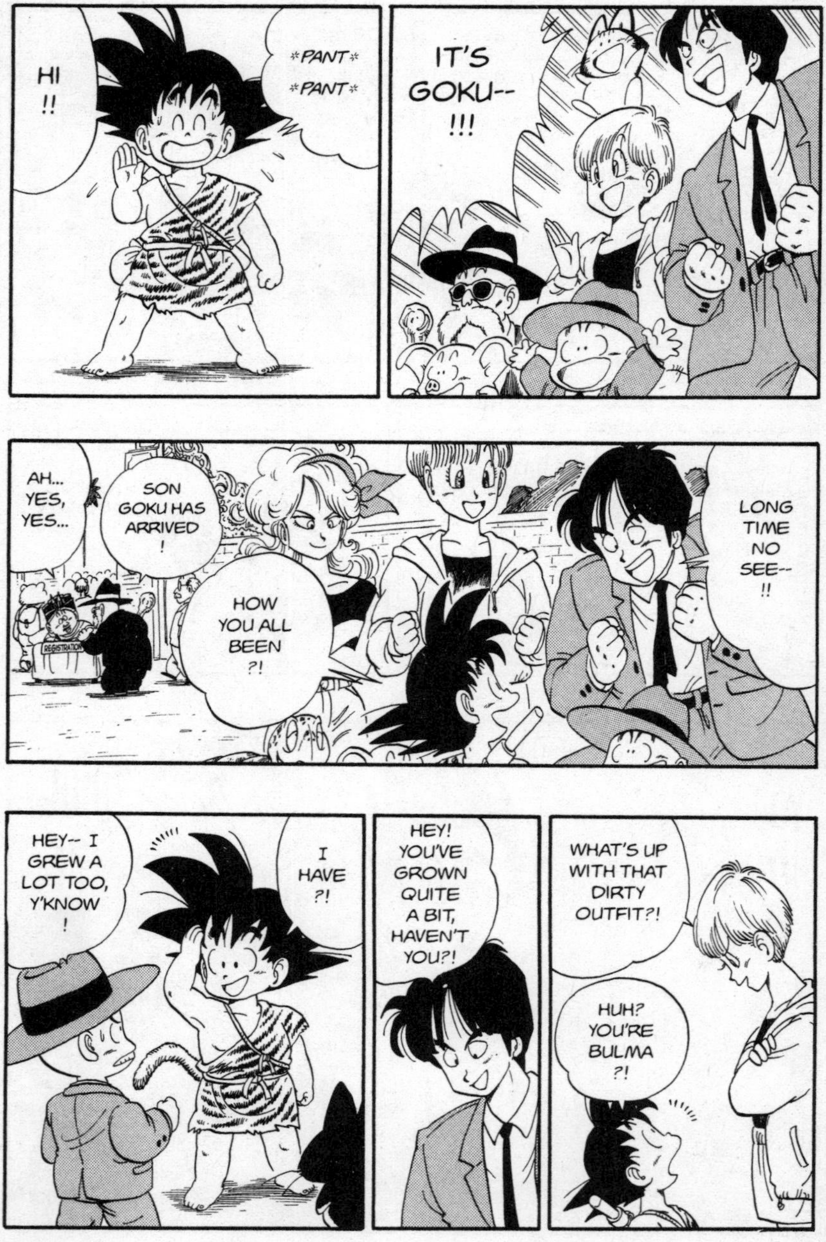
IT'S GOKU-- !!!
PANT *PANT*
HI !!
LONG TIME NO SEE-- !!
HOW YOU ALL BEEN ?!
SON GOKU HAS ARRIVED !
AH... YES, YES...
REGISTRATION
WHAT'S UP WITH THAT DIRTY OUTFIT?!
HUH? YOU'RE BULMA ?!
HEY! YOU'VE GROWN QUITE A BIT, HAVEN'T YOU?!
I HAVE ?!
HEY-- I GREW A LOT TOO, Y'KNOW !

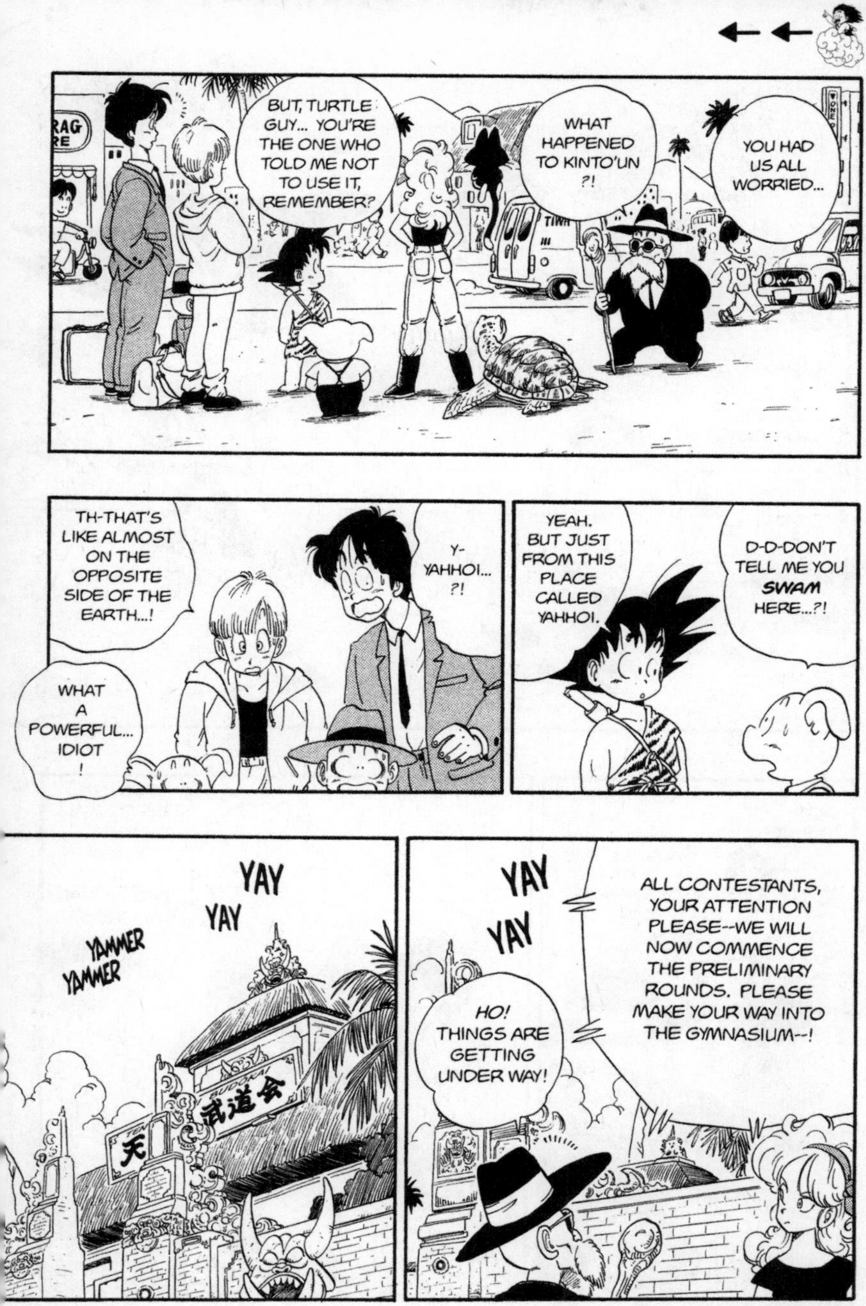
YOU HAD US ALL WORRIED...
WHAT HAPPENED TO KINTO'UN ?!
BUT, TURTLE GUY... YOU'RE THE ONE WHO TOLD ME NOT TO USE IT, REMEMBER?
D-D-DON'T TELL ME YOU **SWAM** HERE...?!
YEAH. BUT JUST FROM THIS PLACE CALLED YAHHOI.
Y-YAHHOI... ?!
TH-THAT'S LIKE ALMOST ON THE OPPOSITE SIDE OF THE EARTH...!
WHAT A POWERFUL... IDIOT !
ALL CONTESTANTS, YOUR ATTENTION PLEASE--WE WILL NOW COMMENCE THE PRELIMINARY ROUNDS. PLEASE MAKE YOUR WAY INTO THE GYMNASIUM--!
YAY
YAY
HO! THINGS ARE GETTING UNDER WAY!
YAY
YAY
YAMMER YAMMER
天
武道会

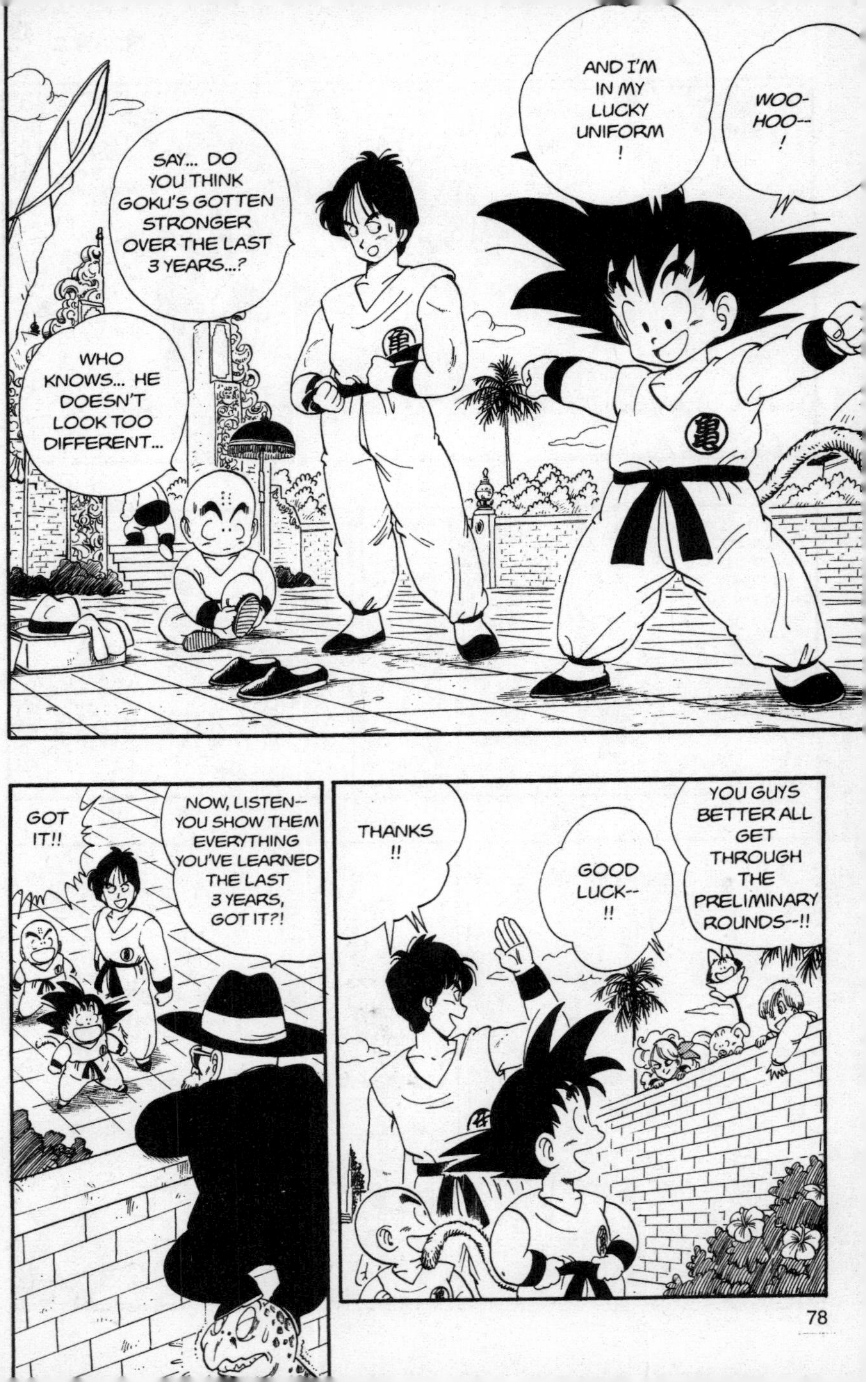
WOO-HOO--!
AND I'M IN MY LUCKY UNIFORM!
SAY... DO YOU THINK GOKU'S GOTTEN STRONGER OVER THE LAST 3 YEARS...?
WHO KNOWS... HE DOESN'T LOOK TOO DIFFERENT...
YOU GUYS BETTER ALL GET THROUGH THE PRELIMINARY ROUNDS--!!
GOOD LUCK--!!
THANKS!!
NOW, LISTEN-- YOU SHOW THEM EVERYTHING YOU'VE LEARNED THE LAST 3 YEARS, GOT IT?!
GOT IT!!

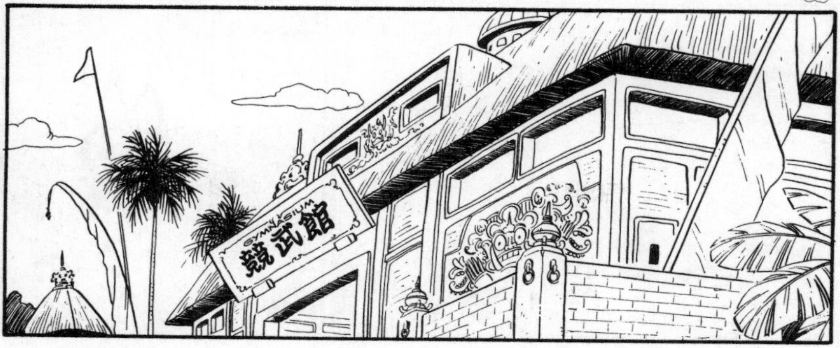
GYMNASIUM
競武館

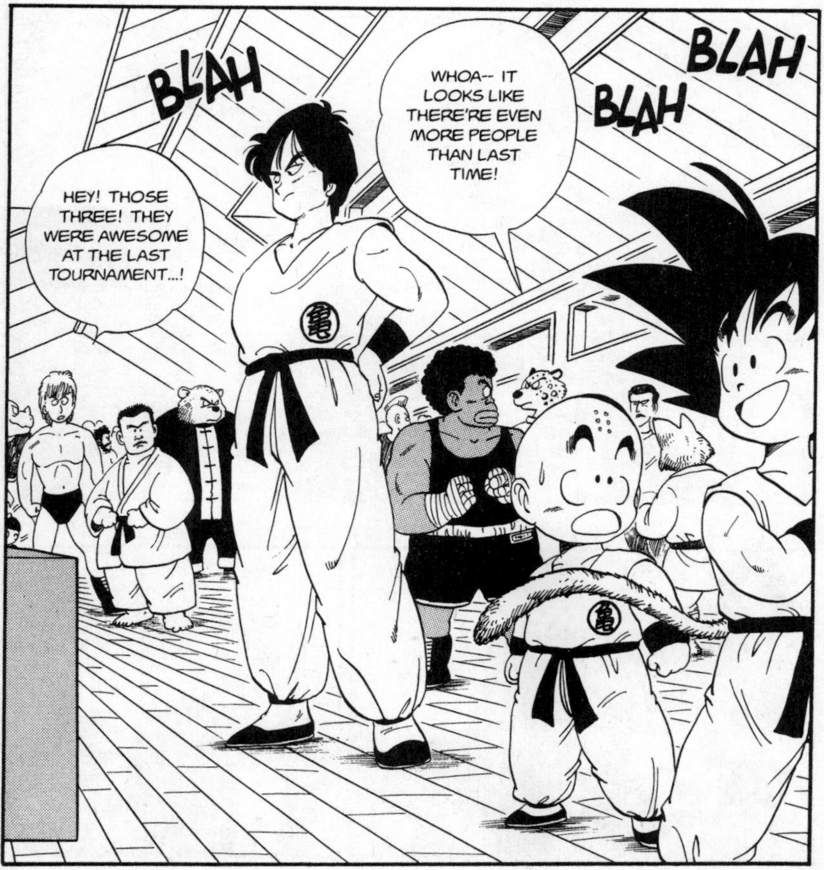
BLAH
BLAH
WHOA-- IT LOOKS LIKE THERE'RE EVEN MORE PEOPLE THAN LAST TIME!
BLAH
HEY! THOSE THREE! THEY WERE AWESOME AT THE LAST TOURNAMENT...!

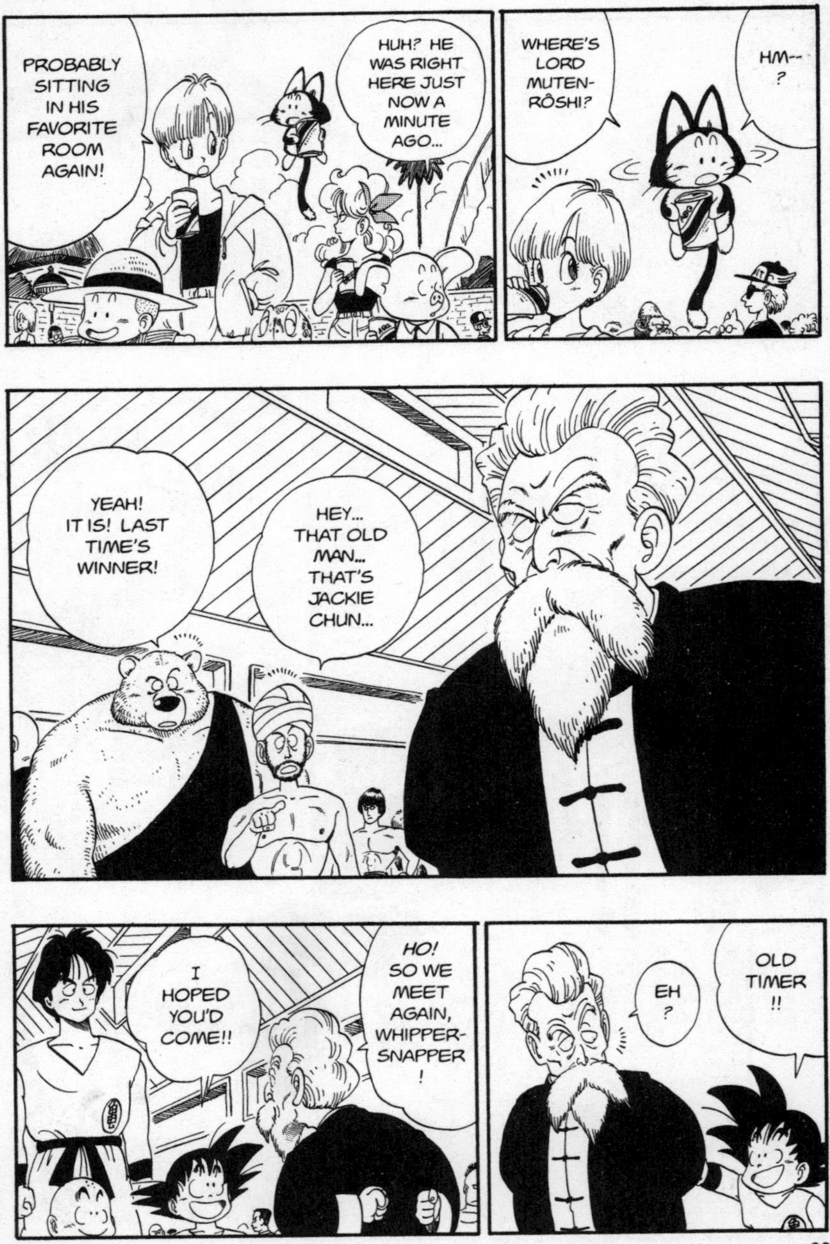
HM-- ?
WHERE'S LORD MUTEN-RÔSHI?
HUH? HE WAS RIGHT HERE JUST NOW A MINUTE AGO...
PROBABLY SITTING IN HIS FAVORITE ROOM AGAIN!
HEY... THAT OLD MAN... THAT'S JACKIE CHUN...
YEAH! IT IS! LAST TIME'S WINNER!
OLD TIMER !!
EH ?
HO! SO WE MEET AGAIN, WHIPPER-SNAPPER !
I HOPED YOU'D COME!!

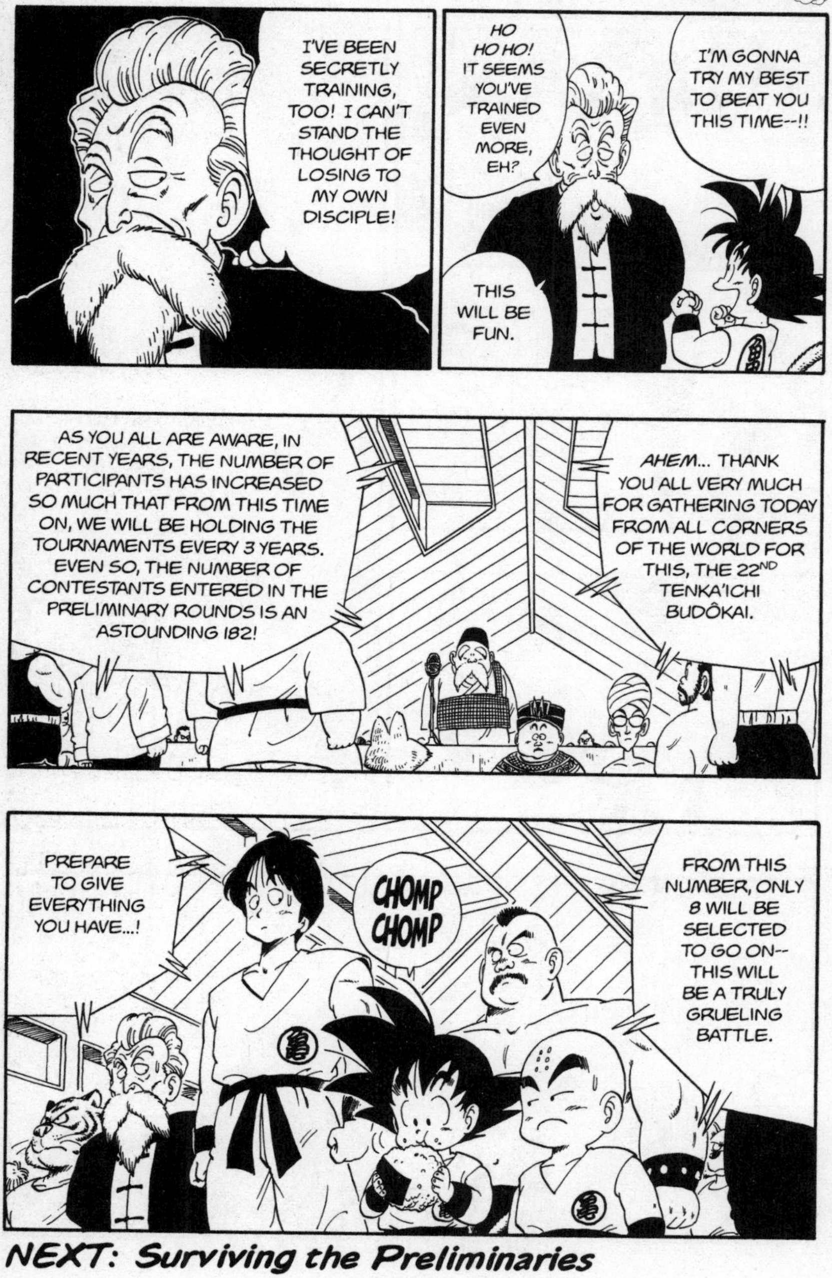
I'M GONNA TRY MY BEST TO BEAT YOU THIS TIME--!!
HO HO HO! IT SEEMS YOU'VE TRAINED EVEN MORE, EH?
THIS WILL BE FUN.
I'VE BEEN SECRETLY TRAINING, TOO! I CAN'T STAND THE THOUGHT OF LOSING TO MY OWN DISCIPLE!
AHEM... THANK YOU ALL VERY MUCH FOR GATHERING TODAY FROM ALL CORNERS OF THE WORLD FOR THIS, THE 22ND TENKA'ICHI BUDÔKAI.
AS YOU ALL ARE AWARE, IN RECENT YEARS, THE NUMBER OF PARTICIPANTS HAS INCREASED SO MUCH THAT FROM THIS TIME ON, WE WILL BE HOLDING THE TOURNAMENTS EVERY 3 YEARS. EVEN SO, THE NUMBER OF CONTESTANTS ENTERED IN THE PRELIMINARY ROUNDS IS AN ASTOUNDING 182!
FROM THIS NUMBER, ONLY 8 WILL BE SELECTED TO GO ON-- THIS WILL BE A TRULY GRUELING BATTLE.
CHOMP CHOMP
PREPARE TO GIVE EVERYTHING YOU HAVE...!

NEXT: ***Surviving the Preliminaries***

The Qualifying Rounds

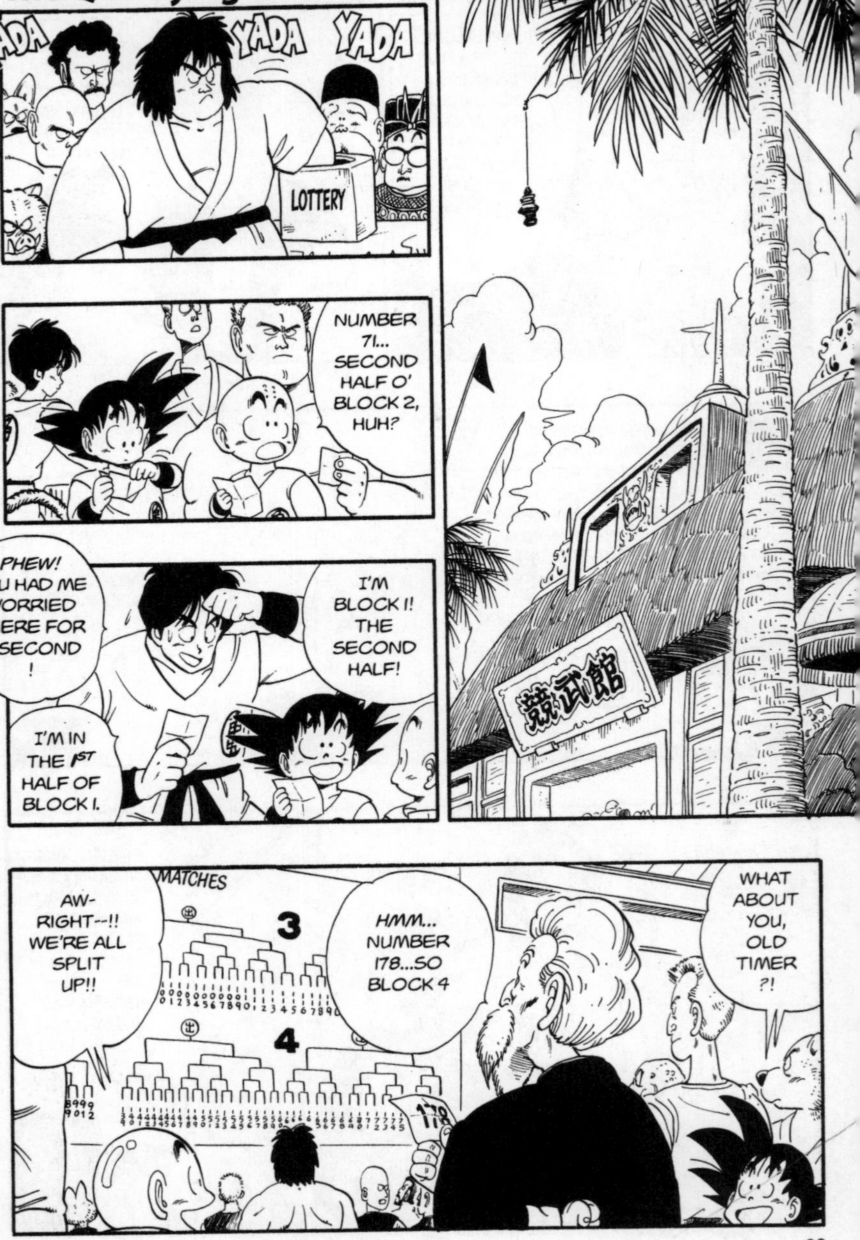
競武館
YADA YADA YADA
LOTTERY
NUMBER 71... SECOND HALF O' BLOCK 2, HUH?
I'M BLOCK 1! THE SECOND HALF!
PHEW! YOU HAD ME WORRIED THERE FOR A SECOND!
I'M IN THE 1ST HALF OF BLOCK 1.
WHAT ABOUT YOU, OLD TIMER?!
HMM... NUMBER 178...SO BLOCK 4
AW-RIGHT--!! WE'RE ALL SPLIT UP!!
MATCHES
3
4
178

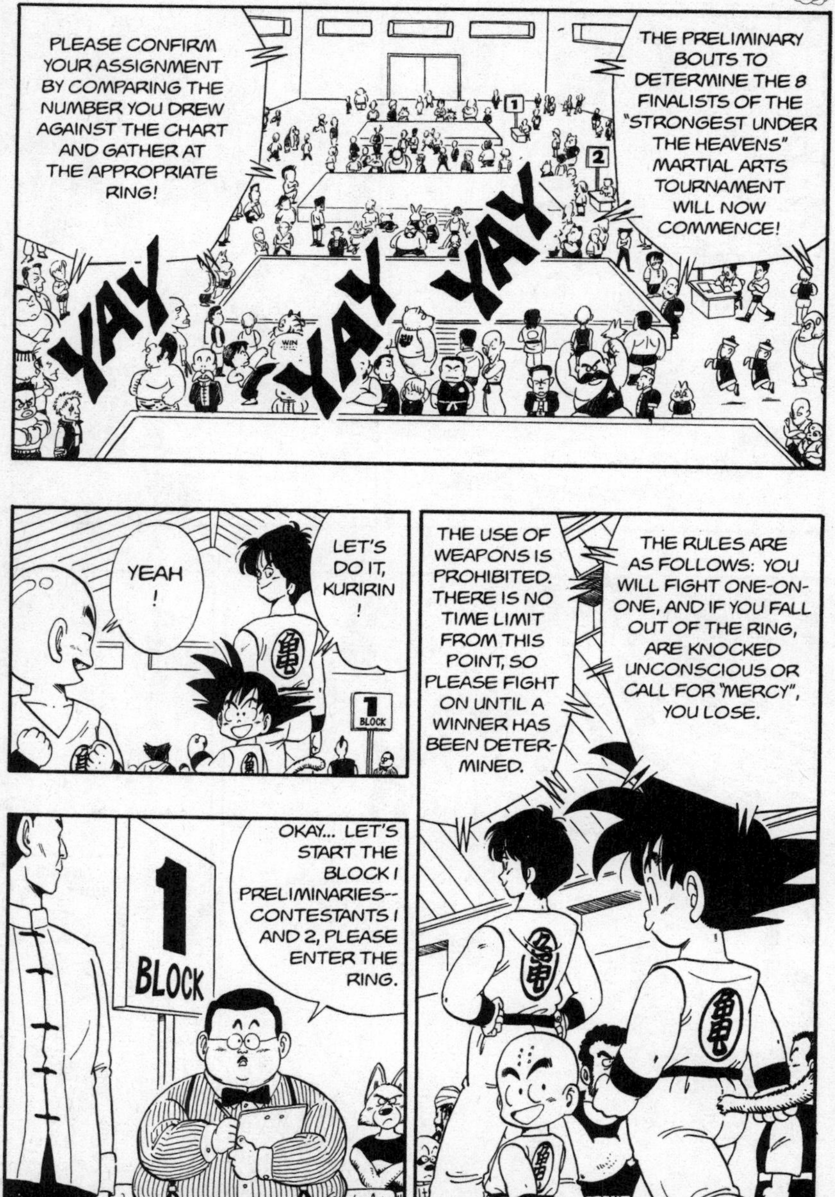
THE PRELIMINARY BOUTS TO DETERMINE THE 8 FINALISTS OF THE "STRONGEST UNDER THE HEAVENS" MARTIAL ARTS TOURNAMENT WILL NOW COMMENCE!
PLEASE CONFIRM YOUR ASSIGNMENT BY COMPARING THE NUMBER YOU DREW AGAINST THE CHART AND GATHER AT THE APPROPRIATE RING!
1
2
YAX
YAX
YAX
WIN
THE RULES ARE AS FOLLOWS: YOU WILL FIGHT ONE-ON-ONE, AND IF YOU FALL OUT OF THE RING, ARE KNOCKED UNCONSCIOUS OR CALL FOR "MERCY", YOU LOSE.
THE USE OF WEAPONS IS PROHIBITED. THERE IS NO TIME LIMIT FROM THIS POINT, SO PLEASE FIGHT ON UNTIL A WINNER HAS BEEN DETER-MINED.
LET'S DO IT, KURIRIN!
YEAH!
1 BLOCK
OKAY... LET'S START THE BLOCK 1 PRELIMINARIES-- CONTESTANTS 1 AND 2, PLEASE ENTER THE RING.
1 BLOCK

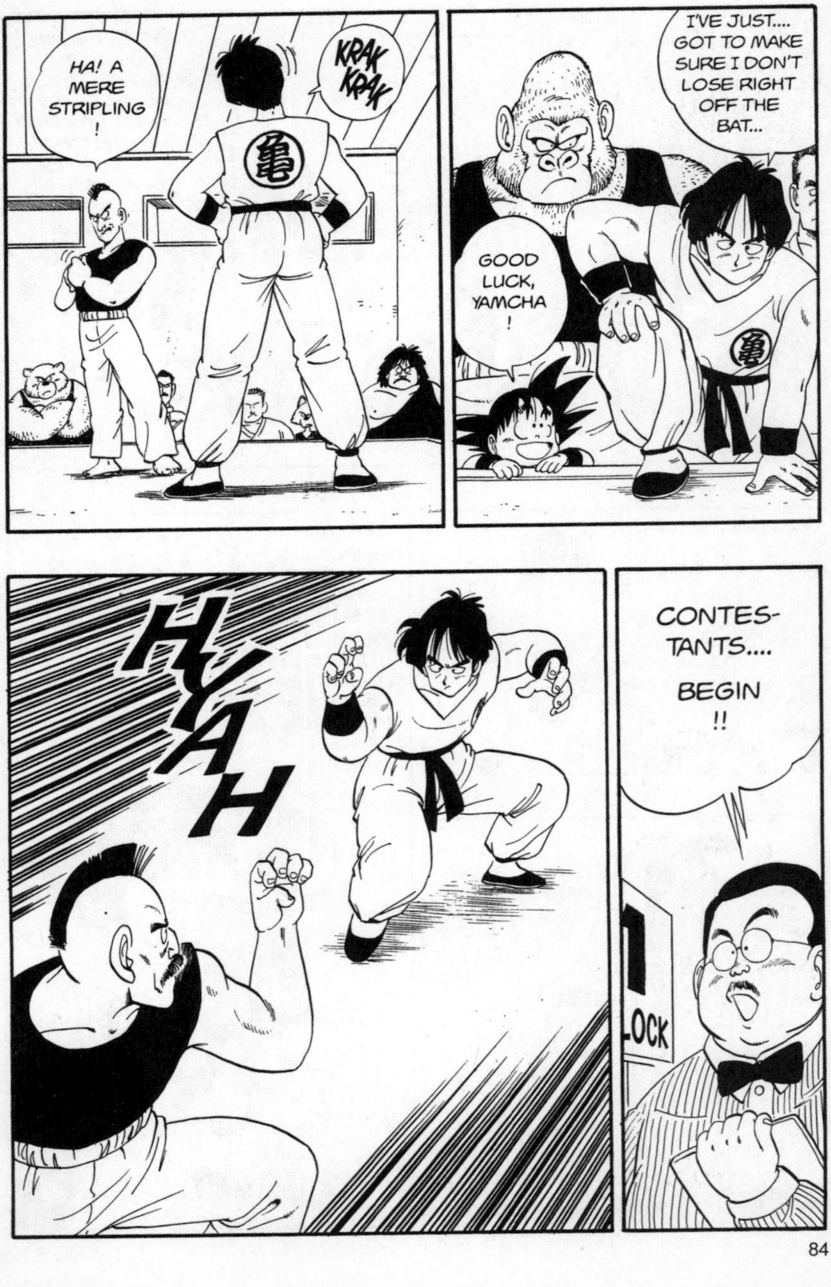
I'VE JUST.... GOT TO MAKE SURE I DON'T LOSE RIGHT OFF THE BAT...
GOOD LUCK, YAMCHA!
HA! A MERE STRIPLING!
KRAK KRAK
CONTES-TANTS.... BEGIN!!
HYAH

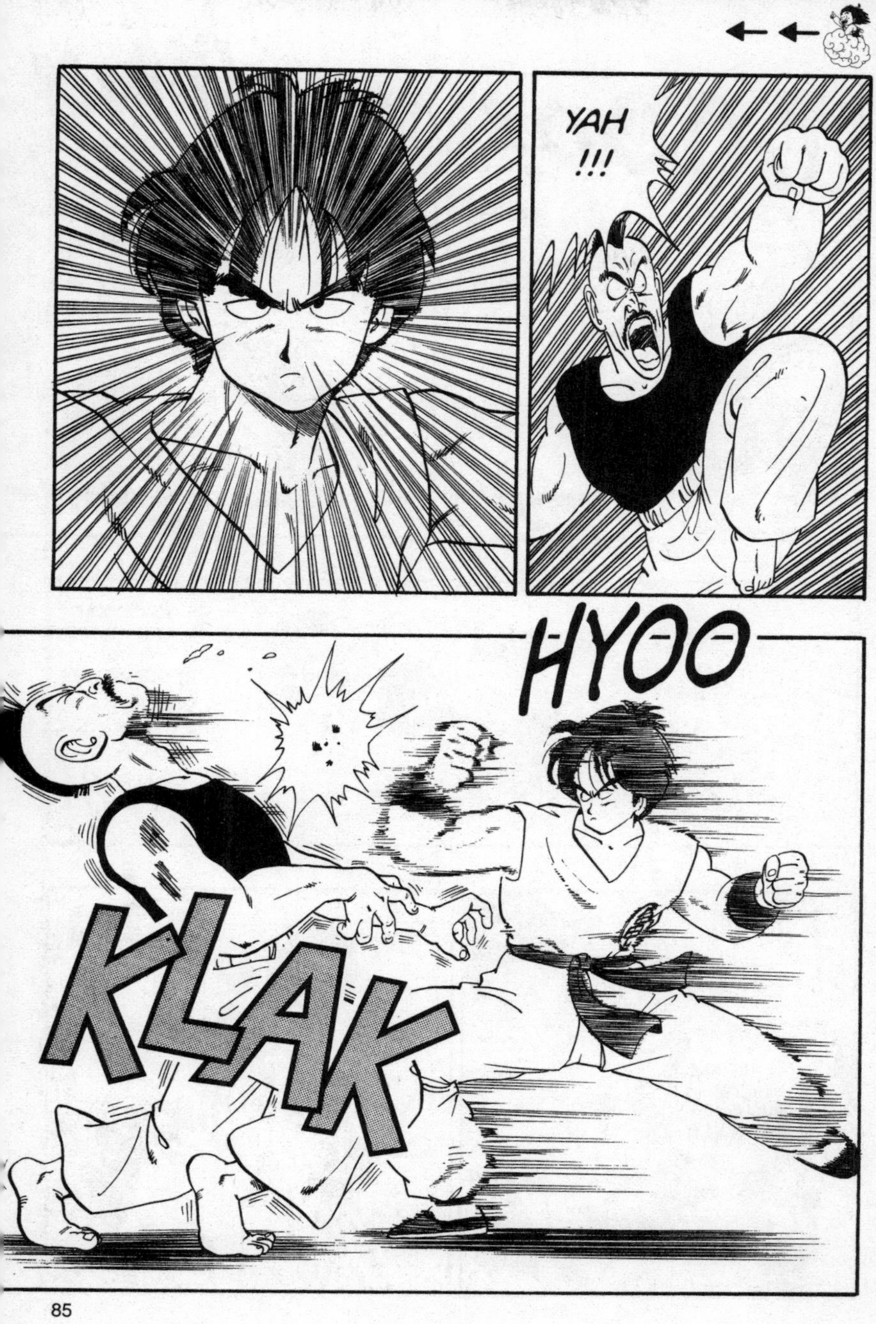
YAH
!!!
HYOO
KLAK

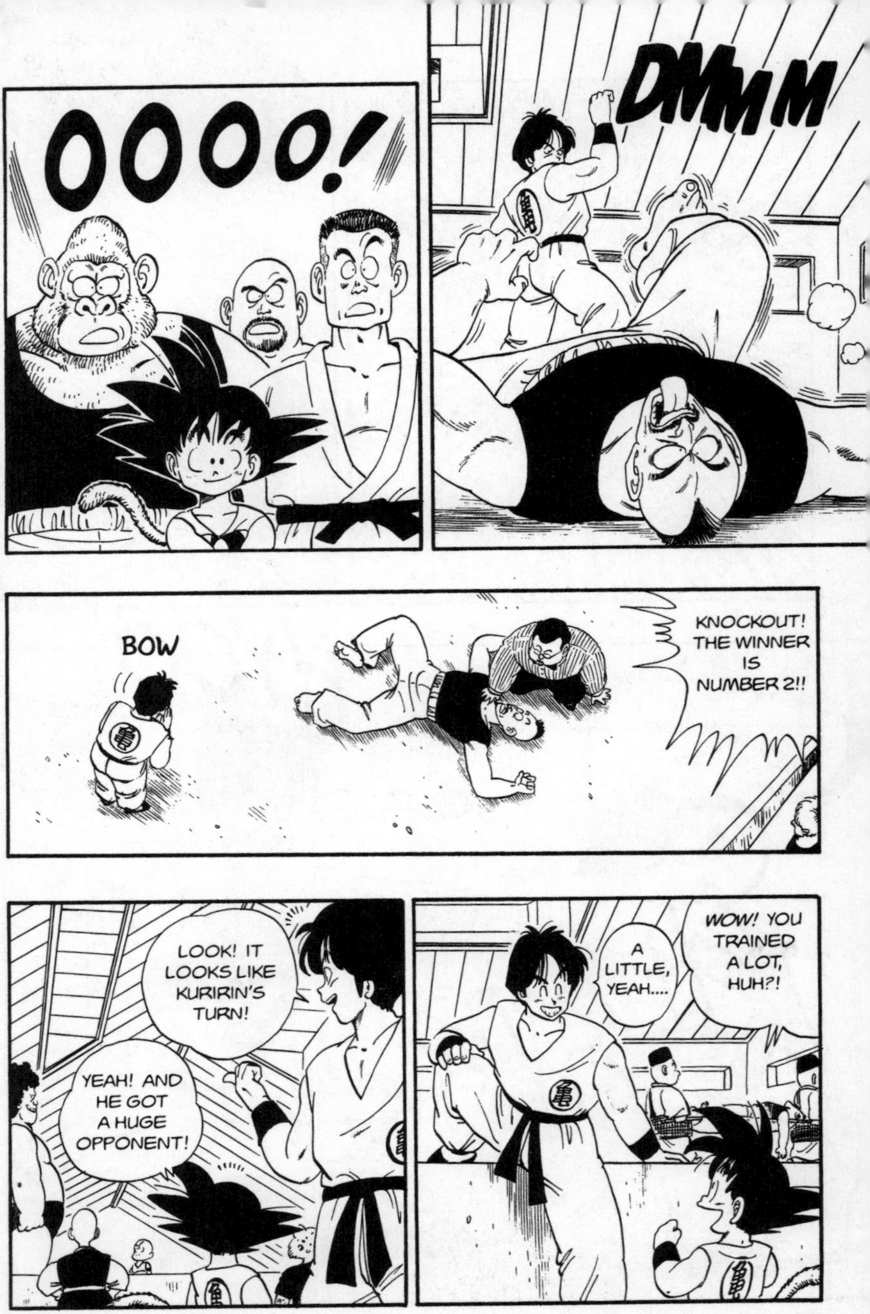

DMMM
OOOO!
KNOCKOUT! THE WINNER IS NUMBER 2!!
BOW
WOW! YOU TRAINED A LOT, HUH?!
A LITTLE, YEAH....
LOOK! IT LOOKS LIKE KURIRIN'S TURN!
YEAH! AND HE GOT A HUGE OPPONENT!

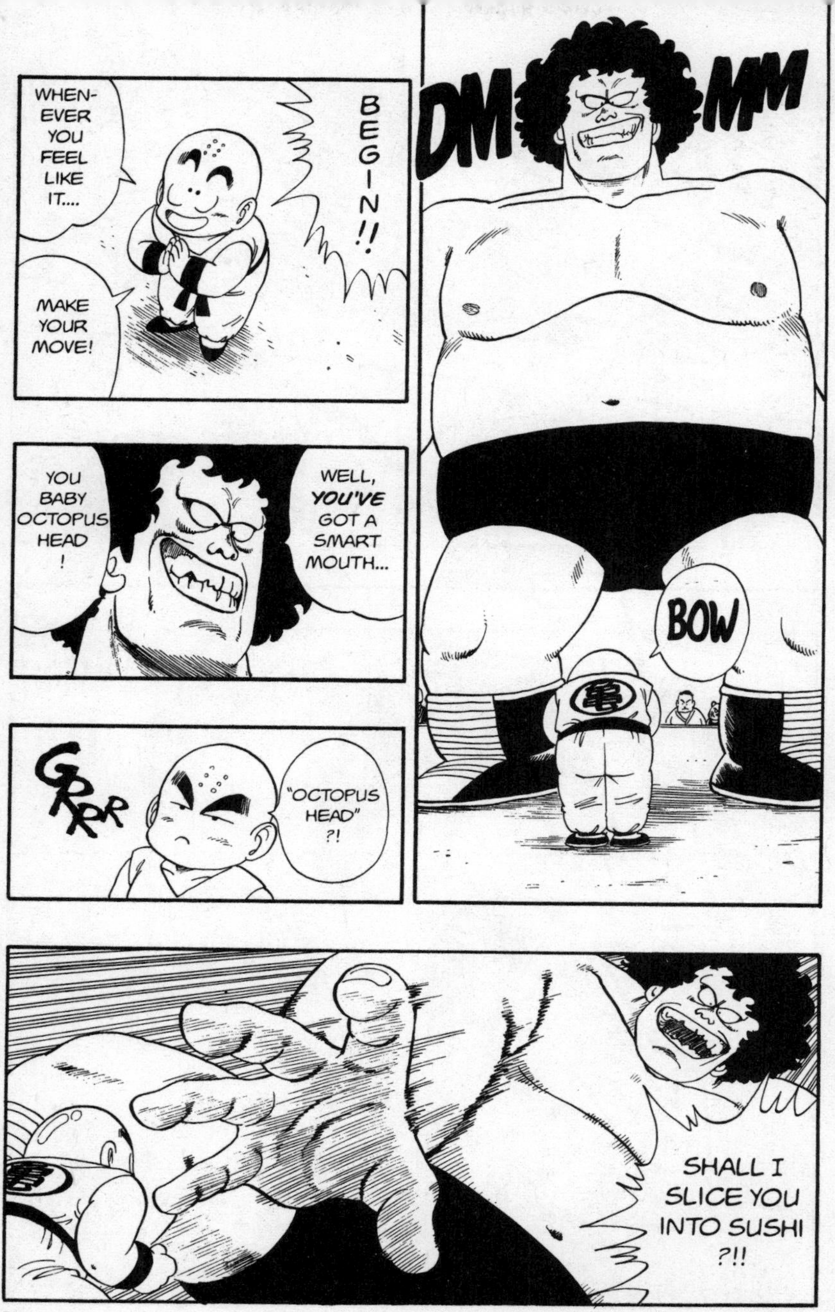
DM MM
BOW
BEGIN!!
WHENEVER YOU FEEL LIKE IT....
MAKE YOUR MOVE!
WELL, *YOU'VE* GOT A SMART MOUTH...
YOU BABY OCTOPUS HEAD!
"OCTOPUS HEAD" ?!
GRRR
SHALL I SLICE YOU INTO SUSHI ?!!

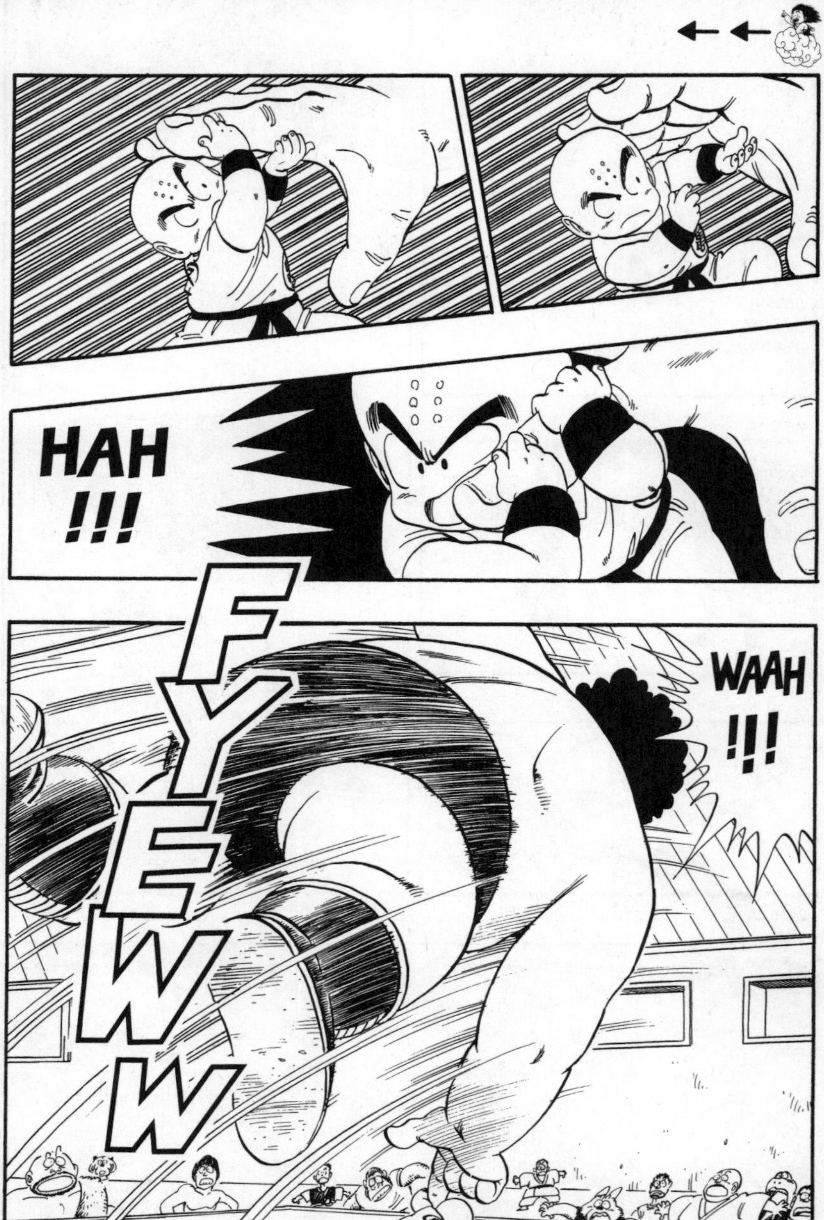
HAH !!!
WAAH !!!
FYEWWW

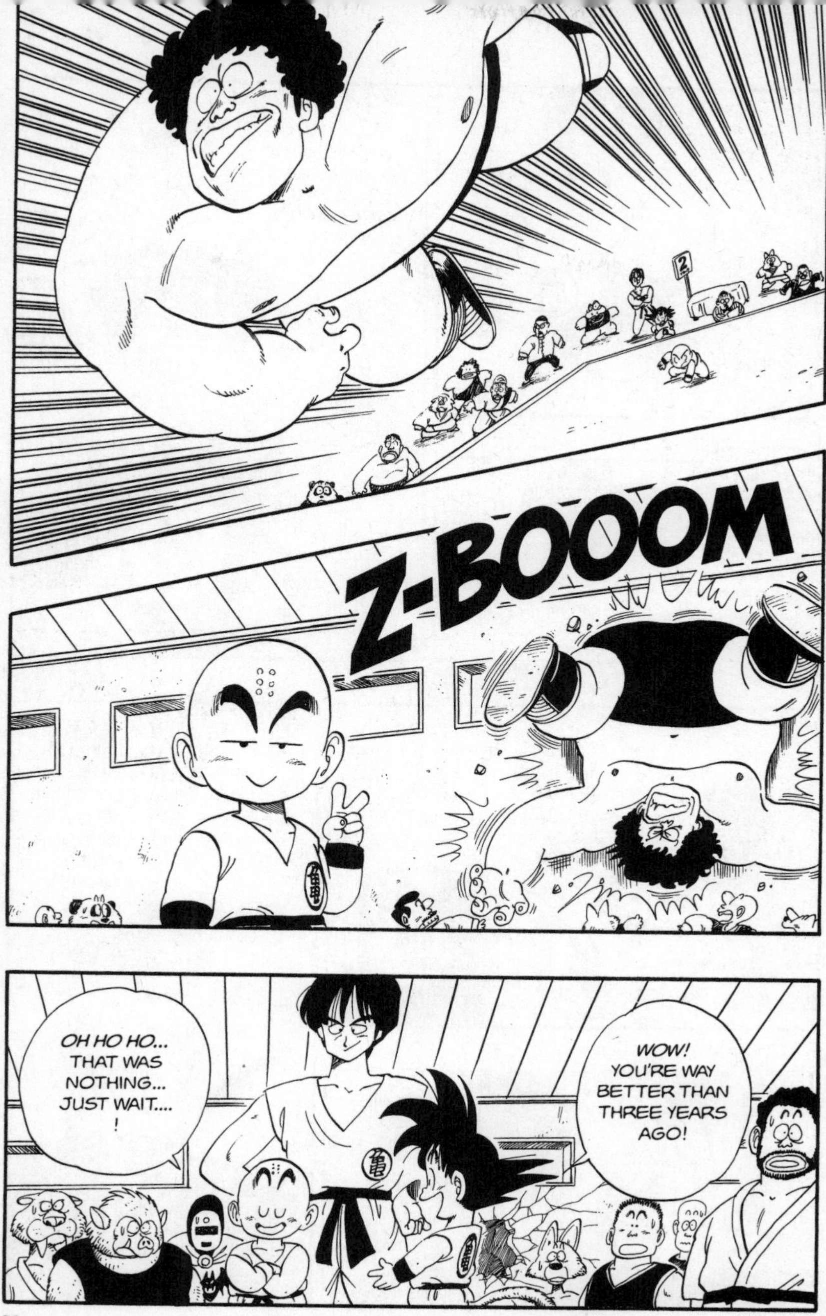
Z-BOOOM
WOW! YOU'RE WAY BETTER THAN THREE YEARS AGO!
OH HO HO... THAT WAS NOTHING... JUST WAIT.... !

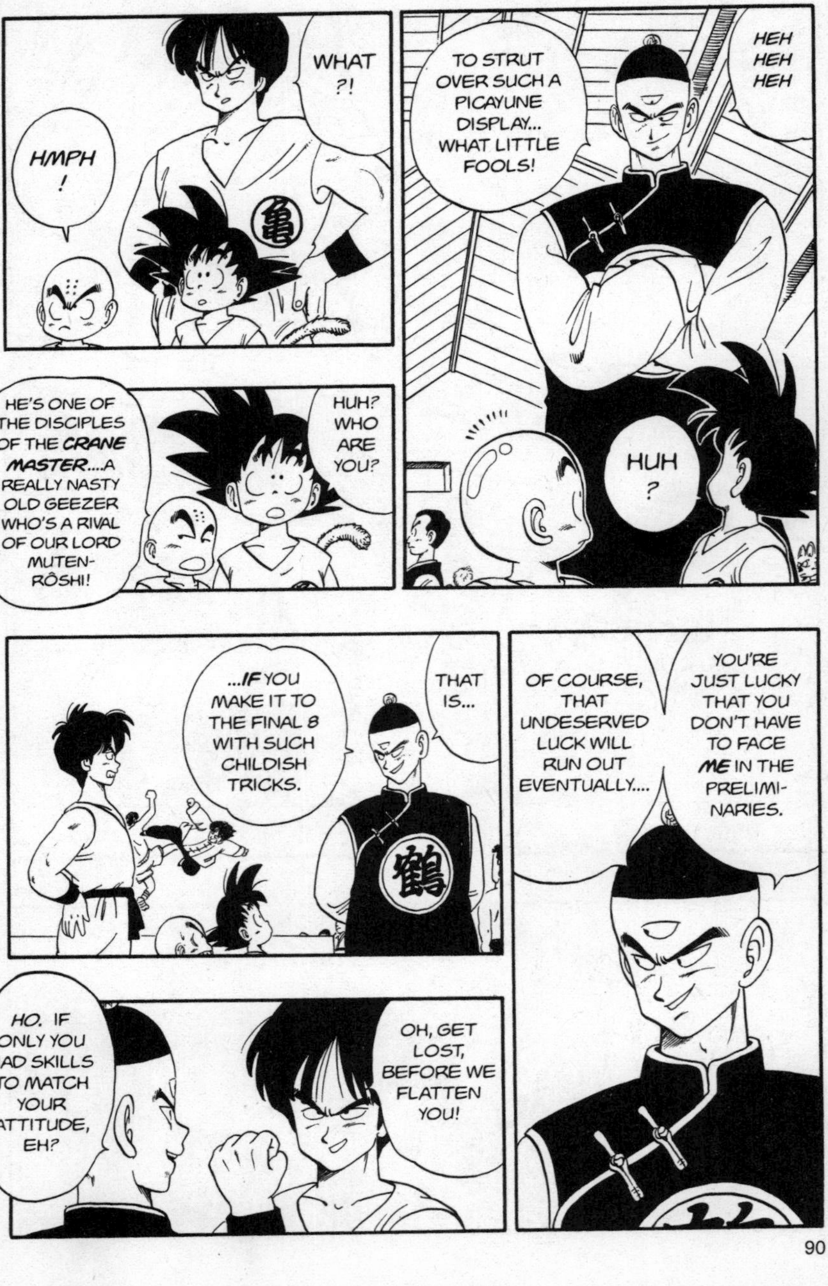
HEH HEH HEH
TO STRUT OVER SUCH A PICAYUNE DISPLAY... WHAT LITTLE FOOLS!
HUH ?
WHAT ?!
HMPH !
HUH? WHO ARE YOU?
HE'S ONE OF THE DISCIPLES OF THE CRANE MASTER....A REALLY NASTY OLD GEEZER WHO'S A RIVAL OF OUR LORD MUTEN-RÔSHI!
YOU'RE JUST LUCKY THAT YOU DON'T HAVE TO FACE ME IN THE PRELIMI-NARIES.
OF COURSE, THAT UNDESERVED LUCK WILL RUN OUT EVENTUALLY....
THAT IS...
...IF YOU MAKE IT TO THE FINAL 8 WITH SUCH CHILDISH TRICKS.
OH, GET LOST, BEFORE WE FLATTEN YOU!
HO. IF ONLY YOU HAD SKILLS TO MATCH YOUR ATTITUDE, EH?

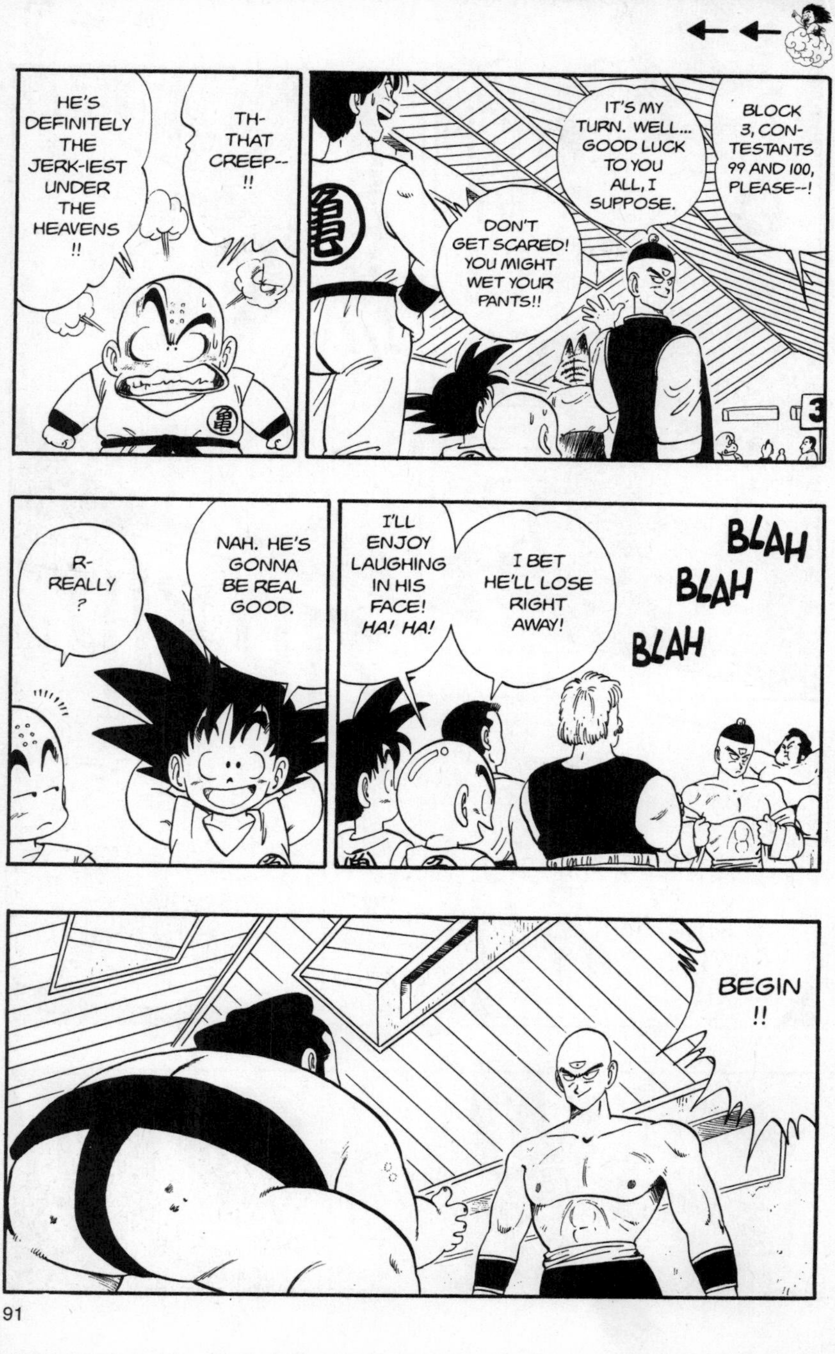
BLOCK 3, CON-TESTANTS 99 AND 100, PLEASE--!
IT'S MY TURN. WELL... GOOD LUCK TO YOU ALL, I SUPPOSE.
DON'T GET SCARED! YOU MIGHT WET YOUR PANTS!!
TH-THAT CREEP--!!
HE'S DEFINITELY THE JERK-IEST UNDER THE HEAVENS!!
BLAH BLAH BLAH
I BET HE'LL LOSE RIGHT AWAY!
I'LL ENJOY LAUGHING IN HIS FACE! HA! HA!
NAH. HE'S GONNA BE REAL GOOD.
R-REALLY?
BEGIN!!

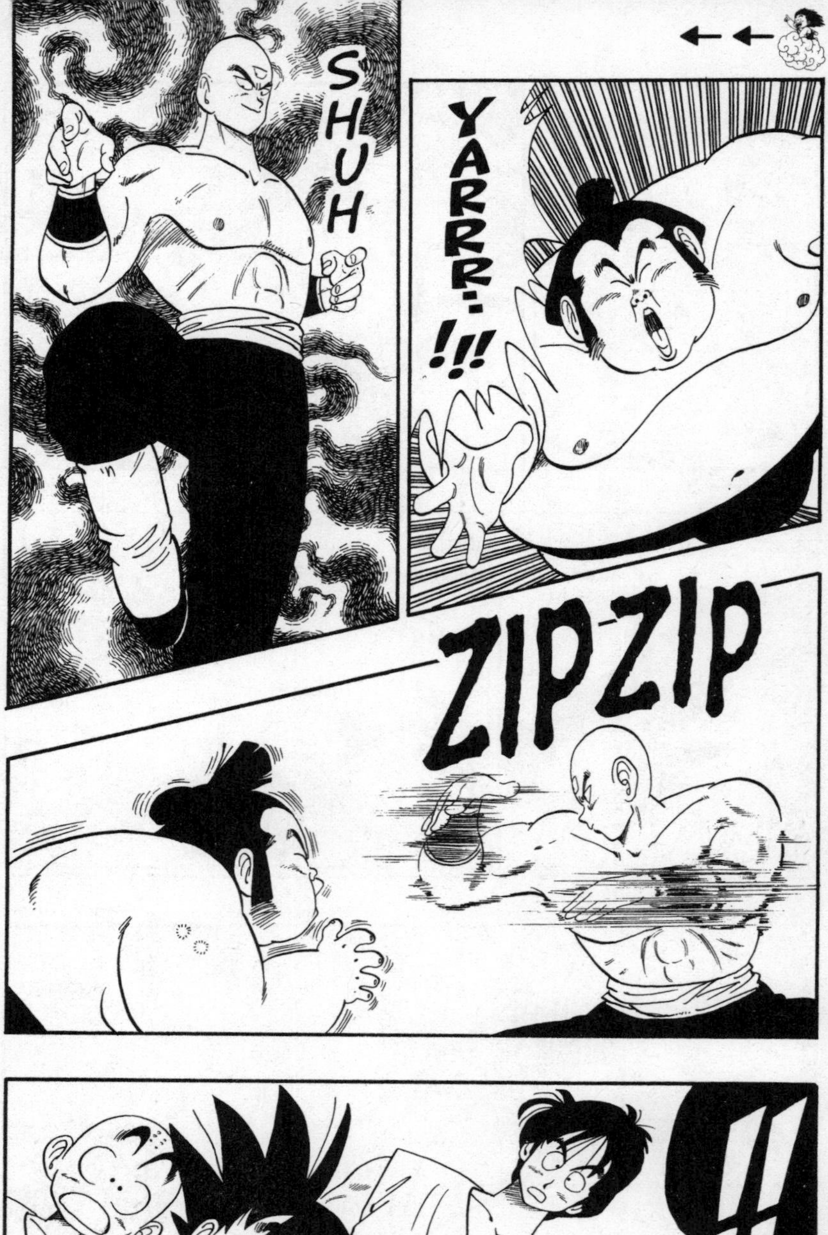
YARRR!!!
SHUH
ZIP ZIP
!!

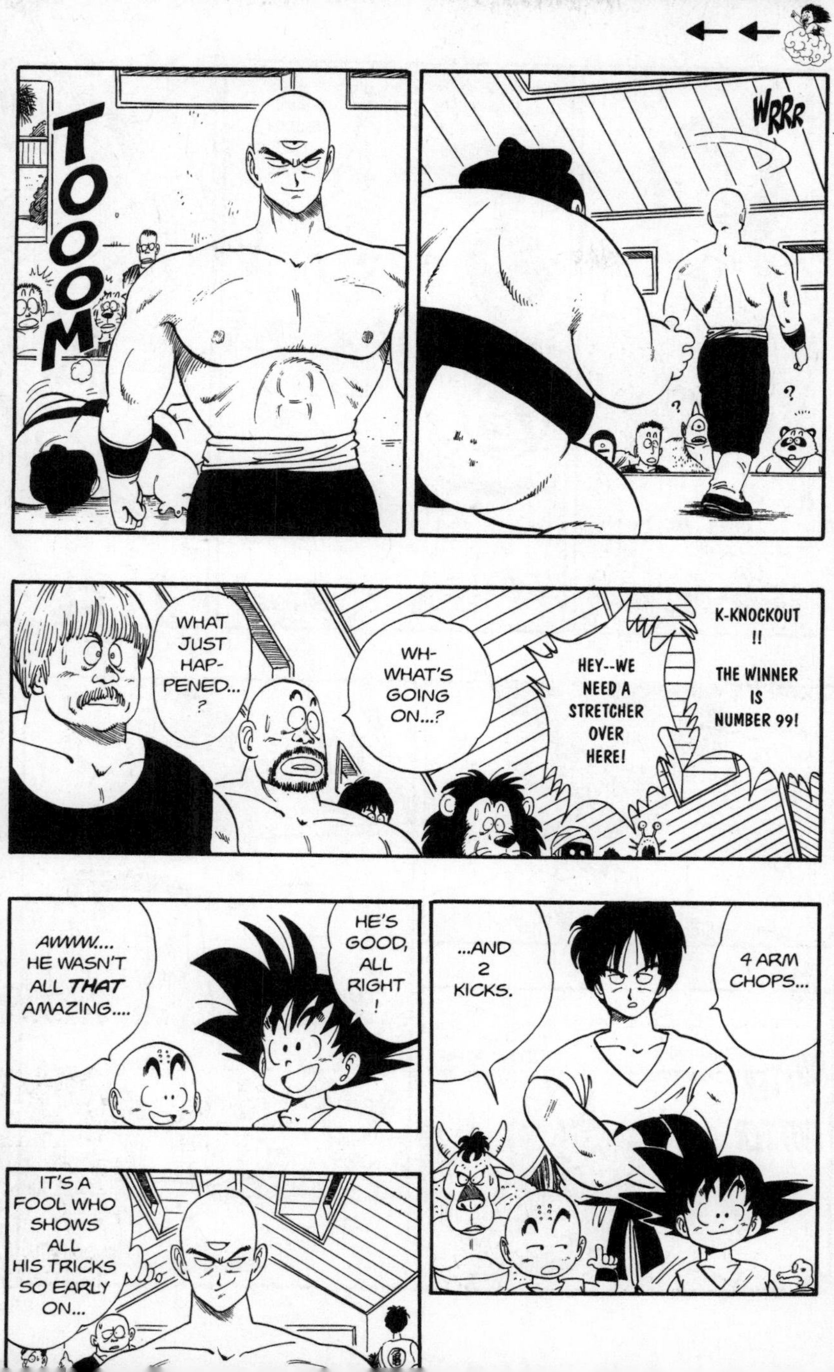
WRRR
TOOOM
K-KNOCKOUT!! THE WINNER IS NUMBER 99!
HEY--WE NEED A STRETCHER OVER HERE!
WH-WHAT'S GOING ON...?
WHAT JUST HAPPENED...?
4 ARM CHOPS...
...AND 2 KICKS.
HE'S GOOD, ALL RIGHT!
AWWW.... HE WASN'T ALL *THAT* AMAZING....
IT'S A FOOL WHO SHOWS ALL HIS TRICKS SO EARLY ON...

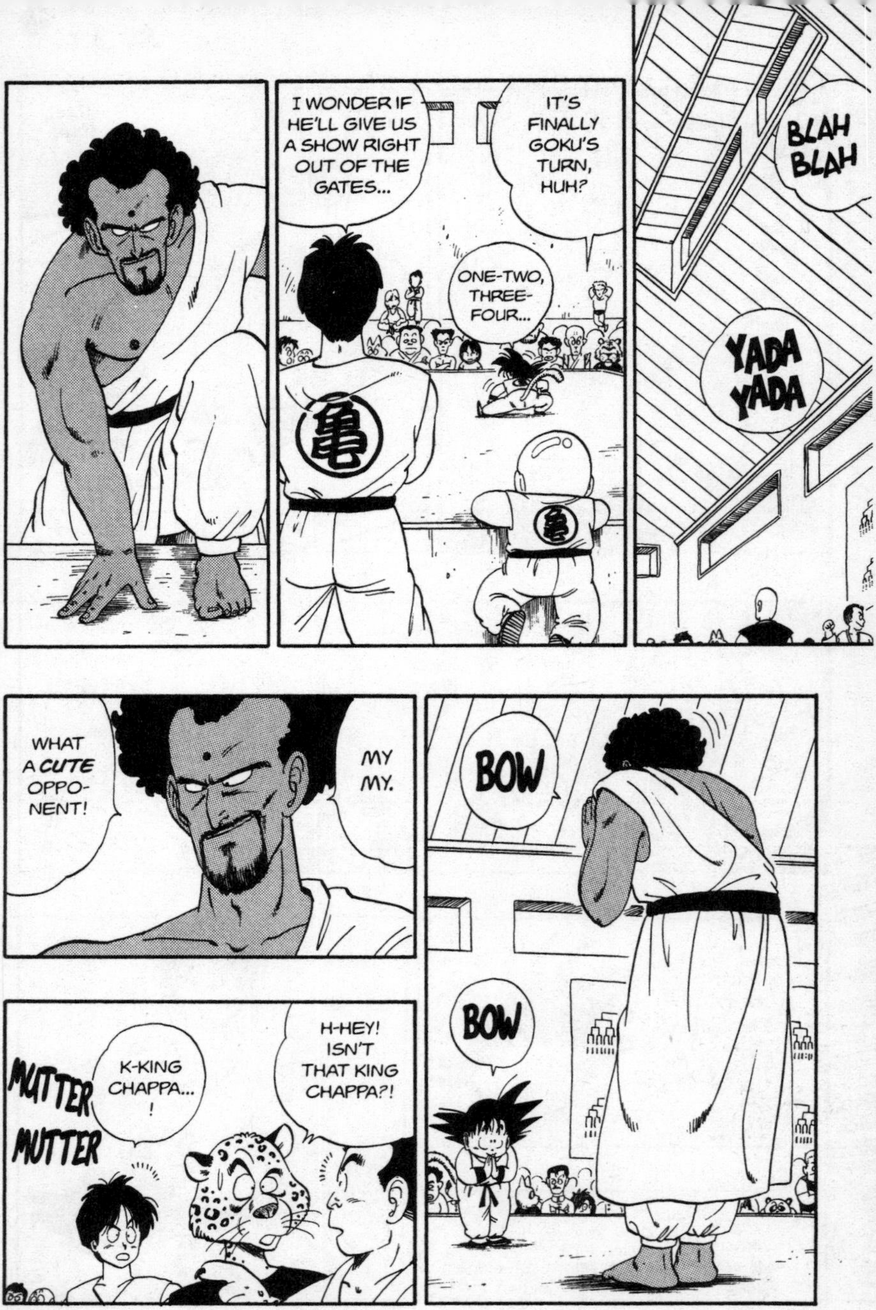
BLAH BLAH
YADA YADA
IT'S FINALLY GOKU'S TURN, HUH?
I WONDER IF HE'LL GIVE US A SHOW RIGHT OUT OF THE GATES...
ONE-TWO, THREE-FOUR...
BOW
BOW
MY MY.
WHAT A *CUTE* OPPONENT!
H-HEY! ISN'T THAT KING CHAPPA?!
K-KING CHAPPA... !
MUTTER MUTTER

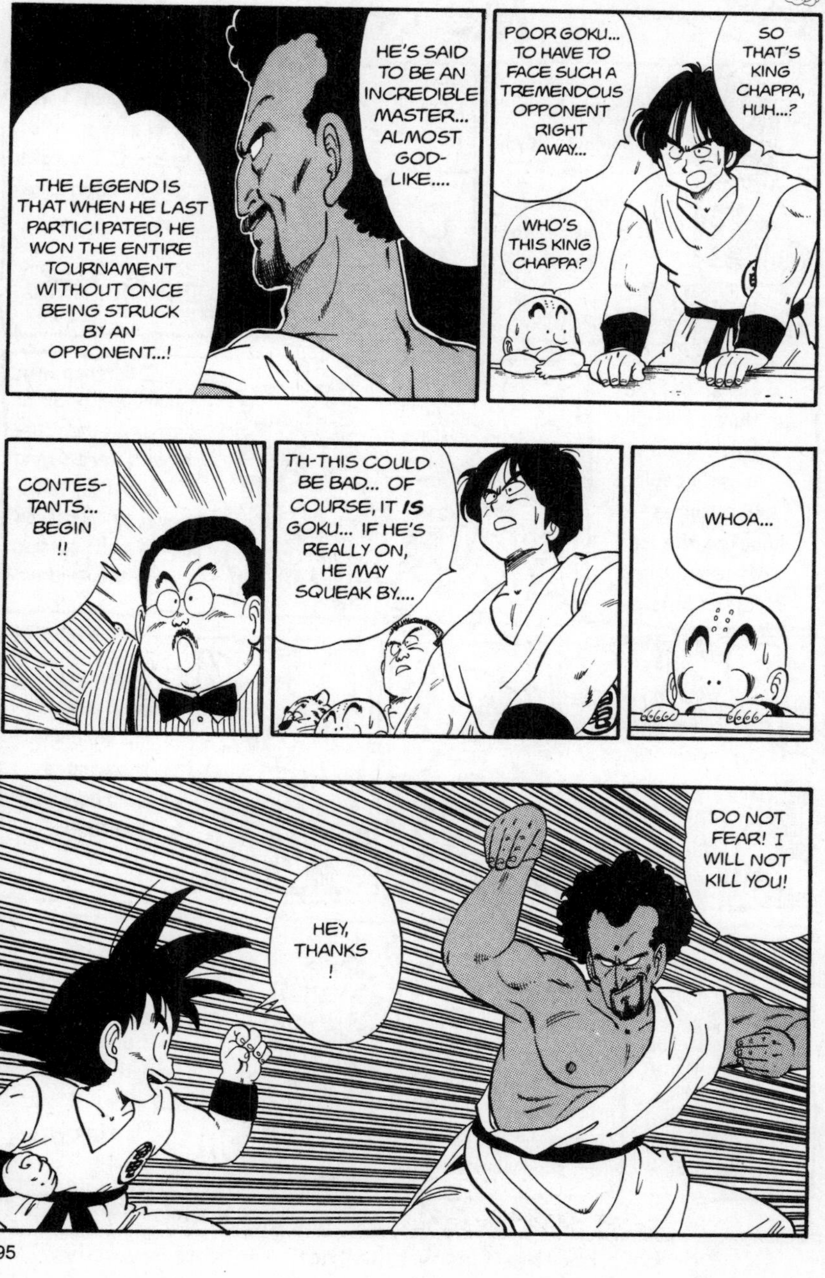
SO THAT'S KING CHAPPA, HUH...?
POOR GOKU... TO HAVE TO FACE SUCH A TREMENDOUS OPPONENT RIGHT AWAY...
WHO'S THIS KING CHAPPA?
HE'S SAID TO BE AN INCREDIBLE MASTER... ALMOST GOD-LIKE....
THE LEGEND IS THAT WHEN HE LAST PARTICIPATED, HE WON THE ENTIRE TOURNAMENT WITHOUT ONCE BEING STRUCK BY AN OPPONENT...!
WHOA...
TH-THIS COULD BE BAD... OF COURSE, IT *IS* GOKU... IF HE'S REALLY ON, HE MAY SQUEAK BY....
CONTES-TANTS... BEGIN !!
DO NOT FEAR! I WILL NOT KILL YOU!
HEY, THANKS !

True Story— "ME BACK THEN"

By Akira Toriyama

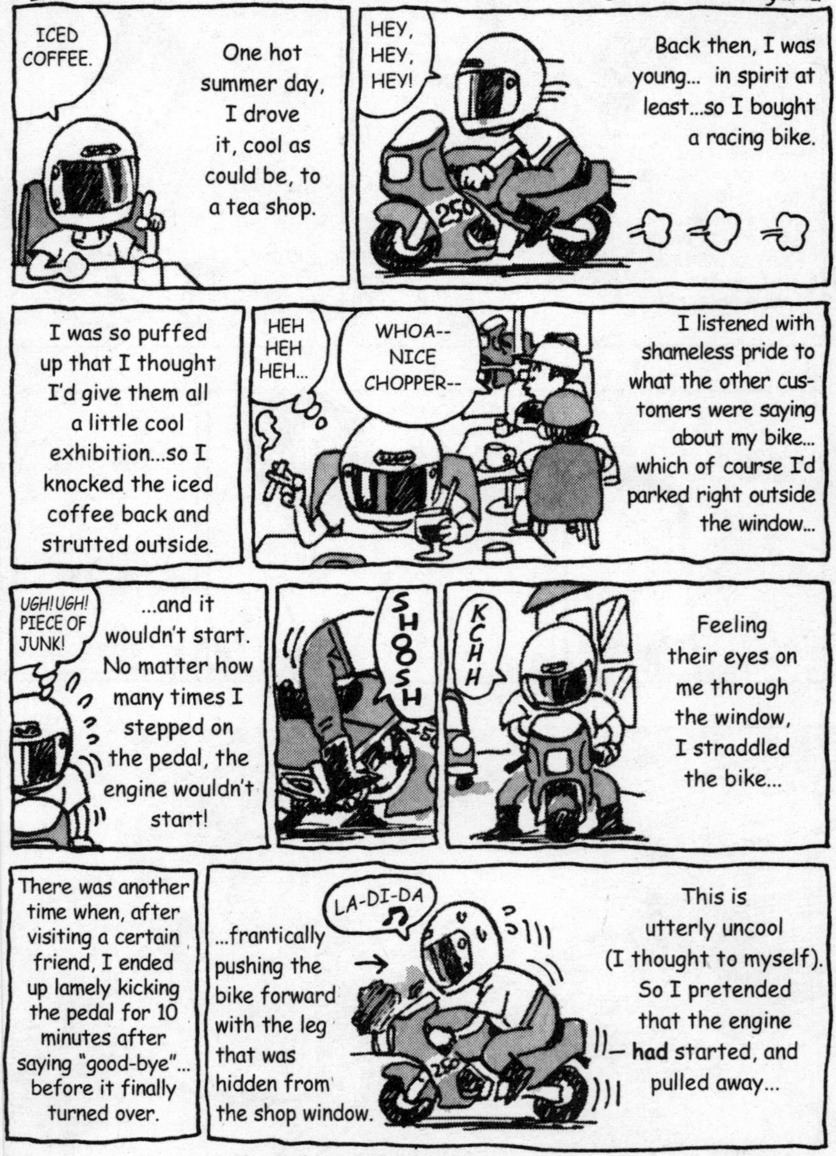
Back then, I was young... in spirit at least...so I bought a racing bike.
HEY, HEY, HEY!
250
ICED COFFEE.
One hot summer day, I drove it, cool as could be, to a tea shop.
I listened with shameless pride to what the other customers were saying about my bike... which of course I'd parked right outside the window...
WHOA-- NICE CHOPPER--
HEH HEH HEH...
I was so puffed up that I thought I'd give them all a little cool exhibition...so I knocked the iced coffee back and strutted outside.
Feeling their eyes on me through the window, I straddled the bike...
KCHH
SHOOSH
...and it wouldn't start. No matter how many times I stepped on the pedal, the engine wouldn't start!
UGH!UGH! PIECE OF JUNK!
This is utterly uncool (I thought to myself). So I pretended that the engine **had** started, and pulled away...
LA-DI-DA
...frantically pushing the bike forward with the leg that was hidden from the shop window.
250
There was another time when, after visiting a certain friend, I ended up lamely kicking the pedal for 10 minutes after saying "good-bye"... before it finally turned over.

I don't have that bike any more...
But I do have **another** flashy bike that starts more easily....

DRAGON BALL

Tale 115
King Chappa

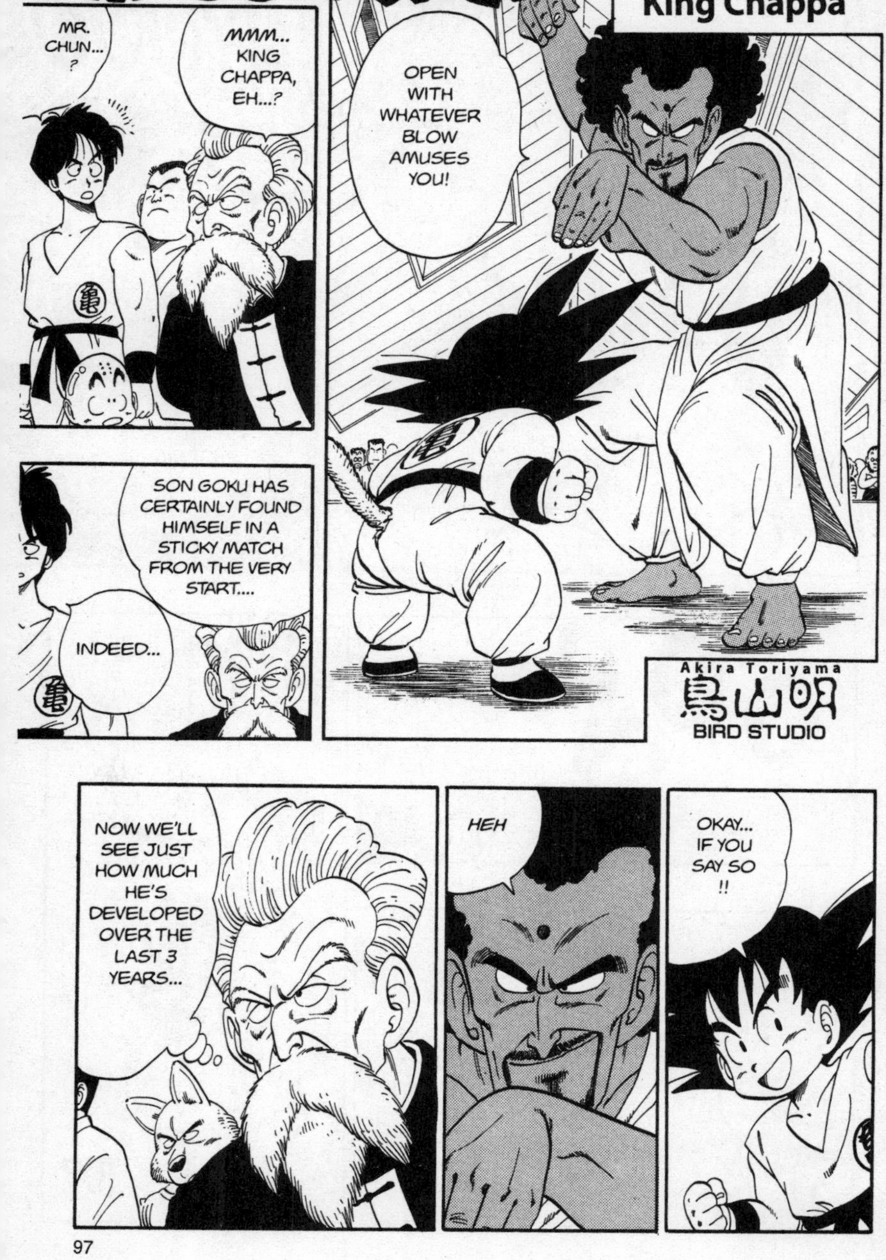

OPEN WITH WHATEVER BLOW AMUSES YOU!
Akira Toriyama
鳥山明
BIRD STUDIO
MMM... KING CHAPPA, EH...?
MR. CHUN... ?
SON GOKU HAS CERTAINLY FOUND HIMSELF IN A STICKY MATCH FROM THE VERY START....
INDEED...
OKAY... IF YOU SAY SO !!
HEH
NOW WE'LL SEE JUST HOW MUCH HE'S DEVELOPED OVER THE LAST 3 YEARS...

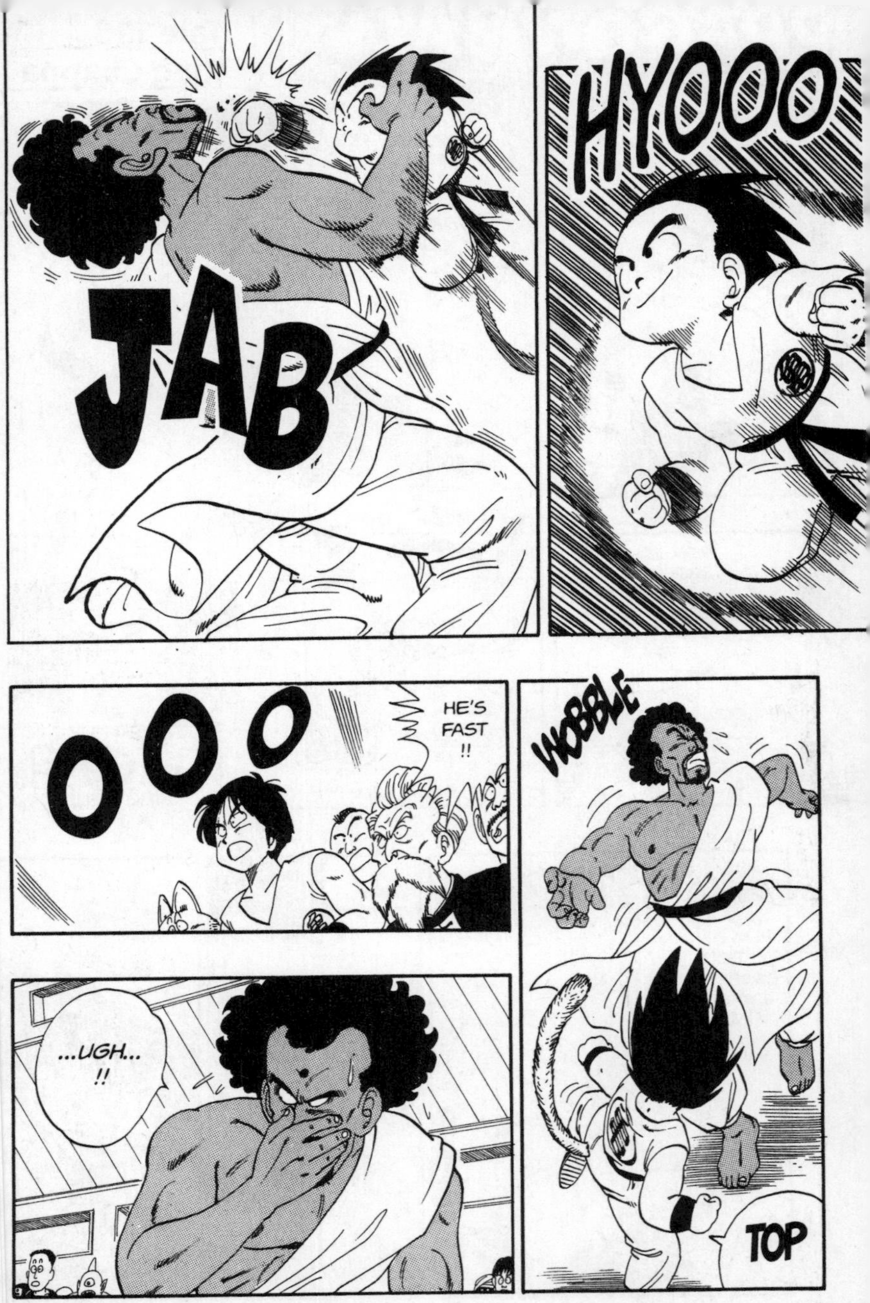
HYOOO
JAB
WOBBLE
TOP
OOO
HE'S FAST !!
...UGH... !!

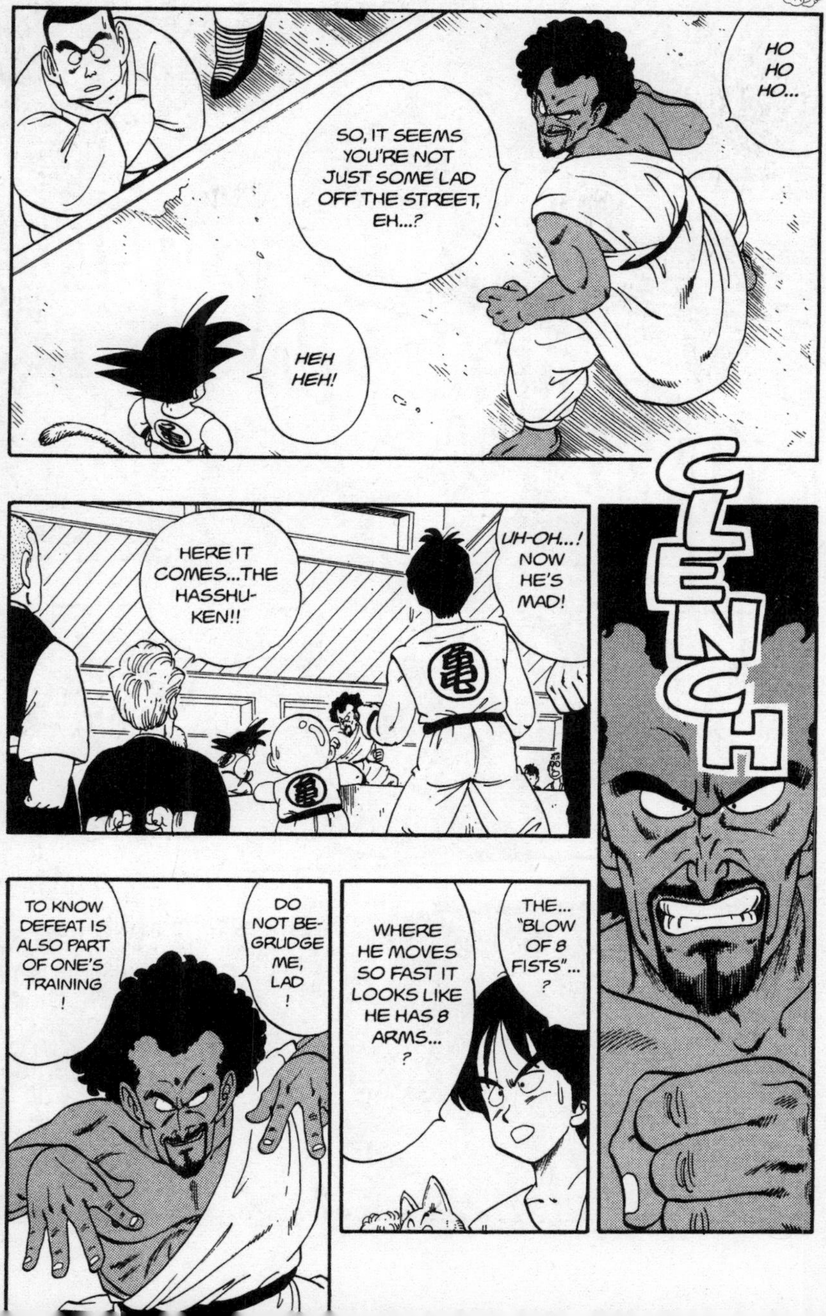
HO HO HO...
SO, IT SEEMS YOU'RE NOT JUST SOME LAD OFF THE STREET, EH...?
HEH HEH!
CLENCH
UH-OH...! NOW HE'S MAD!
HERE IT COMES...THE HASSHU-KEN!!
THE... "BLOW OF 8 FISTS"...?
WHERE HE MOVES SO FAST IT LOOKS LIKE HE HAS 8 ARMS...?
DO NOT BEGRUDGE ME, LAD!
TO KNOW DEFEAT IS ALSO PART OF ONE'S TRAINING!

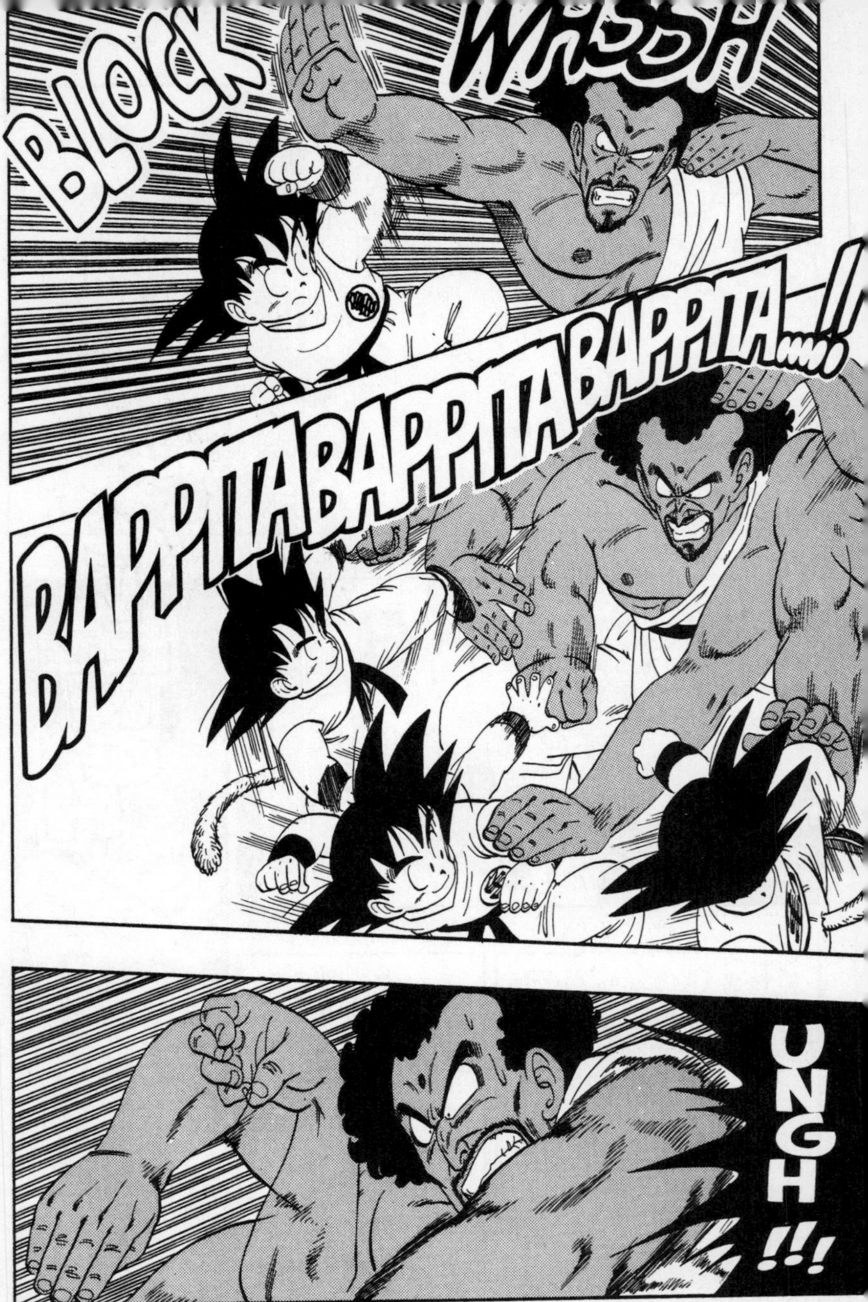
WHSSH
BLOCK
BAPPITABAPPITABAPPITA...!
UNGH!!!

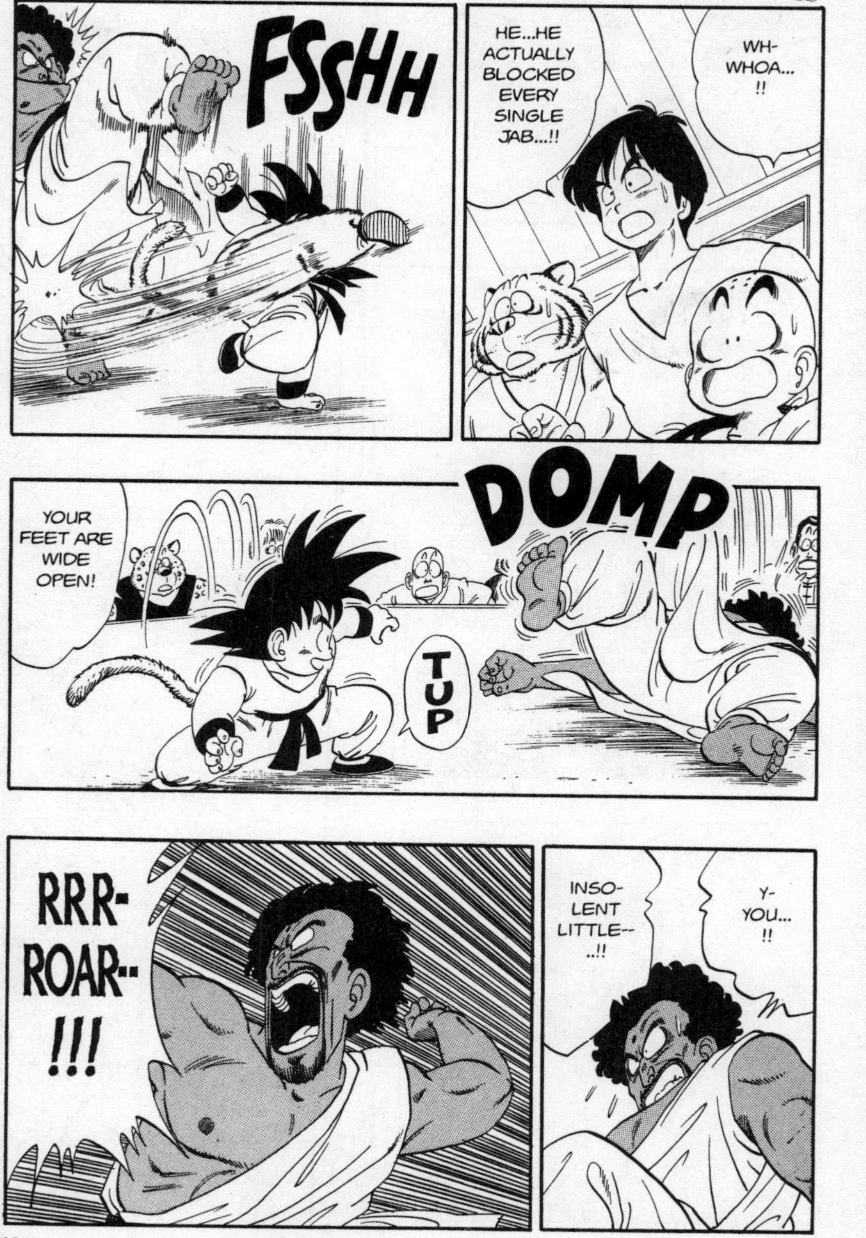
WH-WHOA... !!
HE...HE ACTUALLY BLOCKED EVERY SINGLE JAB...!!
FSSHH
DOMP
TUP
YOUR FEET ARE WIDE OPEN!
Y-YOU... !!
INSO-LENT LITTLE-- ..!!
RRR-ROAR-- !!!

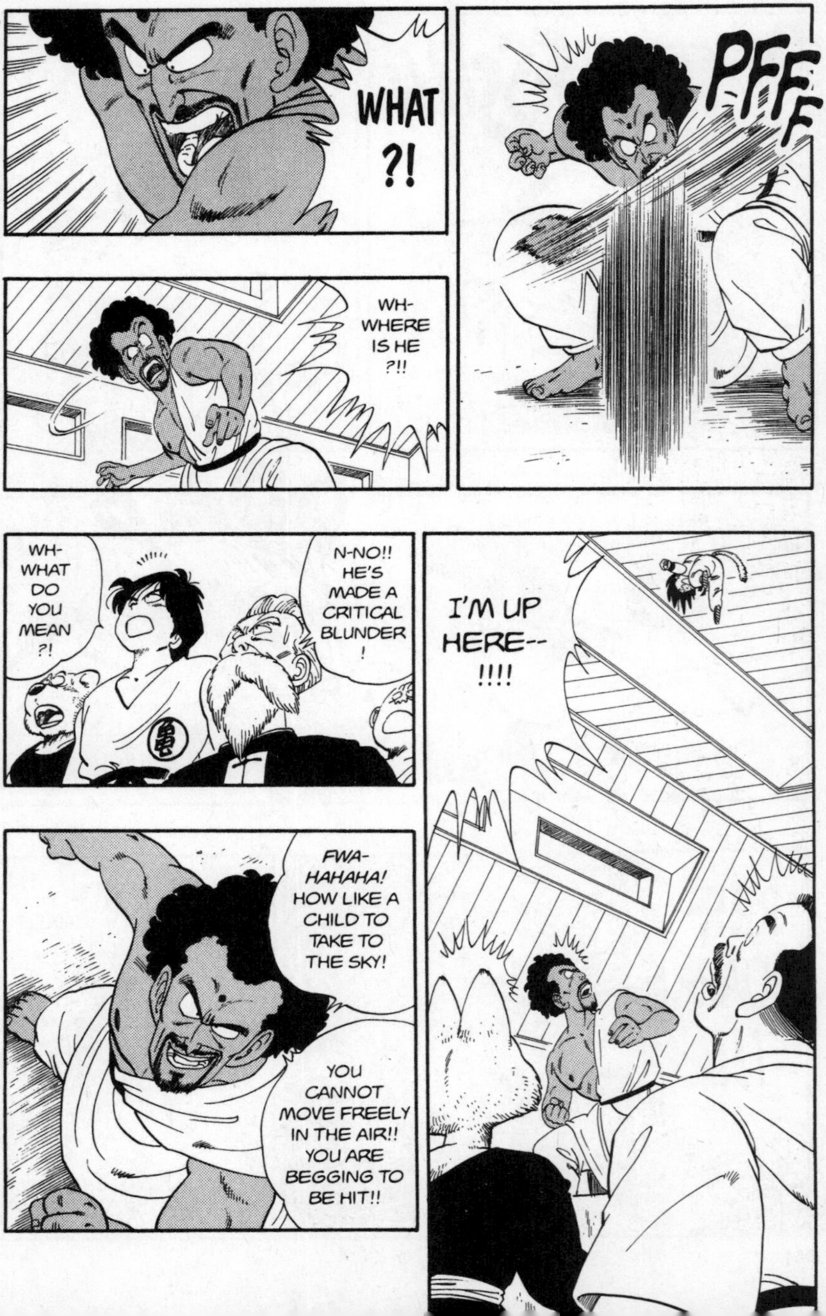
PFFF
WHAT ?!
WH- WHERE IS HE ?!!
I'M UP HERE-- !!!!
N-NO!! HE'S MADE A CRITICAL BLUNDER !
WH- WHAT DO YOU MEAN ?!
FWA- HAHAHA! HOW LIKE A CHILD TO TAKE TO THE SKY!
YOU CANNOT MOVE FREELY IN THE AIR!! YOU ARE BEGGING TO BE HIT!!

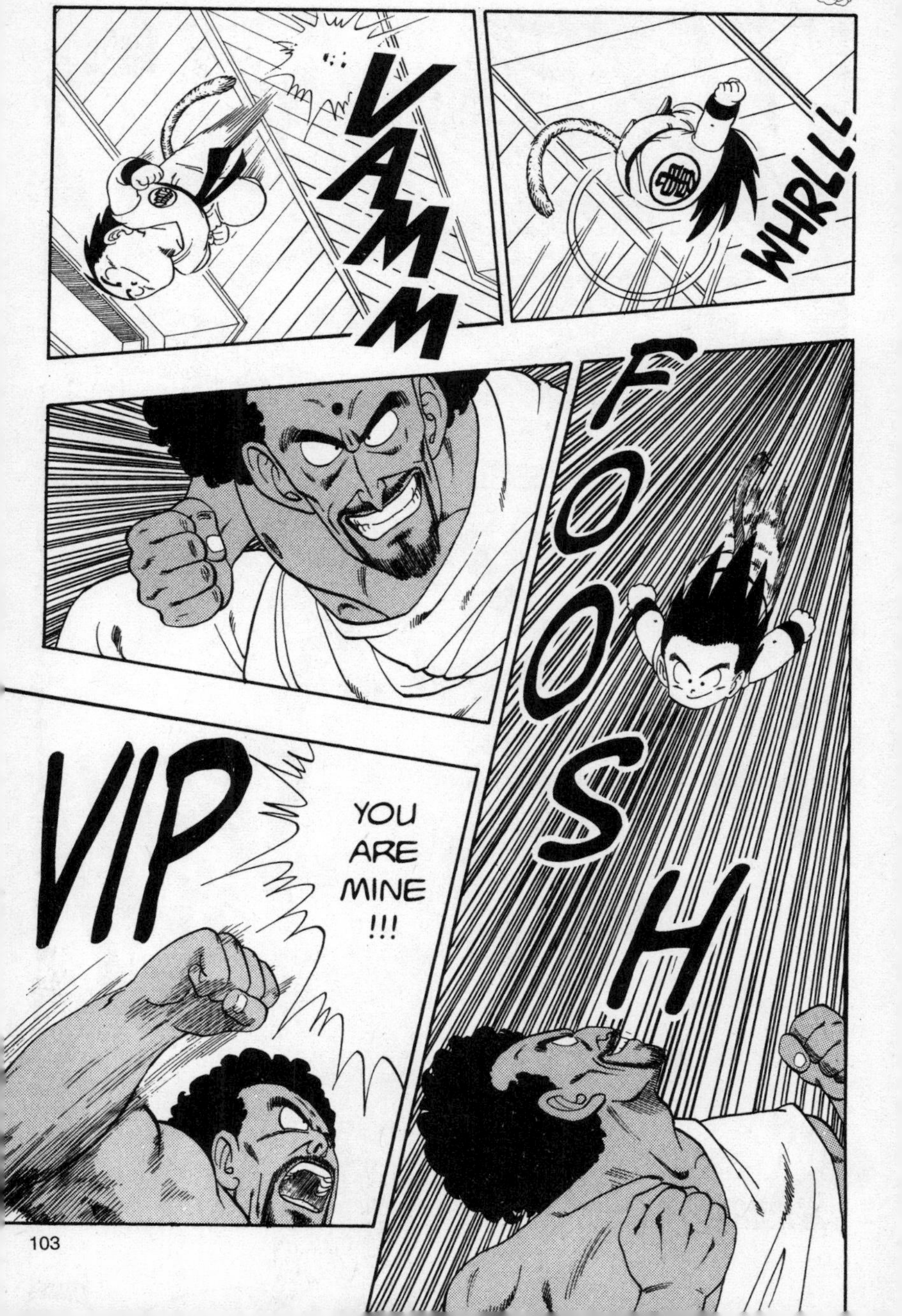
WHRLLL
VAMM
FOOOSH
VIP
YOU ARE MINE !!!

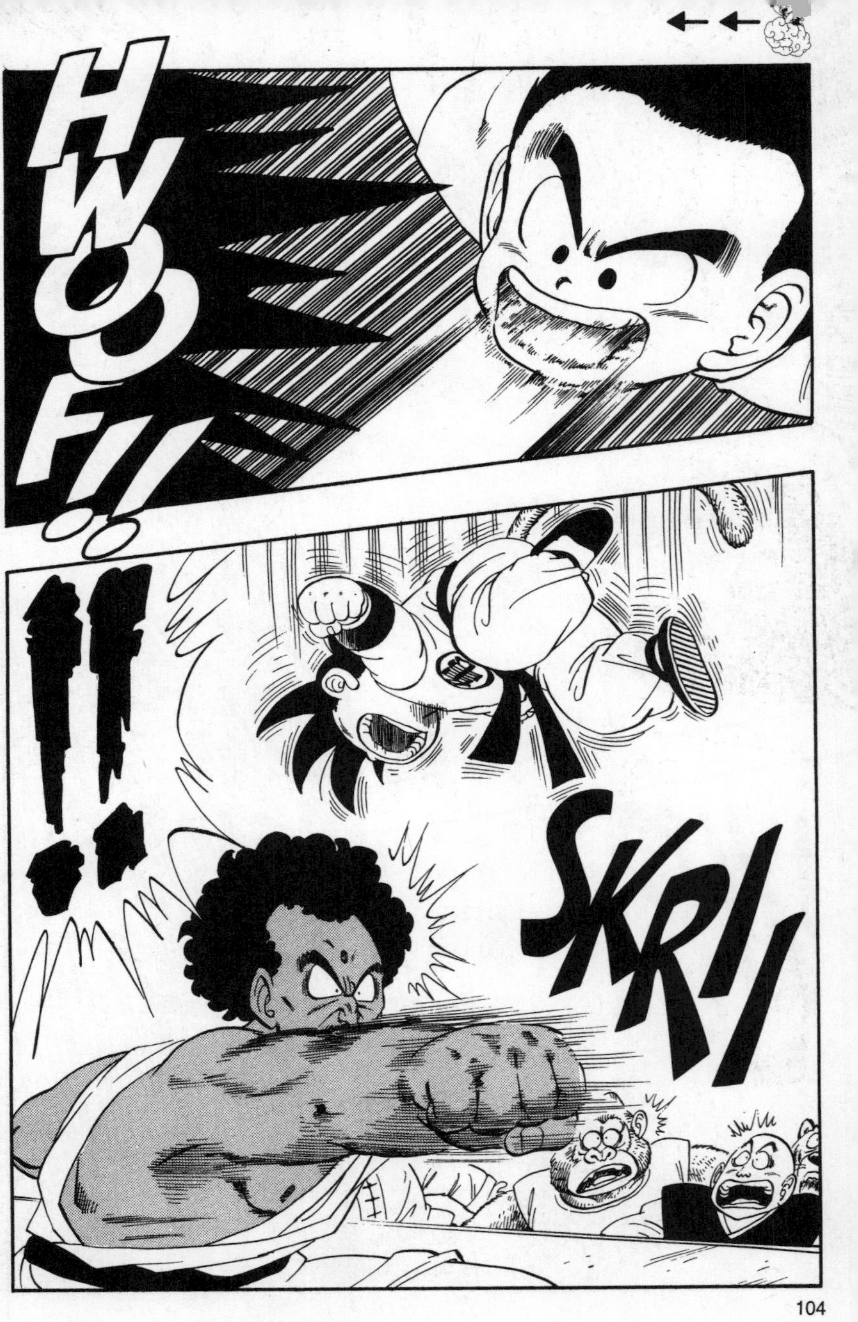
HWOOF!!
!!
SKRIIII

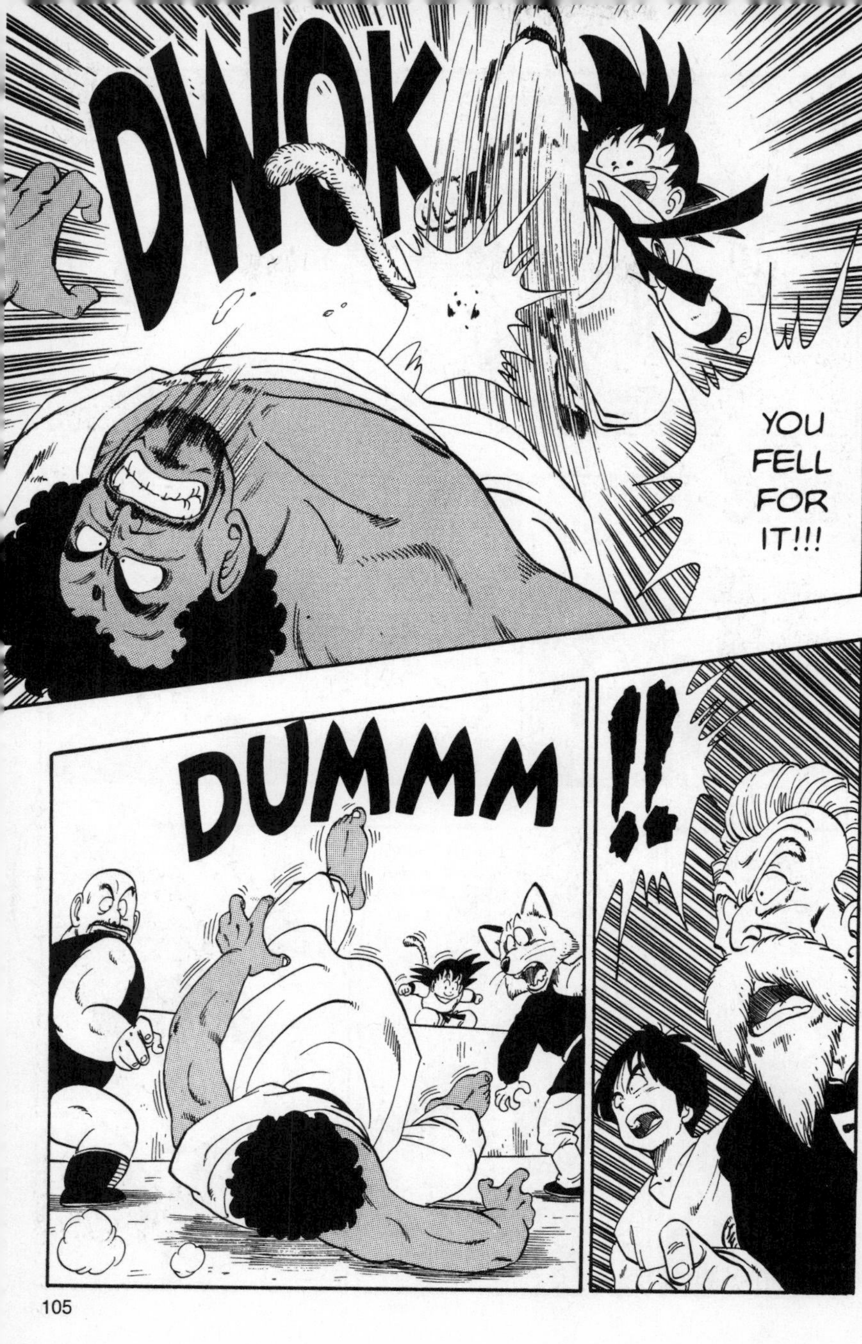
DWOK
YOU FELL FOR IT!!!
!!
DUMMM

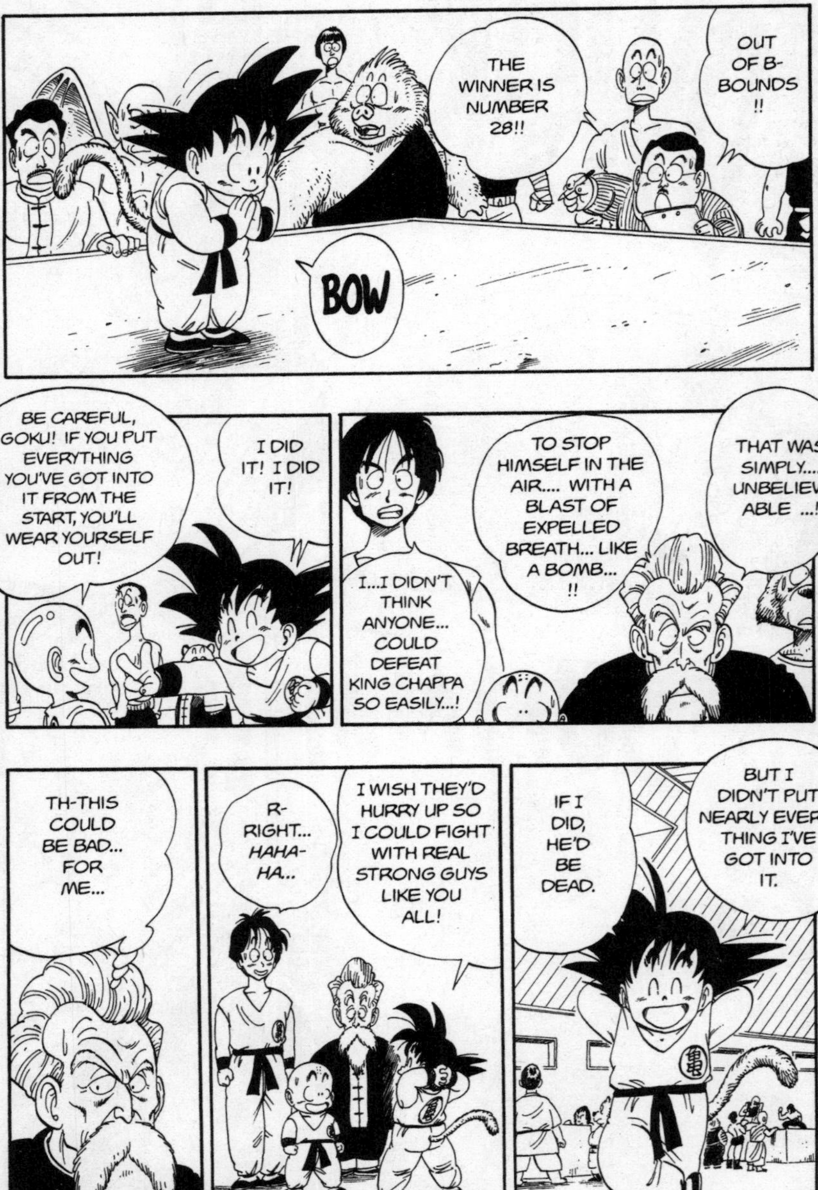
OUT OF B-BOUNDS !!
THE WINNER IS NUMBER 28!!
BOW
THAT WAS SIMPLY.... UNBELIEV-ABLE ...!
TO STOP HIMSELF IN THE AIR.... WITH A BLAST OF EXPELLED BREATH... LIKE A BOMB... !!
I...I DIDN'T THINK ANYONE... COULD DEFEAT KING CHAPPA SO EASILY...!
I DID IT! I DID IT!
BE CAREFUL, GOKU! IF YOU PUT EVERYTHING YOU'VE GOT INTO IT FROM THE START, YOU'LL WEAR YOURSELF OUT!
BUT I DIDN'T PUT NEARLY EVERY-THING I'VE GOT INTO IT.
IF I DID, HE'D BE DEAD.
I WISH THEY'D HURRY UP SO I COULD FIGHT WITH REAL STRONG GUYS LIKE YOU ALL!
R-RIGHT... *HAHA-HA...*
TH-THIS COULD BE BAD... FOR ME...

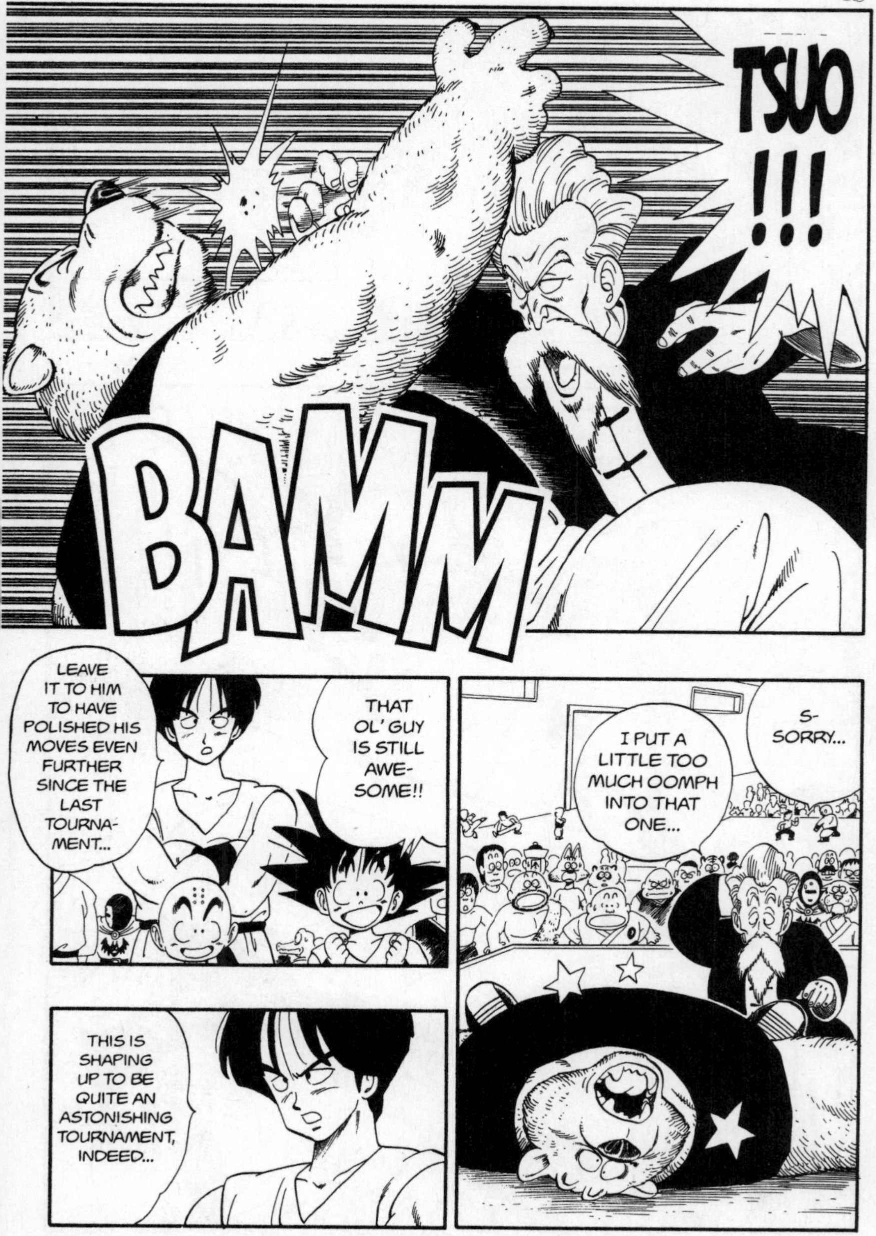
TSUO!!!
BAMM
S-SORRY...
I PUT A LITTLE TOO MUCH OOMPH INTO THAT ONE...
THAT OL' GUY IS STILL AWESOME!!
LEAVE IT TO HIM TO HAVE POLISHED HIS MOVES EVEN FURTHER SINCE THE LAST TOURNAMENT...
THIS IS SHAPING UP TO BE QUITE AN ASTONISHING TOURNAMENT, INDEED...

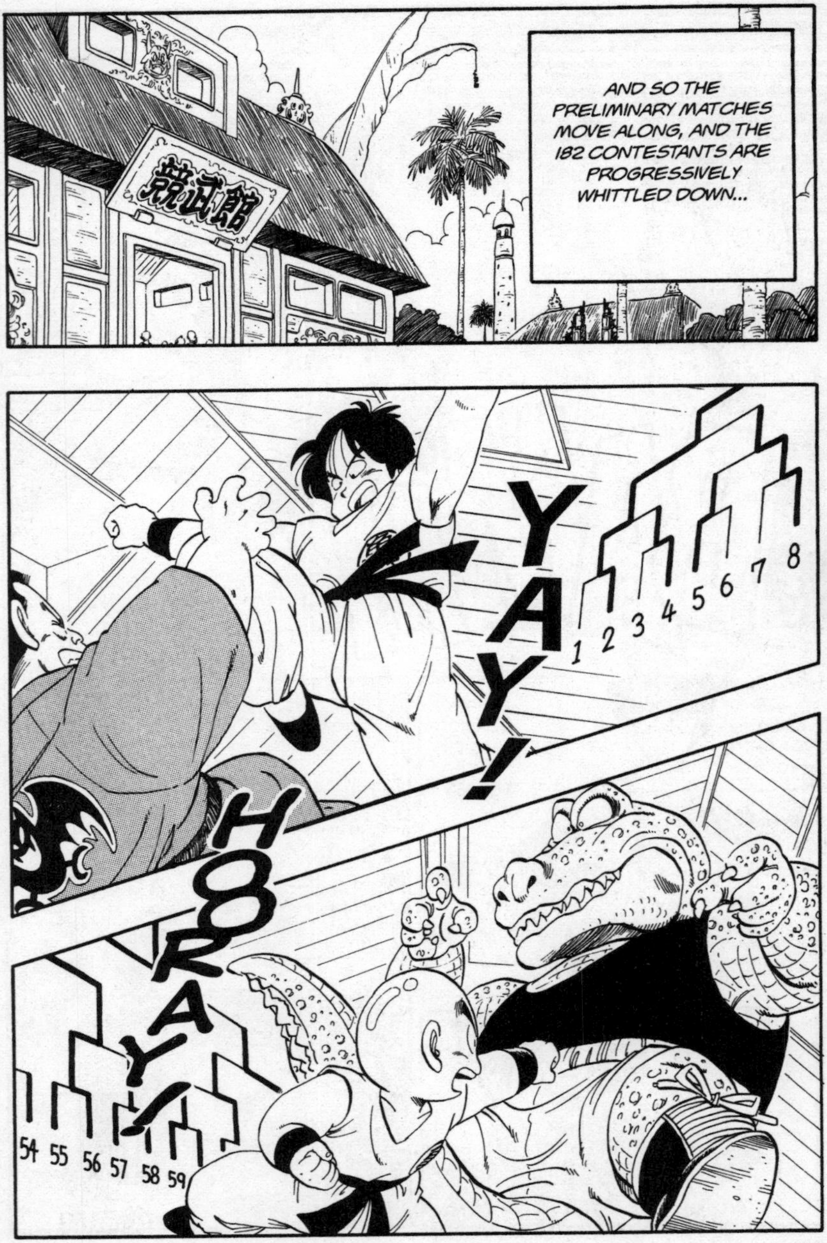
AND SO THE PRELIMINARY MATCHES MOVE ALONG, AND THE 182 CONTESTANTS ARE PROGRESSIVELY WHITTLED DOWN...
YAY!
1 2 3 4 5 6 7 8
HOORAY!
54 55 56 57 58 59

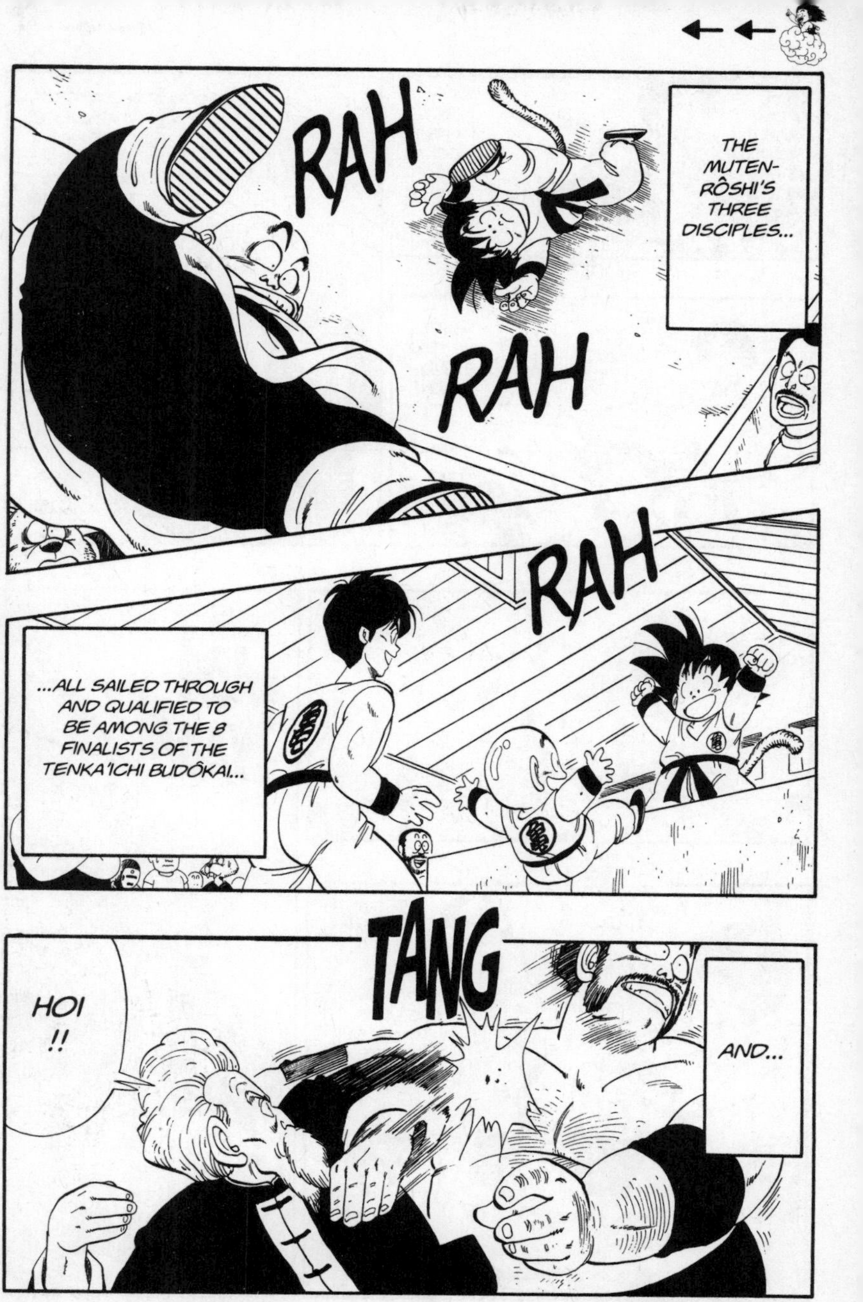
THE MUTEN-RÔSHI'S THREE DISCIPLES...
RAH
RAH
RAH
...ALL SAILED THROUGH AND QUALIFIED TO BE AMONG THE 8 FINALISTS OF THE TENKA'ICHI BUDÔKAI...
AND...
TANG
HOI !!

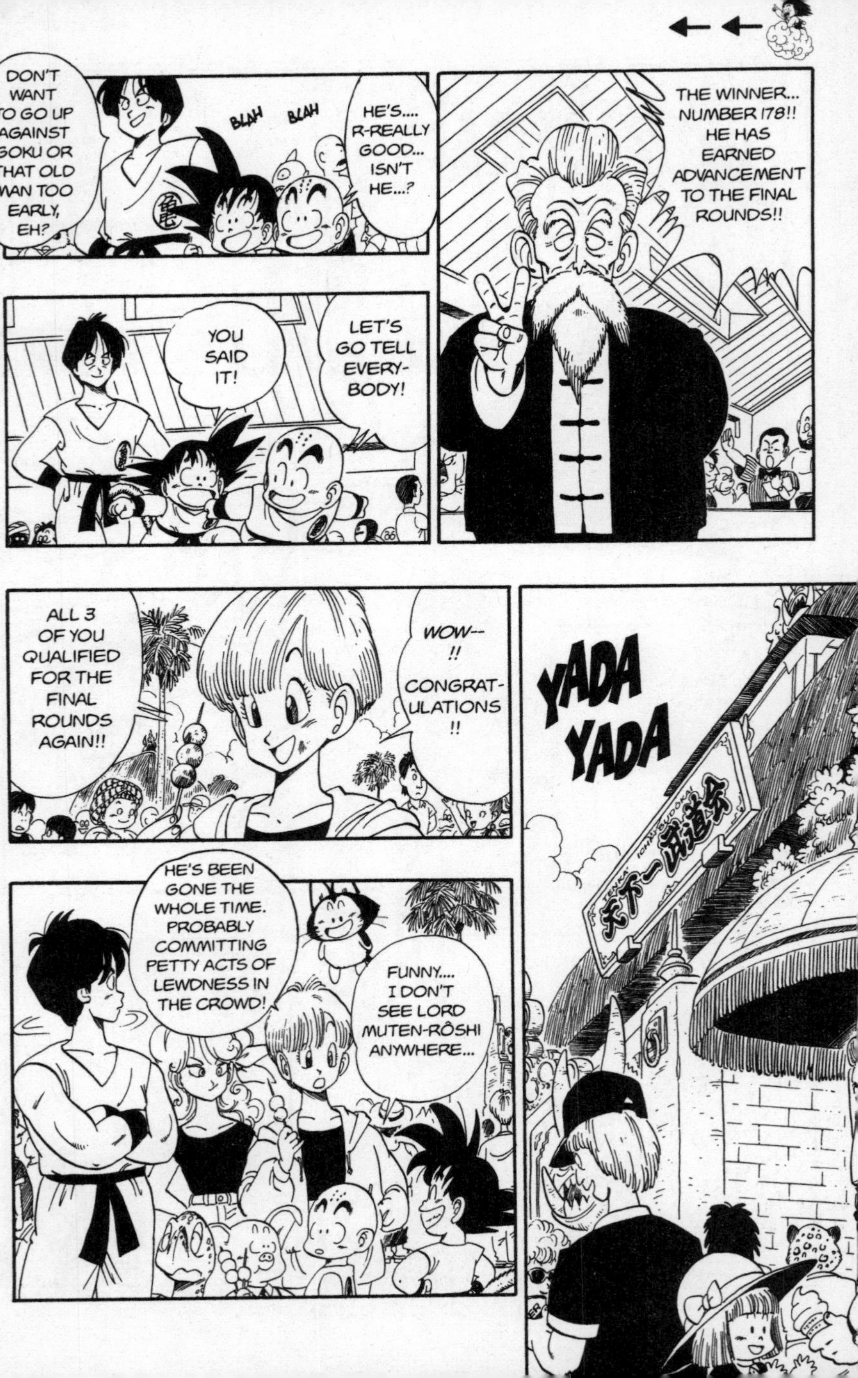
THE WINNER... NUMBER 178!! HE HAS EARNED ADVANCEMENT TO THE FINAL ROUNDS!!
HE'S.... R-REALLY GOOD... ISN'T HE...?
BLAH BLAH
DON'T WANT TO GO UP AGAINST GOKU OR THAT OLD MAN TOO EARLY, EH?
LET'S GO TELL EVERY-BODY!
YOU SAID IT!
YADA YADA
天下一武道会
WOW--!! CONGRAT-ULATIONS!!
ALL 3 OF YOU QUALIFIED FOR THE FINAL ROUNDS AGAIN!!
FUNNY.... I DON'T SEE LORD MUTEN-RÔSHI ANYWHERE...
HE'S BEEN GONE THE WHOLE TIME. PROBABLY COMMITTING PETTY ACTS OF LEWDNESS IN THE CROWD!

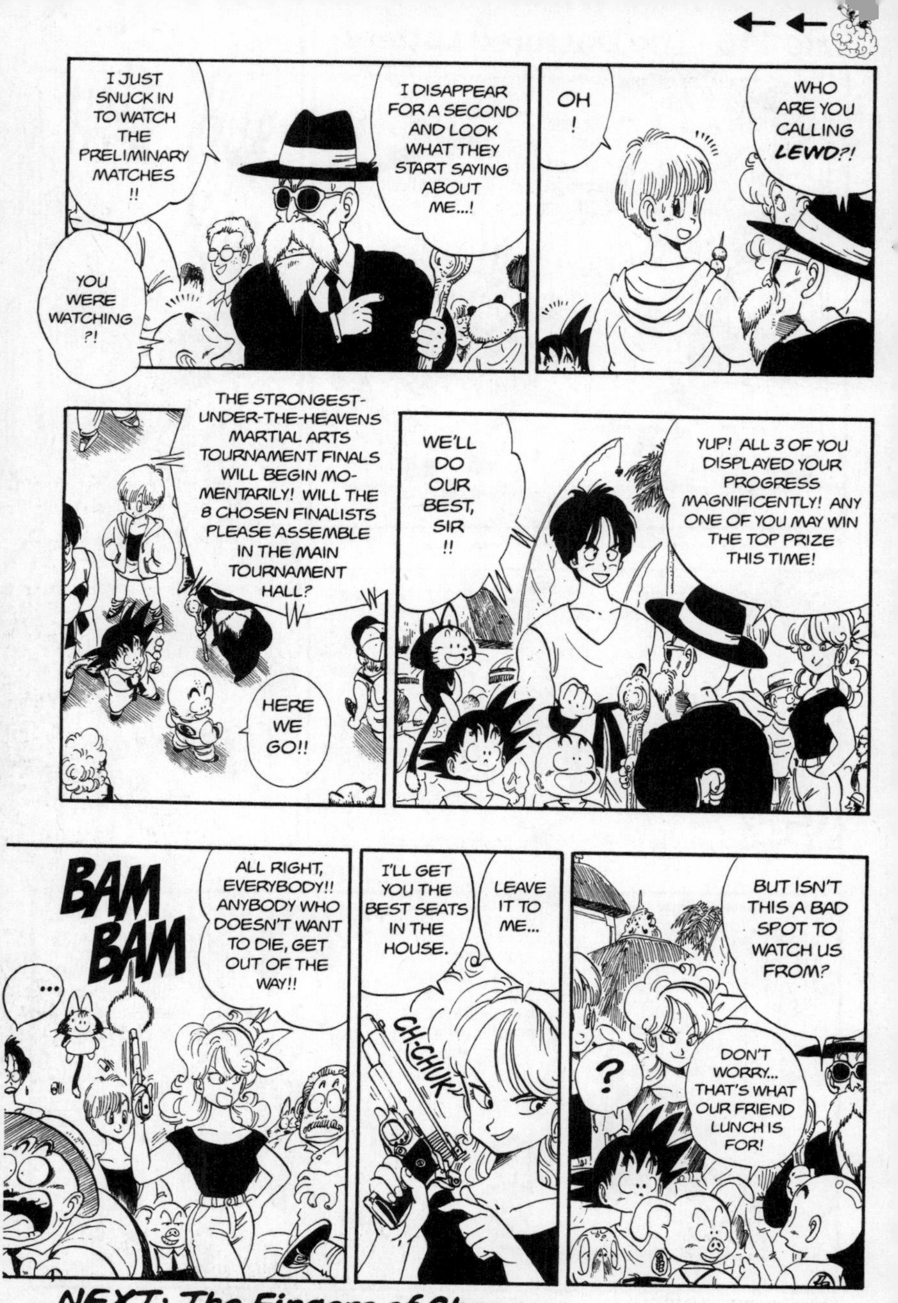
WHO ARE YOU CALLING LEWD?!
OH !
I DISAPPEAR FOR A SECOND AND LOOK WHAT THEY START SAYING ABOUT ME...!
I JUST SNUCK IN TO WATCH THE PRELIMINARY MATCHES !!
YOU WERE WATCHING ?!
YUP! ALL 3 OF YOU DISPLAYED YOUR PROGRESS MAGNIFICENTLY! ANY ONE OF YOU MAY WIN THE TOP PRIZE THIS TIME!
WE'LL DO OUR BEST, SIR !!
THE STRONGEST-UNDER-THE-HEAVENS MARTIAL ARTS TOURNAMENT FINALS WILL BEGIN MO-MENTARILY! WILL THE 8 CHOSEN FINALISTS PLEASE ASSEMBLE IN THE MAIN TOURNAMENT HALL?
HERE WE GO!!
BUT ISN'T THIS A BAD SPOT TO WATCH US FROM?
?
DON'T WORRY... THAT'S WHAT OUR FRIEND LUNCH IS FOR!
LEAVE IT TO ME...
I'LL GET YOU THE BEST SEATS IN THE HOUSE.
CH-CHUK
ALL RIGHT, EVERYBODY!! ANYBODY WHO DOESN'T WANT TO DIE, GET OUT OF THE WAY!!
BAM BAM
...

NEXT: The Fingers of Chaozu

Tale 116 • The Doctored Lottery

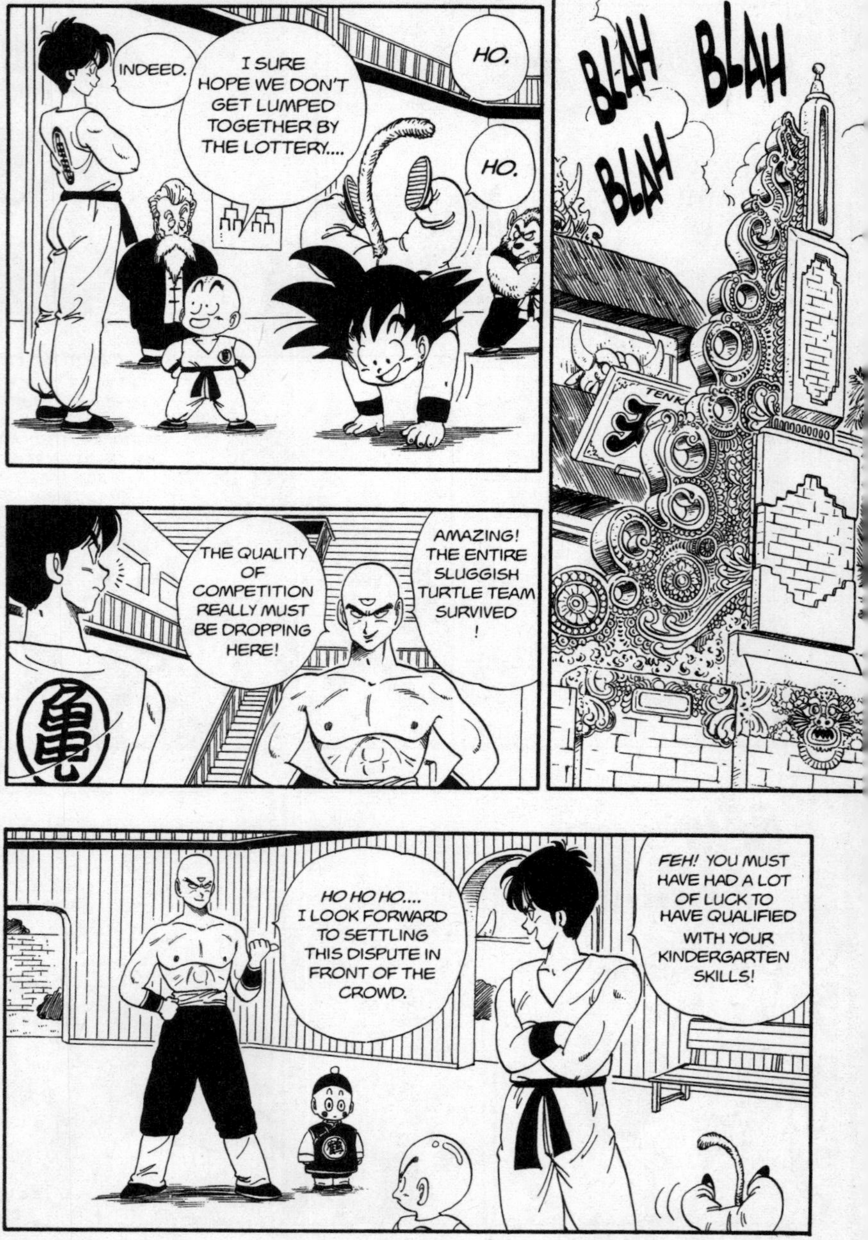

BLAH BLAH
BLAH
TENK
HO.
HO.
I SURE HOPE WE DON'T GET LUMPED TOGETHER BY THE LOTTERY....
INDEED.
AMAZING! THE ENTIRE SLUGGISH TURTLE TEAM SURVIVED!
THE QUALITY OF COMPETITION REALLY MUST BE DROPPING HERE!
FEH! YOU MUST HAVE HAD A LOT OF LUCK TO HAVE QUALIFIED WITH YOUR KINDERGARTEN SKILLS!
HO HO HO.... I LOOK FORWARD TO SETTLING THIS DISPUTE IN FRONT OF THE CROWD.

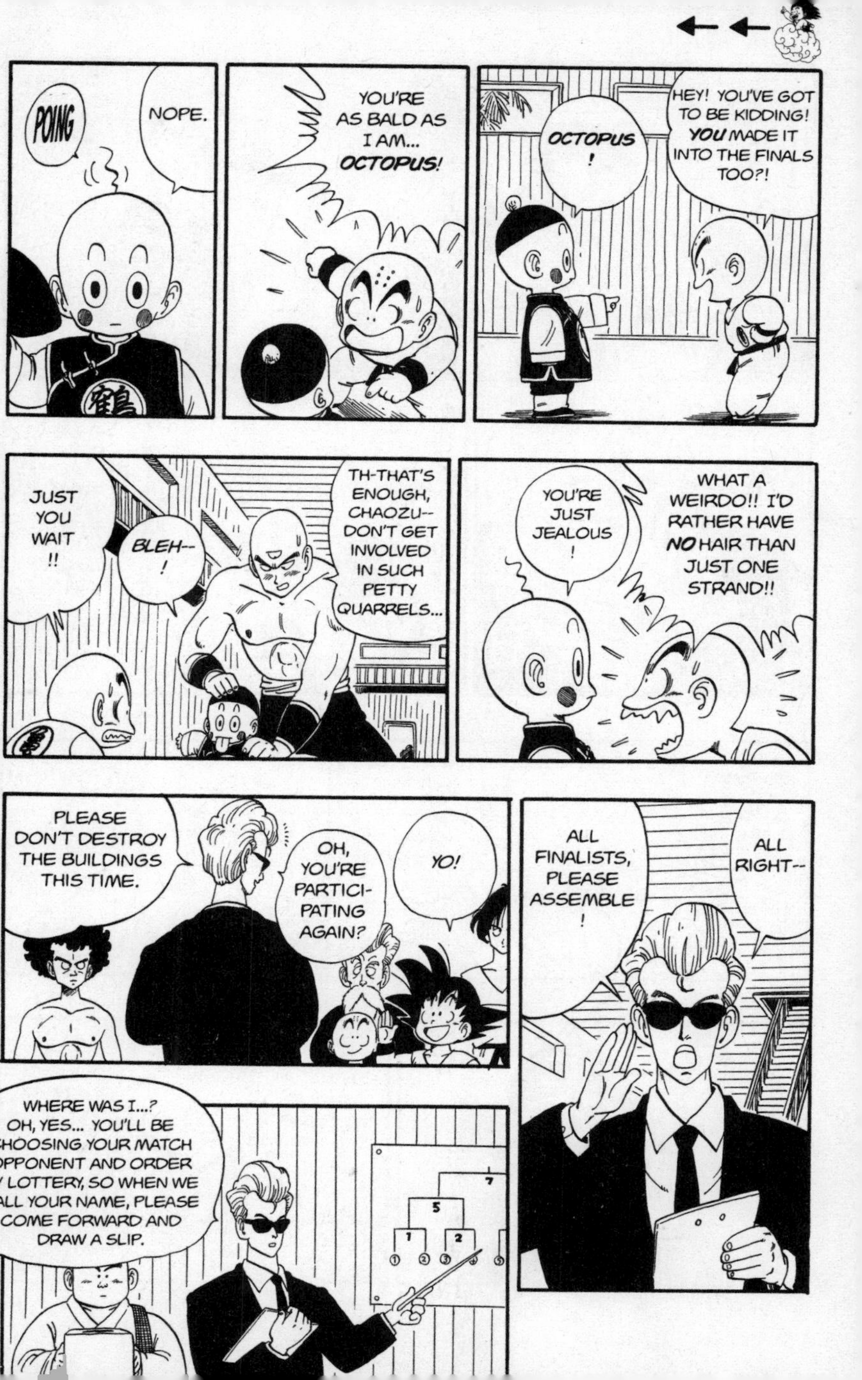
HEY! YOU'VE GOT TO BE KIDDING! *YOU* MADE IT INTO THE FINALS TOO?!
OCTOPUS!
YOU'RE AS BALD AS I AM... OCTOPUS!
POING
NOPE.
WHAT A WEIRDO!! I'D RATHER HAVE *NO* HAIR THAN JUST ONE STRAND!!
YOU'RE JUST JEALOUS!
TH-THAT'S ENOUGH, CHAOZU-- DON'T GET INVOLVED IN SUCH PETTY QUARRELS...
BLEH--!
JUST YOU WAIT!!
ALL RIGHT--
ALL FINALISTS, PLEASE ASSEMBLE!
YO!
OH, YOU'RE PARTICIPATING AGAIN?
PLEASE DON'T DESTROY THE BUILDINGS THIS TIME.
WHERE WAS I...? OH, YES... YOU'LL BE CHOOSING YOUR MATCH OPPONENT AND ORDER BY LOTTERY, SO WHEN WE CALL YOUR NAME, PLEASE COME FORWARD AND DRAW A SLIP.

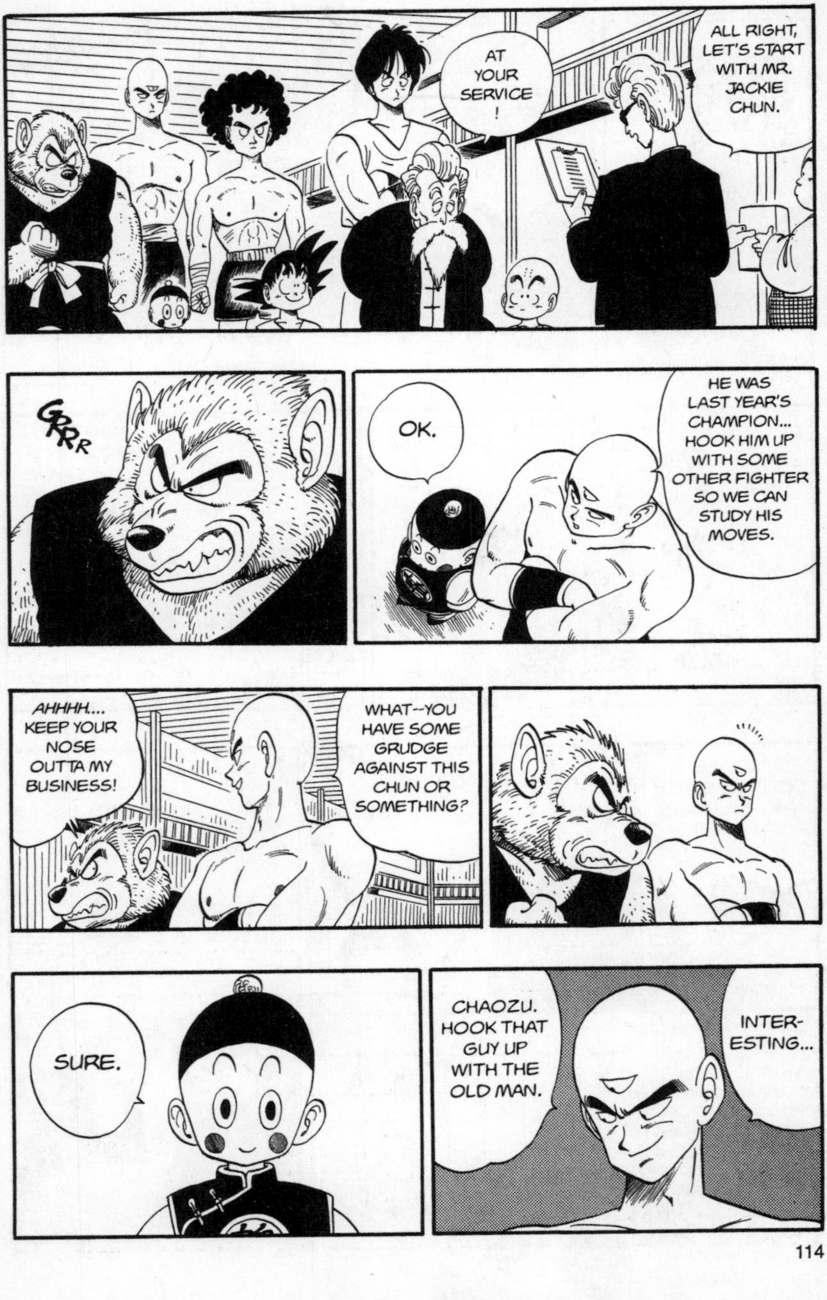
ALL RIGHT, LET'S START WITH MR. JACKIE CHUN.
AT YOUR SERVICE!
HE WAS LAST YEAR'S CHAMPION... HOOK HIM UP WITH SOME OTHER FIGHTER SO WE CAN STUDY HIS MOVES.
OK.
GRRR
WHAT--YOU HAVE SOME GRUDGE AGAINST THIS CHUN OR SOMETHING?
AHHHH.... KEEP YOUR NOSE OUTTA MY BUSINESS!
INTER-ESTING...
CHAOZU. HOOK THAT GUY UP WITH THE OLD MAN.
SURE.

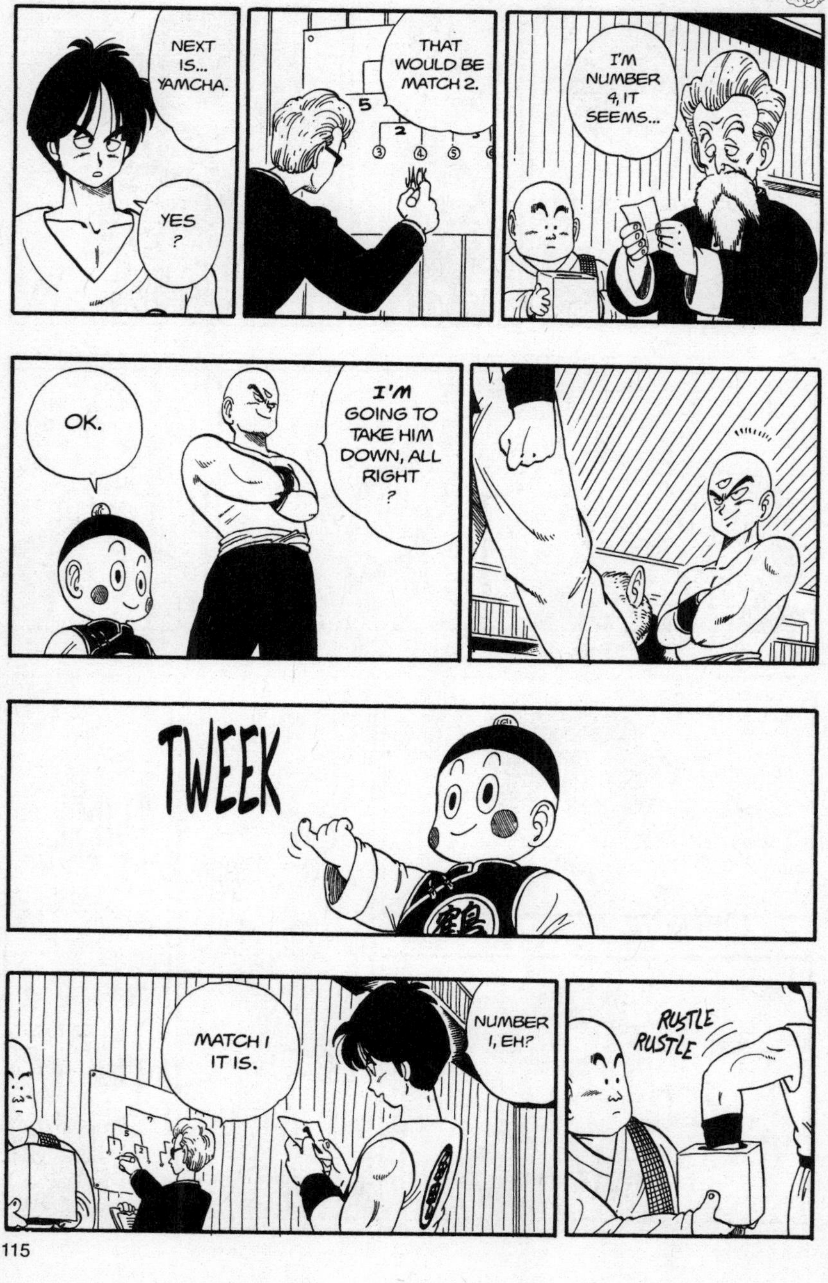
I'M NUMBER 4, IT SEEMS...
THAT WOULD BE MATCH 2.
NEXT IS... YAMCHA.
YES?
I'M GOING TO TAKE HIM DOWN, ALL RIGHT?
OK.
TWEEK
RUSTLE RUSTLE
NUMBER 1, EH?
MATCH 1 IT IS.

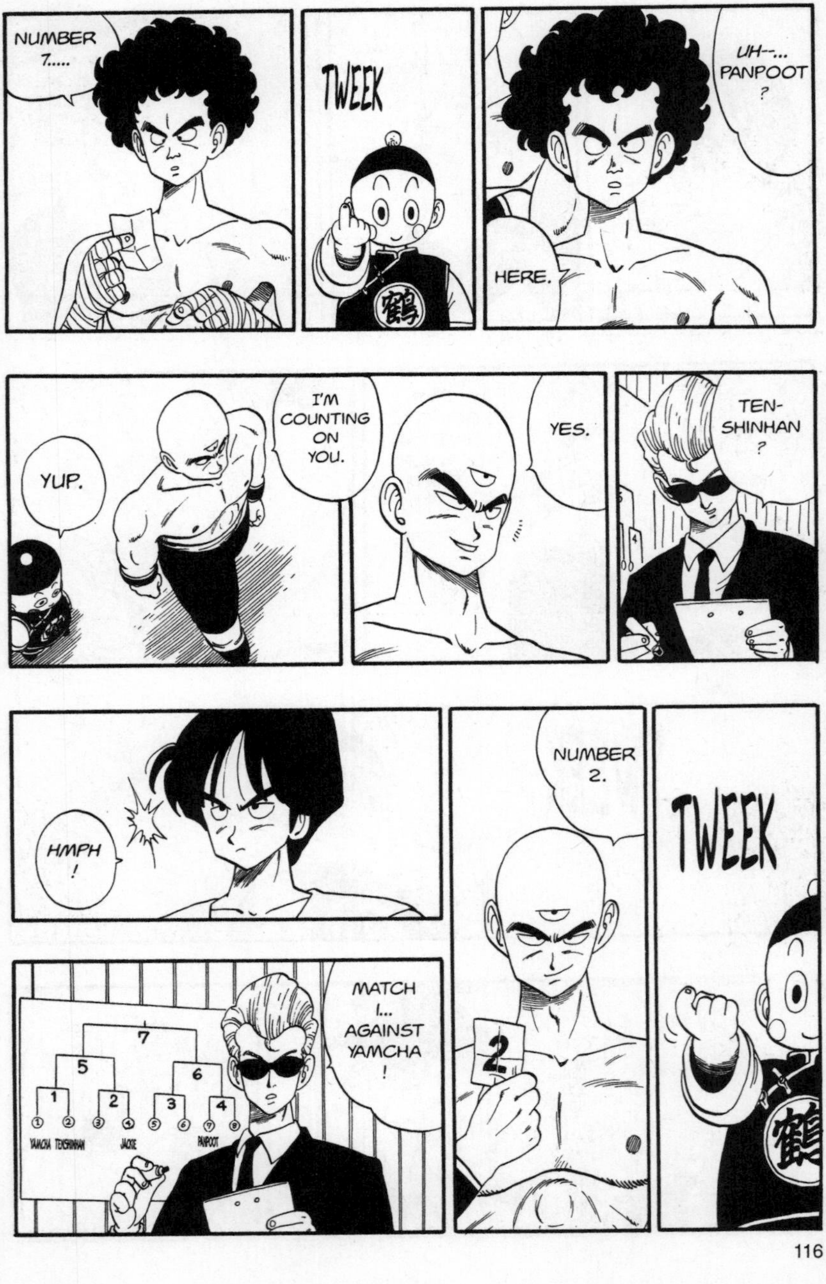
UH--... PANPOOT ?
HERE.
TWEEK
NUMBER 7.....
TEN-SHINHAN ?
YES.
I'M COUNTING ON YOU.
YUP.
TWEEK
NUMBER 2.
HMPH !
MATCH 1... AGAINST YAMCHA !
7
5
6
1
2
3
4
YAMCHA
TENSHINHAN
JACKIE
PANPOOT

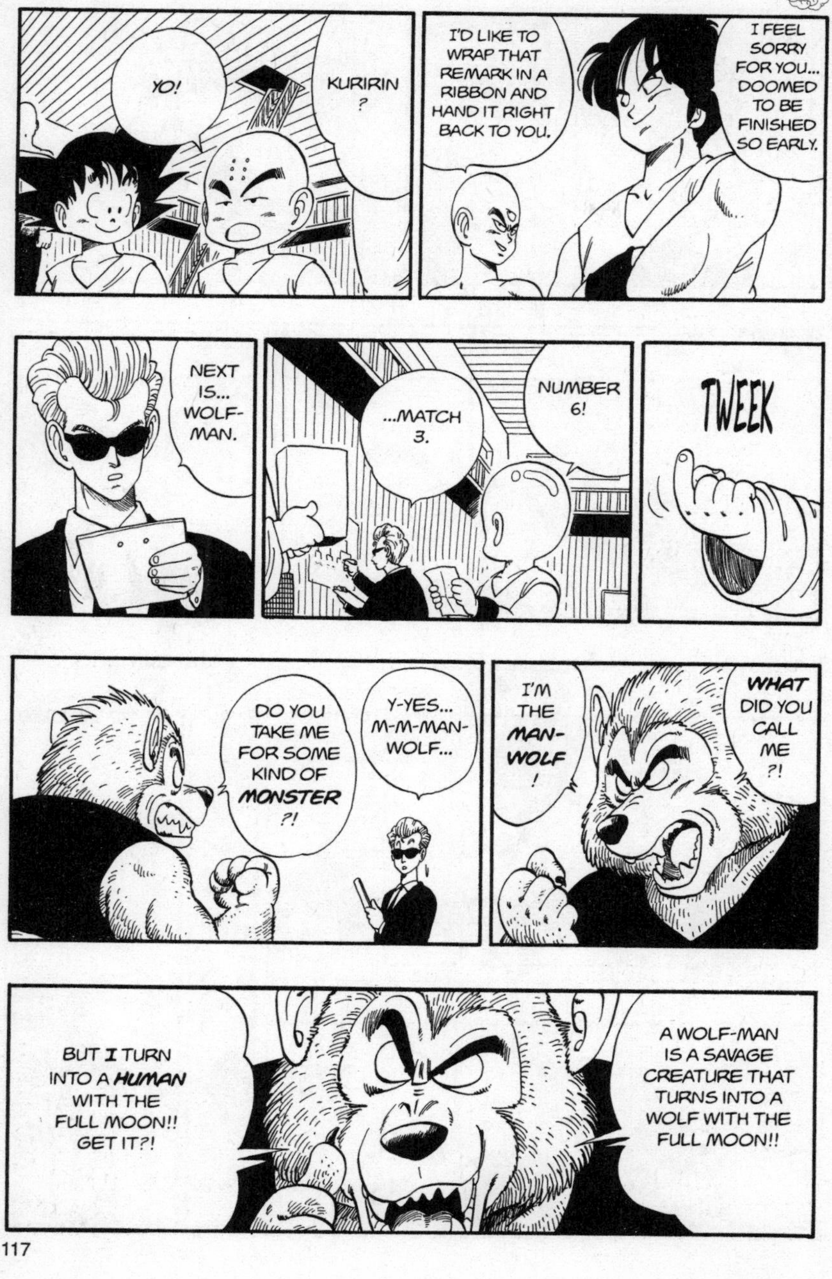
I FEEL SORRY FOR YOU... DOOMED TO BE FINISHED SO EARLY.
I'D LIKE TO WRAP THAT REMARK IN A RIBBON AND HAND IT RIGHT BACK TO YOU.
KURIRIN ?
YO!
TWEEK
NUMBER 6!
...MATCH 3.
NEXT IS... WOLF-MAN.
WHAT DID YOU CALL ME ?!
I'M THE MAN-WOLF !
Y-YES... M-M-MAN-WOLF...
DO YOU TAKE ME FOR SOME KIND OF MONSTER ?!
A WOLF-MAN IS A SAVAGE CREATURE THAT TURNS INTO A WOLF WITH THE FULL MOON!!
BUT I TURN INTO A HUMAN WITH THE FULL MOON!! GET IT?!

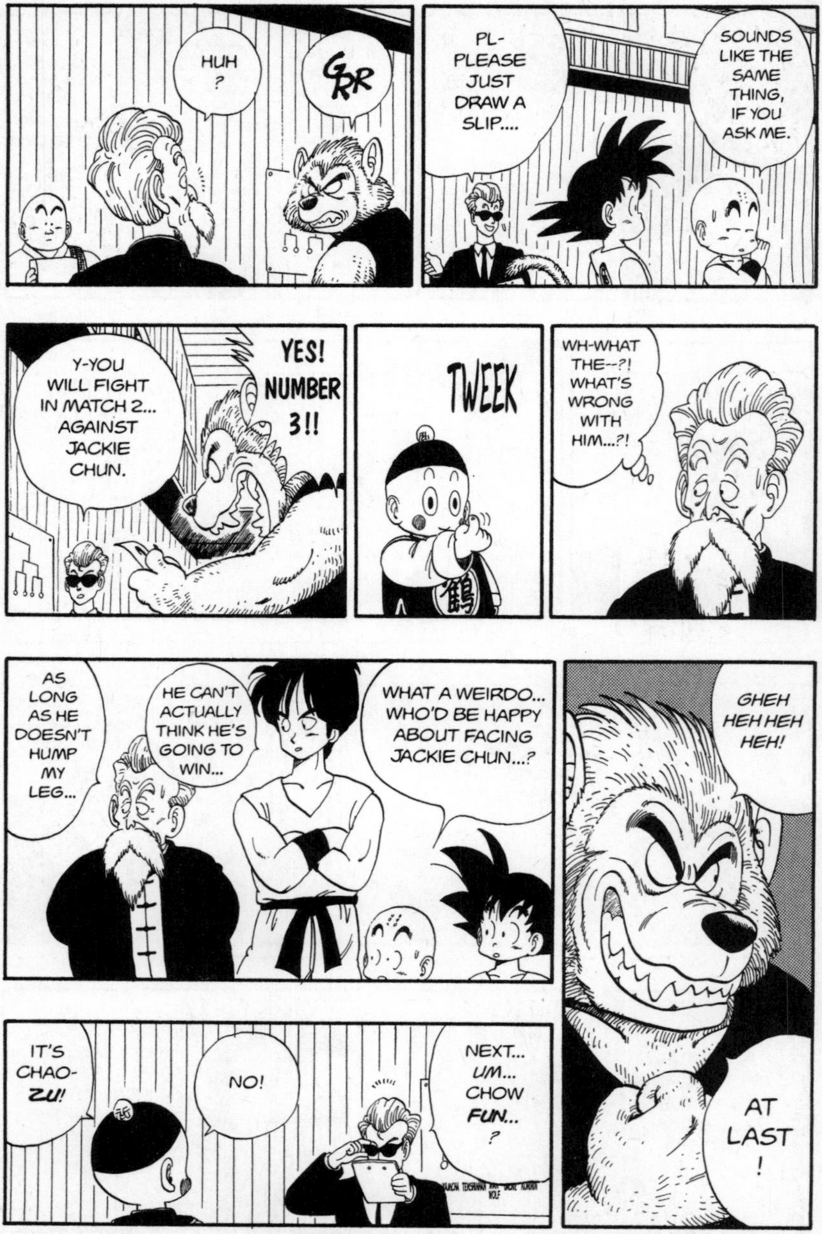
SOUNDS LIKE THE SAME THING, IF YOU ASK ME.
PL- PLEASE JUST DRAW A SLIP....
GRR
HUH ?
WH-WHAT THE--?! WHAT'S WRONG WITH HIM...?!
TWEEK
YES! NUMBER 3!!
Y-YOU WILL FIGHT IN MATCH 2... AGAINST JACKIE CHUN.
GHEH HEH HEH HEH!
AT LAST !
WHAT A WEIRDO... WHO'D BE HAPPY ABOUT FACING JACKIE CHUN...?
HE CAN'T ACTUALLY THINK HE'S GOING TO WIN...
AS LONG AS HE DOESN'T HUMP MY LEG...
NEXT... UM... CHOW FUN... ?
NO!
IT'S CHAO-ZU!

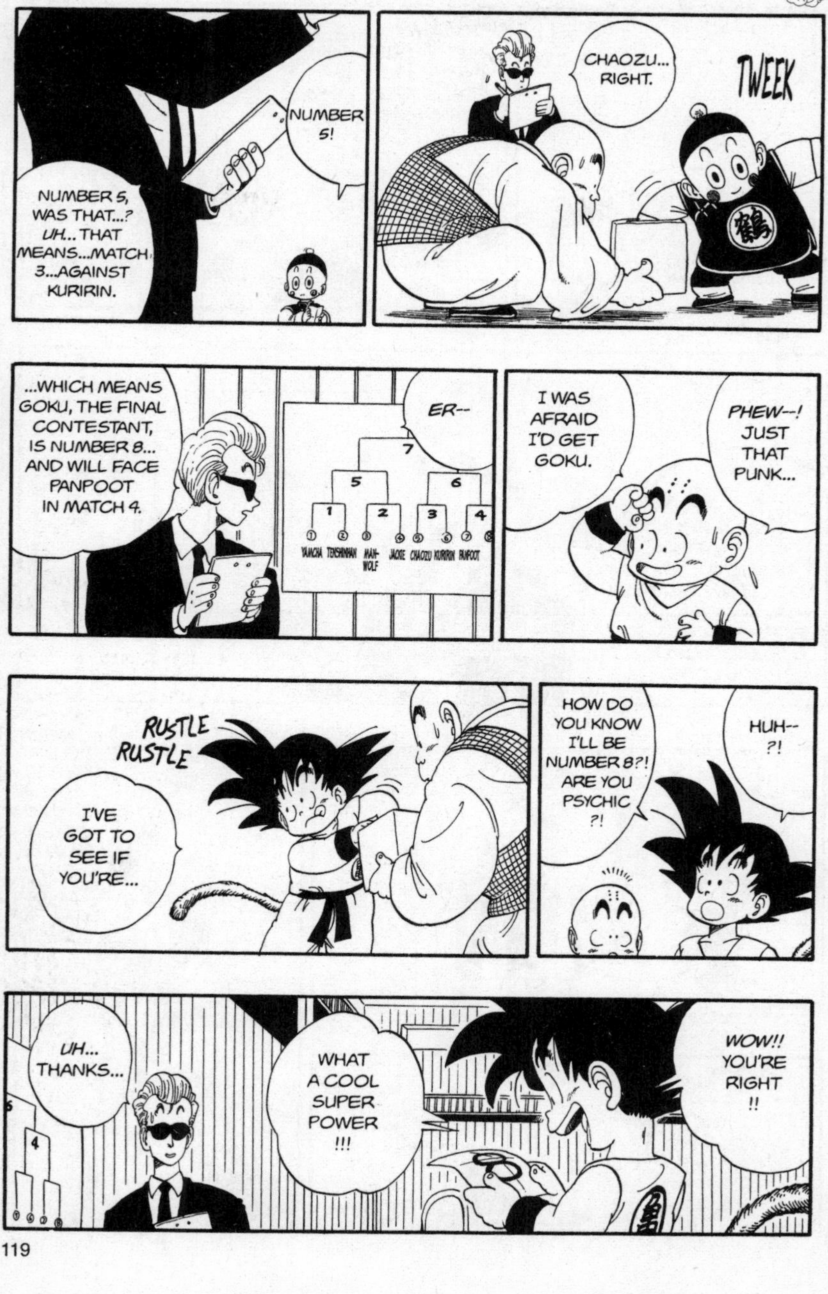

CHAOZU... RIGHT.
TWEEK
NUMBER 5!
NUMBER 5, WAS THAT...? UH... THAT MEANS...MATCH 3...AGAINST KURIRIN.
PHEW--! JUST THAT PUNK...
I WAS AFRAID I'D GET GOKU.
ER--
...WHICH MEANS GOKU, THE FINAL CONTESTANT, IS NUMBER 8... AND WILL FACE PANPOOT IN MATCH 4.
7
5
6
1
2
3
4
YAMCHA
TENSHINHAN
MAN-WOLF
JACKIE
CHAOZU
KURIRIN
PANPOOT
HUH--?!
HOW DO YOU KNOW I'LL BE NUMBER 8?! ARE YOU PSYCHIC?!
RUSTLE RUSTLE
I'VE GOT TO SEE IF YOU'RE...
WOW!! YOU'RE RIGHT!!
WHAT A COOL SUPER POWER!!!
UH... THANKS...

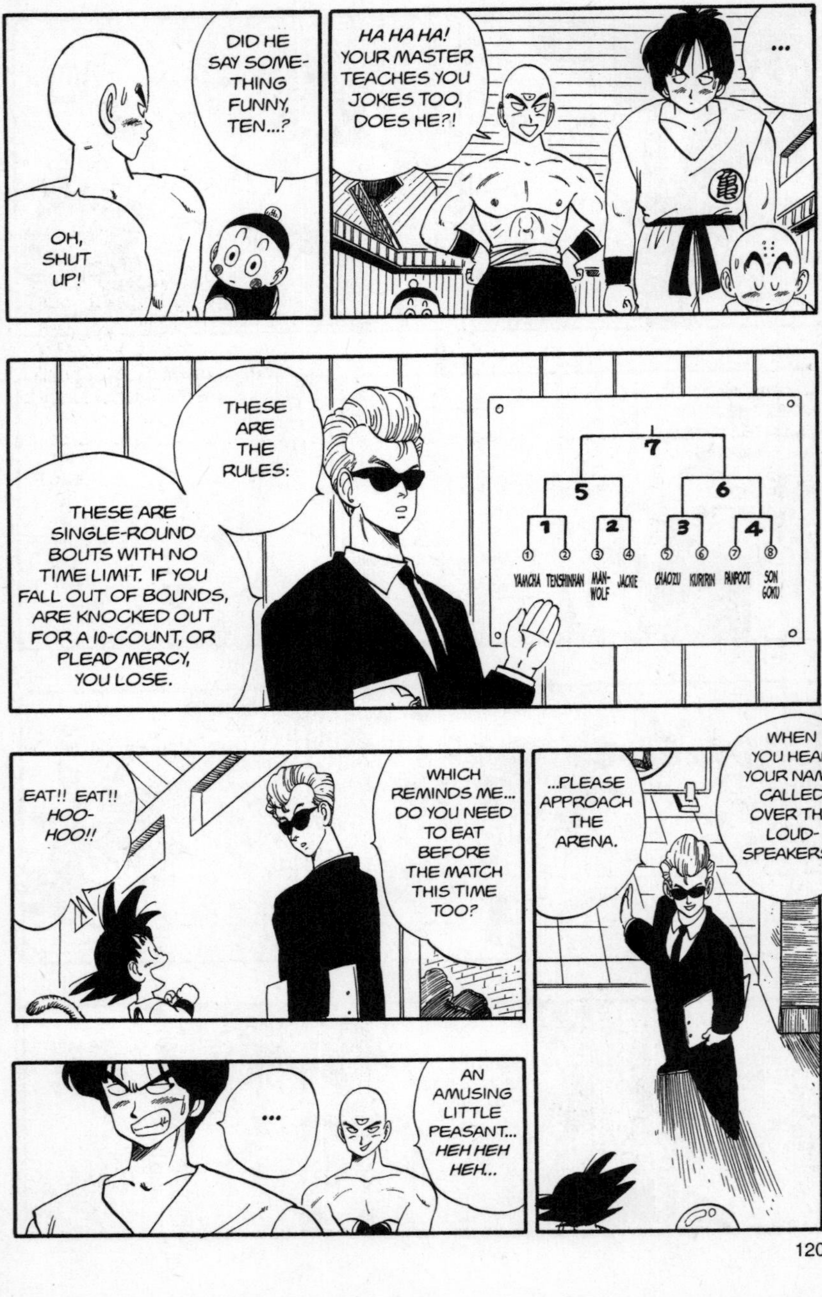
...
HA HA HA! YOUR MASTER TEACHES YOU JOKES TOO, DOES HE?!
DID HE SAY SOME-THING FUNNY, TEN...?
OH, SHUT UP!
THESE ARE THE RULES:
THESE ARE SINGLE-ROUND BOUTS WITH NO TIME LIMIT. IF YOU FALL OUT OF BOUNDS, ARE KNOCKED OUT FOR A 10-COUNT, OR PLEAD MERCY, YOU LOSE.
7
5
6
1 2 3 4
1 2 3 4 5 6 7 8
YAMCHA TENSHINHAN MAN-WOLF JACKIE CHAOZU KURIRIN PANPOOT SON GOKU
WHEN YOU HEAR YOUR NAME CALLED OVER THE LOUD-SPEAKERS...
...PLEASE APPROACH THE ARENA.
WHICH REMINDS ME... DO YOU NEED TO EAT BEFORE THE MATCH THIS TIME TOO?
EAT!! EAT!! HOO-HOO!!
AN AMUSING LITTLE PEASANT... HEH HEH HEH...
...

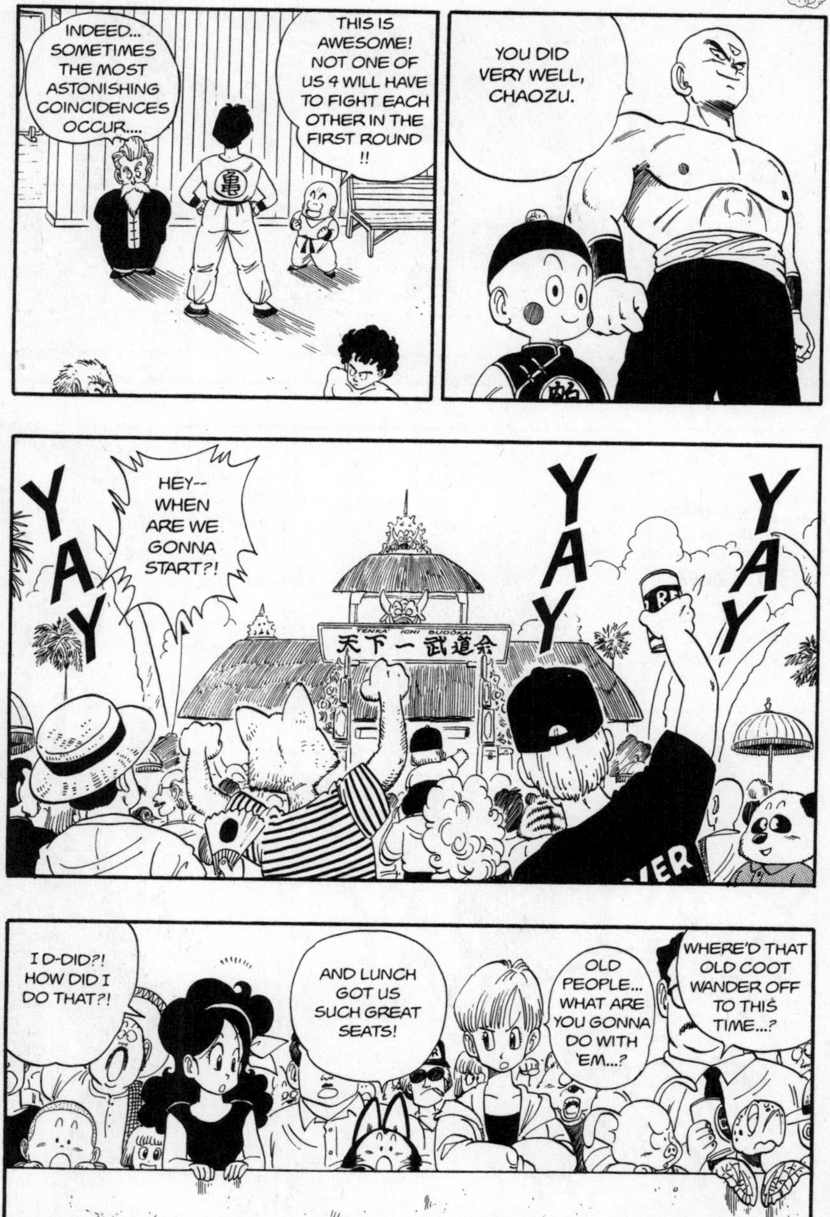
YOU DID VERY WELL, CHAOZU.
THIS IS AWESOME! NOT ONE OF US 4 WILL HAVE TO FIGHT EACH OTHER IN THE FIRST ROUND !!
INDEED... SOMETIMES THE MOST ASTONISHING COINCIDENCES OCCUR....
YAY
YAY
天下一武道会
TENKA' ICHI BUDOKAI
HEY-- WHEN ARE WE GONNA START?!
YAY
WHERE'D THAT OLD COOT WANDER OFF TO THIS TIME...?
OLD PEOPLE... WHAT ARE YOU GONNA DO WITH 'EM...?
AND LUNCH GOT US SUCH GREAT SEATS!
I D-DID?! HOW DID I DO THAT?!

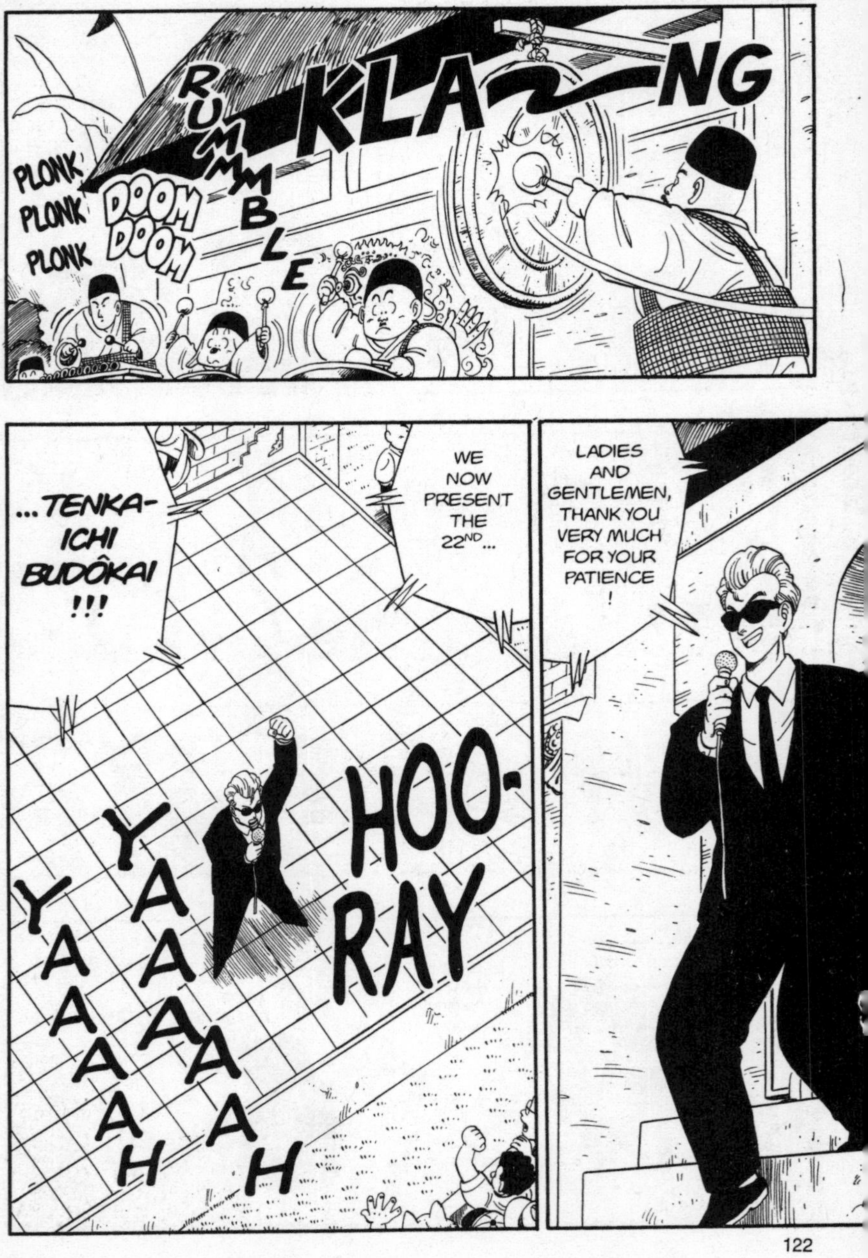
KLA—NG
RUMMMBLE
DOOM DOOM
PLONK PLONK PLONK
LADIES AND GENTLEMEN, THANK YOU VERY MUCH FOR YOUR PATIENCE!
WE NOW PRESENT THE 22ND...
...TENKA-ICHI BUDÔKAI!!!
HOO-RAY
YAAAAAH
YAAAAAH

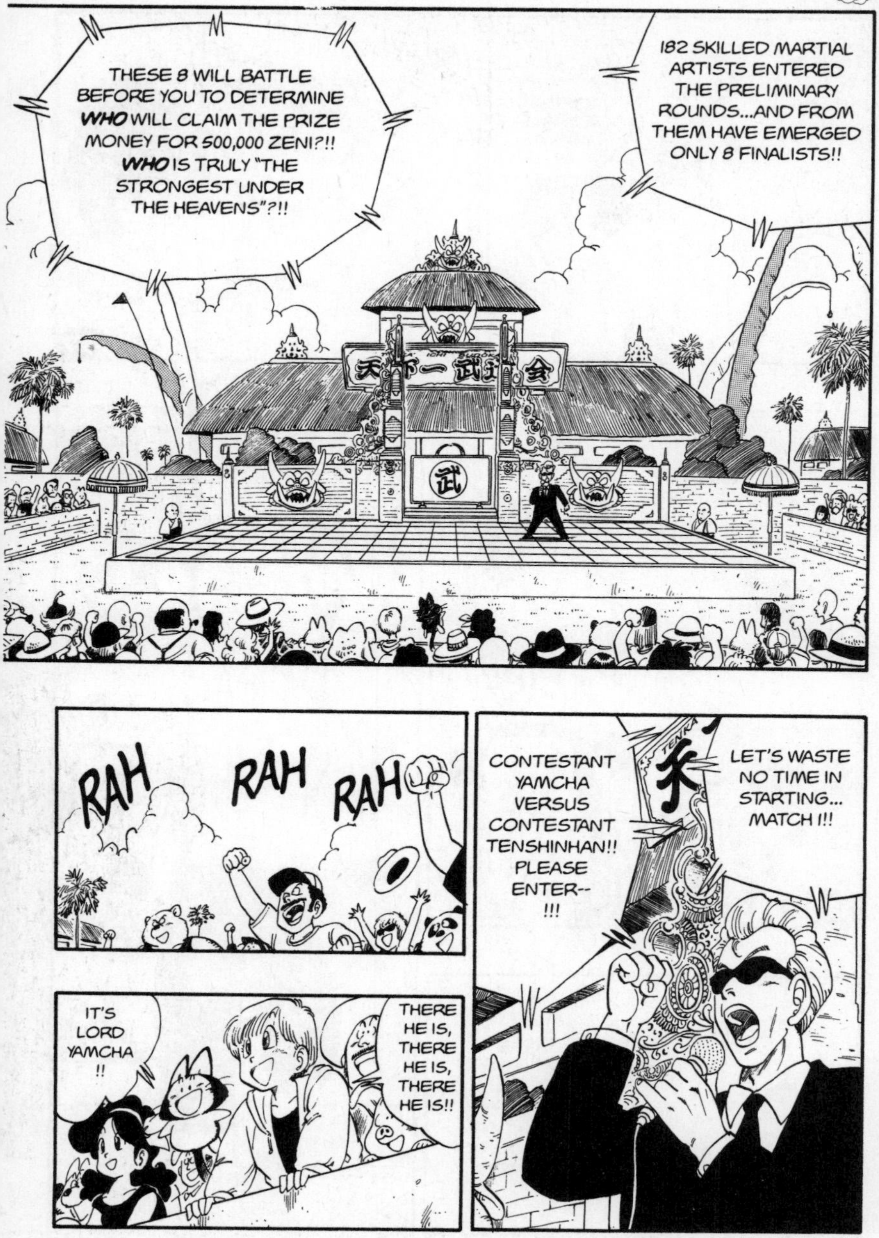
182 SKILLED MARTIAL ARTISTS ENTERED THE PRELIMINARY ROUNDS...AND FROM THEM HAVE EMERGED ONLY 8 FINALISTS!!
THESE 8 WILL BATTLE BEFORE YOU TO DETERMINE WHO WILL CLAIM THE PRIZE MONEY FOR 500,000 ZENI?!! WHO IS TRULY "THE STRONGEST UNDER THE HEAVENS"?!!
LET'S WASTE NO TIME IN STARTING... MATCH 1!!
CONTESTANT YAMCHA VERSUS CONTESTANT TENSHINHAN!! PLEASE ENTER-- !!!
RAH RAH RAH
THERE HE IS, THERE HE IS, THERE HE IS!!
IT'S LORD YAMCHA !!

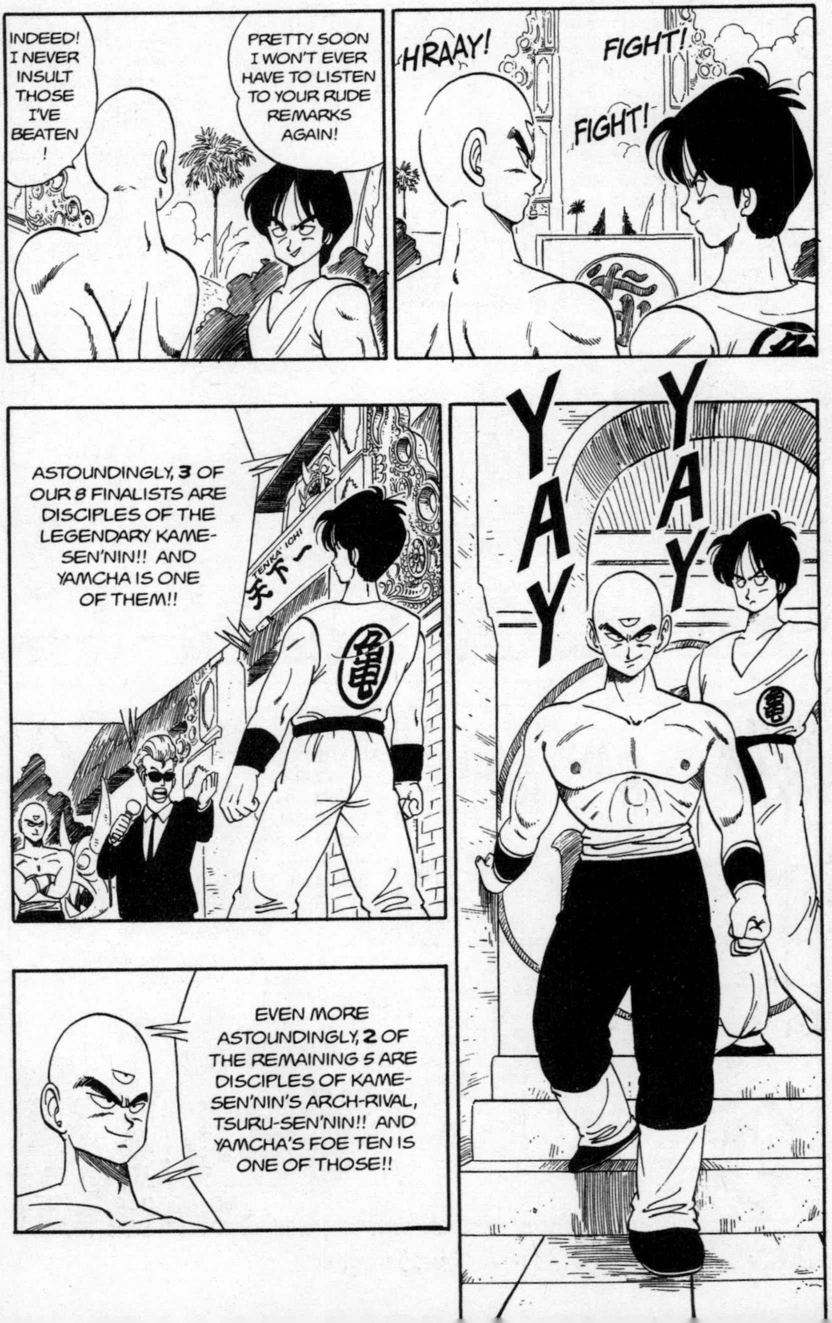
HRAAY!
FIGHT!
FIGHT!
PRETTY SOON I WON'T EVER HAVE TO LISTEN TO YOUR RUDE REMARKS AGAIN!
INDEED! I NEVER INSULT THOSE I'VE BEATEN!
YAY
YAY
ASTOUNDINGLY, 3 OF OUR 8 FINALISTS ARE DISCIPLES OF THE LEGENDARY KAME-SEN'NIN!! AND YAMCHA IS ONE OF THEM!!
TENKA' ICHI
天下一
EVEN MORE ASTOUNDINGLY, 2 OF THE REMAINING 5 ARE DISCIPLES OF KAME-SEN'NIN'S ARCH-RIVAL, TSURU-SEN'NIN!! AND YAMCHA'S FOE TEN IS ONE OF THOSE!!

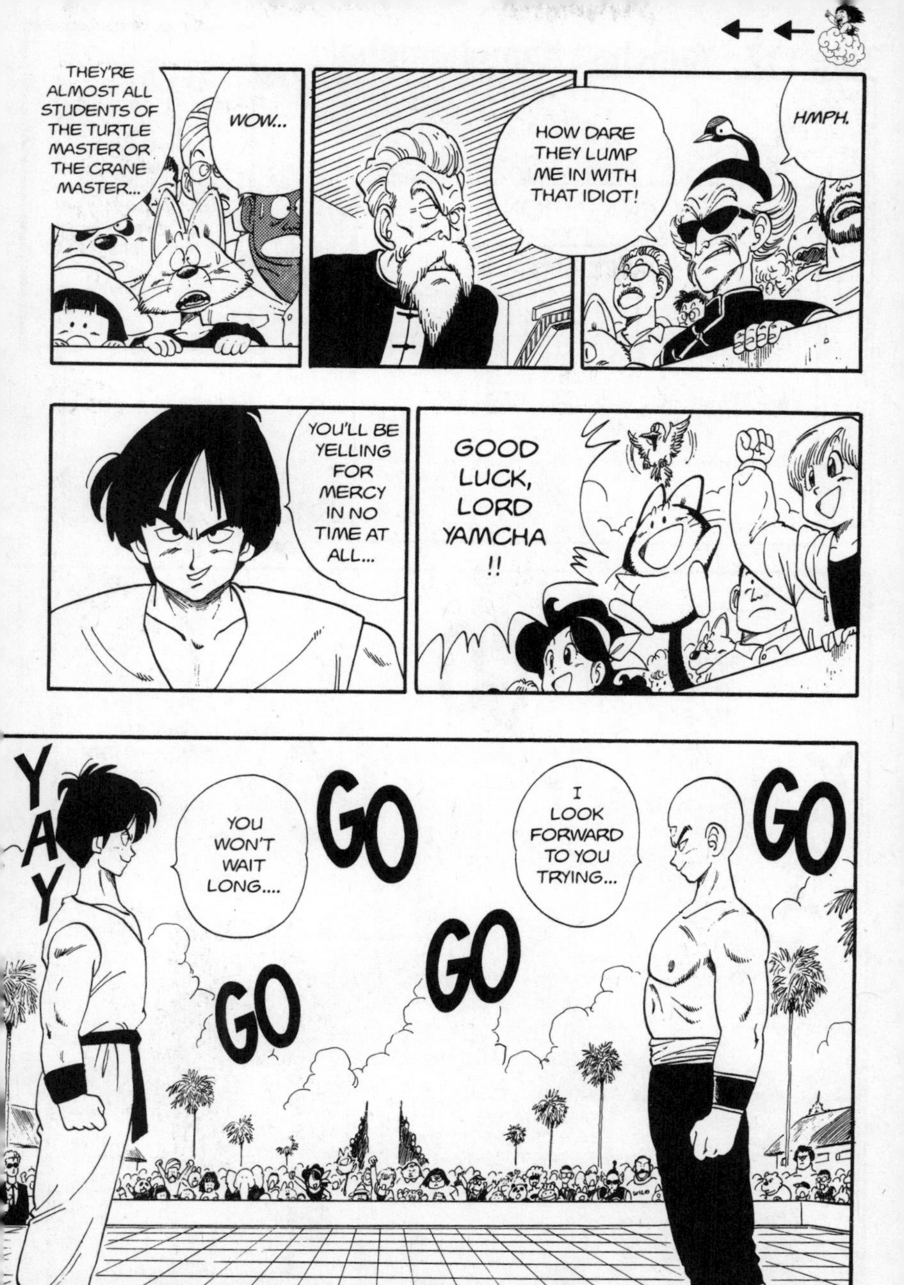
THEY'RE ALMOST ALL STUDENTS OF THE TURTLE MASTER OR THE CRANE MASTER...
WOW...
HOW DARE THEY LUMP ME IN WITH THAT IDIOT!
HMPH.
YOU'LL BE YELLING FOR MERCY IN NO TIME AT ALL...
GOOD LUCK, LORD YAMCHA !!
YAY
YOU WON'T WAIT LONG....
GO
GO
GO
I LOOK FORWARD TO YOU TRYING...
GO

NEXT: Yamcha's New Technique!

Tale 117 • Yamcha's Kamehameha!

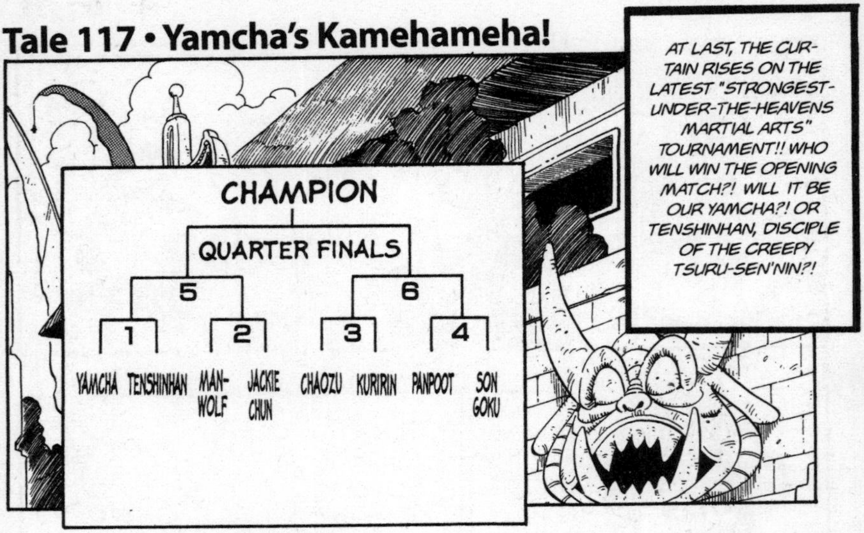

AT LAST, THE CURTAIN RISES ON THE LATEST "STRONGEST-UNDER-THE-HEAVENS MARTIAL ARTS" TOURNAMENT!! WHO WILL WIN THE OPENING MATCH?! WILL IT BE OUR YAMCHA?! OR TENSHINHAN, DISCIPLE OF THE CREEPY TSURU-SEN'NIN?!
CHAMPION
QUARTER FINALS
5
6
1
2
3
4
YAMCHA
TENSHINHAN
MAN-WOLF
JACKIE CHUN
CHAOZU
KURIRIN
PANPOOT
SON GOKU

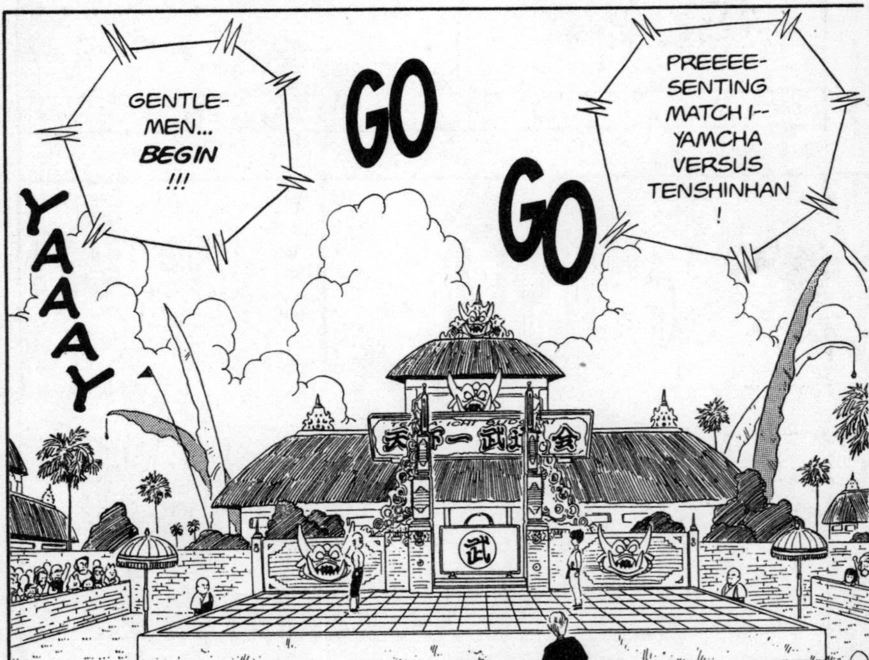

PREEEE-SENTING MATCH I-- YAMCHA VERSUS TENSHINHAN !
GO
GO
GENTLEMEN... ***BEGIN*** !!!
YAAAY

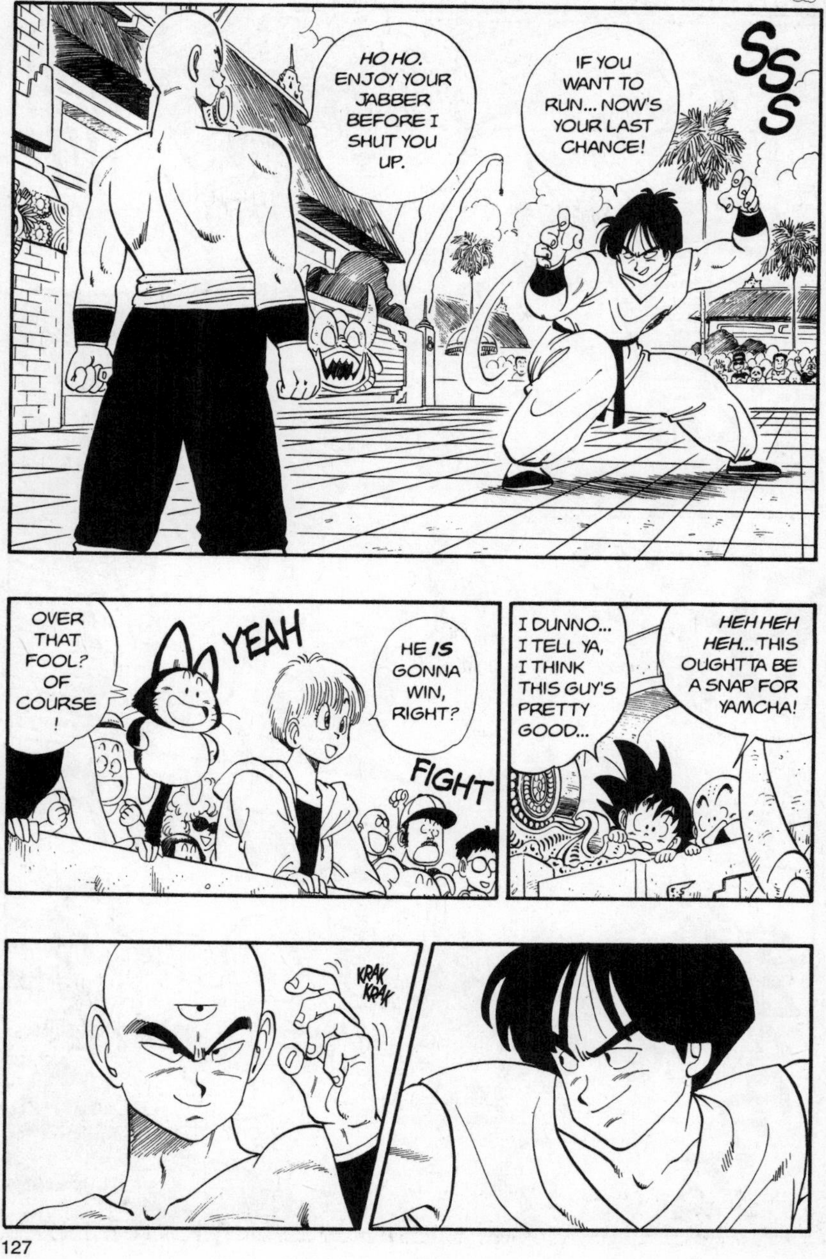
SSS
IF YOU WANT TO RUN... NOW'S YOUR LAST CHANCE!
HO HO. ENJOY YOUR JABBER BEFORE I SHUT YOU UP.
HEH HEH HEH... THIS OUGHTTA BE A SNAP FOR YAMCHA!
I DUNNO... I TELL YA, I THINK THIS GUY'S PRETTY GOOD...
YEAH
HE *IS* GONNA WIN, RIGHT?
OVER THAT FOOL? OF COURSE!
FIGHT
KRAK KRAK

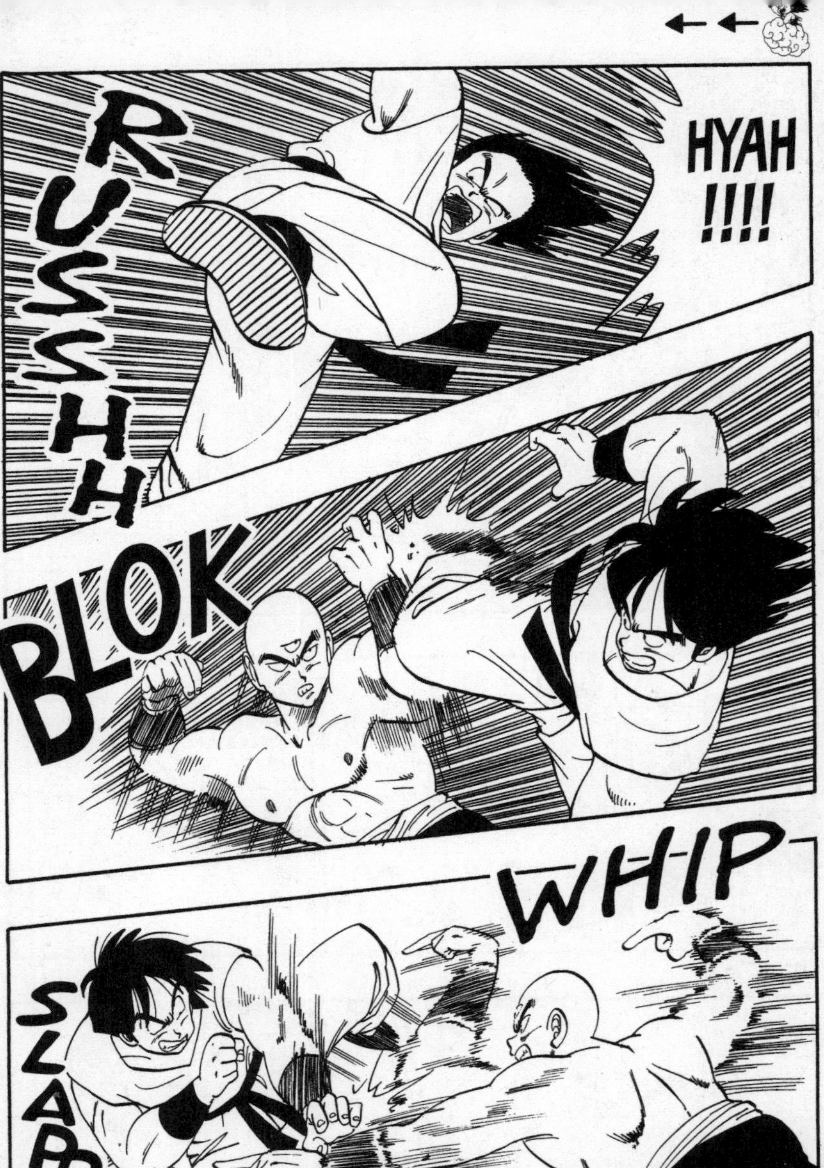
HYAH !!!!
RUSSHH
BLOK
WHIP
SLAPPITA

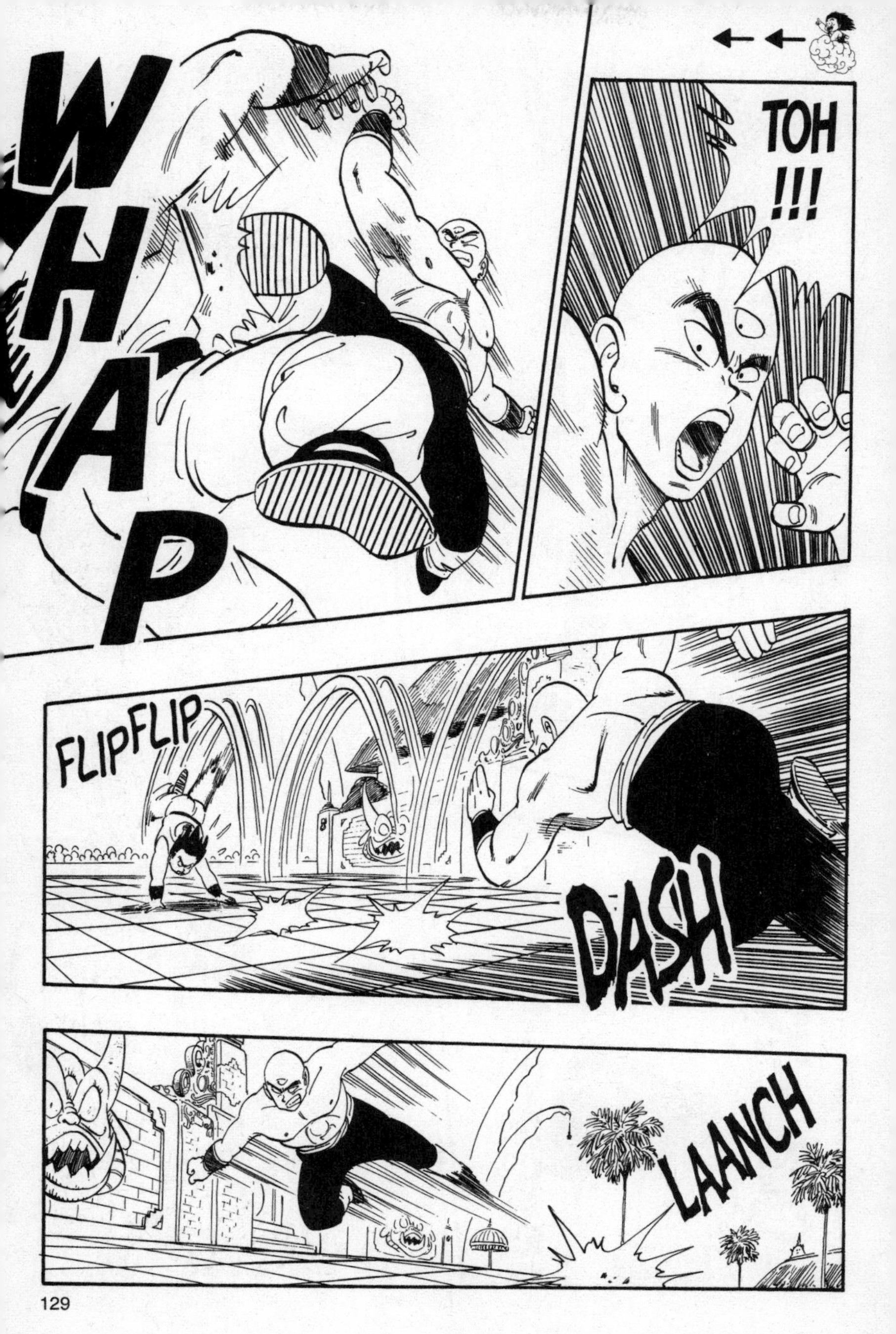
TOH !!!
WHAP
FLIPFLIP
DASH
LAANCH

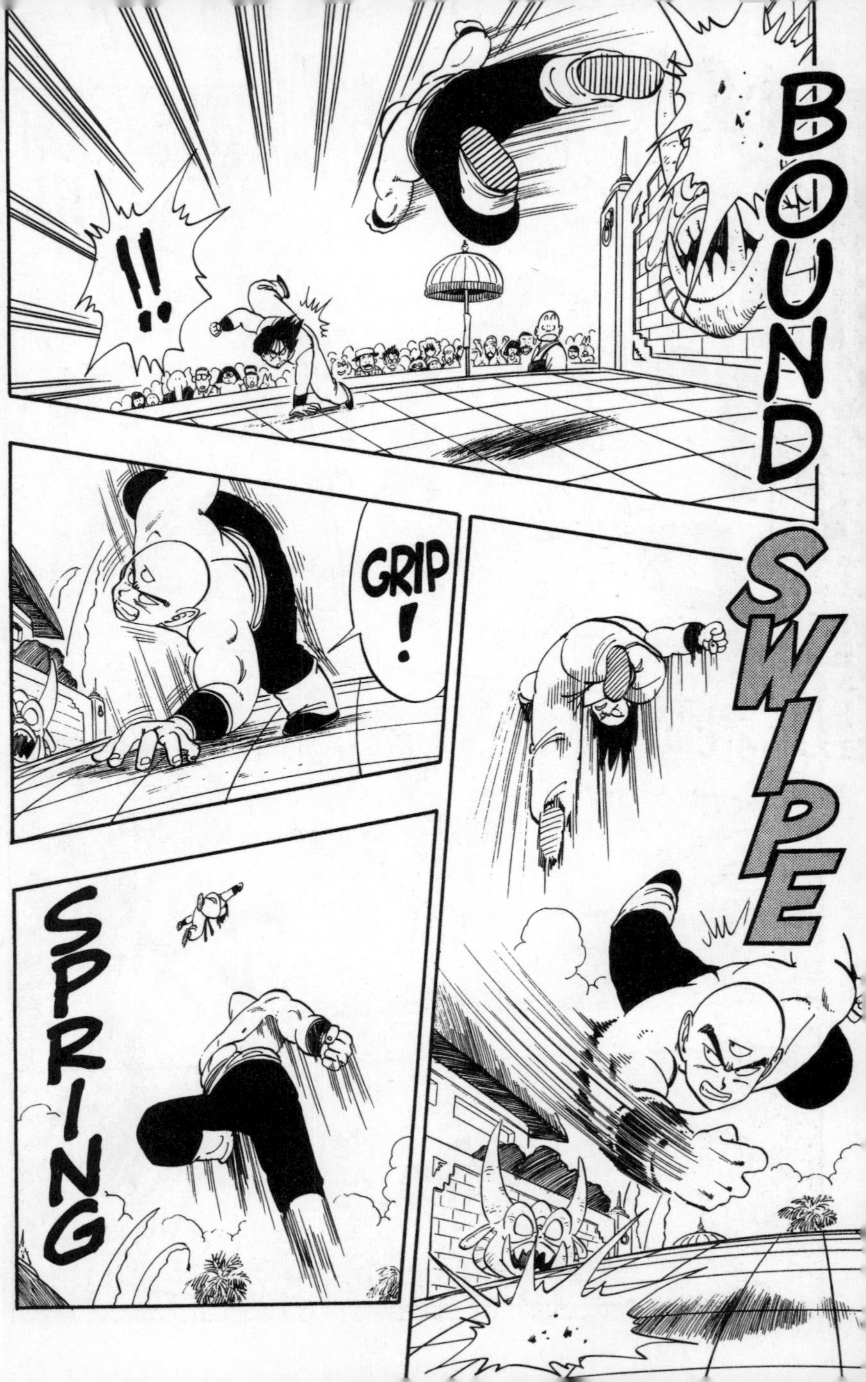
BOUND
!!
SWIPE
GRIP!
SPRING

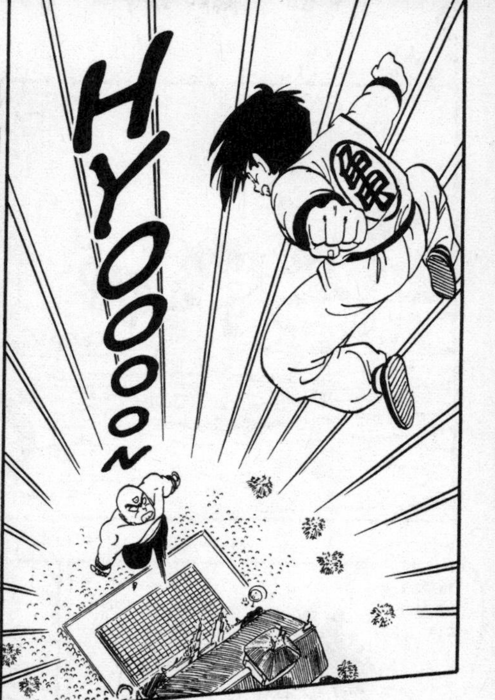
HYOOOOON
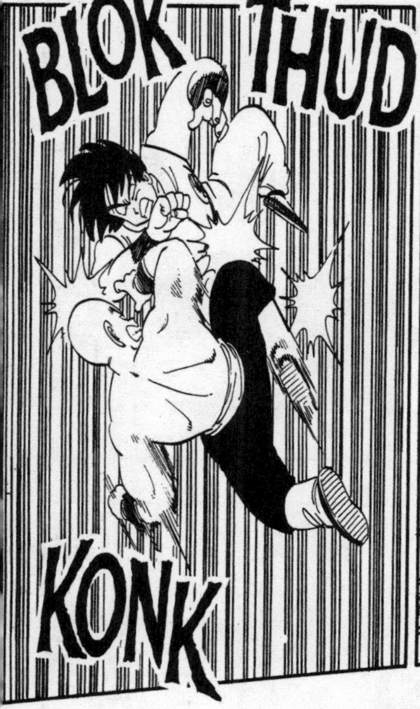
BLOK
THUD
KONK
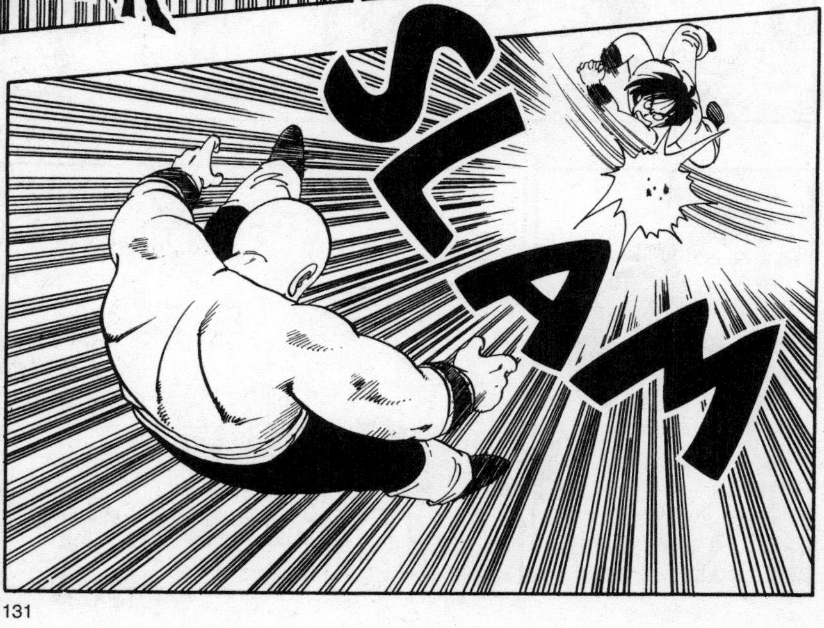
SLAM

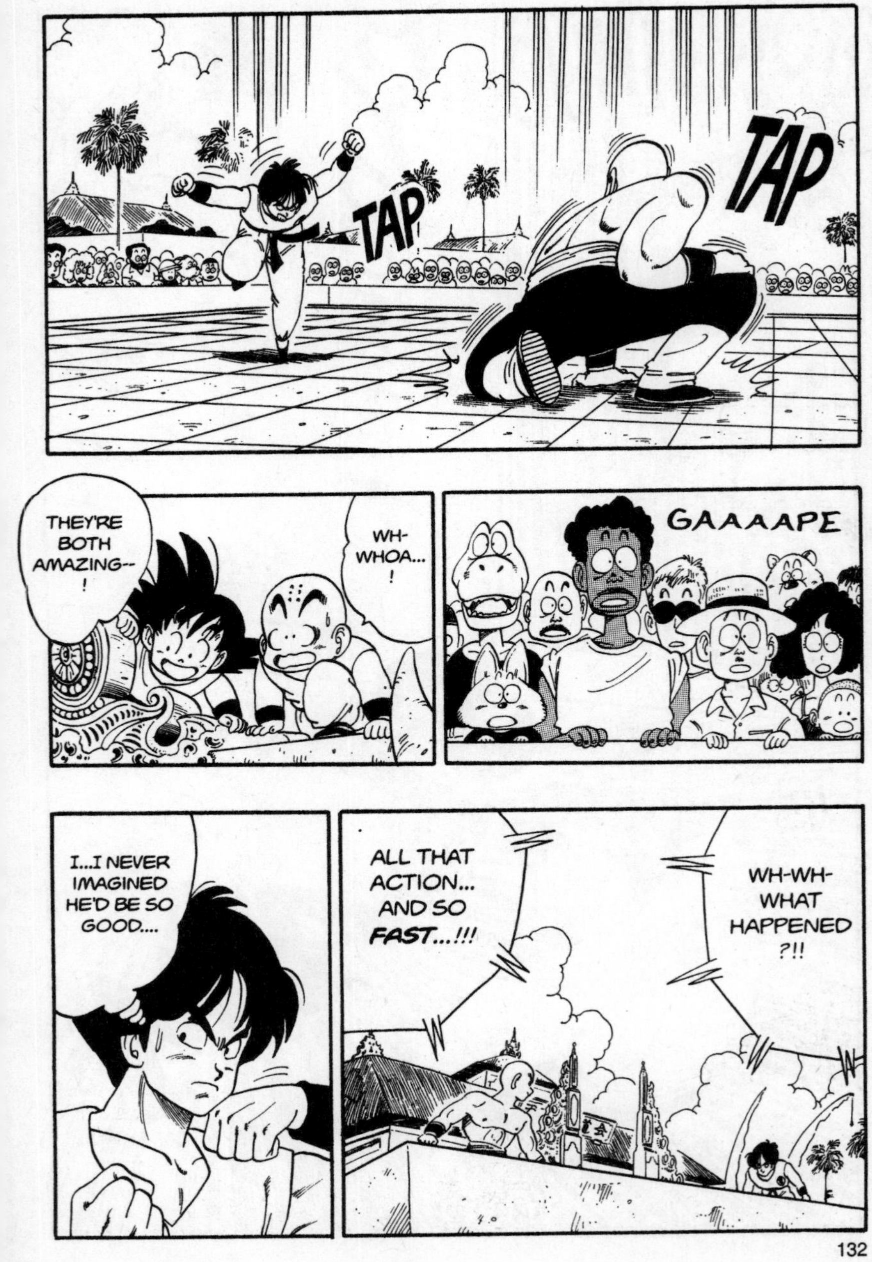
TAP
TAP
GAAAAPE
WH- WHOA... !
THEY'RE BOTH AMAZING-- !
WH-WH- WHAT HAPPENED ?!!
ALL THAT ACTION... AND SO FAST...!!!
I...I NEVER IMAGINED HE'D BE SO GOOD....

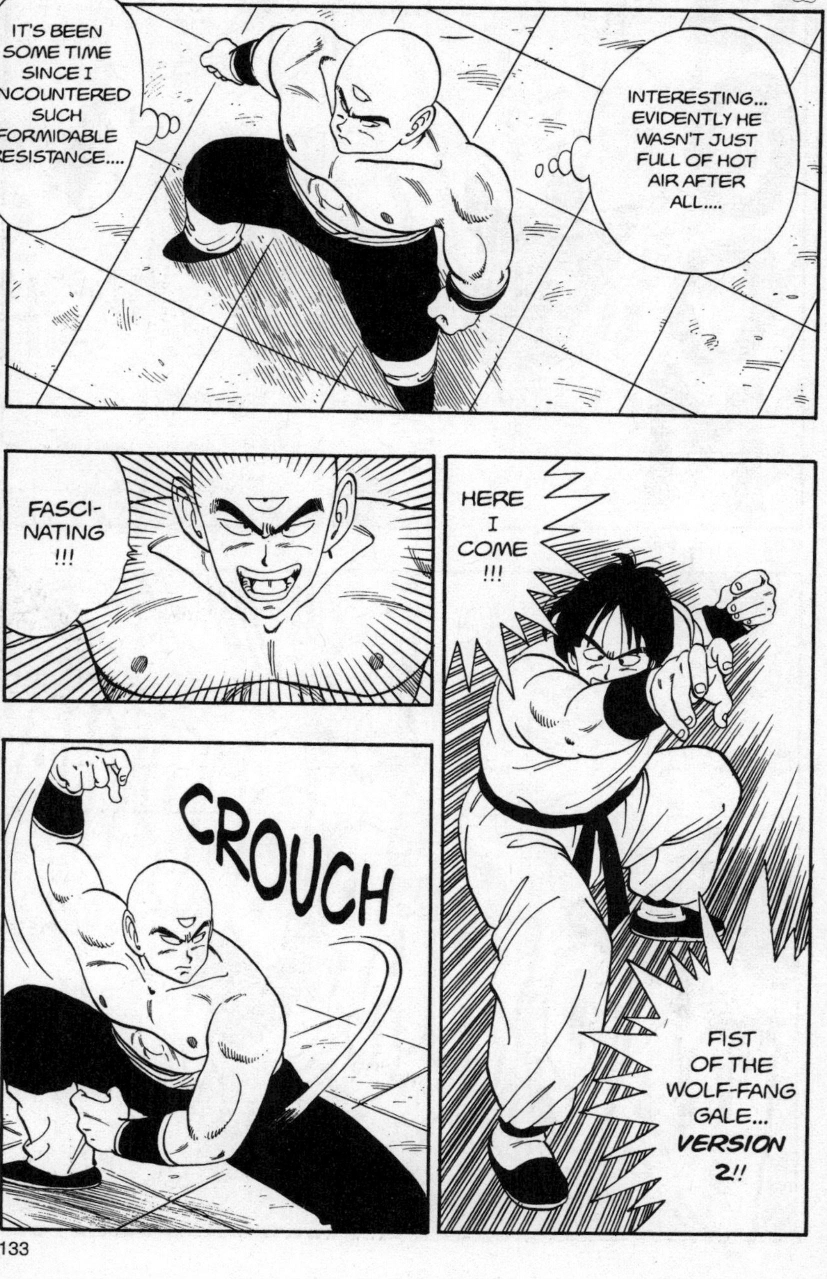
INTERESTING... EVIDENTLY HE WASN'T JUST FULL OF HOT AIR AFTER ALL....
IT'S BEEN SOME TIME SINCE I ENCOUNTERED SUCH FORMIDABLE RESISTANCE....
HERE I COME!!!
FIST OF THE WOLF-FANG GALE... ***VERSION 2!!***
FASCI-NATING!!!
CROUCH

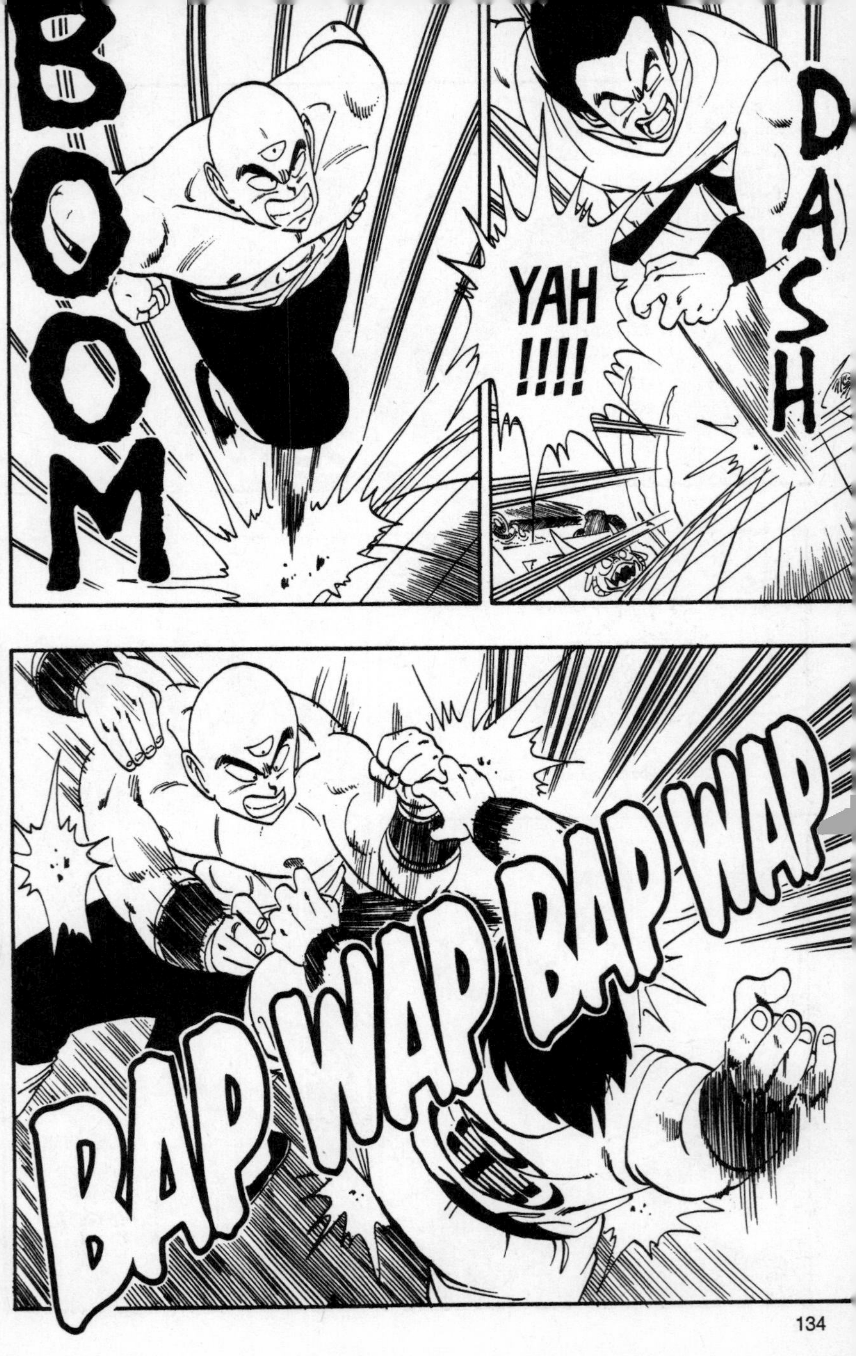
DASH
YAH !!!!
BOOM
BAP WAP BAP WAP

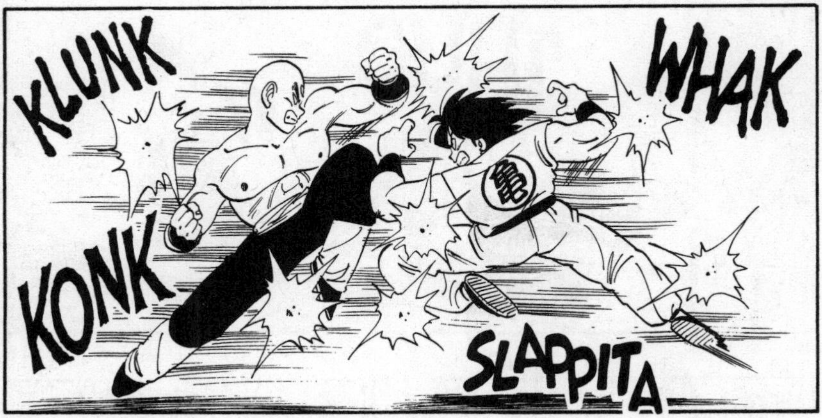
WHAK
KLUNK
KONK
SLAPPITA

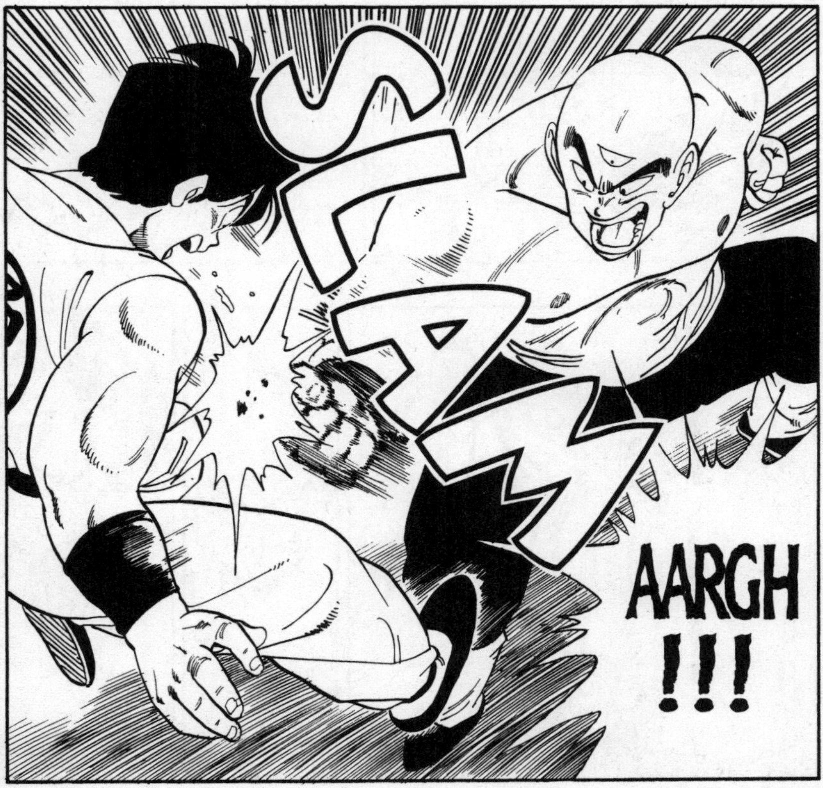
SLAM
AARGH!!!

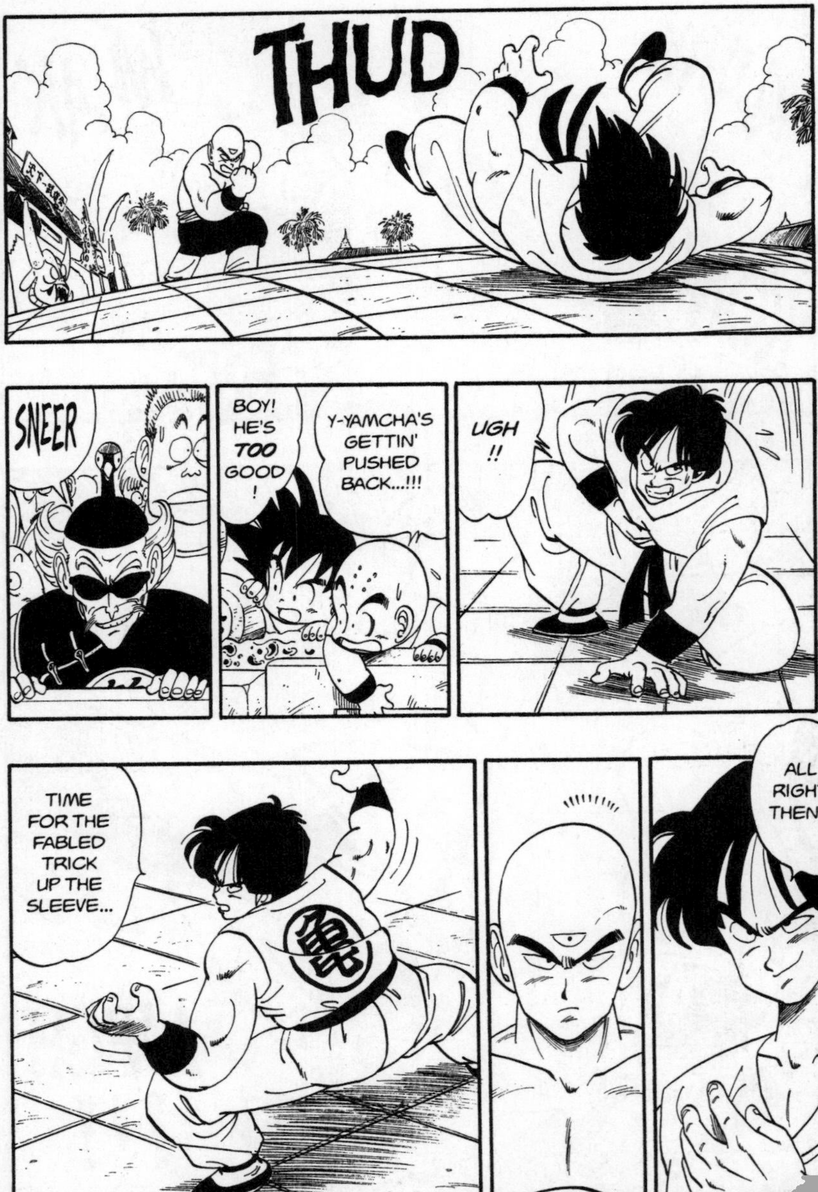
THUD
UGH !!
Y-YAMCHA'S GETTIN' PUSHED BACK...!!!
BOY! HE'S TOO GOOD !
SNEER
ALL RIGHT, THEN...
TIME FOR THE FABLED TRICK UP THE SLEEVE...

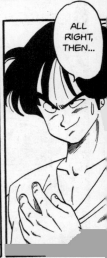

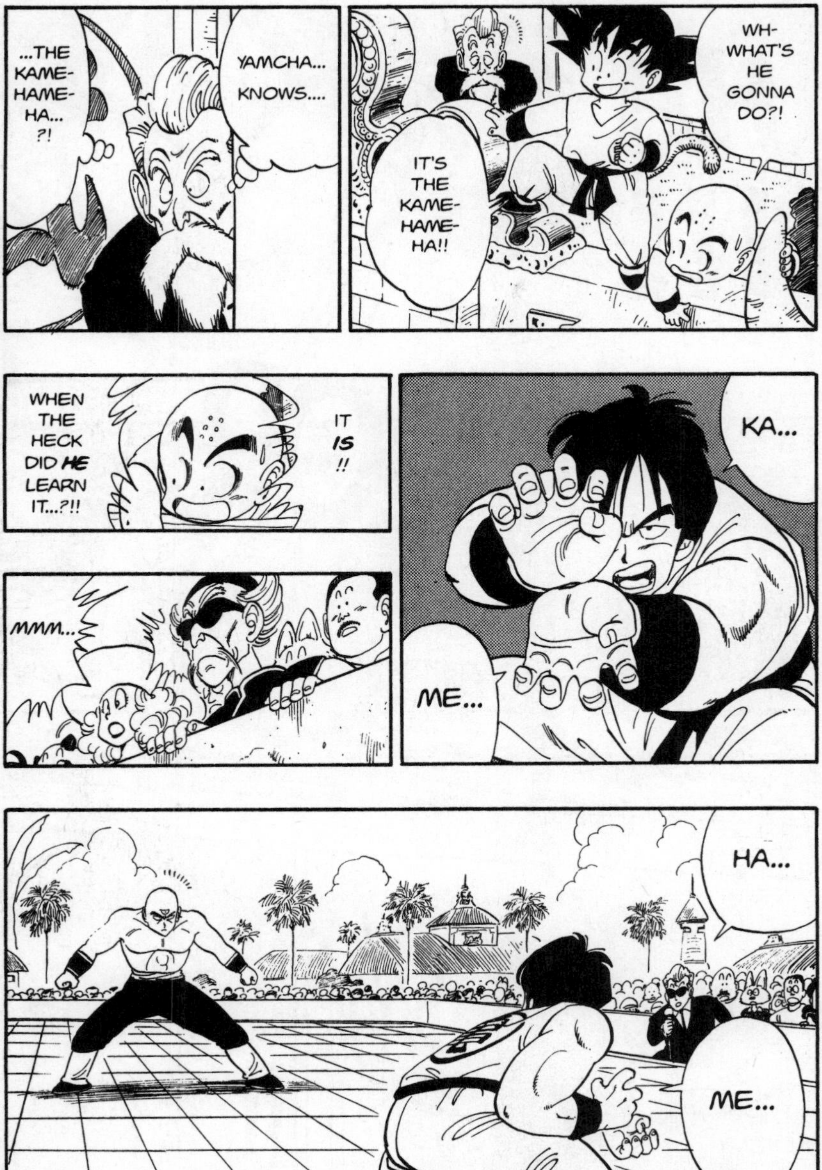
WH- WHAT'S HE GONNA DO?!
IT'S THE KAME-HAME-HA!!
YAMCHA... KNOWS....
...THE KAME-HAME-HA...?!
KA...
ME...
IT IS!!
WHEN THE HECK DID HE LEARN IT...?!!
MMM...
HA...
ME...

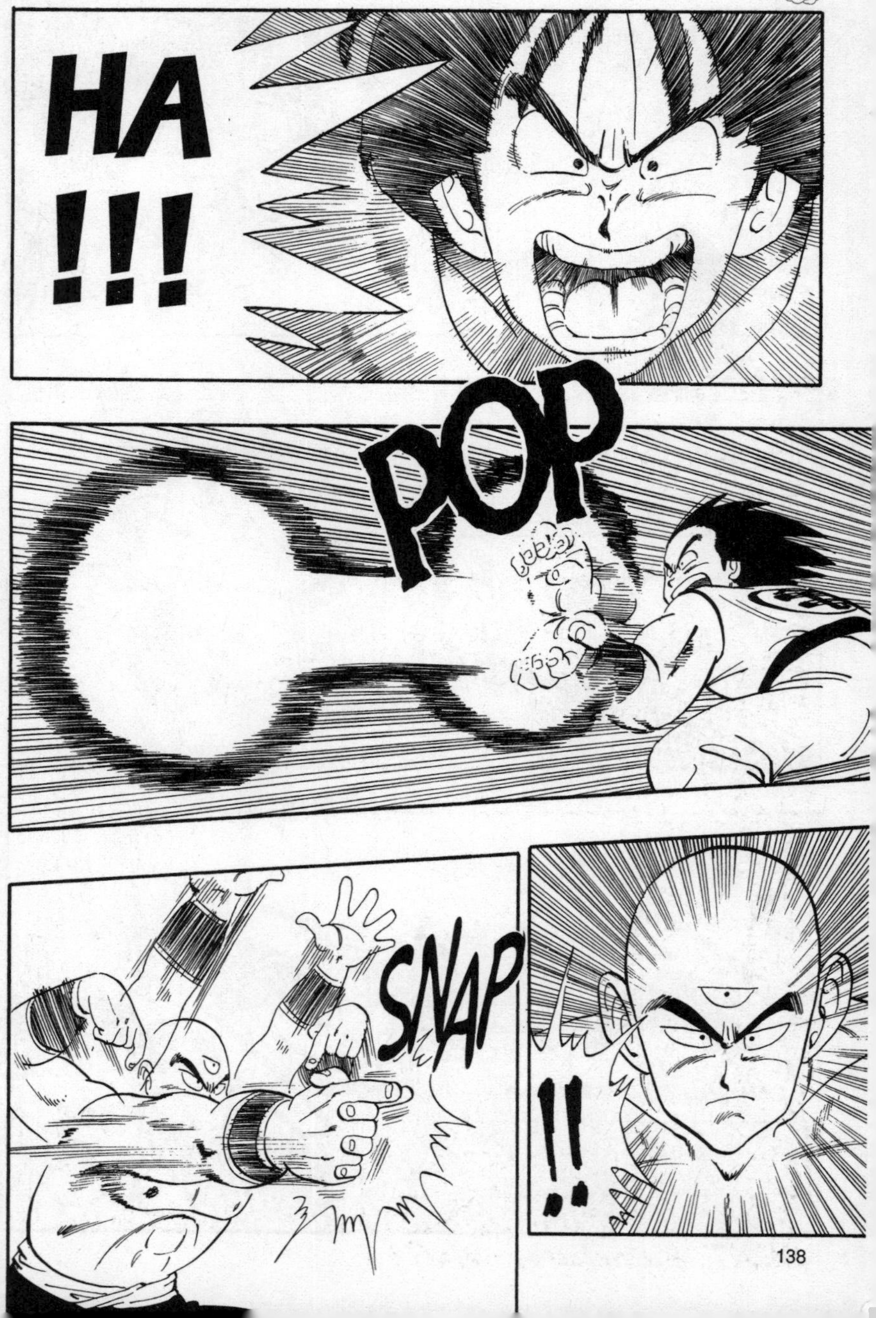
HA!!!
POP
!!
SNAP

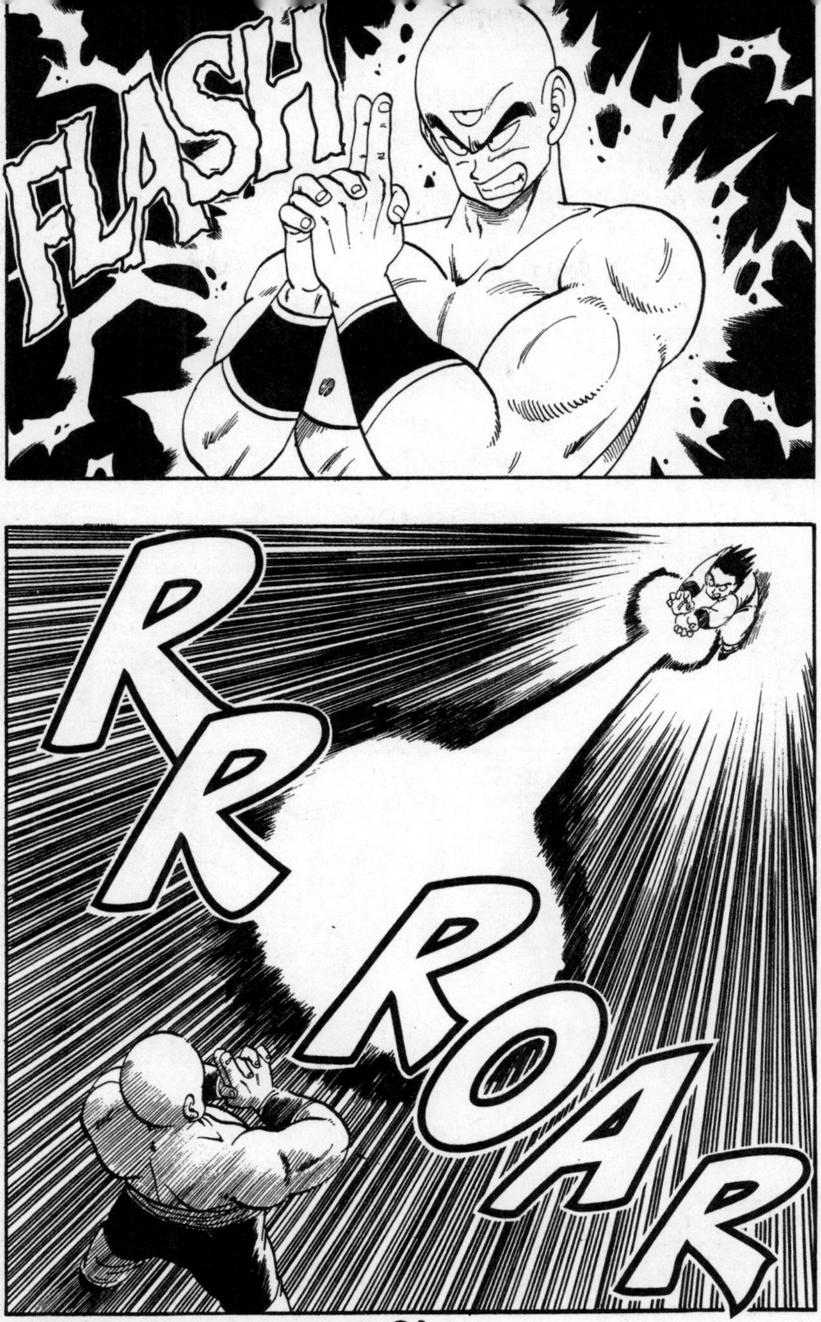
FLASH
RRROAR

NEXT: Kamehame-wha?!

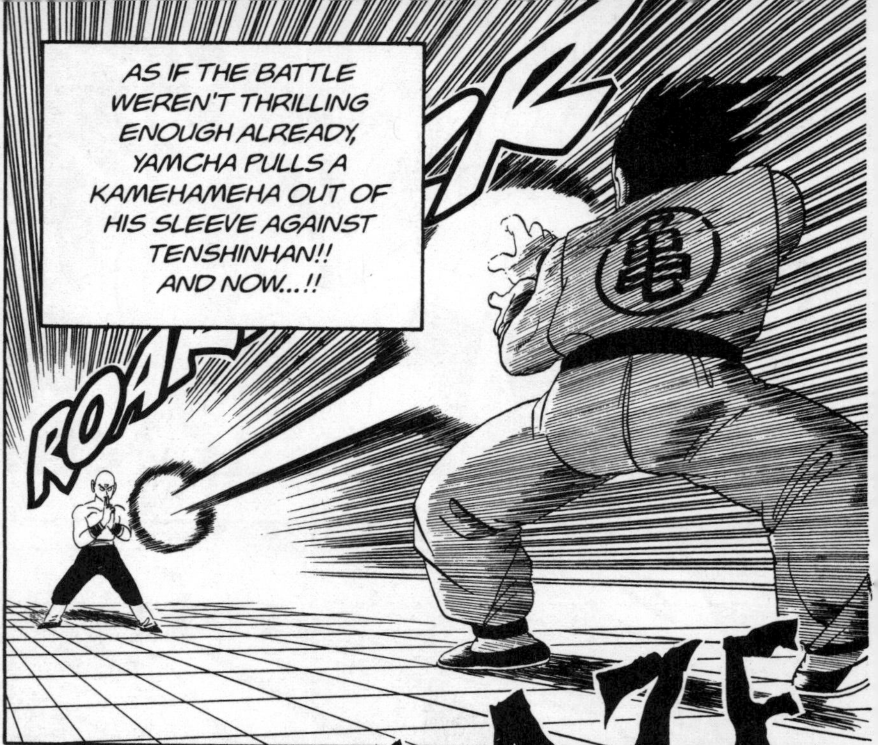
AS IF THE BATTLE WEREN'T THRILLING ENOUGH ALREADY, YAMCHA PULLS A KAMEHAMEHA OUT OF HIS SLEEVE AGAINST TENSHINHAN!! AND NOW...!!
ROA

Tale 118 • The Cruelty of Tenshinhan

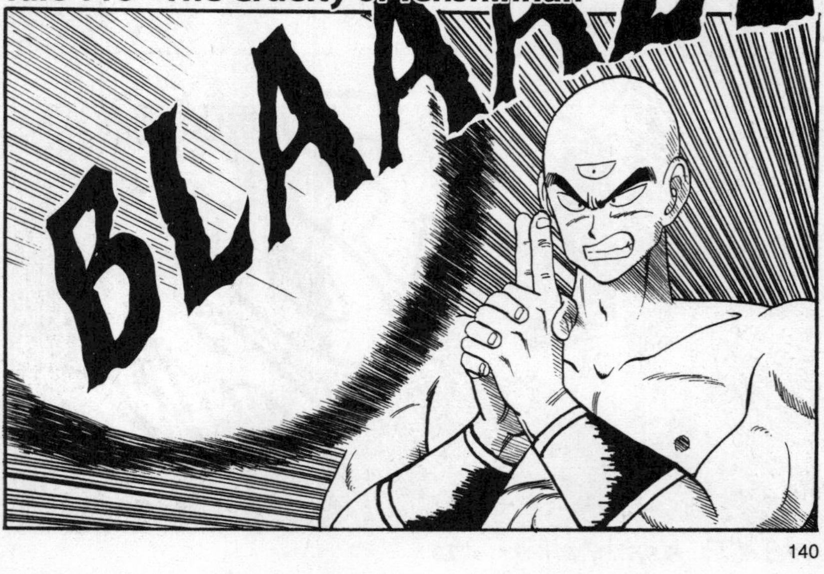
BLAAAZE

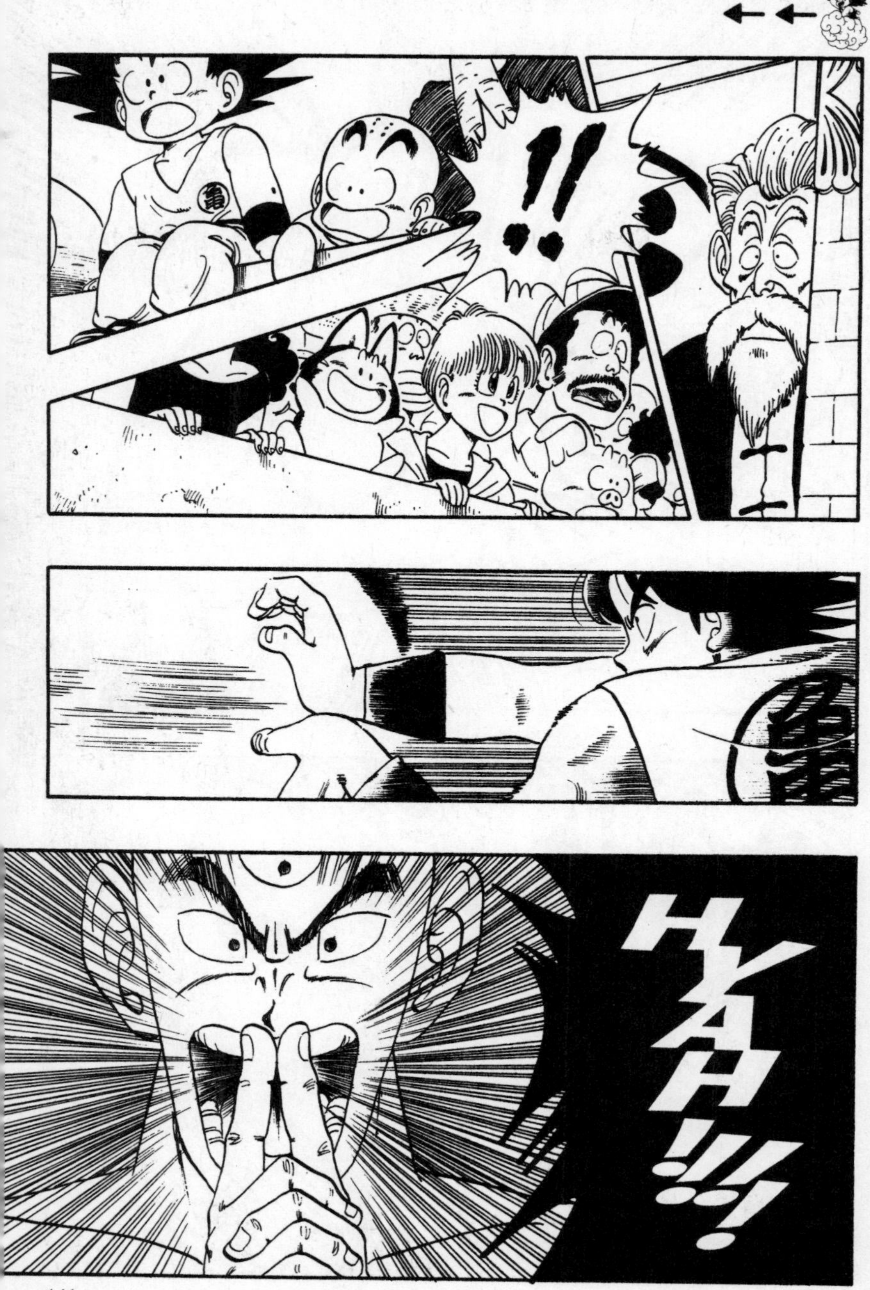
!!
HYAH!!!!

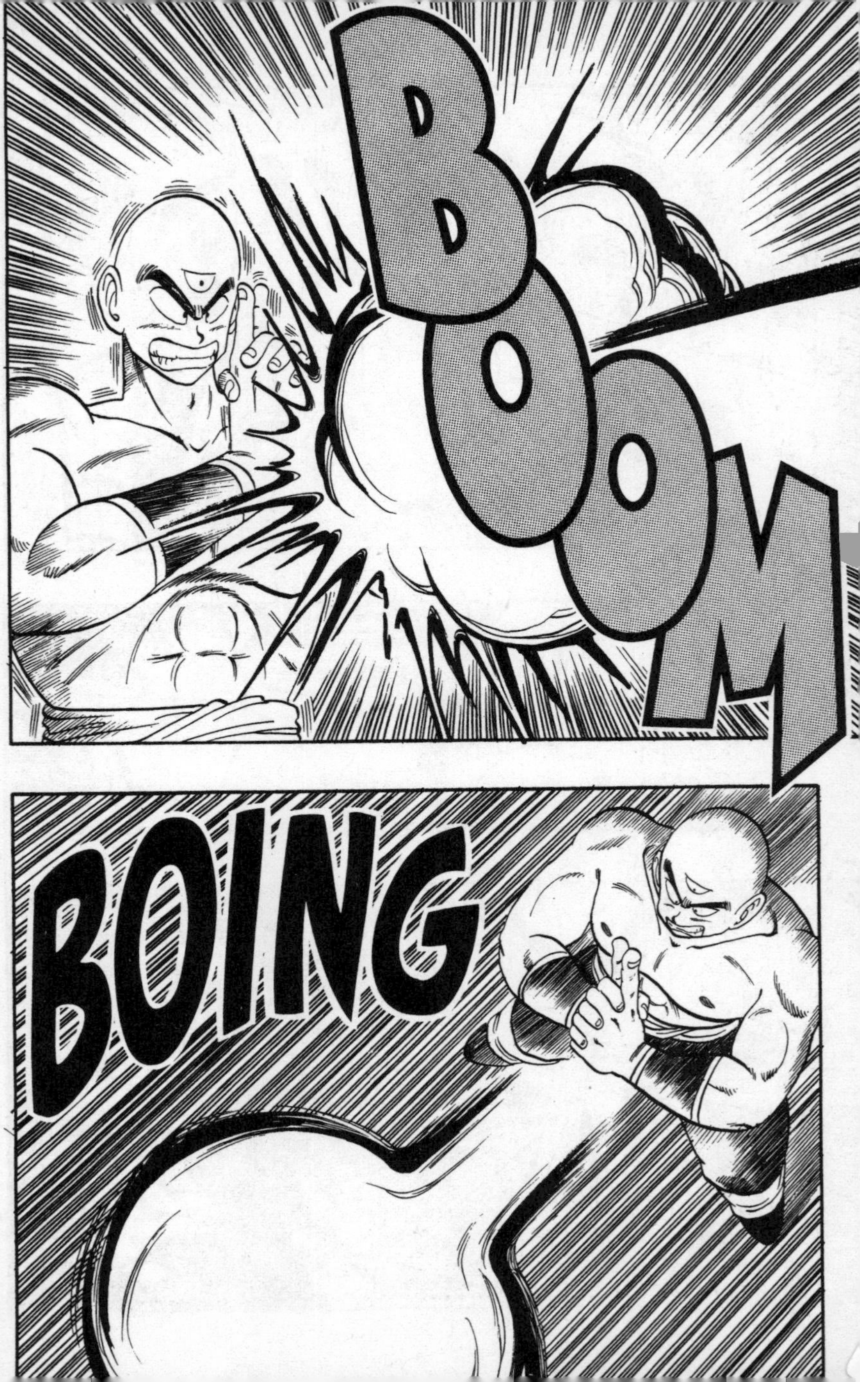
BOOOM
BOING

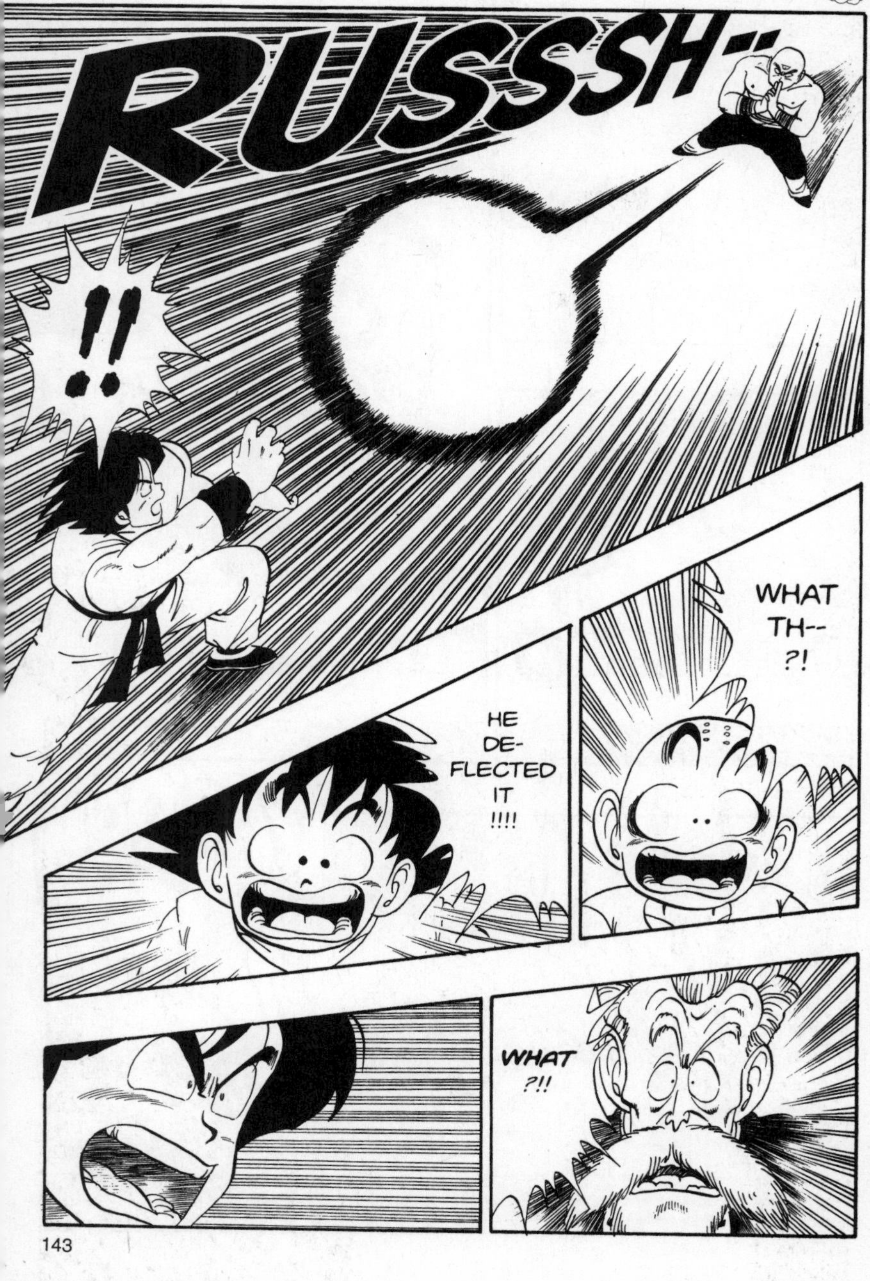
RUSSSH--
!!
WHAT TH-- ?!
HE DE-FLECTED IT !!!!
WHAT ?!!

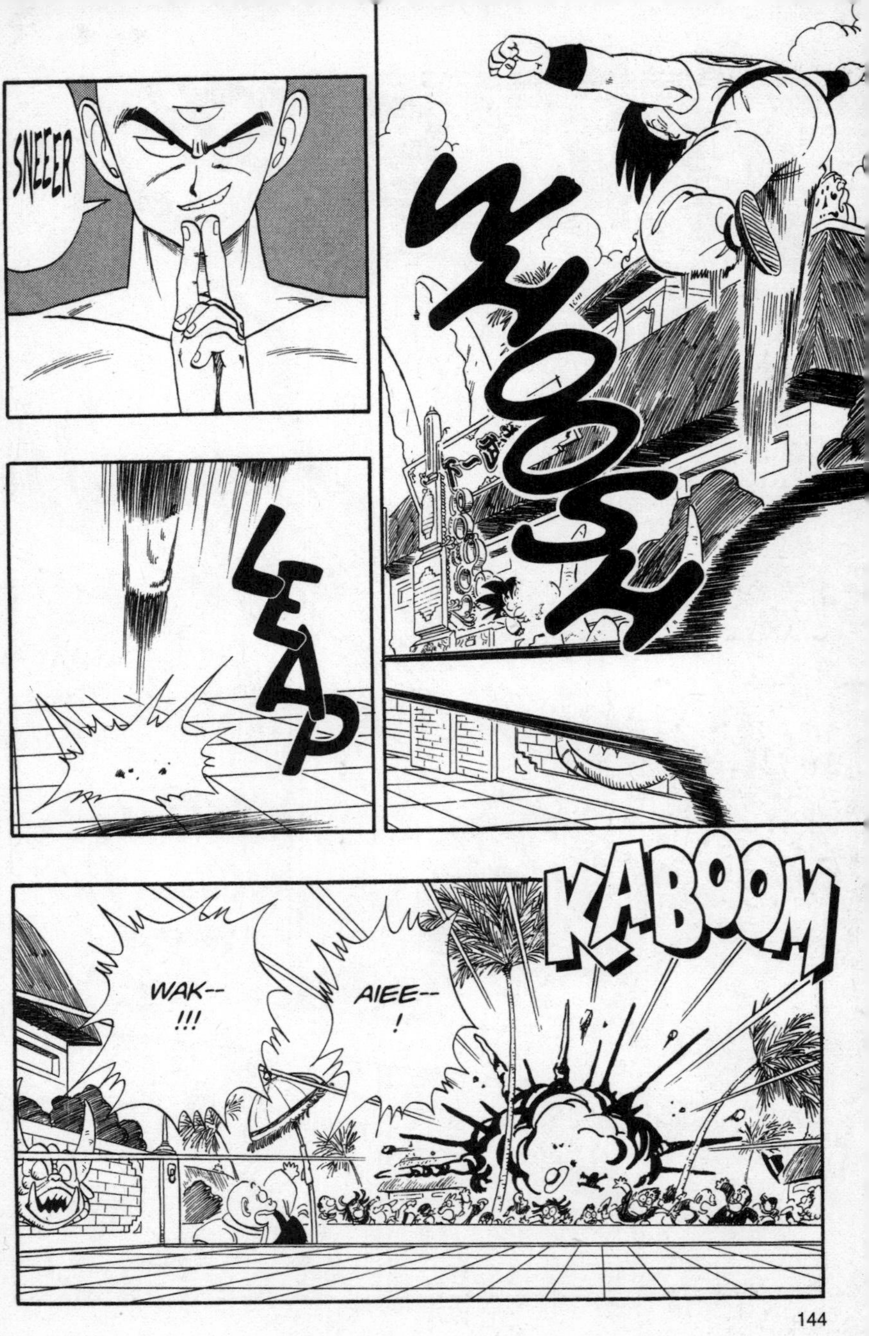
WHOOSH
SNEEER
LEAP
KABOOM
AIEE--!
WAK--!!!

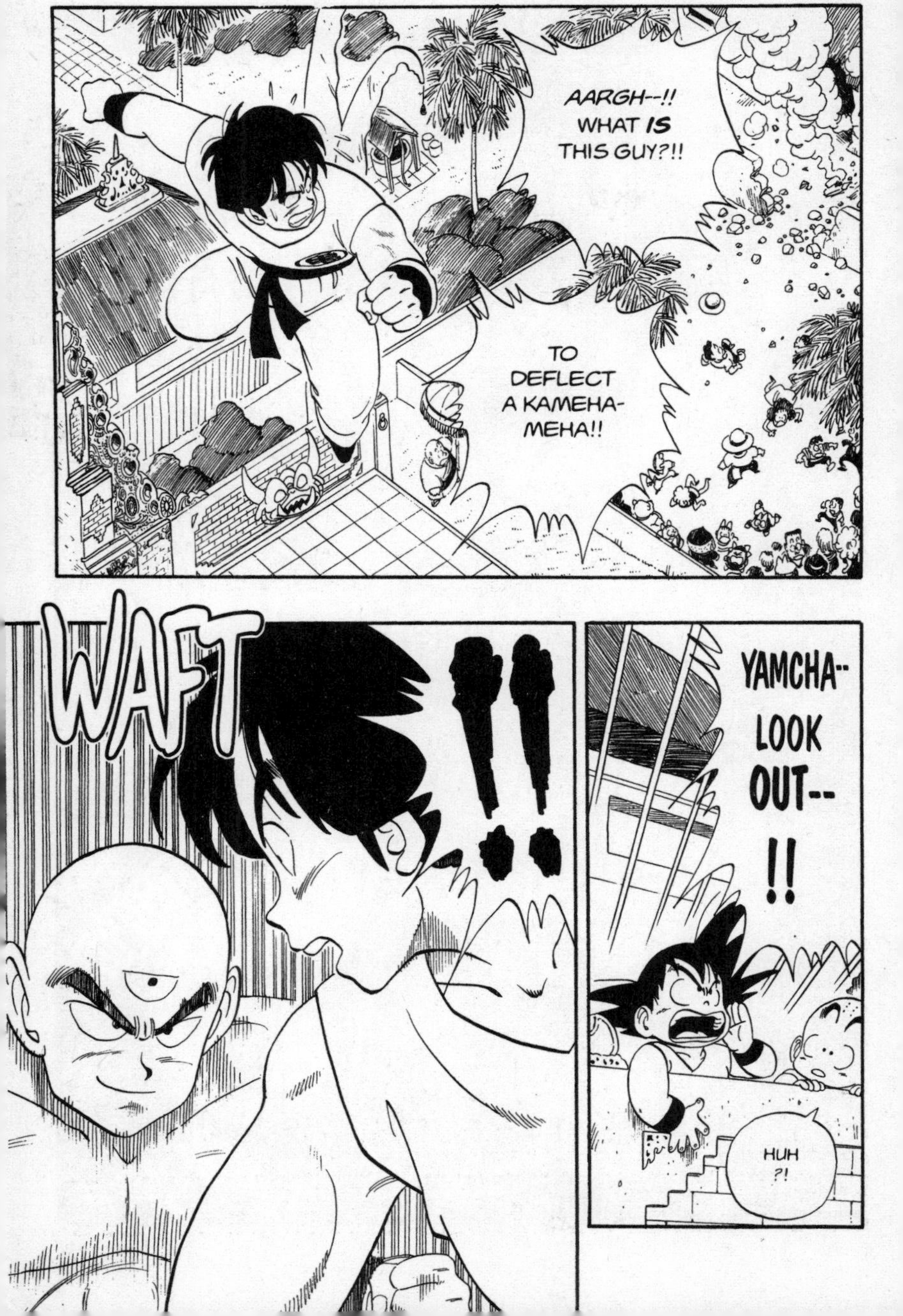
AARGH--!! WHAT **IS** THIS GUY?!!
TO DEFLECT A KAMEHA-MEHA!!
YAMCHA-- LOOK OUT-- !!
HUH ?!
WAFT
!!

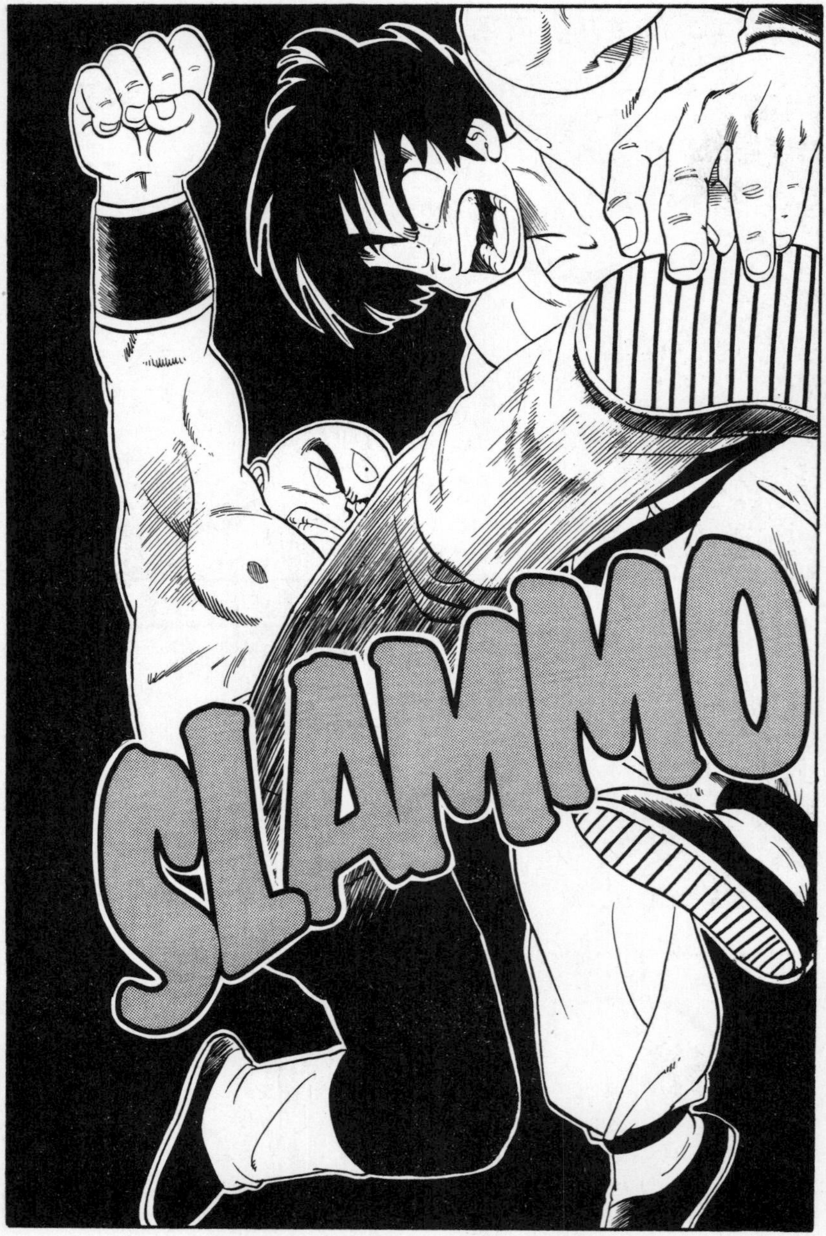
SLAMMO

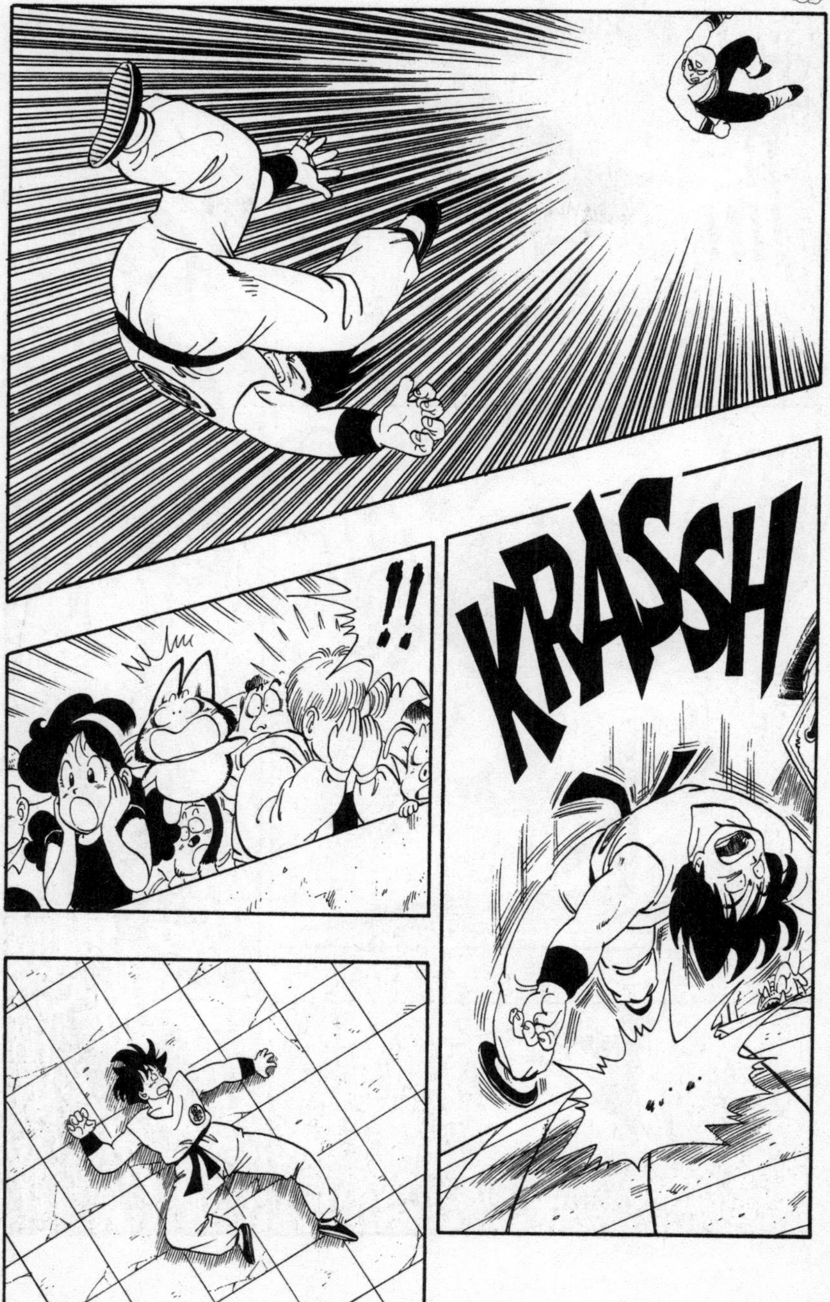
KRASSH
!!

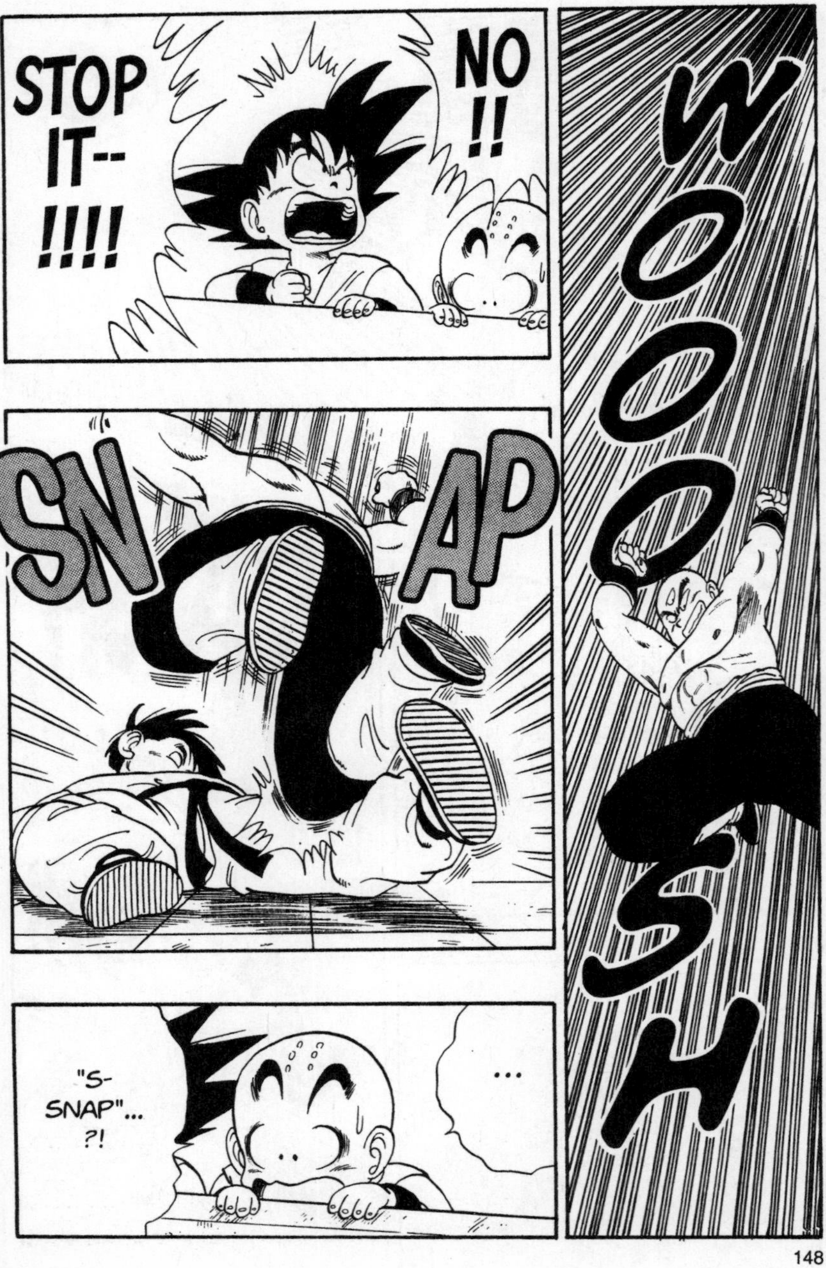
WOOOOSH
NO!!
STOP IT--!!!!
SNAP
...
"S-SNAP"...?!

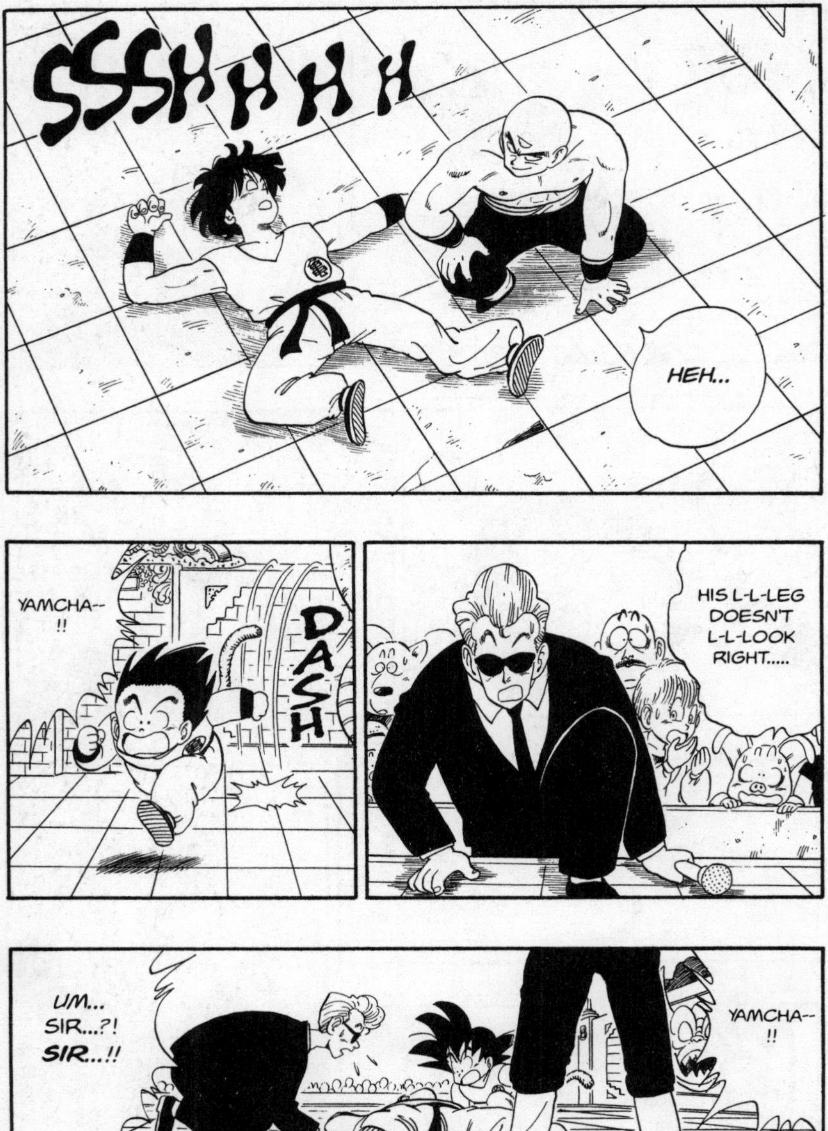

SSSHHHH
HEH...
HIS L-L-LEG DOESN'T L-L-LOOK RIGHT.....
YAMCHA-- !!
DASH
YAMCHA-- !!
UM... SIR...?! SIR...!!

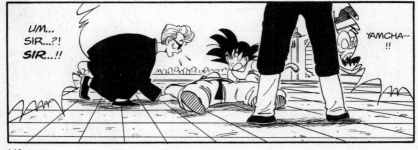

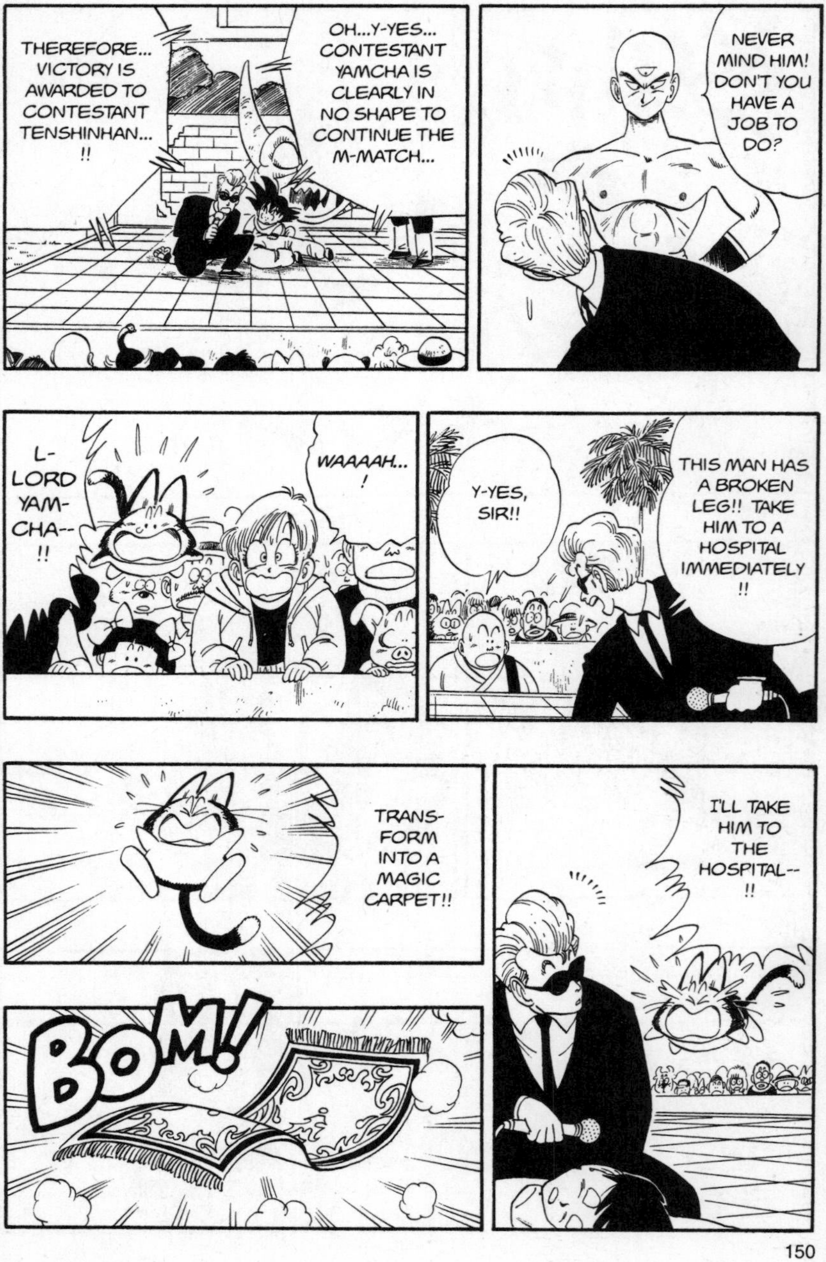
NEVER MIND HIM! DON'T YOU HAVE A JOB TO DO?
OH...Y-YES... CONTESTANT YAMCHA IS CLEARLY IN NO SHAPE TO CONTINUE THE M-MATCH...
THEREFORE... VICTORY IS AWARDED TO CONTESTANT TENSHINHAN... !!
THIS MAN HAS A BROKEN LEG!! TAKE HIM TO A HOSPITAL IMMEDIATELY !!
Y-YES, SIR!!
WAAAAH... !
L- LORD YAM- CHA-- !!
I'LL TAKE HIM TO THE HOSPITAL-- !!
TRANS- FORM INTO A MAGIC CARPET!!
BOM!

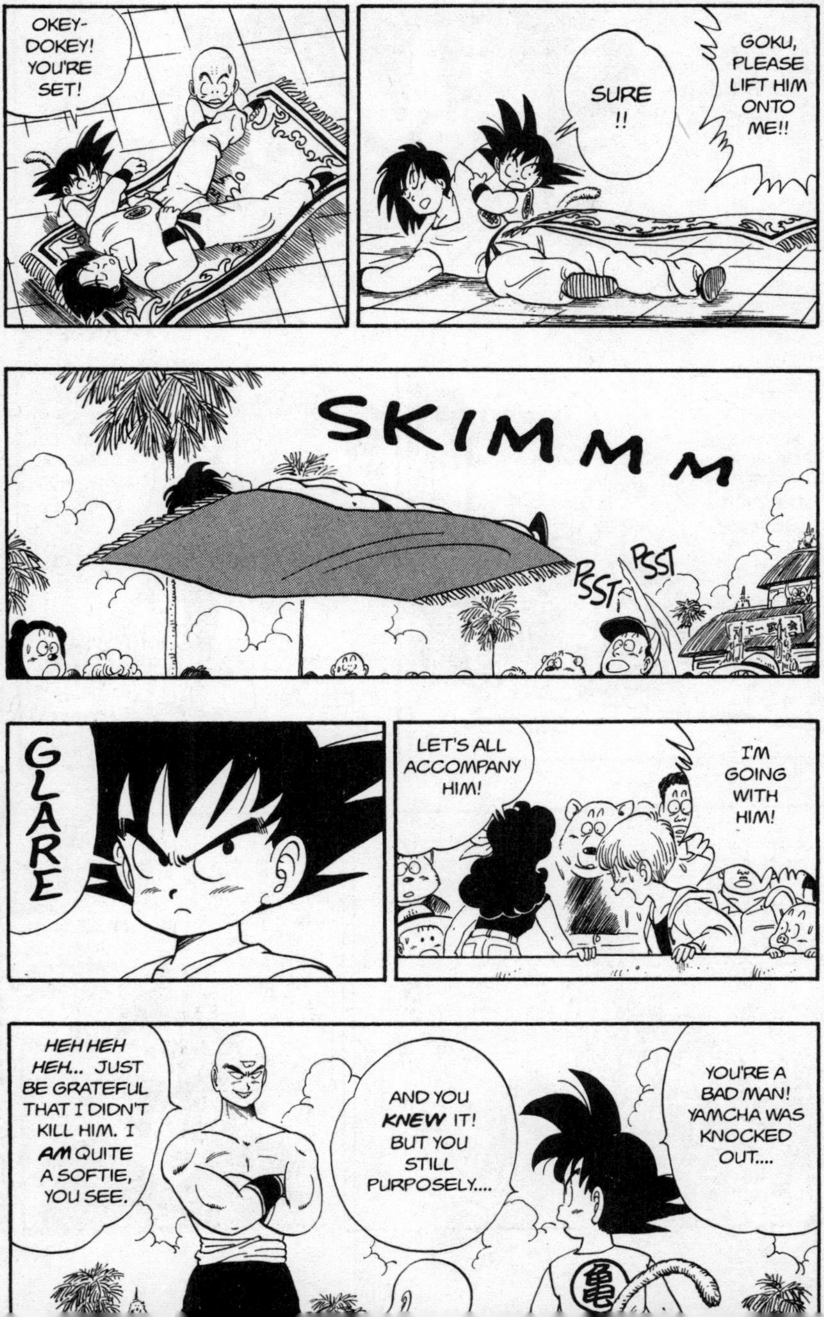
GOKU, PLEASE LIFT HIM ONTO ME!!
SURE!!
OKEY-DOKEY! YOU'RE SET!
SKIMMMM
PSST
PSST
I'M GOING WITH HIM!
LET'S ALL ACCOMPANY HIM!
GLARE
YOU'RE A BAD MAN! YAMCHA WAS KNOCKED OUT....
AND YOU KNEW IT! BUT YOU STILL PURPOSELY....
HEH HEH HEH... JUST BE GRATEFUL THAT I DIDN'T KILL HIM. I AM QUITE A SOFTIE, YOU SEE.

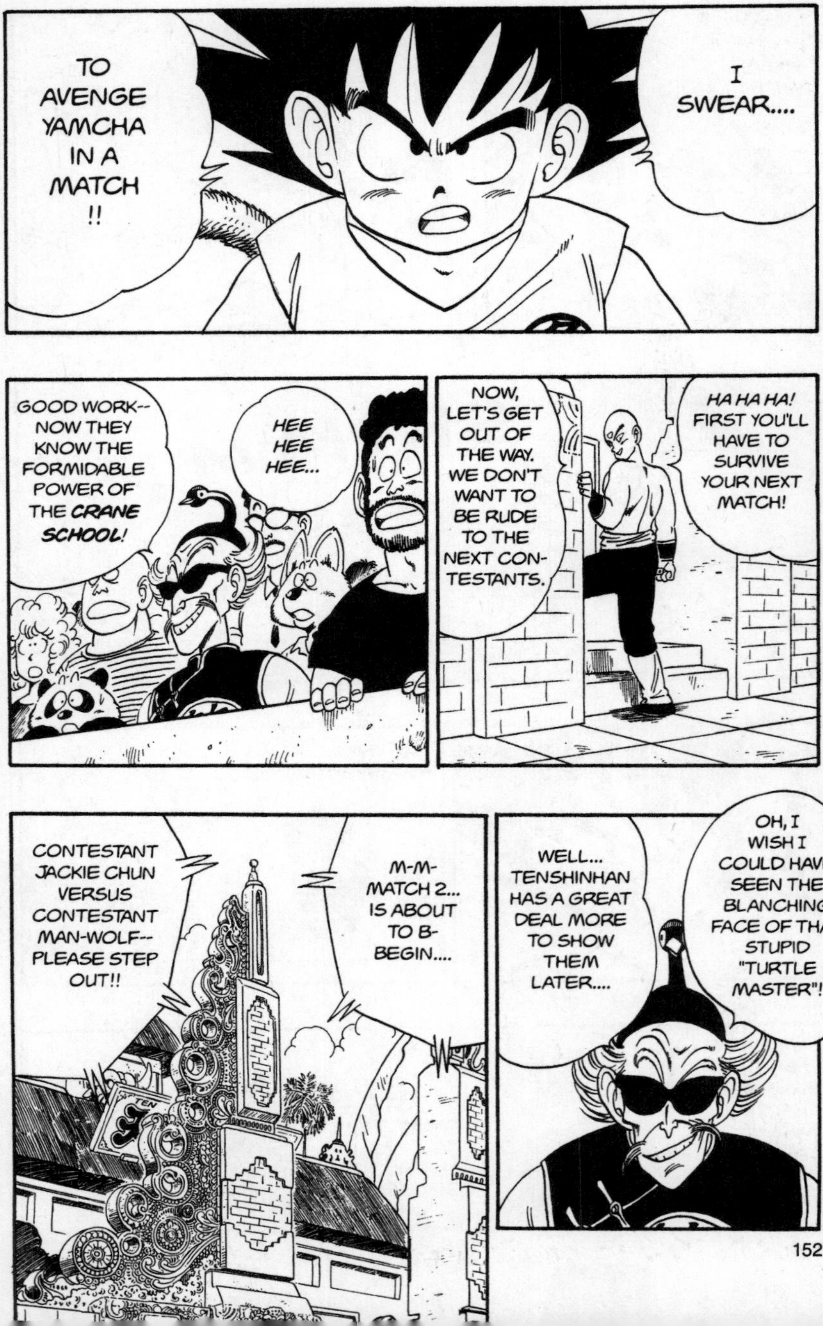
I SWEAR....
TO AVENGE YAMCHA IN A MATCH !!
HA HA HA! FIRST YOU'LL HAVE TO SURVIVE YOUR NEXT MATCH!
NOW, LET'S GET OUT OF THE WAY. WE DON'T WANT TO BE RUDE TO THE NEXT CONTESTANTS.
HEE HEE HEE...
GOOD WORK-- NOW THEY KNOW THE FORMIDABLE POWER OF THE CRANE SCHOOL!
OH, I WISH I COULD HAVE SEEN THE BLANCHING FACE OF THAT STUPID "TURTLE MASTER"!
WELL... TENSHINHAN HAS A GREAT DEAL MORE TO SHOW THEM LATER....
M-M-MATCH 2... IS ABOUT TO B-BEGIN....
CONTESTANT JACKIE CHUN VERSUS CONTESTANT MAN-WOLF-- PLEASE STEP OUT!!

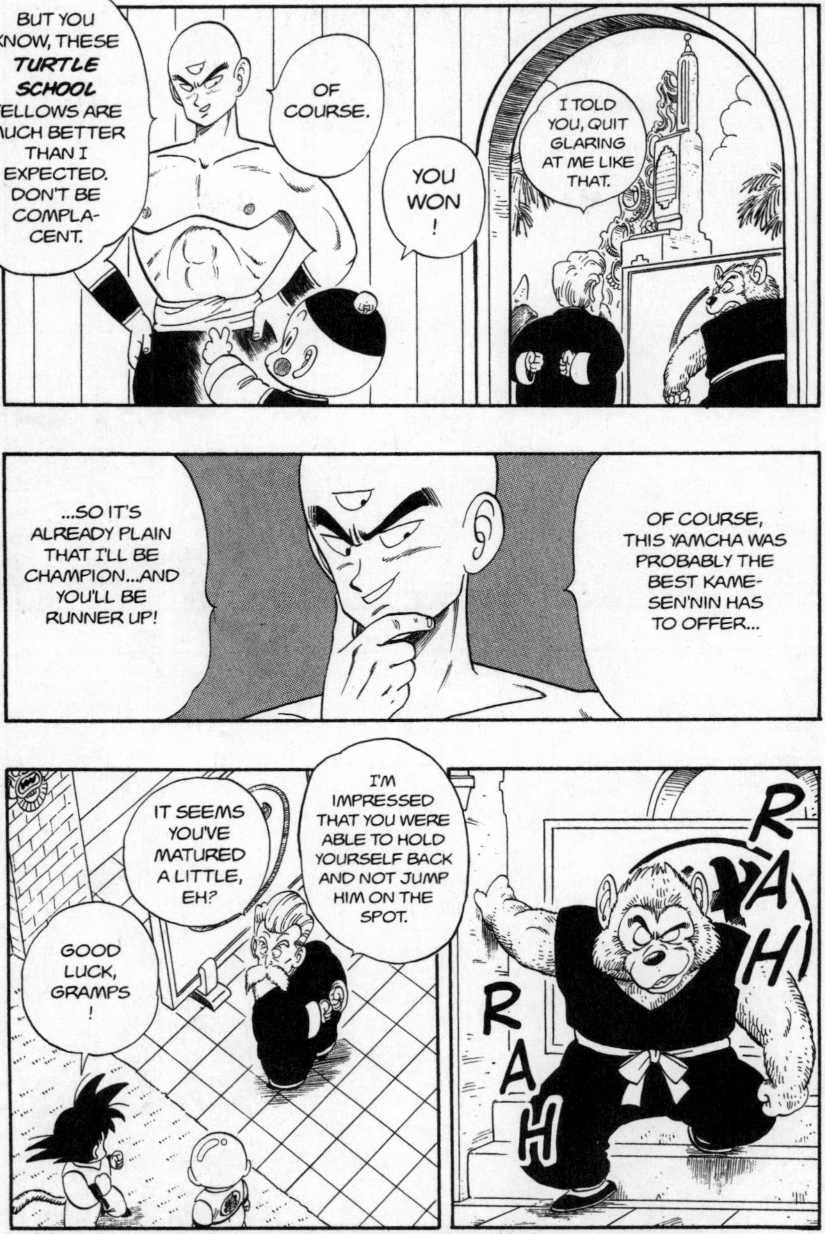
I TOLD YOU, QUIT GLARING AT ME LIKE THAT.
YOU WON!
OF COURSE.
BUT YOU KNOW, THESE **TURTLE SCHOOL** FELLOWS ARE MUCH BETTER THAN I EXPECTED. DON'T BE COMPLA-CENT.
OF COURSE, THIS YAMCHA WAS PROBABLY THE BEST KAME-SEN'NIN HAS TO OFFER...
...SO IT'S ALREADY PLAIN THAT I'LL BE CHAMPION...AND YOU'LL BE RUNNER UP!
RAHRAH
I'M IMPRESSED THAT YOU WERE ABLE TO HOLD YOURSELF BACK AND NOT JUMP HIM ON THE SPOT.
IT SEEMS YOU'VE MATURED A LITTLE, EH?
GOOD LUCK, GRAMPS!

NEXT: The Moon Belongs to Man-Wolves

Tale 11
The Full Moon Grudge

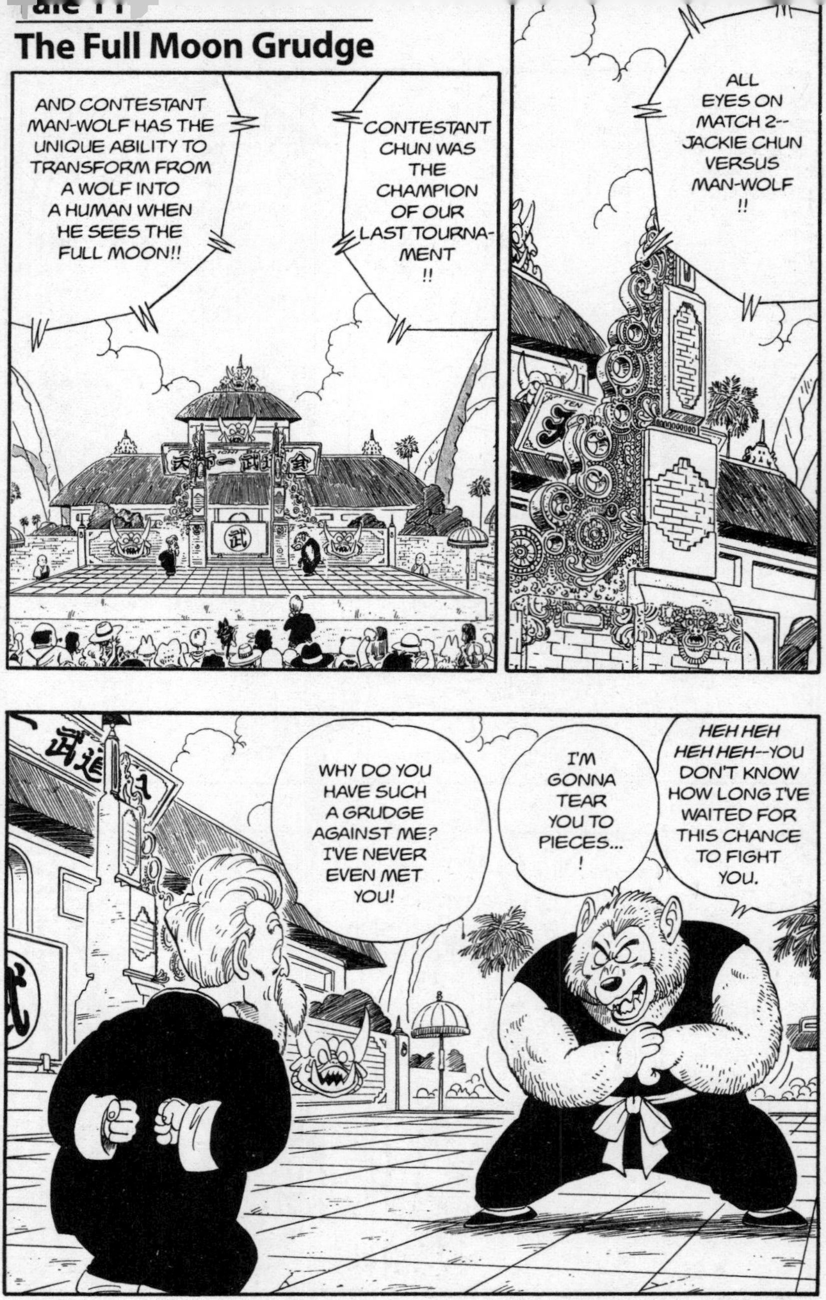
ALL EYES ON MATCH 2-- JACKIE CHUN VERSUS MAN-WOLF !!
CONTESTANT CHUN WAS THE CHAMPION OF OUR LAST TOURNAMENT !!
AND CONTESTANT MAN-WOLF HAS THE UNIQUE ABILITY TO TRANSFORM FROM A WOLF INTO A HUMAN WHEN HE SEES THE FULL MOON!!
HEH HEH HEH HEH--YOU DON'T KNOW HOW LONG I'VE WAITED FOR THIS CHANCE TO FIGHT YOU.
I'M GONNA TEAR YOU TO PIECES... !
WHY DO YOU HAVE SUCH A GRUDGE AGAINST ME? I'VE NEVER EVEN MET YOU!

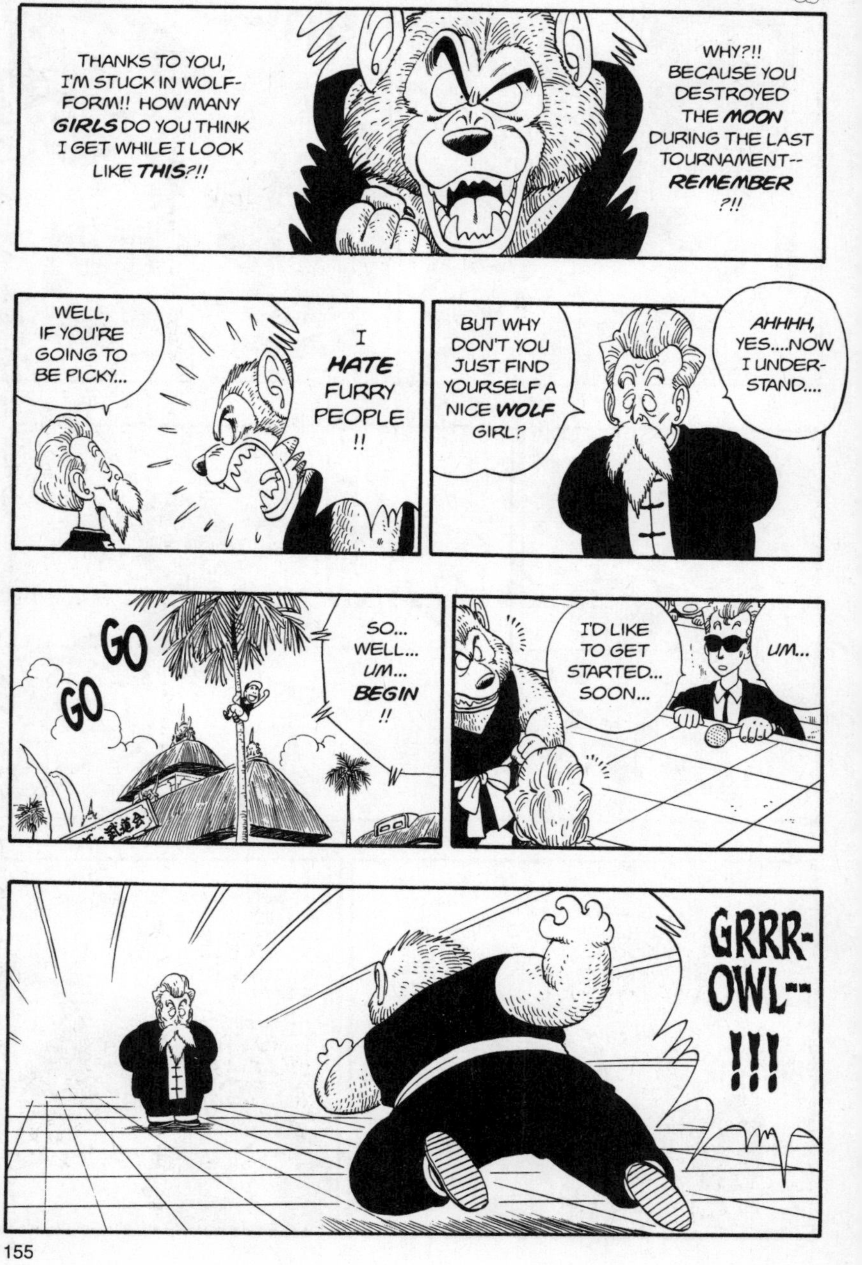
WHY?!! BECAUSE YOU DESTROYED THE MOON DURING THE LAST TOURNAMENT-- REMEMBER ?!!
THANKS TO YOU, I'M STUCK IN WOLF-FORM!! HOW MANY GIRLS DO YOU THINK I GET WHILE I LOOK LIKE THIS?!!
AHHHH, YES....NOW I UNDERSTAND....
BUT WHY DON'T YOU JUST FIND YOURSELF A NICE WOLF GIRL?
I HATE FURRY PEOPLE !!
WELL, IF YOU'RE GOING TO BE PICKY...
UM...
I'D LIKE TO GET STARTED... SOON...
SO... WELL... UM... BEGIN !!
GO
GO
GRRR-OWL-- !!!

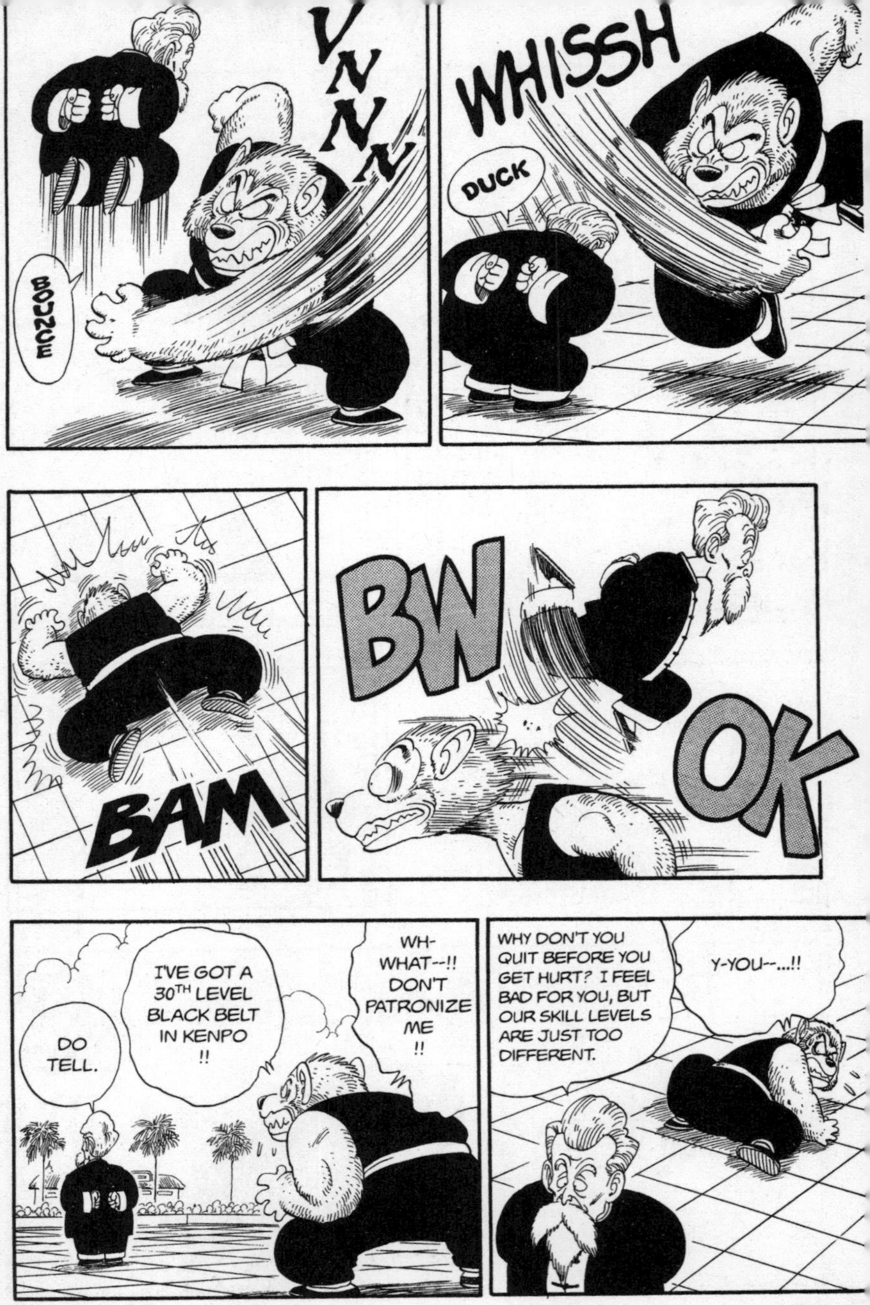
WHISSH
DUCK
VNNN
BOUNCE
BW
OK
BAM
WHY DON'T YOU QUIT BEFORE YOU GET HURT? I FEEL BAD FOR YOU, BUT OUR SKILL LEVELS ARE JUST TOO DIFFERENT.
Y-YOU--...!!
WH- WHAT--!! DON'T PATRONIZE ME !!
I'VE GOT A 30TH LEVEL BLACK BELT IN KENPO !!
DO TELL.

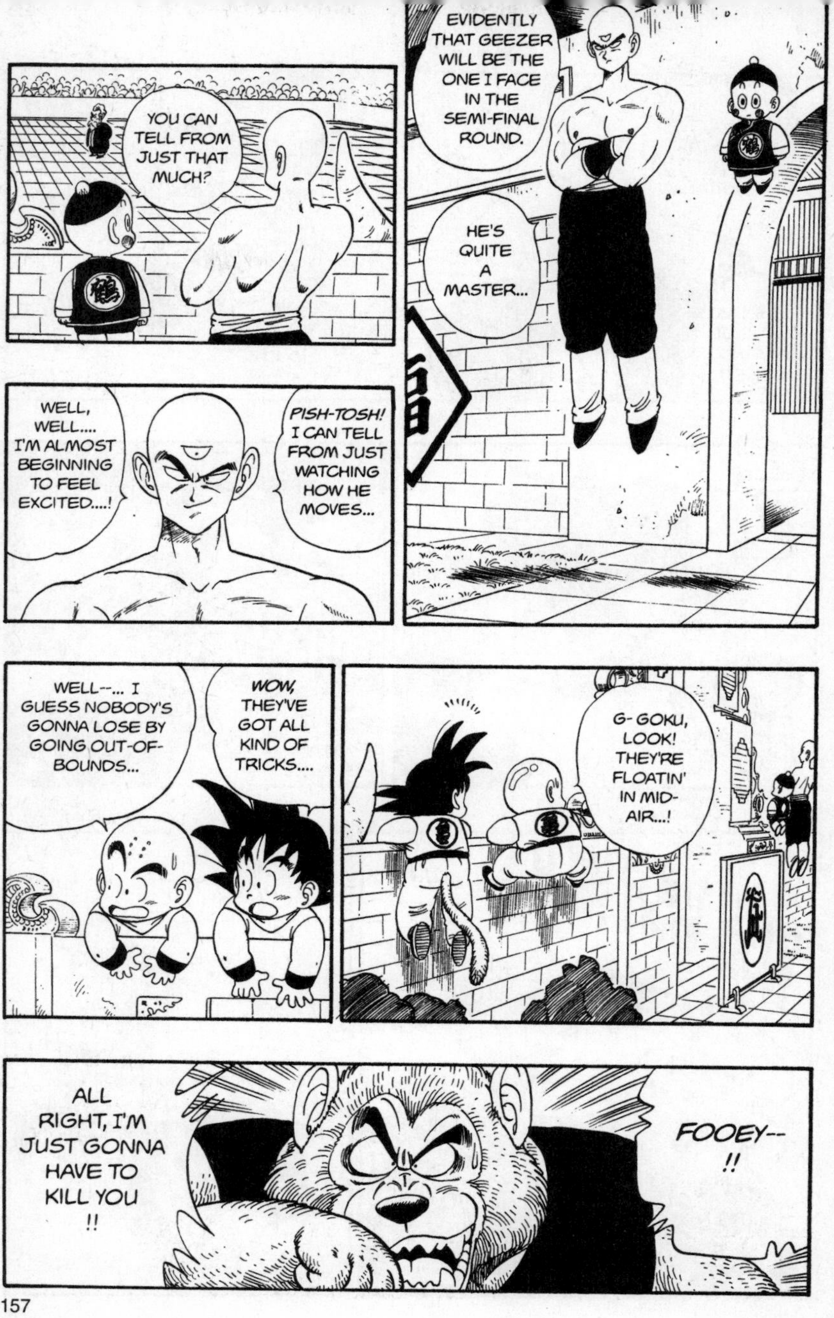
EVIDENTLY THAT GEEZER WILL BE THE ONE I FACE IN THE SEMI-FINAL ROUND.
HE'S QUITE A MASTER...
YOU CAN TELL FROM JUST THAT MUCH?
PISH-TOSH! I CAN TELL FROM JUST WATCHING HOW HE MOVES...
WELL, WELL.... I'M ALMOST BEGINNING TO FEEL EXCITED....!
G- GOKU, LOOK! THEY'RE FLOATIN' IN MID-AIR...!
WOW, THEY'VE GOT ALL KIND OF TRICKS....
WELL--... I GUESS NOBODY'S GONNA LOSE BY GOING OUT-OF-BOUNDS...
FOOEY--!!
ALL RIGHT, I'M JUST GONNA HAVE TO KILL YOU !!

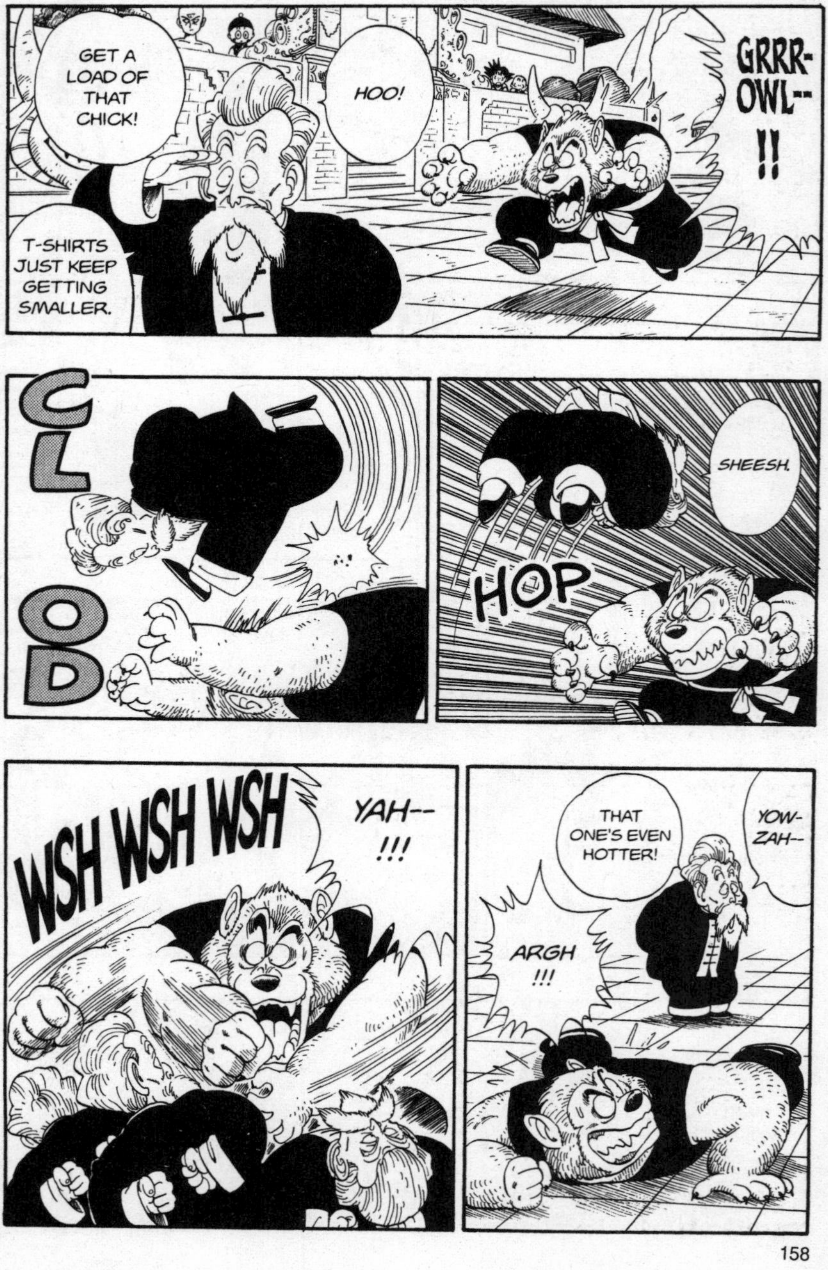
GRRR-OWL--!!
HOO!
GET A LOAD OF THAT CHICK!
T-SHIRTS JUST KEEP GETTING SMALLER.
SHEESH.
HOP
CLOD
YOW-ZAH--
THAT ONE'S EVEN HOTTER!
ARGH!!!
YAH--!!!
WSH WSH WSH

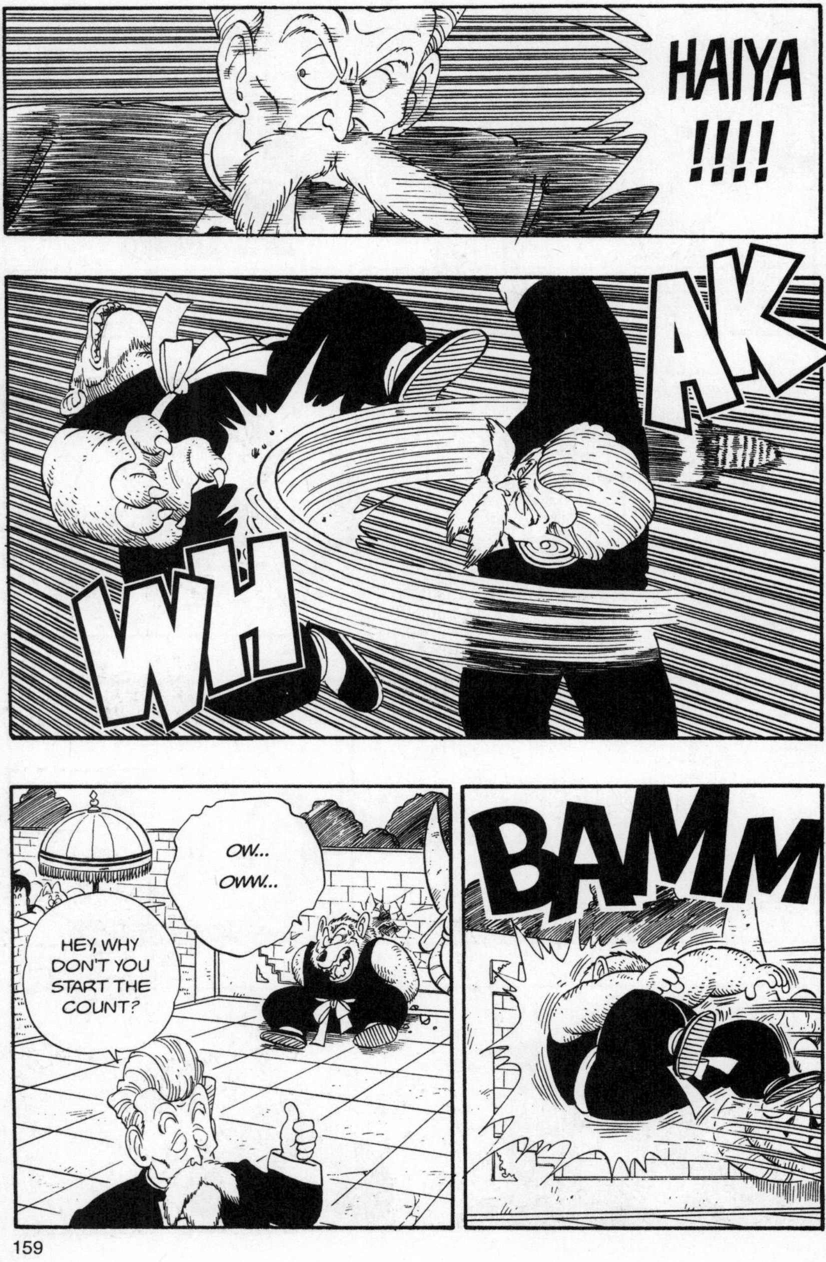
HAIYA !!!!
AK
WH
BAMM
OW... OWW...
HEY, WHY DON'T YOU START THE COUNT?

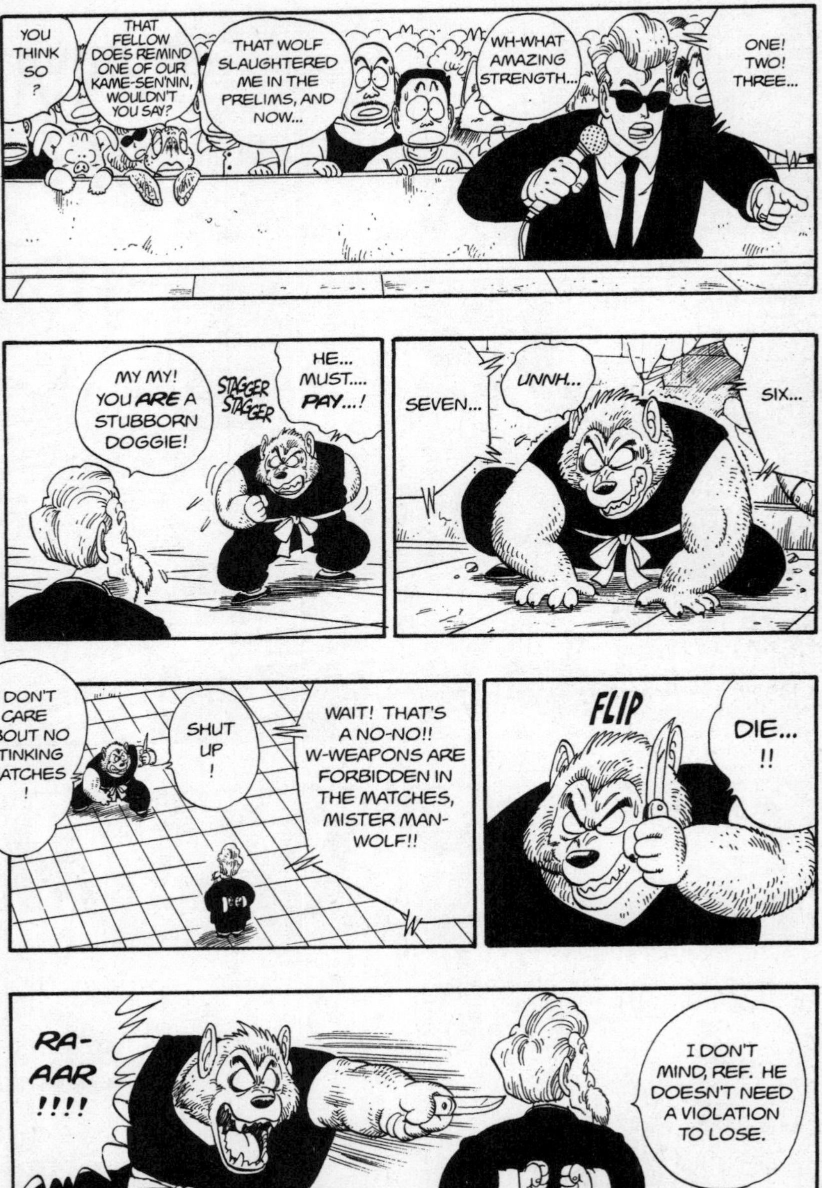
ONE! TWO! THREE...
WH-WHAT AMAZING STRENGTH...
THAT WOLF SLAUGHTERED ME IN THE PRELIMS, AND NOW...
THAT FELLOW DOES REMIND ONE OF OUR KAME-SEN'NIN, WOULDN'T YOU SAY?
YOU THINK SO?
SIX...
UNNH...
SEVEN...
HE... MUST.... PAY...!
STAGGER STAGGER
MY MY! YOU ARE A STUBBORN DOGGIE!
FLIP
DIE... !!
WAIT! THAT'S A NO-NO!! W-WEAPONS ARE FORBIDDEN IN THE MATCHES, MISTER MAN-WOLF!!
SHUT UP!
I DON'T CARE ABOUT NO STINKING MATCHES!
I DON'T MIND, REF. HE DOESN'T NEED A VIOLATION TO LOSE.
RA-AAR!!!!

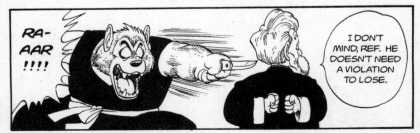

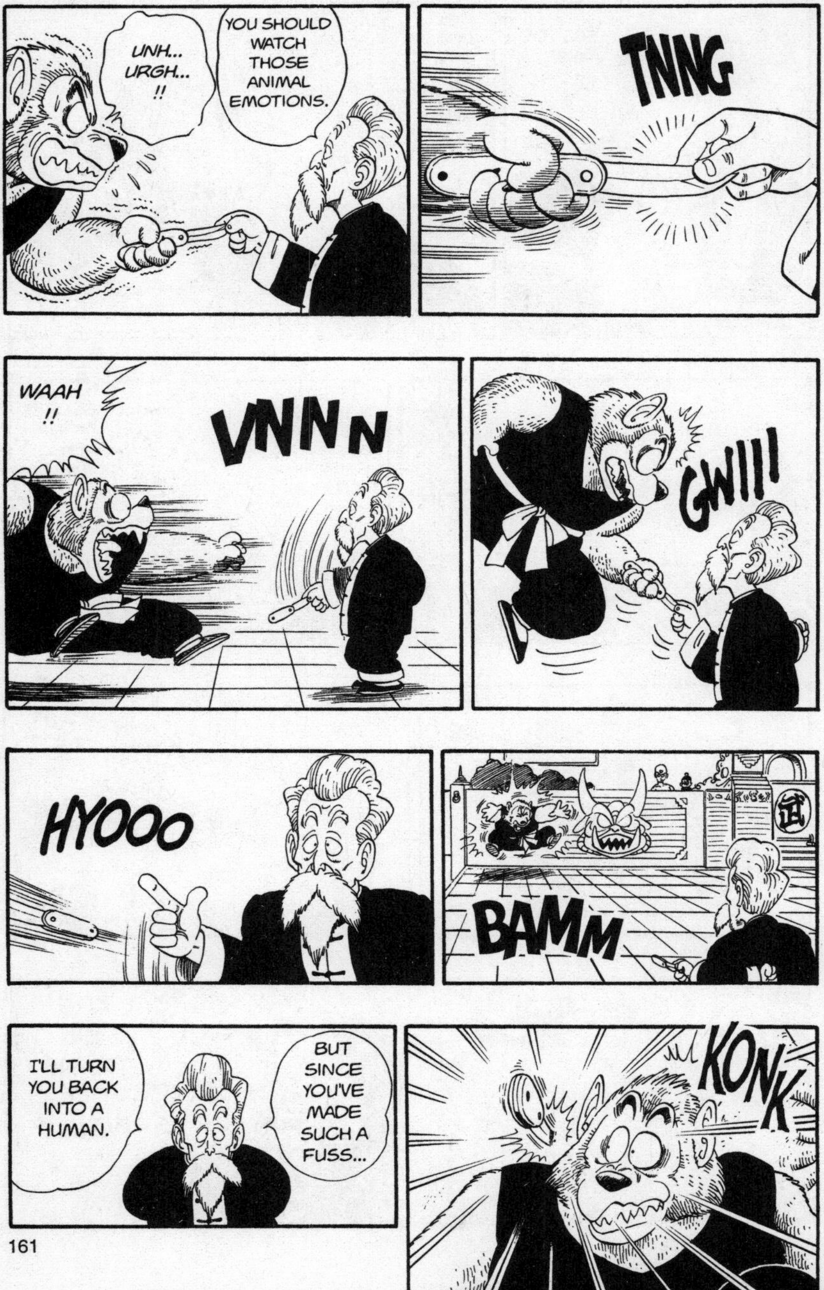
TNNG
YOU SHOULD WATCH THOSE ANIMAL EMOTIONS.
UNH... URGH... !!
GWIII
VNNN
WAAH !!
BAMM
HYOOO
KONK
BUT SINCE YOU'VE MADE SUCH A FUSS...
I'LL TURN YOU BACK INTO A HUMAN.

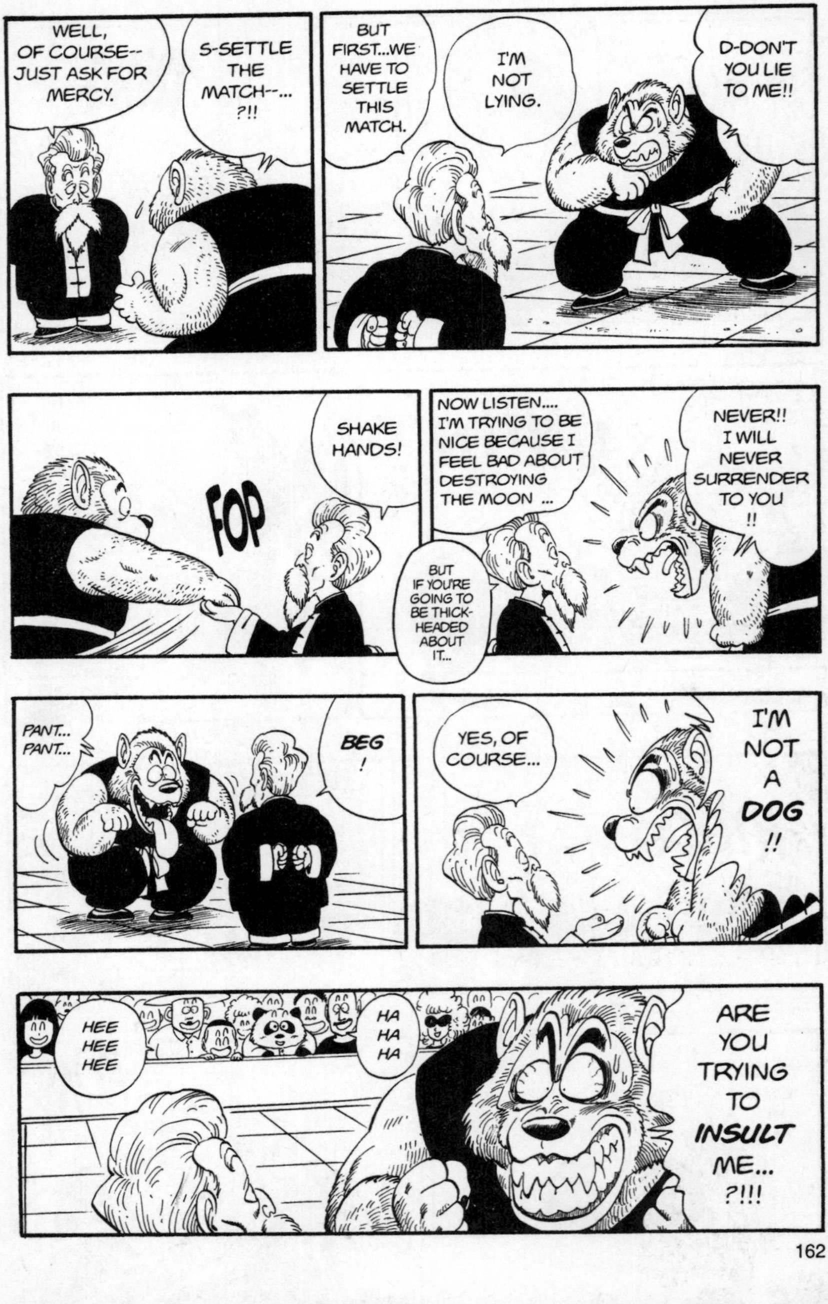
D-DON'T YOU LIE TO ME!!
I'M NOT LYING.
BUT FIRST...WE HAVE TO SETTLE THIS MATCH.
S-SETTLE THE MATCH--...?!!
WELL, OF COURSE-- JUST ASK FOR MERCY.
NEVER!! I WILL NEVER SURRENDER TO YOU!!
NOW LISTEN.... I'M TRYING TO BE NICE BECAUSE I FEEL BAD ABOUT DESTROYING THE MOON ...
BUT IF YOU'RE GOING TO BE THICK-HEADED ABOUT IT...
SHAKE HANDS!
FOP
I'M NOT A DOG!!
YES, OF COURSE...
BEG!
PANT... PANT...
ARE YOU TRYING TO INSULT ME...?!!!
HA HA HA
HEE HEE HEE

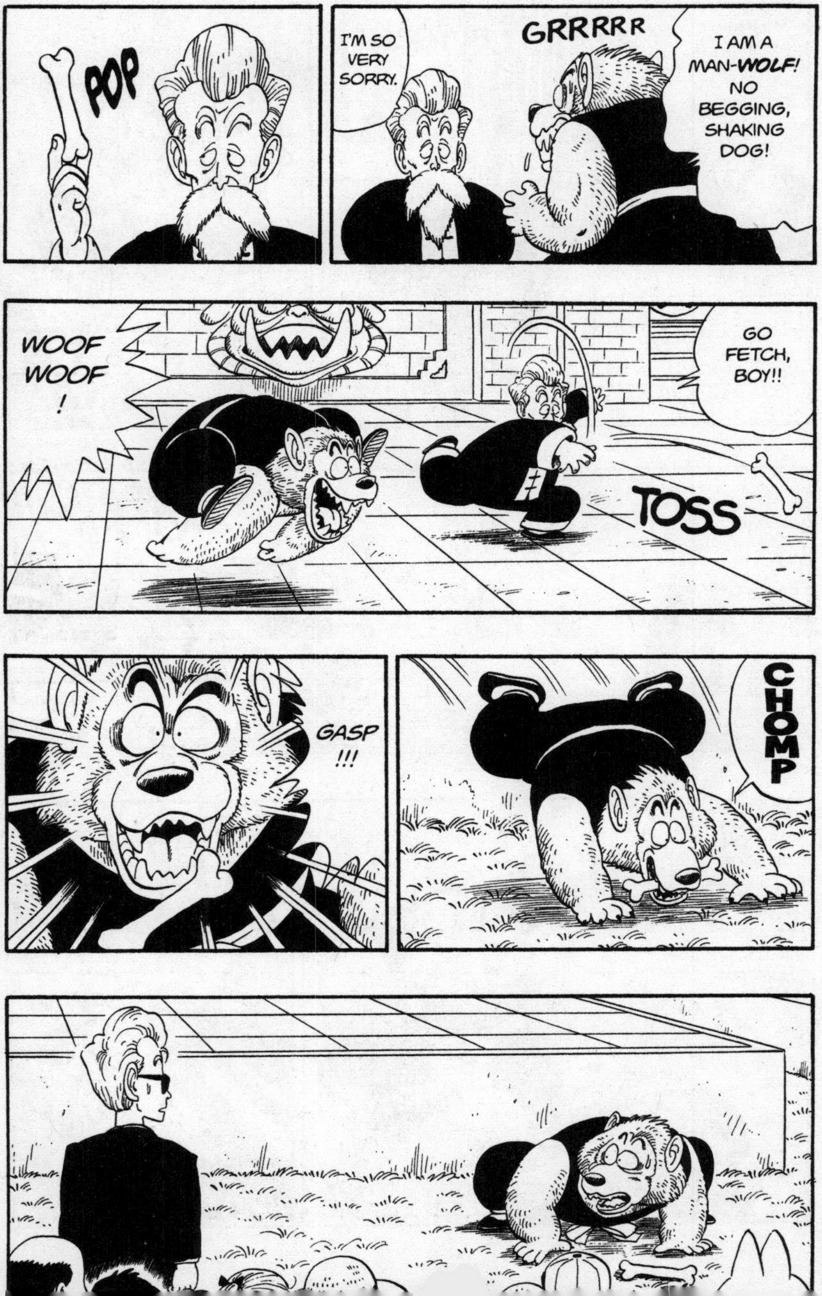
I AM A MAN-WOLF! NO BEGGING, SHAKING DOG!
GRRRRR
I'M SO VERY SORRY.
POP
GO FETCH, BOY!!
TOSS
WOOF WOOF !
CHOMP
GASP !!!

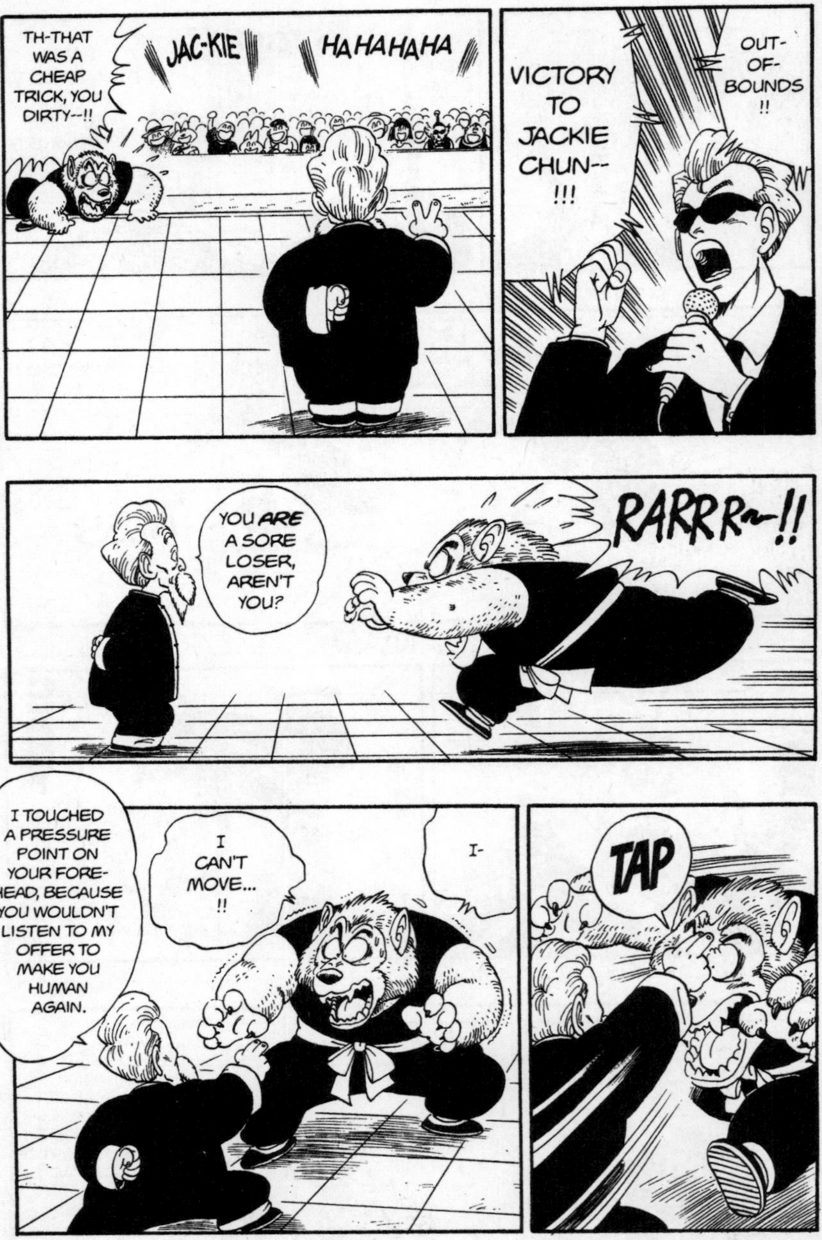
OUT-OF-BOUNDS !!
VICTORY TO JACKIE CHUN-- !!!
HAHAHAHA
JAC-KIE
TH-THAT WAS A CHEAP TRICK, YOU DIRTY--!!
RARRR~!!
YOU *ARE* A SORE LOSER, AREN'T YOU?
TAP
I-
I CAN'T MOVE... !!
I TOUCHED A PRESSURE POINT ON YOUR FORE-HEAD, BECAUSE YOU WOULDN'T LISTEN TO MY OFFER TO MAKE YOU HUMAN AGAIN.

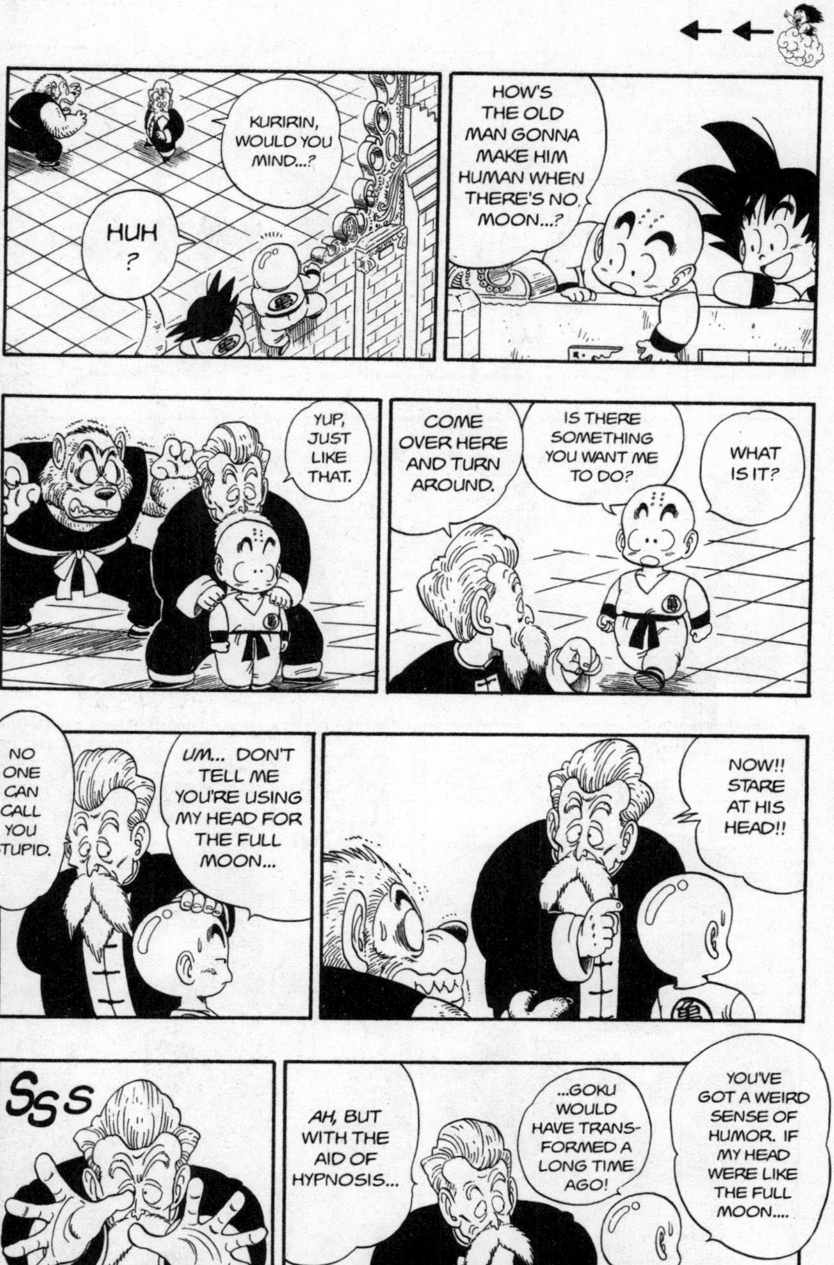
HOW'S THE OLD MAN GONNA MAKE HIM HUMAN WHEN THERE'S NO MOON...?
KURIRIN, WOULD YOU MIND...?
HUH ?
WHAT IS IT?
IS THERE SOMETHING YOU WANT ME TO DO?
COME OVER HERE AND TURN AROUND.
YUP, JUST LIKE THAT.
NOW!! STARE AT HIS HEAD!!
UM... DON'T TELL ME YOU'RE USING MY HEAD FOR THE FULL MOON...
NO ONE CAN CALL YOU STUPID.
YOU'VE GOT A WEIRD SENSE OF HUMOR. IF MY HEAD WERE LIKE THE FULL MOON....
...GOKU WOULD HAVE TRANSFORMED A LONG TIME AGO!
AH, BUT WITH THE AID OF HYPNOSIS...
SSS

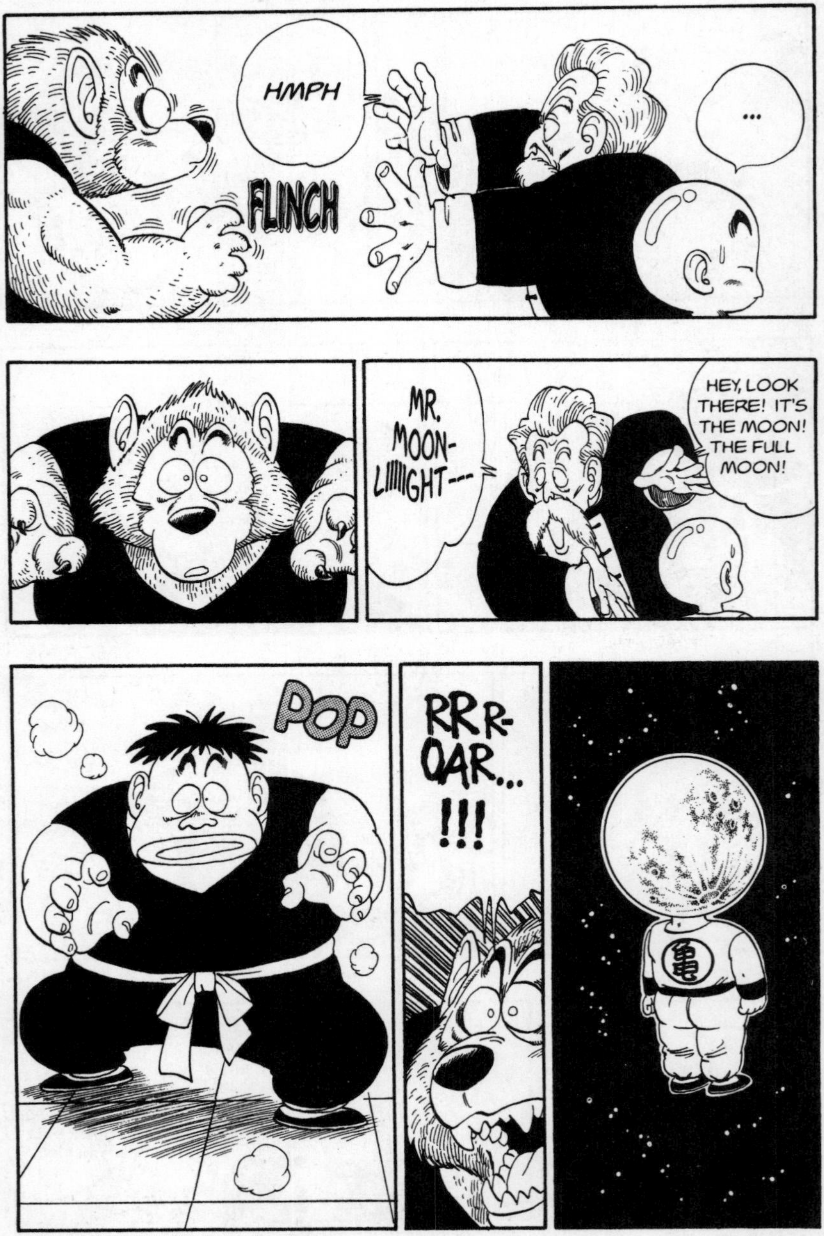
...
HMPH
FLINCH
HEY, LOOK THERE! IT'S THE MOON! THE FULL MOON!
MR. MOON-LIIIIGHT---
RRR-OAR... !!!
POP

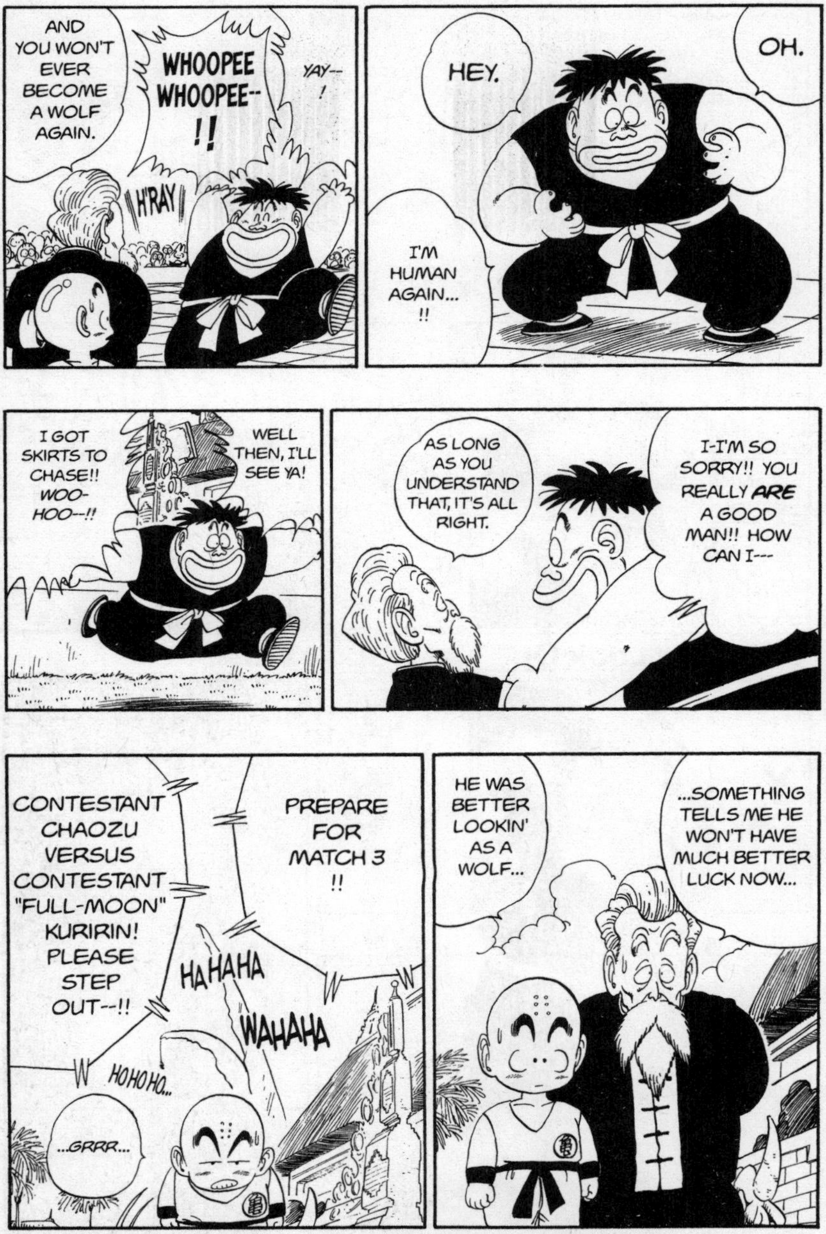
OH.
HEY.
I'M HUMAN AGAIN... !!
YAY-- !
WHOOPEE WHOOPEE-- !!
AND YOU WON'T EVER BECOME A WOLF AGAIN.
H'RAY
I-I'M SO SORRY!! YOU REALLY ARE A GOOD MAN!! HOW CAN I---
AS LONG AS YOU UNDERSTAND THAT, IT'S ALL RIGHT.
WELL THEN, I'LL SEE YA!
I GOT SKIRTS TO CHASE!! WOO-HOO--!!
...SOMETHING TELLS ME HE WON'T HAVE MUCH BETTER LUCK NOW...
HE WAS BETTER LOOKIN' AS A WOLF...
PREPARE FOR MATCH 3 !!
CONTESTANT CHAOZU VERSUS CONTESTANT "FULL-MOON" KURIRIN! PLEASE STEP OUT--!!
HAHAHA
WAHAHA
HOHOHO...
...GRRR...

NEXT: Once Again... The Dodon Blast!

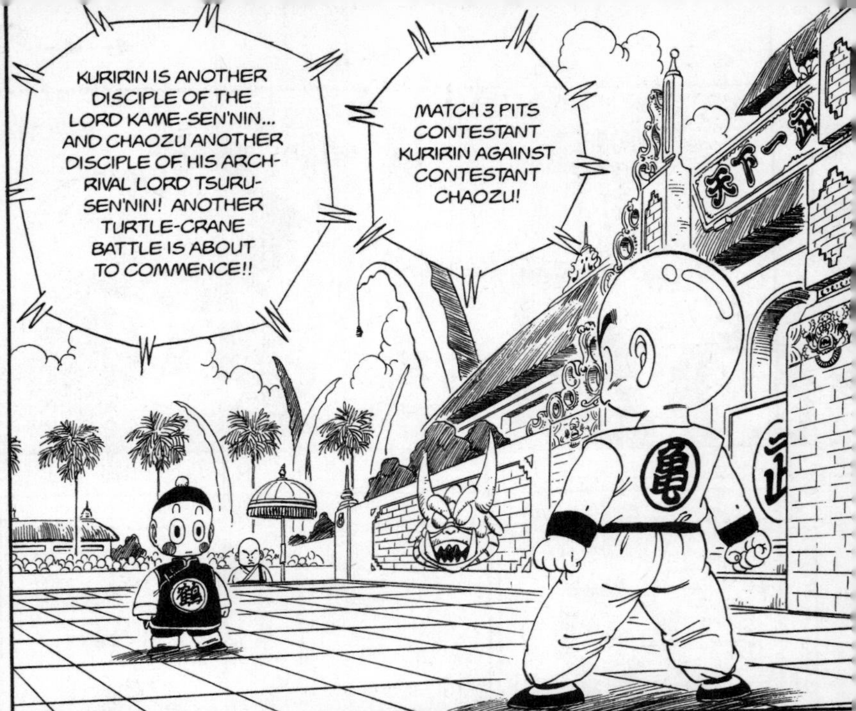
MATCH 3 PITS CONTESTANT KURIRIN AGAINST CONTESTANT CHAOZU!
KURIRIN IS ANOTHER DISCIPLE OF THE LORD KAME-SEN'NIN... AND CHAOZU ANOTHER DISCIPLE OF HIS ARCH-RIVAL LORD TSURU-SEN'NIN! ANOTHER TURTLE-CRANE BATTLE IS ABOUT TO COMMENCE!!

Tale 120 • Look Out! The Dodon Blast!

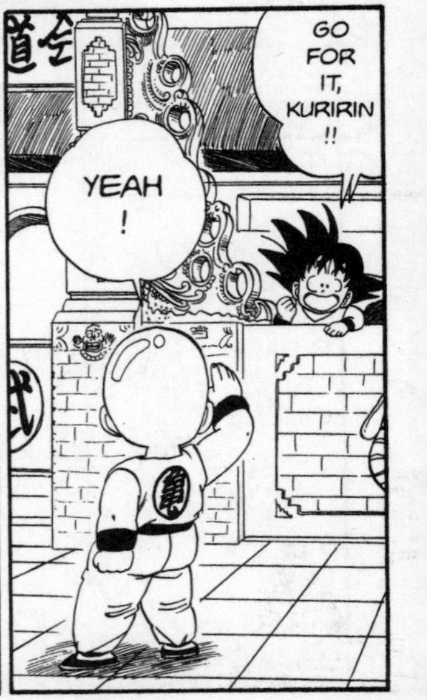
GO FOR IT, KURIRIN!!
YEAH!

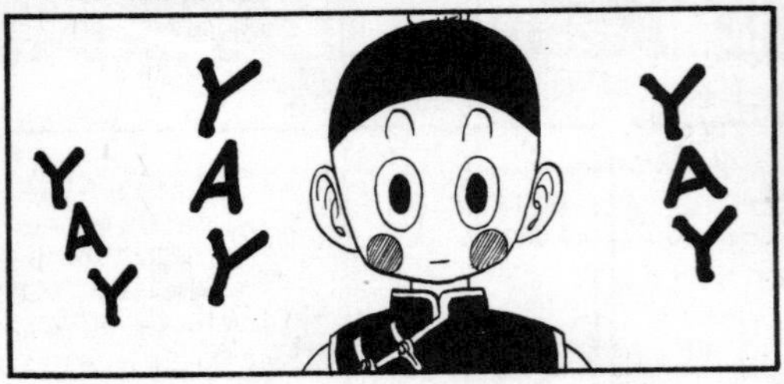
YAY
YAY
YAY

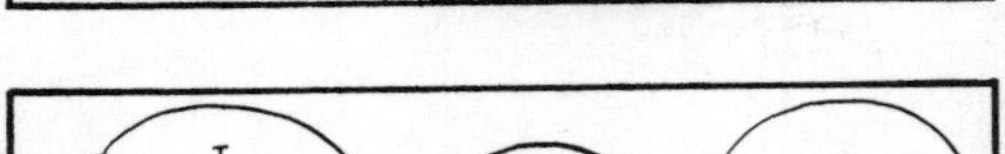
...I CAN'T TELL WHAT THIS GUY'S THINKING...
I SHOULDA PAID ATTENTION TO HIS FIGHTING STYLE DURING THE PRELIMS...

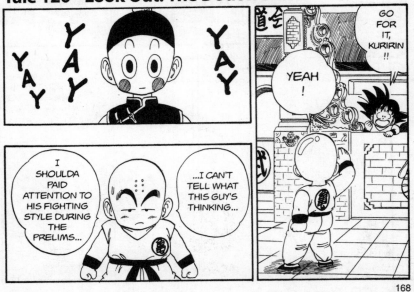

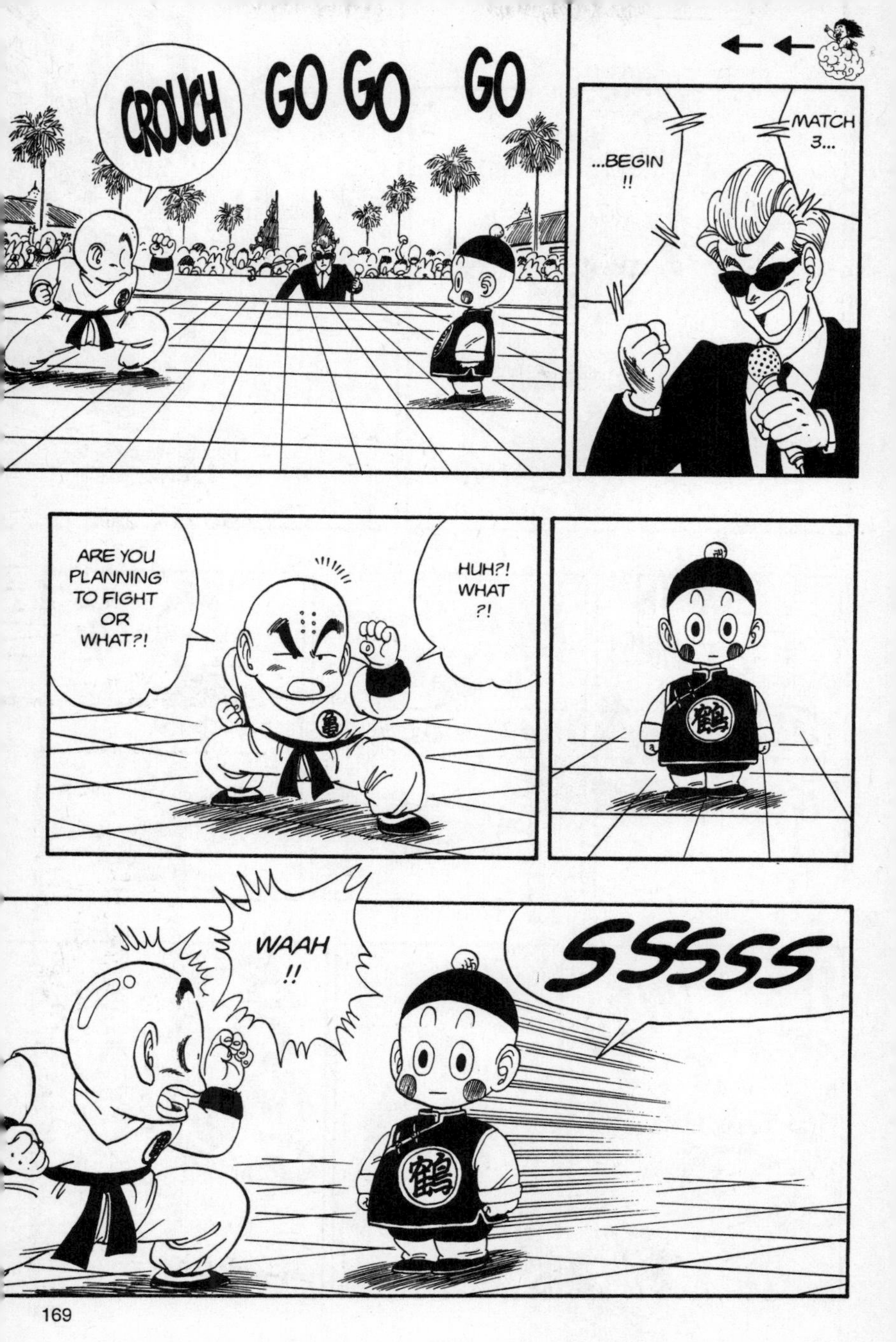
MATCH 3...
...BEGIN !!
CROUCH
GO GO GO
HUH?! WHAT?!
ARE YOU PLANNING TO FIGHT OR WHAT?!
SSSSS
WAAH !!

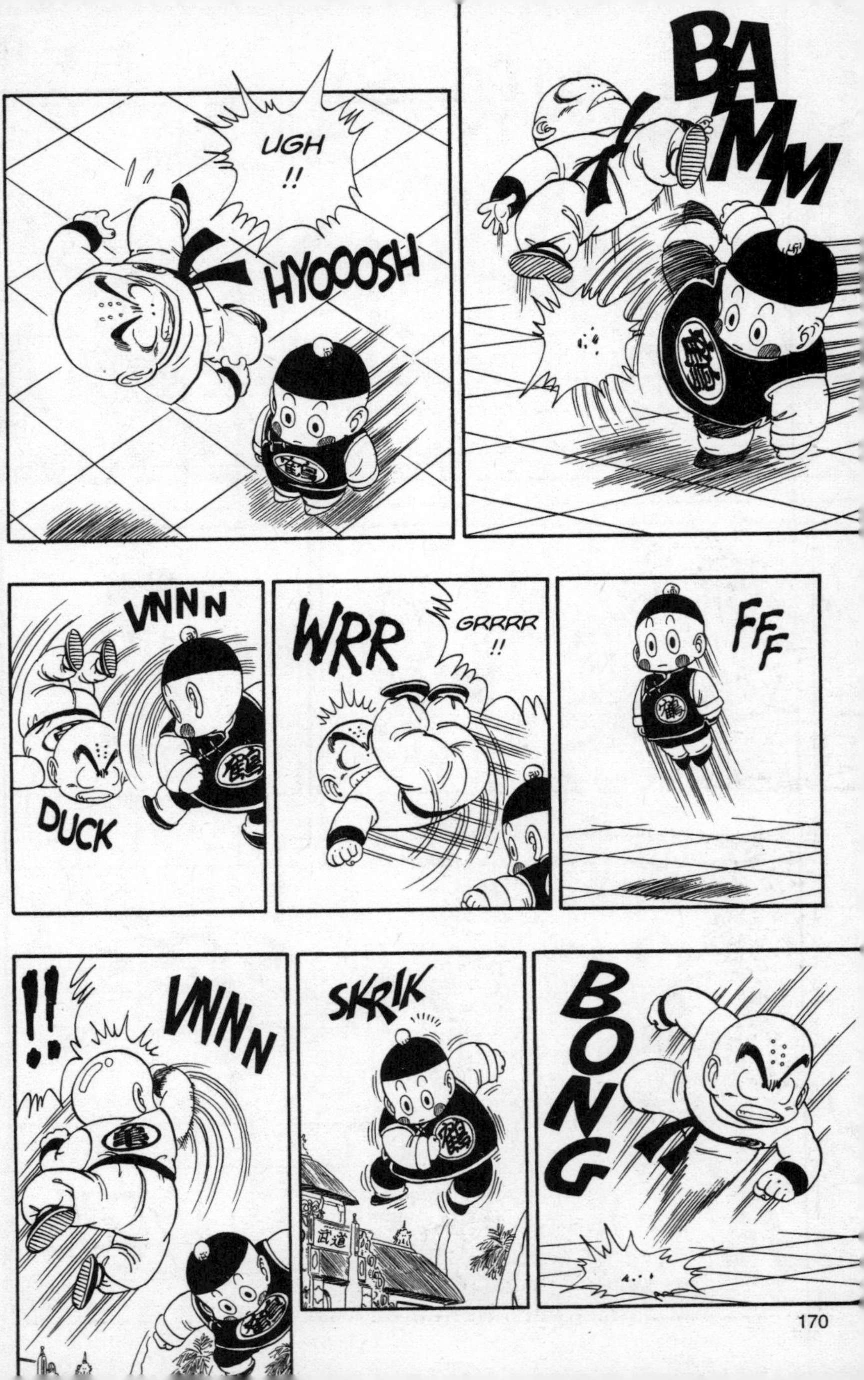

BAMM
UGH !!
HYOOOSH
FFF
WRR
GRRRR !!
VNNn
DUCK
BONG
SKRIK
!!
VNNn

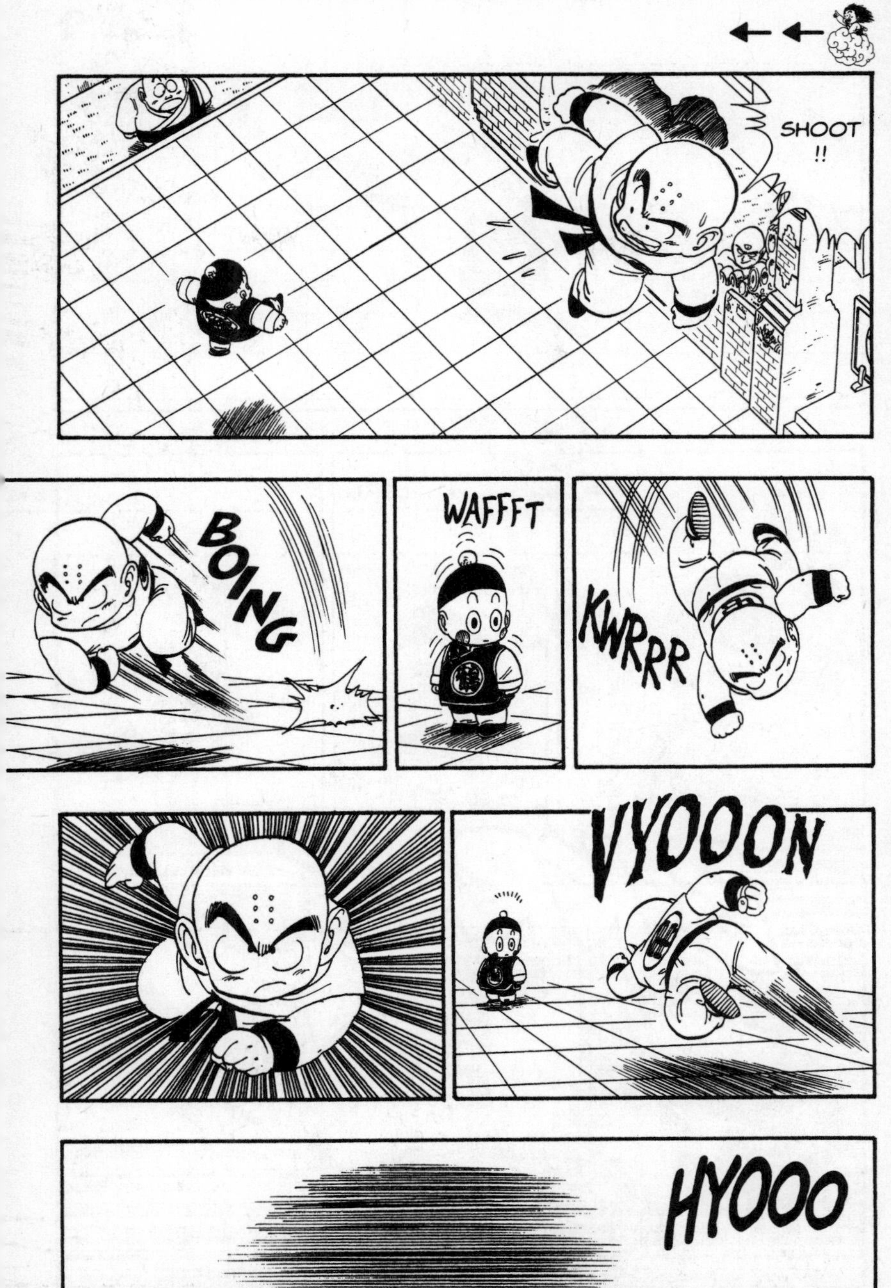
SHOOT
!!
KWRRR
WAFFFT
BOING
VYOOON
HYOOO

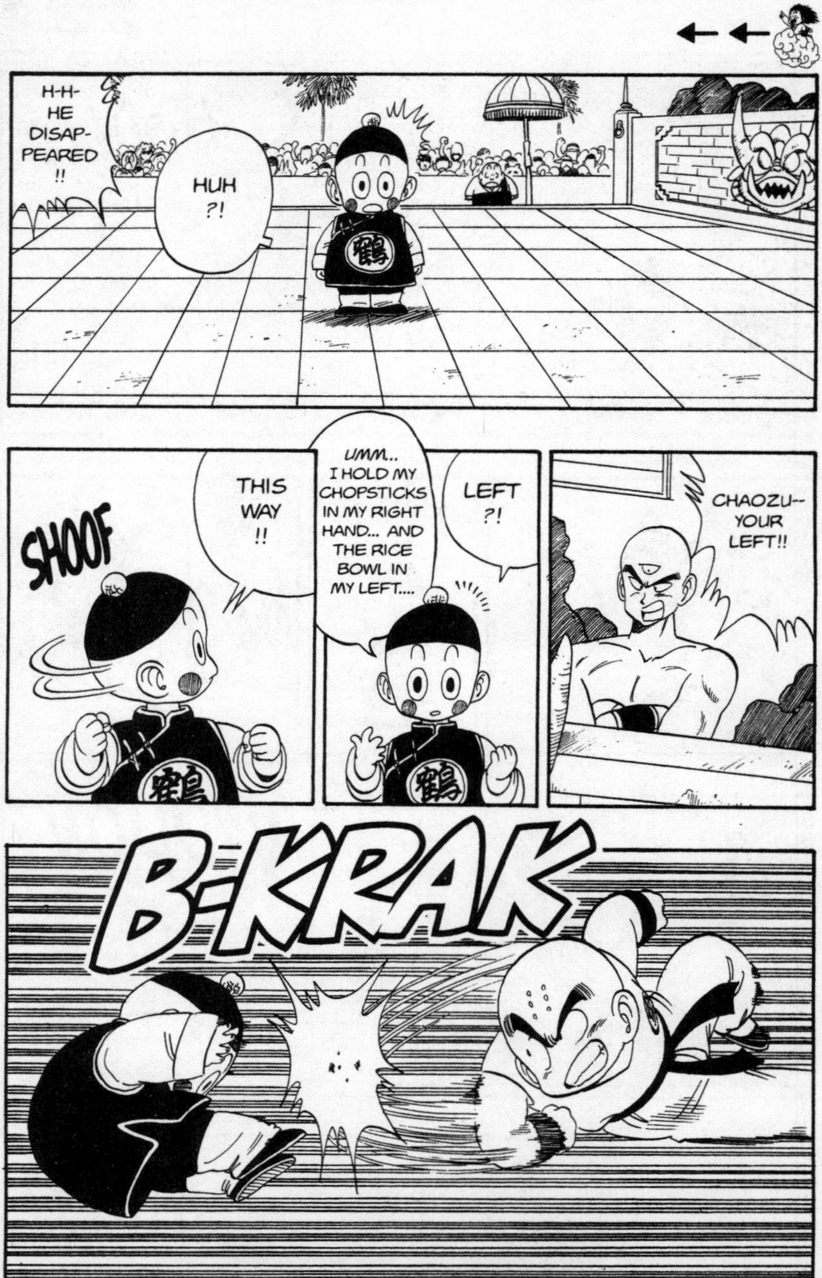
HUH ?!
H-H-HE DISAPPEARED !!
CHAOZU-- YOUR LEFT!!
LEFT ?!
UMM... I HOLD MY CHOPSTICKS IN MY RIGHT HAND... AND THE RICE BOWL IN MY LEFT....
THIS WAY !!
SHOOF
B-KRAK

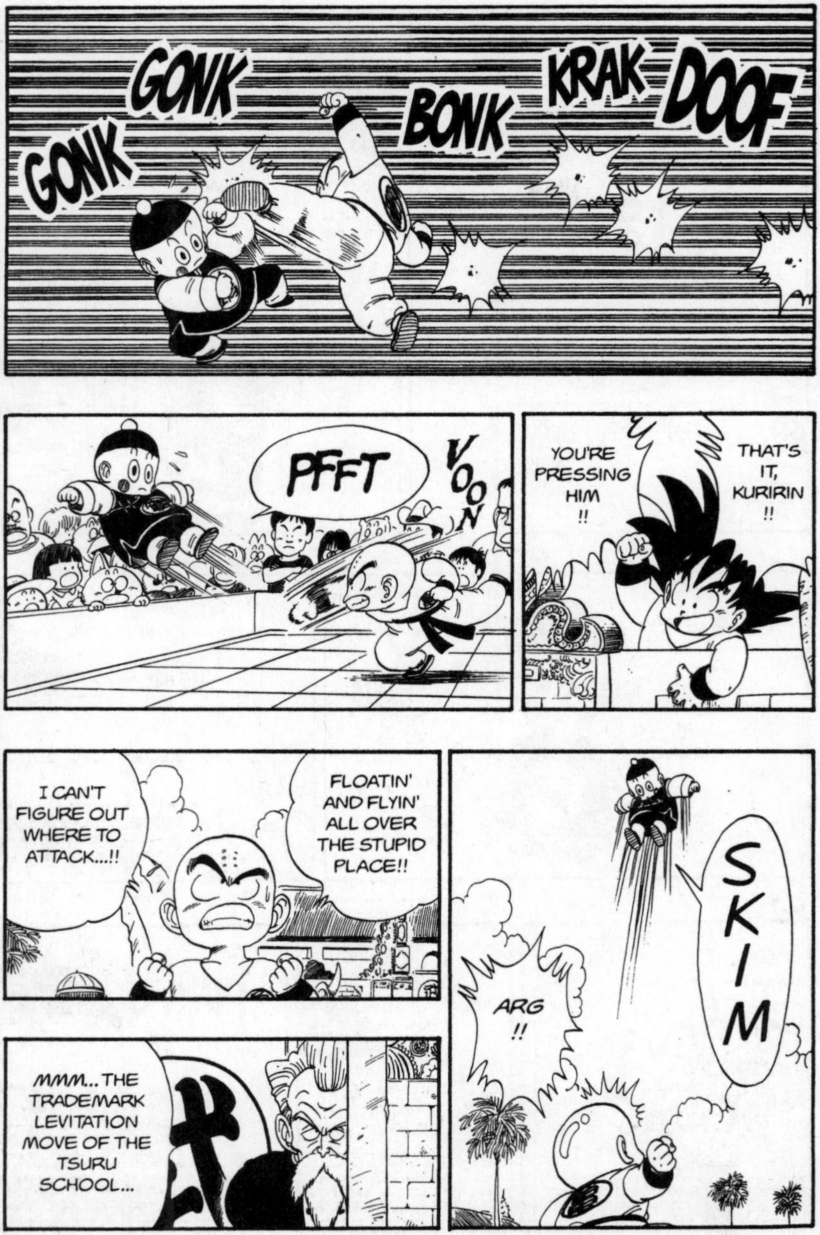
DOOF
KRAK
BONK
GONK
GONK
THAT'S IT, KURIRIN!!
YOU'RE PRESSING HIM!!
VOON
PFFT
SKIM
ARG!!
FLOATIN' AND FLYIN' ALL OVER THE STUPID PLACE!!
I CAN'T FIGURE OUT WHERE TO ATTACK...!!
MMM... THE TRADEMARK LEVITATION MOVE OF THE TSURU SCHOOL...

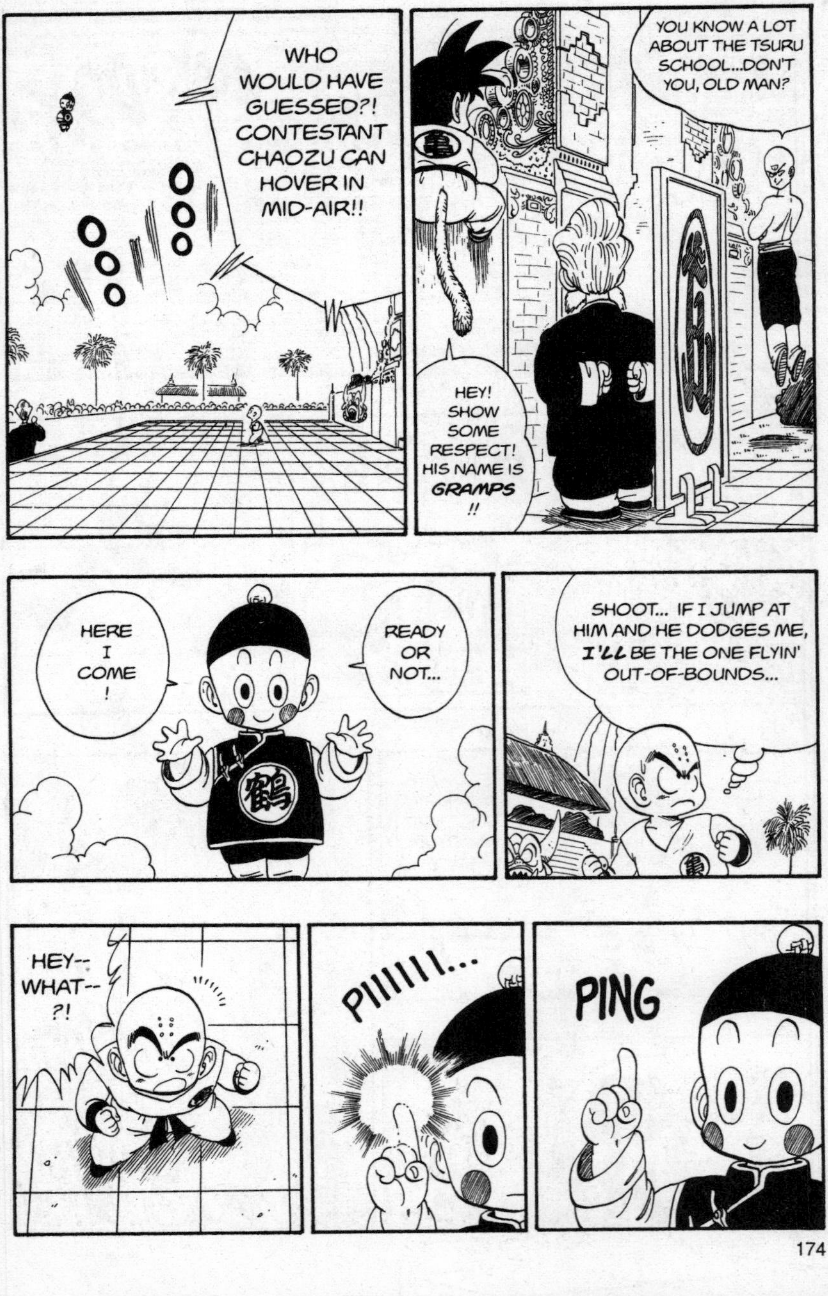
YOU KNOW A LOT ABOUT THE TSURU SCHOOL...DON'T YOU, OLD MAN?
HEY! SHOW SOME RESPECT! HIS NAME IS *GRAMPS*!!
WHO WOULD HAVE GUESSED?! CONTESTANT CHAOZU CAN HOVER IN MID-AIR!!
SHOOT... IF I JUMP AT HIM AND HE DODGES ME, *I'LL* BE THE ONE FLYIN' OUT-OF-BOUNDS...
READY OR NOT...
HERE I COME!
PING
PIIIIII...
HEY--WHAT--?!

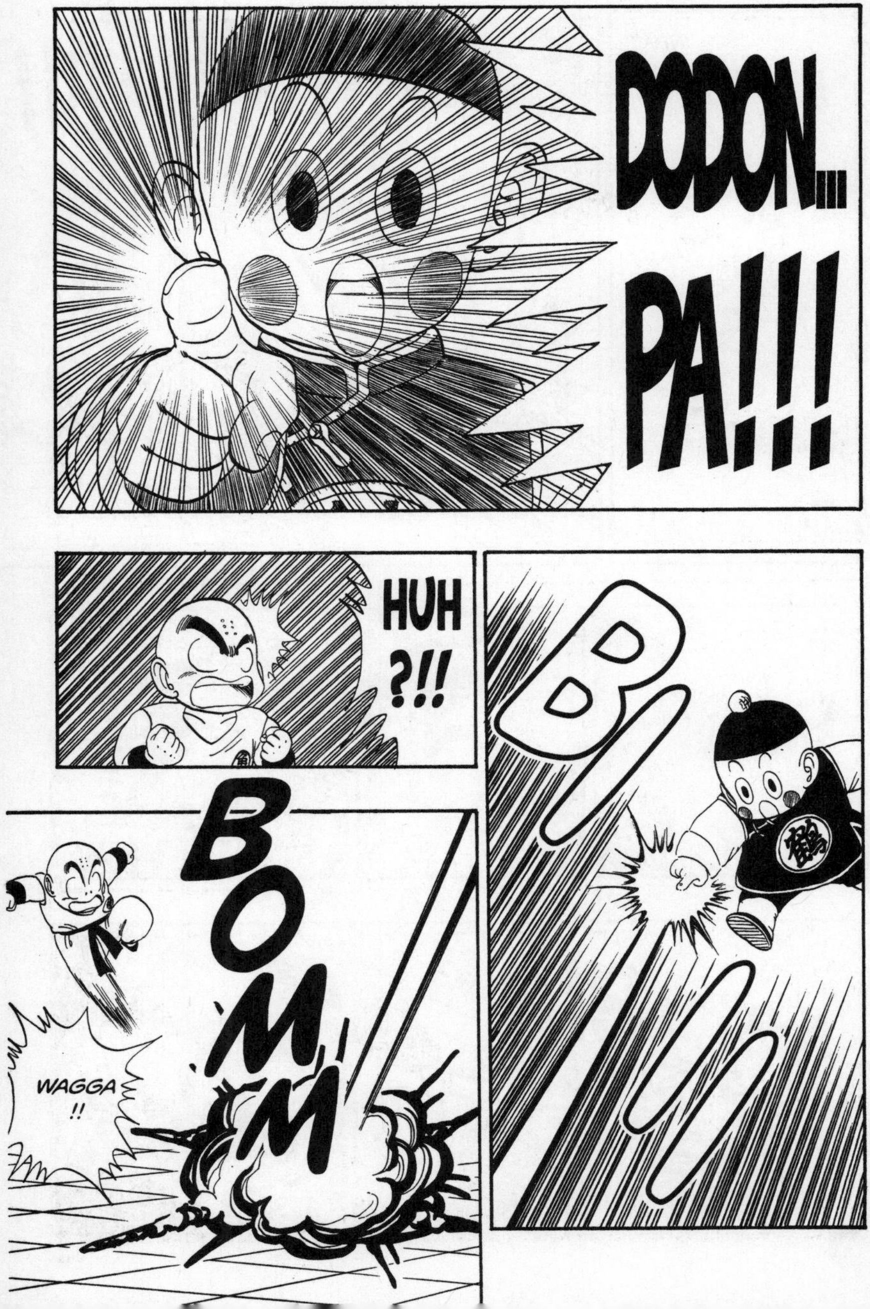
DODON...
PA!!!
HUH ?!!
BOMM
WAGGA !!

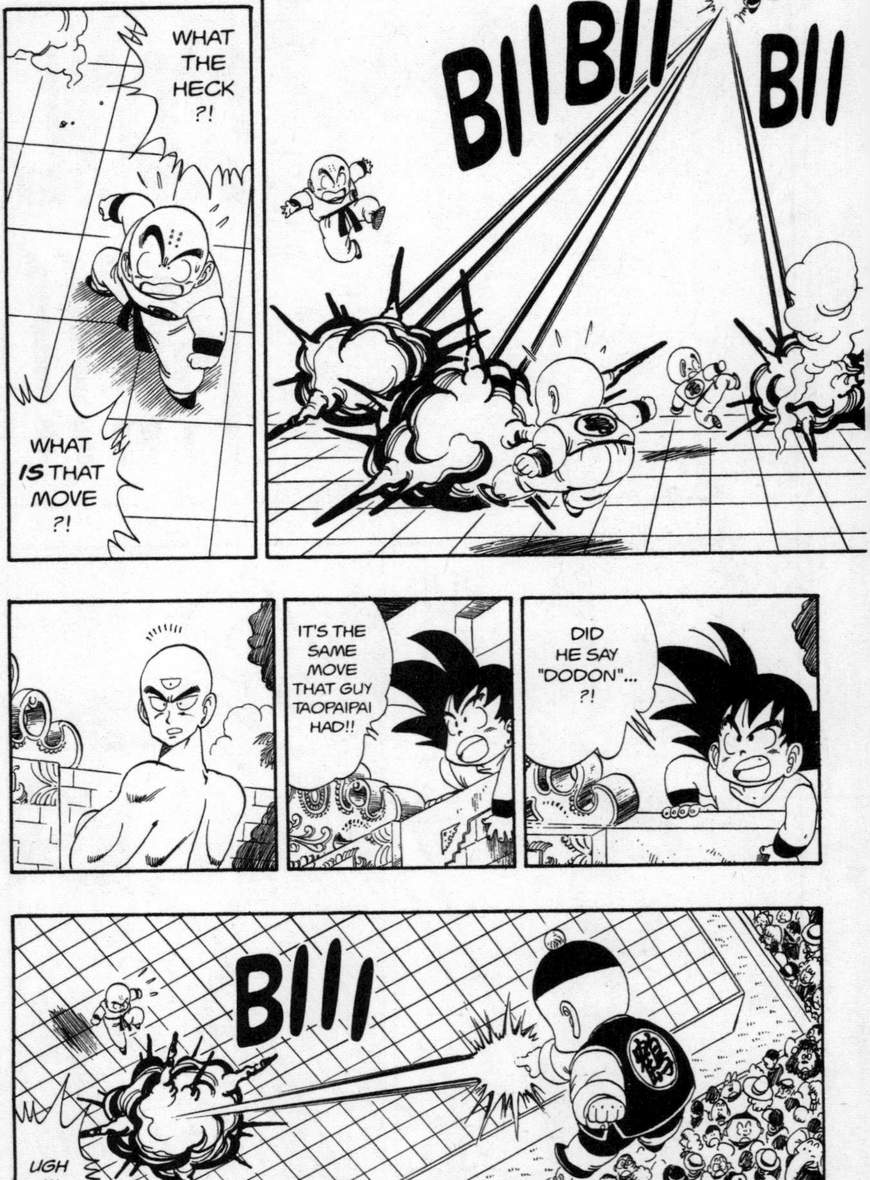

BII
BII
BII
WHAT THE HECK ?!
WHAT *IS* THAT MOVE ?!
DID HE SAY "DODON"... ?!
IT'S THE SAME MOVE THAT GUY TAOPAIPAI HAD!!
BIII
UGH !!!

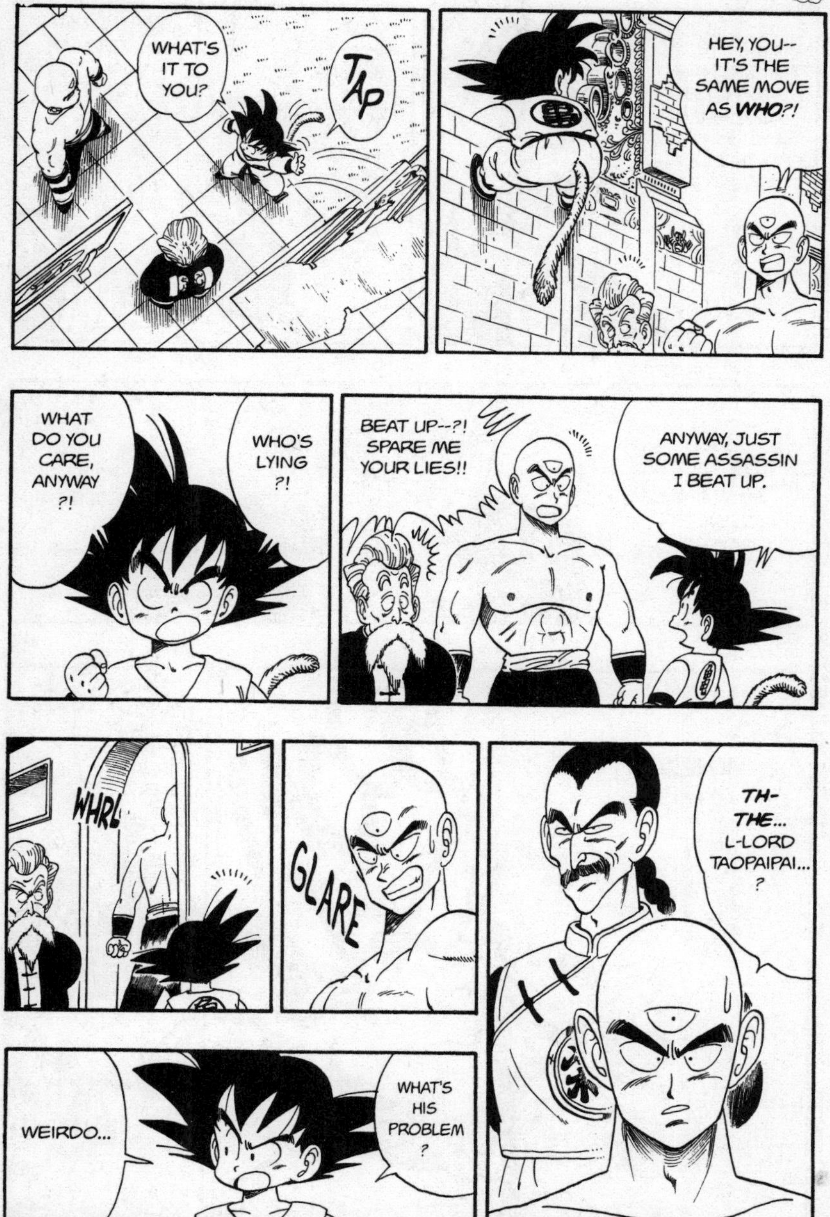
HEY, YOU-- IT'S THE SAME MOVE AS **WHO**?!
TAP
WHAT'S IT TO YOU?
ANYWAY, JUST SOME ASSASSIN I BEAT UP.
BEAT UP--?! SPARE ME YOUR LIES!!
WHO'S LYING ?!
WHAT DO YOU CARE, ANYWAY ?!
TH- THE... L-LORD TAOPAIPAI... ?
GLARE
WHRL
WHAT'S HIS PROBLEM ?
WEIRDO...

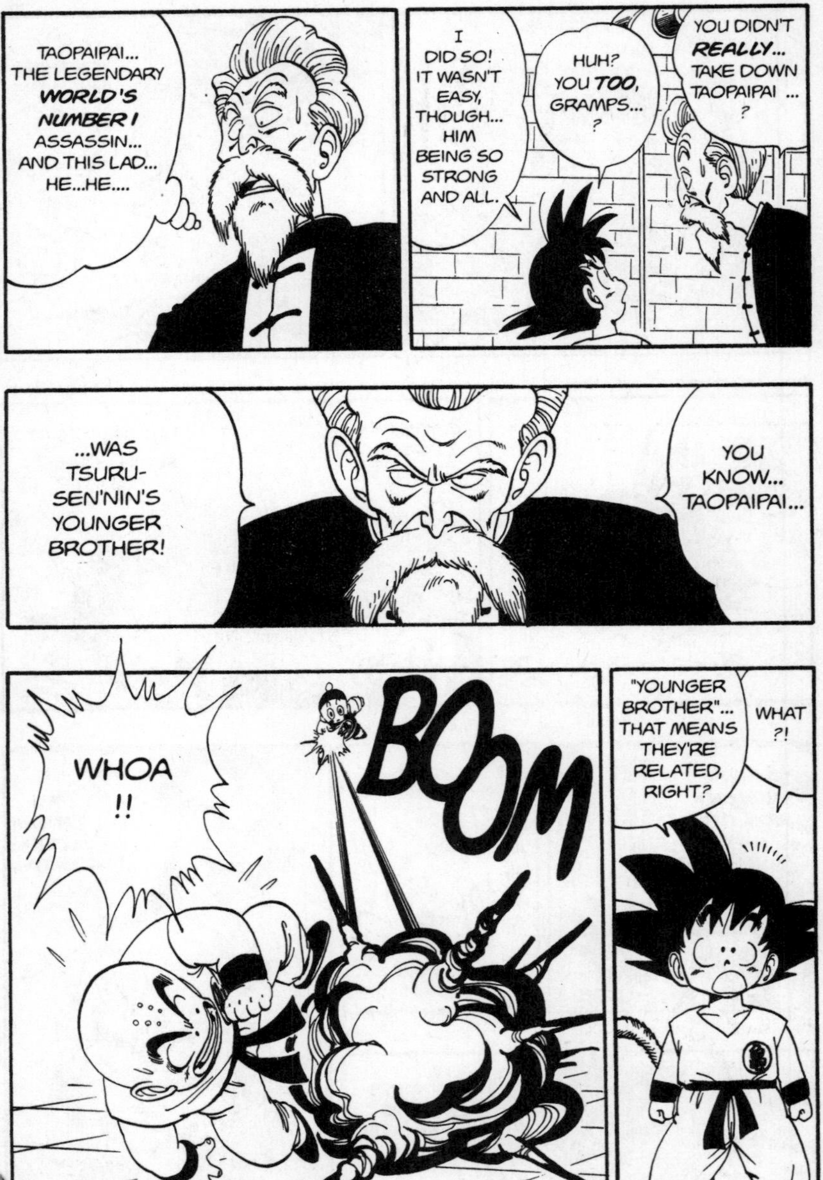
YOU DIDN'T REALLY... TAKE DOWN TAOPAIPAI ...?
HUH? YOU TOO, GRAMPS...?
I DID SO! IT WASN'T EASY, THOUGH... HIM BEING SO STRONG AND ALL.
TAOPAIPAI... THE LEGENDARY WORLD'S NUMBER 1 ASSASSIN... AND THIS LAD... HE...HE....
YOU KNOW... TAOPAIPAI...
...WAS TSURU-SEN'NIN'S YOUNGER BROTHER!
WHAT?!
"YOUNGER BROTHER"... THAT MEANS THEY'RE RELATED, RIGHT?
BOOM
WHOA!!

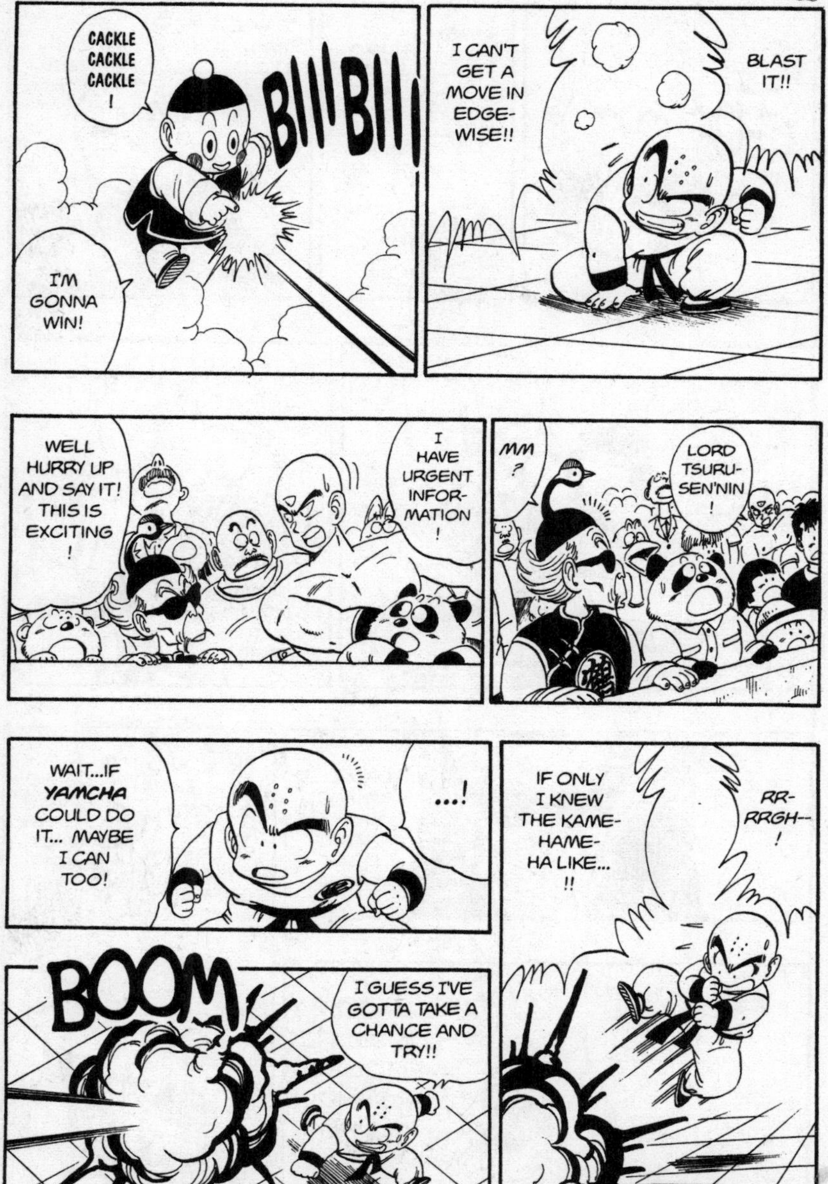
BLAST IT!!
I CAN'T GET A MOVE IN EDGE-WISE!!
CACKLE CACKLE CACKLE !
BIIIBIII
I'M GONNA WIN!
LORD TSURU-SEN'NIN !
MM ?
I HAVE URGENT INFOR-MATION !
WELL HURRY UP AND SAY IT! THIS IS EXCITING !
RR-RRGH-- !
IF ONLY I KNEW THE KAME-HAME-HA LIKE... !!
...!
WAIT...IF *YAMCHA* COULD DO IT... MAYBE I CAN TOO!
I GUESS I'VE GOTTA TAKE A CHANCE AND TRY!!
BOOM

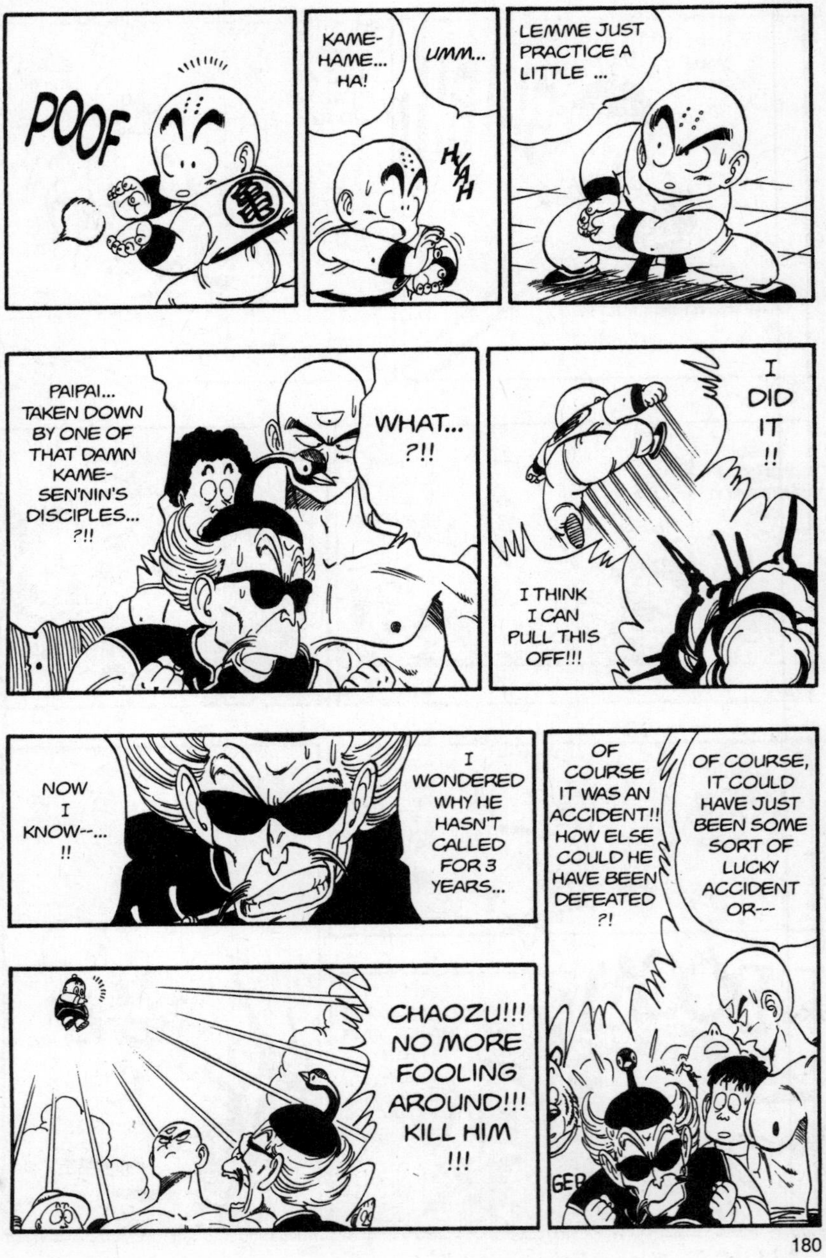
LEMME JUST PRACTICE A LITTLE ...
UMM...
KAME-HAME... HA!
HYAH
POOF
I DID IT !!
I THINK I CAN PULL THIS OFF!!!
WHAT... ?!!
PAIPAI... TAKEN DOWN BY ONE OF THAT DAMN KAME-SEN'NIN'S DISCIPLES... ?!!
OF COURSE, IT COULD HAVE JUST BEEN SOME SORT OF LUCKY ACCIDENT OR---
OF COURSE IT WAS AN ACCIDENT!! HOW ELSE COULD HE HAVE BEEN DEFEATED ?!
GEB
I WONDERED WHY HE HASN'T CALLED FOR 3 YEARS...
NOW I KNOW--... !!
CHAOZU!!! NO MORE FOOLING AROUND!!! KILL HIM !!!

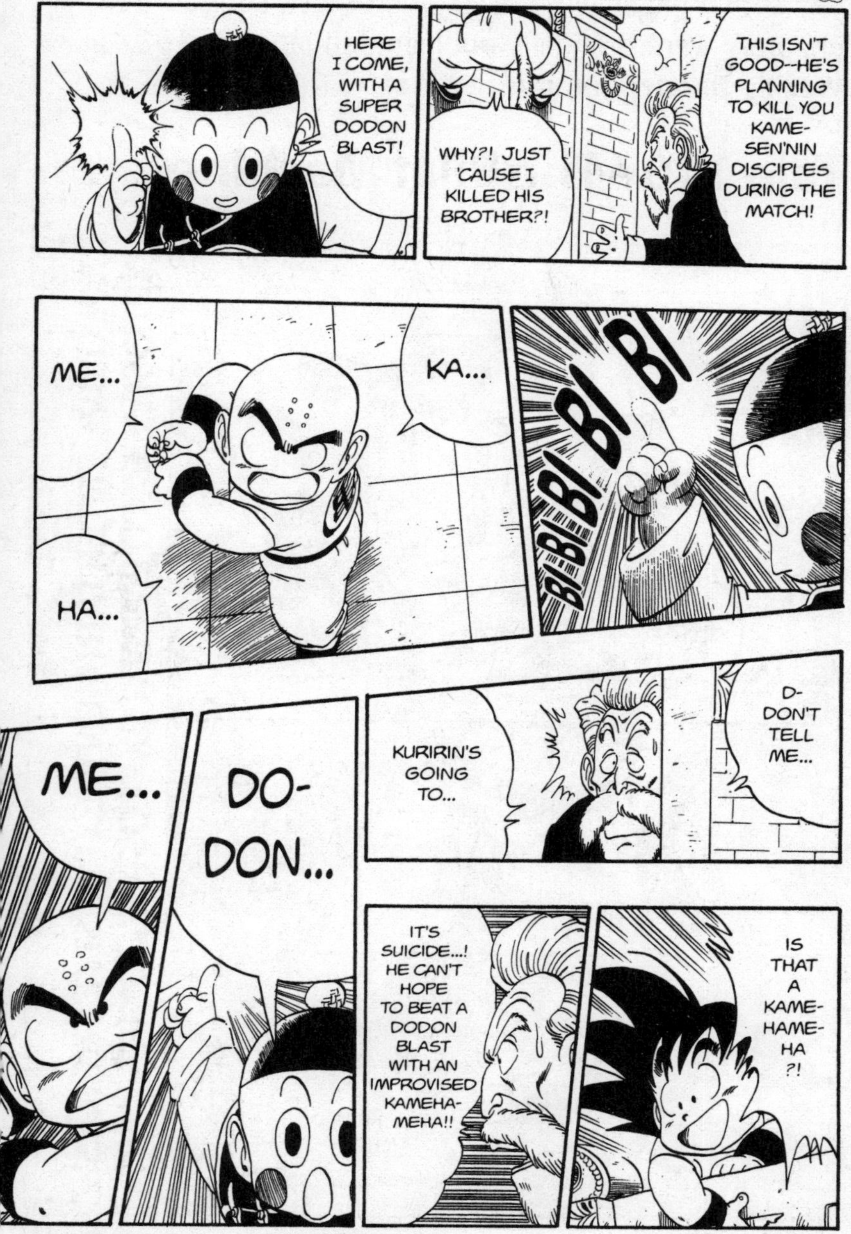
THIS ISN'T GOOD--HE'S PLANNING TO KILL YOU KAME-SEN'NIN DISCIPLES DURING THE MATCH!
WHY?! JUST 'CAUSE I KILLED HIS BROTHER?!
HERE I COME, WITH A SUPER DODON BLAST!
BI BI BI BI BI BI
KA...
ME...
HA...
D- DON'T TELL ME...
KURIRIN'S GOING TO...
IS THAT A KAME-HAME-HA ?!
IT'S SUICIDE...! HE CAN'T HOPE TO BEAT A DODON BLAST WITH AN IMPROVISED KAMEHA-MEHA!!
DO- DON...
ME...

NEXT: Countdown!!!

These title pages were used when these **Dragon Ball** chapters were originally published in Japan in 1987 in **Weekly Shonen Jump** magazine.

Tale 110 • The Pilaf Machine

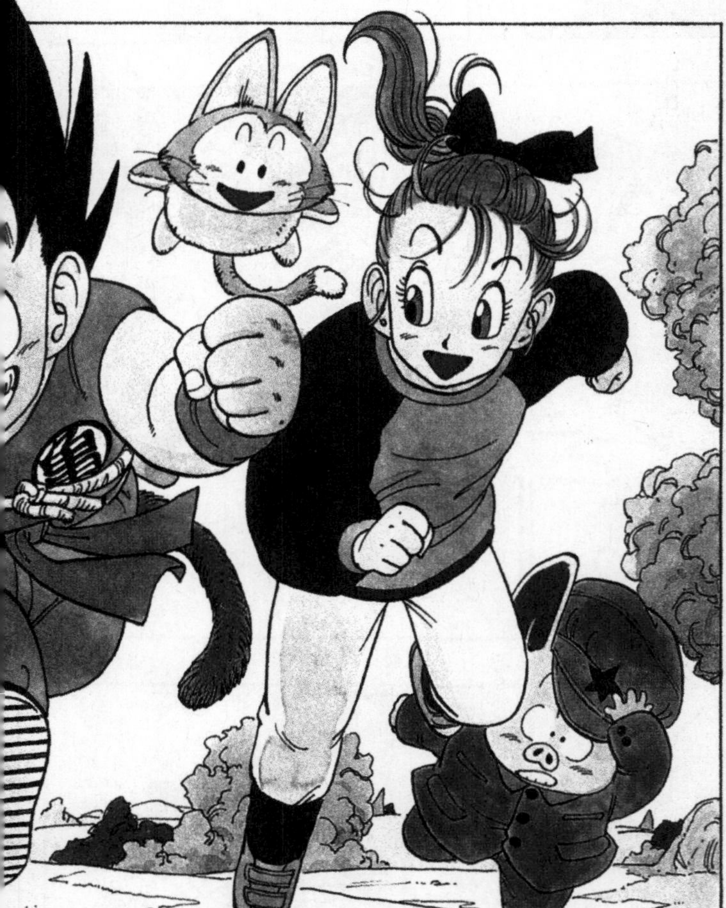

EXPLOSIVE ENTERTAINMENT! EXPLOSIVE THRILLS! EXPLOSIVE EXCITEMENT! EXPLOSIVE GOKU!

TITLE PAGE GALLERY

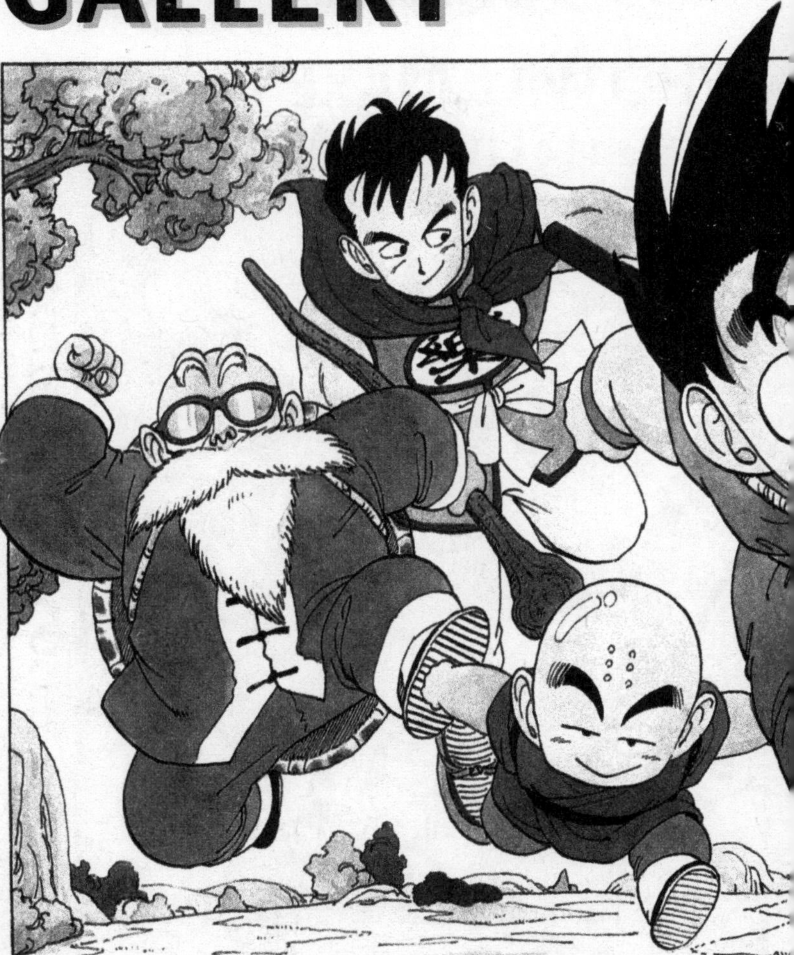

ドラゴンボール

DRAGON BALL

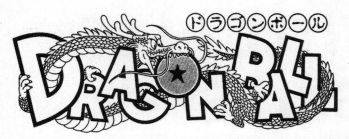

WHO WILL MAKE THE CUT?

Tale 114 • The Qualifying Rounds

競武館

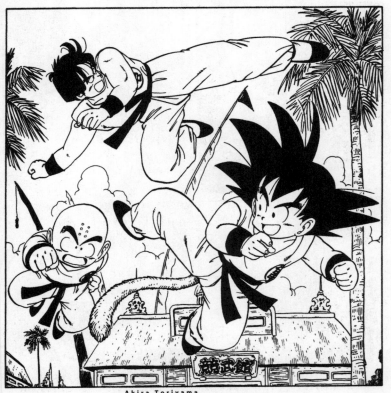

Akira Toriyama

鳥山明 BIRD STUDIO

WHO WILL FIGHT WHO?

Tale 116 • The Doctored Lottery

Akira Toriyama
鳥山明 BIRD STUDIO

ドラゴンボール

DRAGON BALL

THRILLING FROM THE FIRST BLOW!

Tale 117 • Yamcha's Kamehameha!

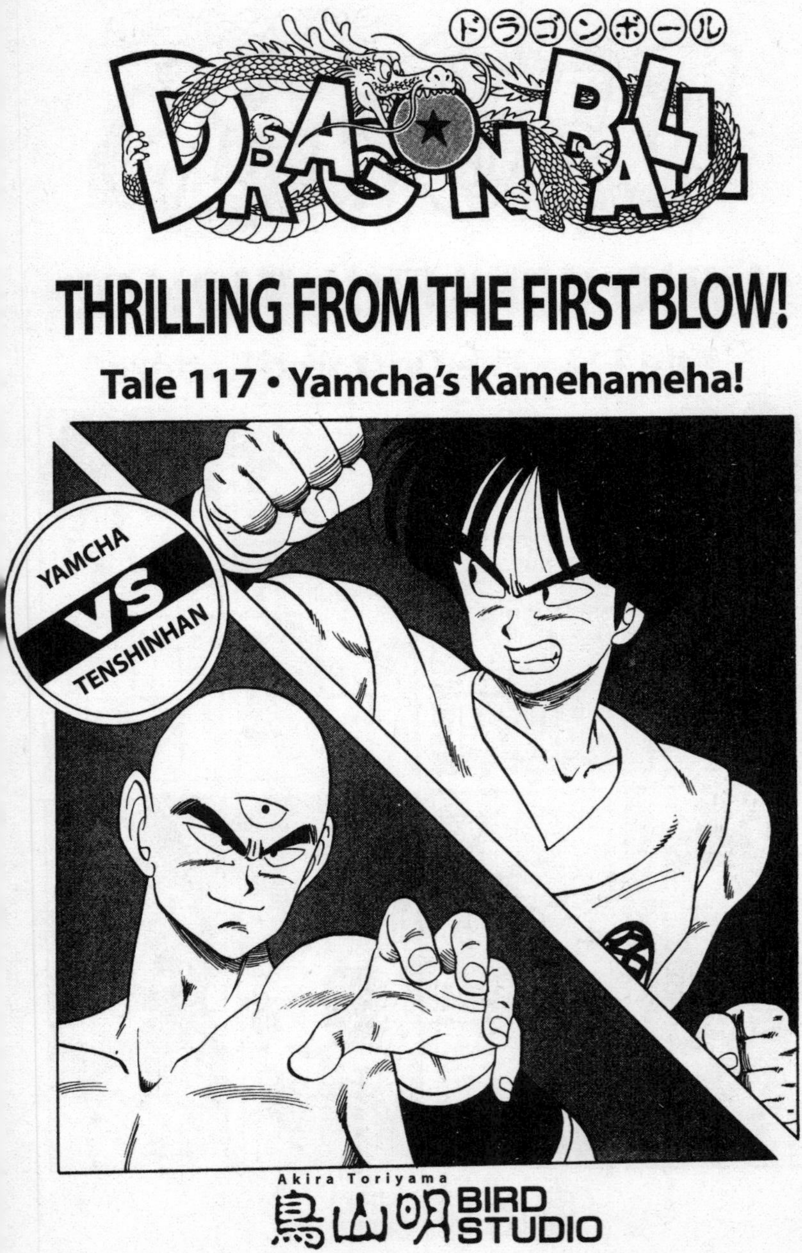
YAMCHA
VS
TENSHINHAN

Akira Toriyama
鳥山明 BIRD STUDIO

ドラゴンボール

DRAGON BALL

HAS YAMCHA WON?

Tale 118 • The Cruelty of Tenshinhan

Akira Toriyama
鳥山明
BIRD STUDIO

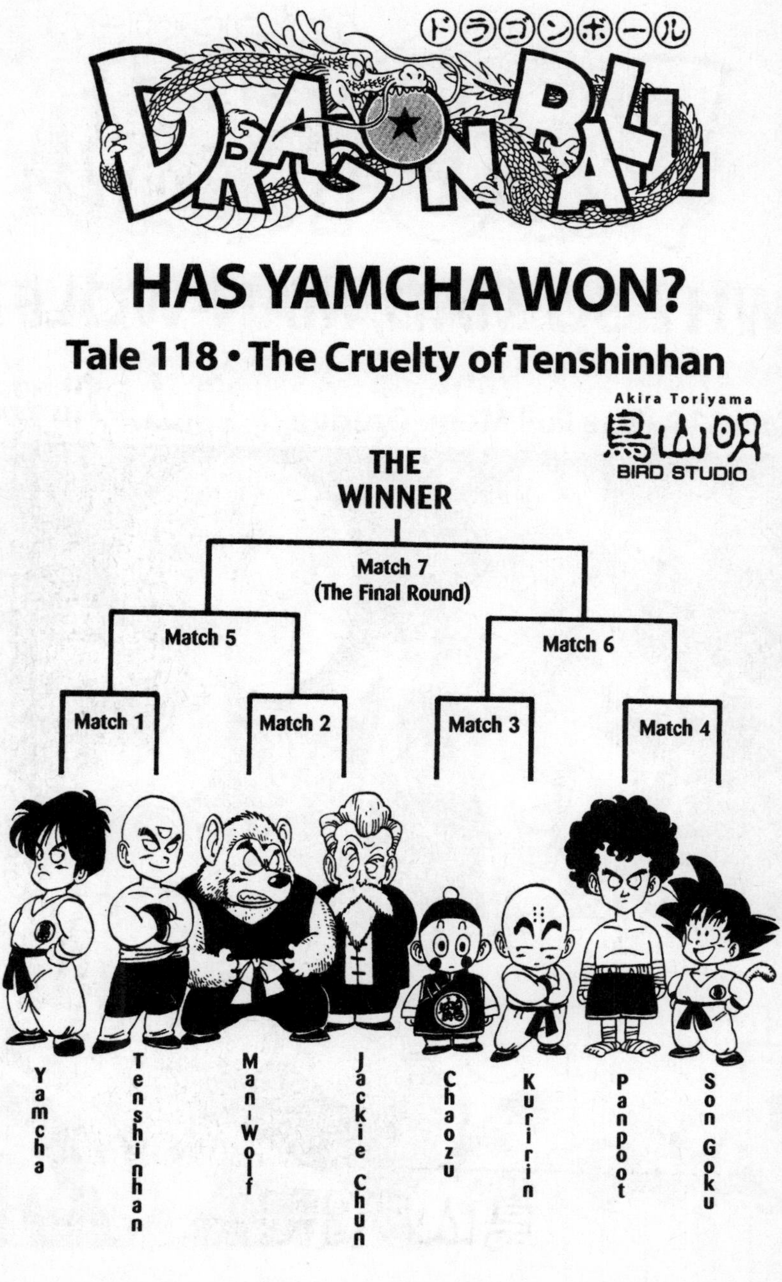
THE WINNER
Match 7
(The Final Round)
Match 5
Match 6
Match 1
Match 2
Match 3
Match 4
Yamcha
Tenshinhan
Man-Wolf
Jackie Chun
Chaozu
Kuririn
Panpoot
Son Goku

WHY SO MAD, MAN-WOLF?

Tale 119 • The Full Moon Grudge

Akira Toriyama
鳥山明 BIRD STUDIO

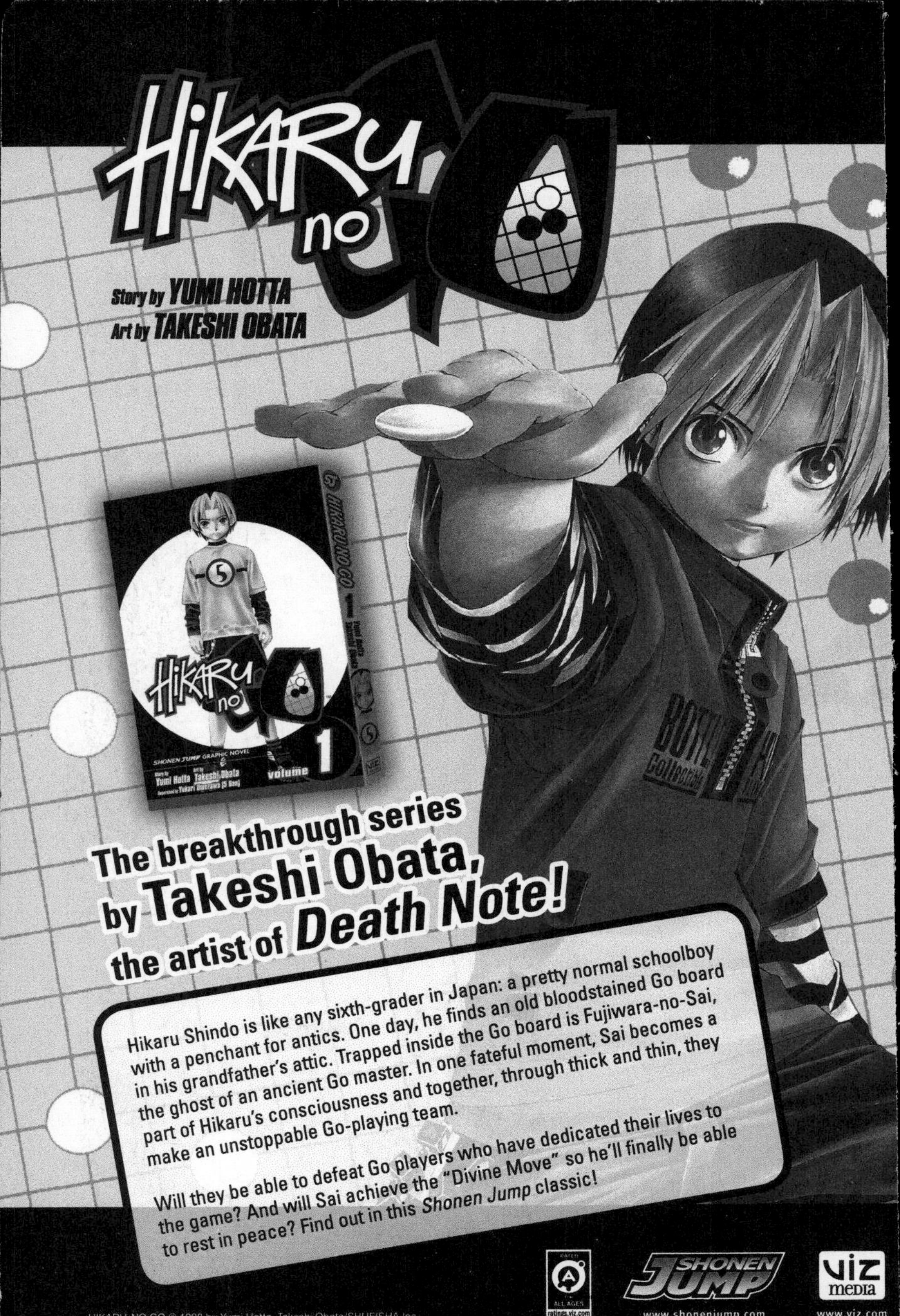
HIKARU no GO
Story by YUMI HOTTA
Art by TAKESHI OBATA
HIKARU no GO
SHONEN JUMP GRAPHIC NOVEL
volume 1
The breakthrough series by Takeshi Obata, the artist of Death Note!
Hikaru Shindo is like any sixth-grader in Japan: a pretty normal schoolboy with a penchant for antics. One day, he finds an old bloodstained Go board in his grandfather's attic. Trapped inside the Go board is Fujiwara-no-Sai, the ghost of an ancient Go master. In one fateful moment, Sai becomes a part of Hikaru's consciousness and together, through thick and thin, they make an unstoppable Go-playing team.
Will they be able to defeat Go players who have dedicated their lives to the game? And will Sai achieve the "Divine Move" so he'll finally be able to rest in peace? Find out in this Shonen Jump classic!
RATED A ALL AGES
ratings.viz.com
SHONEN JUMP
www.shonenjump.com
viz media
www.viz.com

THE BEST SELLING MANGA SERIES IN THE WORLD!

ONE PIECE

Story & Art by **EIICHIRO ODA**

As a child, **Monkey D. Luffy** was inspired to become a pirate by listening to the tales of the buccaneer "Red-Haired" Shanks. But Luffy's life changed when he accidentally ate the Gum-Gum Devil Fruit and gained the power to stretch like rubber...at the cost of never being able to swim again! Years later, still vowing to become the king of the pirates, Luffy sets out on his adventure in search of the legendary "One Piece," said to be the greatest treasure in the world...

ONE PIECE © 1997 by Eiichiro Oda/SHUEISHA Inc.

Story and Art by

KOYOHARU GOTOUGE

In Taisho-era Japan, kindhearted Tanjiro Kamado makes a living selling charcoal. But his peaceful life is shattered when a demon slaughters his entire family. His little sister Nezuko is the only survivor, but she has been transformed into a demon herself! Tanjiro sets out on a dangerous journey to find a way to return his sister to normal and destroy the demon who ruined his life.

You're Reading in the Wrong Direction!!

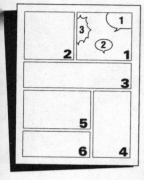

Whoops! Guess what? You're starting at the wrong end of the comic!

...It's true! In keeping with the original Japanese format, Akira Toriyama's world-famous **Dragon Ball** series is meant to be read from right to left, starting in the upper-right corner.

Unlike English, which is read from left to right, Japanese is read from right to left, meaning that action, sound-effects, and word-balloon order are completely reversed...something which can make readers unfamiliar with Japanese feel pretty backwards themselves. For this reason, manga or Japanese comics published in the U.S. in English have traditionally been published "flopped"—that is, printed in exact reverse order, as though seen from the other side of a mirror.

By flopping pages, U.S. publishers can avoid confusing readers, but the compromise is not without its downside. For one thing, a character in a flopped manga series who once wore in the original Japanese version a T-shirt emblazoned with "M A Y" (as in "the merry month of") now wears one which reads "Y A M"! Additionally, many manga creators in Japan are themselves unhappy with the process, as some feel the mirror-imaging of their art reveals otherwise unnoticeable flaws or skews in perspective.

In recognition of the importance and popularity of **Dragon Ball**, we are proud to bring it to you in the original unflopped format.

For now, though, turn to the other side of the book and let the adventure begin...!

—Editor